Praise for **Red Weather**

"If I could stand in the Cuyahoga County juvenile court-house and give one book to each of the more than 8,000 youngsters commanded to appear each year, it would be *Red Weather*. Not because this is a young adult novel—it's not—but because it tells a wry, cant-free story of a boy who gets drunk, breaks the law, does significant damage, and, bit by bit, finds a unique way to square things. . . . Rolls along with a David Sedaris–flavored drollness; it's a flat-out pleasure to read. Writer Pauls Toutonghi has a wonderful ear."

—*Cleveland Plain Dealer*

"A bittersweet love letter to a father and a city. It's prose fiction that might just make Milwaukee famous again."

—*Chicago Tribune*

"Sure-footed . . . Tender as it is comic. . . . In Toutonghi's vivid prose, Yuri's discovery is as bittersweet as life itself."

—*Miami Herald*

"*Red Weather* is a tale of teenage angst . . . What sets the story apart from countless other tales of miserable youth is its perspective."

—*San Francisco Chronicle*

"It's hilarious and touching, unpretentious yet incisive, instantly recognizable both geographically and emotionally, and tells an American story—the perennially American story of trying to become an American—while also presenting an unsentimental father-son bond."

—*Milwaukee Journal Sentinel*

"Toutonghi's vibrant first novel, lyrical and rich in human insight, celebrates the essential experience of the first-generation American—whose struggle for full nativeness is always joined within the dizzying, tragic, and exuberant campaign to become an adult."

—Ken Kalfus, author of *A Disorder Peculiar to the Country*

"Toutonghi is such an original, it seems almost blasphemous to try comparing him to others, but here goes: Gary Shteyngart meets David Sedaris meets Frank McCourt. In other words, he's whip-smart and hilarious and *Red Weather* is a guaranteed knockout."

—Darin Strauss, author of *The Real McCoy* and *Chang and Eng*

"I laughed. I cried. I ate borscht."

—Hannah Tinti, author of *Animal Crackers*

"Toutonghi's humor is imbued with a rare generosity of spirit. And, with his debut novel, he has written a moving and entertaining love letter to youth, to family, to his heritage, and perhaps most important, to Milwaukee, a city that is woefully underrepresented in contemporary fiction."

—Adam Langer, author of *Crossing California*

Red weather

A NOVEL

PAULS TOUTONGHI

THREE RIVERS PRESS
NEW YORK

Grateful acknowledgment is made to Alfred A. Knopf for permission to reprint excerpts from the poems "The Man with the Blue Guitar" and "Disillusionment of Ten O'Clock" from *The Collected Poems of Wallace Stevens* by Wallace Stevens. Copyright © 1954 by Wallace Stevens and renewed 1982 by Holly Stevens. Reprinted by permission of Alfred A. Knopf, a division of Random House, Inc.

Published in the United States by Three Rivers Press, an imprint of the Crown Publishing Group, a division of Random House, Inc., New York.
www.crownpublishing.com

Novel Thoughts colophon is a trademark of Random House, Inc. Three Rivers Press and the Tugboat design are registered trademarks of Random House, Inc.

Originally published in hardcover in the United States by Shaye Areheart Books, an imprint of the Crown Publishing Group, a division of Random House, Inc., New York, in 2006.

Library of Congress Cataloging-in-Publication Data
Toutonghi, Pauls.
  Red weather : a novel / Pauls Toutonghi
1. Teenage boys—Fiction. 2. Poor families—Fiction. 3. Milwaukee (Wis.)—Fiction.
4. Latvian Americans—Fiction. 5. Children of immigrants—Fiction. 6. Conflict of generations—Fiction. I. Title.
  PS3620.O92R43 2006
  813'.6—dc22   2005011604

ISBN: 978-0-307-33676-7

Printed in the United States of America

DESIGN BY ELINA D. NUDELMAN

10 9 8 7 6 5 4 3 2 1

First Paperback Edition

for my parents,
real and imaginary

Red Weather

PROLOGUE

My dad, drunk again and singing.

In a previous life, my dad dreamed of becoming a country and western singer. The fact that he'd lived this life in a concrete apartment tower in a suburb of Riga, Latvia, seems not to have mattered.

In his dreams of the country and western life, my dad would wear rhinestone-crusted spurs and a black Stetson. He'd make his home on the outskirts of Nashville, Tennessee. He'd have a bluetick hound, or perhaps even two bluetick hounds, and at sunset when the light was just so, he'd drink bourbon and mourn the loss of the old American music. He (Rudolfs Balodis, the Lonely Latvian) and his band (the Tragic Trio) would win Grammy after Grammy after Grammy. He would not live in Milwaukee, Wisconsin.

He never said this explicitly, of course. But I could infer. He would drink the bourbon—always Heaven Hill Kentucky Bourbon—and sing the classics. They'd pour out along with the alcohol, delivered in an impenetrable Soviet accent: Hank Williams, Jimmie Rodgers, Bob Wills and His Texas Playboys, Moon Mullican and his Texas Wanderers. And he yodeled—how could he *not* yodel? His pursed lips will forever be with me, meaty and sweaty, clean shaven to the point of razor burn, laboring over this foreign vocabulary.

Good air, good friend, what is there in life?

Is it ideas that I believe?
Good air, my only friend, believe.

Believe would be a brother full
Of love, believe would be a friend,

friendlier than my only friend,
Good air. Poor pale, poor pale guitar.

—Wallace Stevens, "The Man with the Blue Guitar"

part 1

1

wednesday, august 16, 1989

Milwaukee is not famous. Don't believe the Joseph Schlitz Brewing Company, which has claimed since 1871 that Schlitz is "the beer that made Milwaukee famous." This is an indisputable lie. As a teenage resident of downtown Milwaukee—as an inhabitant of the zip code 53202—I was as anonymous as anyone else in America. There was no fame magically coursing through my city's rusted water pipes. There was no fame in the boarded-up homes and concrete warehouses of my neighborhood.

Schlitz or no Schlitz, my family lived in a four-story building on the border of a Section 8 housing development. We inhabited one wing of the top floor. My mom posted this sign just above our mailbox, in cheerful red ink and Scotch tape:

The Balodis Family Welcome You!
Come into our home in Apartment Number 7!
Greeting!

In Latvian, *Balodis* means pigeon. We were a small roost of Soviet immigrant pigeons—just the three of us—huddled together amid the urban decay.

Yes, the apartment was dingy. But dingy in a hopeful way, dingy with a heart. Looking back on it fifteen years later, I recognize that it did have certain low-budget flair. There were posters tacked to the walls, or rather, 8½-by-11 advertisements that my mom had carefully torn out of the magazines in the library. These were advertisements of many different sorts: Coca-Cola, Wrangler Jeans, the Toyota Camry. Anything with bright colors or a sense of consumer wealth. She tacked them up behind sheets of plastic, and at night the plastic would catch the lamplight and shimmer. "That, my darling," she liked to say, "is the most beautiful advertising bulletin, do you not think?"

On the main living room wall there was an enormous *vainags,* a yellow wreath that was made mostly from straw and dried flowers. This *vainags* supposedly brought good luck if you rubbed it, and so there was perpetually a trail of crumbled straw on the floor. That, coupled with the open jar of salt on the dinner table—salt to bring flavor and fertility to our house—made me feel something like a barnyard animal.

We had five rooms: a kitchen, a bathroom, two bedrooms, and a living room. We ate our meals at a table in the kitchen, just the three of us—at times it would get a little lonely. But to my dad, this was the extreme of luxury. "Yuri," he once told me, "for an apartment similar to this in Riga, you would have to turn in at least four neighbors to the KGB." He loved the thick, olive-colored shag carpeting. Barefoot—this is how he liked to be when he was home. His feet were enormous and hairy, and slightly redolent of decay. He liked to shuffle through the carpet, to luxuriate his decaying feet in the petroleum fibers.

Invariably, though, my dad would end up drinking on the balcony. I do believe that if the weather had been more cooperative he would have slept there, covered in his nylon sleeping bag, staring up at the stars. Some summer evenings when my parents weren't fighting they'd drink wine outside and stand uncomfortably close to each other. This would force me to hurry to my bedroom, where I'd burrow under the covers, embarrassed by their affection, and try to read with a flashlight.

The first Latvians, my dad would often tell me, came to Wisconsin in 1903. The Wisconsin Valley Land Company lured them to the farmland west of Milwaukee. They came with the Croats and the Lithuanians, the Bulgarians and the Slovaks, the Armenians and the Fins, the Poles and the Ukrainians and the Montenegrins. Part of an Eastern European exodus—a steady stream of immigrants from east of the Danube—the Latvians became factory workers and farmers and solid middle-class citizens of middle America. They founded their own Latvian Lutheran Evangelical Church—all the way out in Wauwatosa—a little suburb twenty miles to the west. They opened a small group of specialty stores and started printing a Latvian-language newspaper.

But by 1989, most of the stores had closed. The newspaper had shut its doors in 1971. The few elderly parishioners who gathered each Sunday to warble through "A Mighty Fortress Is Our God" did so with increasing frailty. And as Latvians living downtown, anyway, we were out of luck. My dad preferred to go to the Catholic Church that was two blocks from our apartment building. "The communion wafers taste better there," he told me. "More like bread, and not so much like paste and suffering." When we did go to mass—mostly on the holiest of Holy Days—we bundled our way over to St. Philippe's. The spires of this cathedral rose magnificently over Lake Michigan, a tribute to Victorian Gothic architecture, in all its gargoyle-laden glory.

Because of the lack of Latvian merchants in downtown Milwaukee, my mom shopped instead at the Polish specialty stores on South Kinnickinnic Avenue. In her years in the city she'd managed to pick up a few Polish phrases, and so she'd haggle with the retailers, demanding better prices in her scornful, but limited, Polish. When I was free from school I'd accompany her. On this particular Wednesday, we crossed the Milwaukee River twice, taking both the Wisconsin Avenue lift bridge and the steel-truss bridge that followed it. By the time we reached Zigorski's—her favorite of the little shops—my feet ached and throbbed. But, then again, she was my mom, and she demanded a certain amount of Eastern European foodstuffs.

Zigorski's was a Polish delicatessen of the first order. Ropes of sausage dangled from the ceiling. The refrigerated case overflowed with a variety of pickled products—eggs, cucumbers, mushrooms, even a big jar that held the brain of pig, bobbing in a dill-studded brine. No one bought the pig's brain. I guessed that it was a decoration. My mom was looking for fresh herring. She didn't want herring that came in a tin—this you could buy, she told me, at any supermarket. "We will have a good meal that I have been craving recently," she'd said.

When my mom asked the man behind the counter for herring, he frowned and said that they were out. They might have some next week, he indicated, and crossed his heavy arms over his chest. He wore a white apron and a small triangular cap. The apron was stained with broad streaks of blood. His graying sideburns, I noticed, reached the lowest portion of his jaw.

"You bastard," my mom said. "Don't lie to me."

If I'd been inexperienced in the ways of shopping with my mom, I would have been nervous at this point. As it was, a woman standing near the baked goods gasped and dropped a cake on the floor. The cake exploded, scattering frosting in a wide white arc. Another Zigorski's employee scurried out of a back room with a mop.

"Don't call me names," the attendant said. Then, raising the volume of his voice: "Does anyone else need help?" Though there were several other customers, none of them seemed eager to get involved in this particular confrontation. My mother stood there, resolute.

"I know you have it, you bastard," she said again. She then added a few phrases of Polish. They sounded guttural and malicious, and from the expression on the man's face, I guessed that they weren't overly polite. He shook his head and disappeared wordlessly into the back.

This was, then, the old way of shopping. My mom took the lessons she'd learned in Soviet Latvia and applied them to the American grocery marketplace. When the counter attendant vanished, she patted my arm gently. "Do not worry, Yuri," she said, "he will return in a moment with our herring."

Zigorski's also had an extensive selection of olives. They sat in open barrels near the door, green and black and brown. I liked standing next to the olives and inhaling deeply. I'd bring the scent of the vinegar into my lungs, wincing as it made me slightly dizzy. I looked at the walls. Every available space was overflowing with goods—with packaged crackers and cookies and strips of dehydrated meat, sold in bulk. The store carried products from a variety of Eastern European countries. The ceiling was decorated with a series of flags, flags I recognized as Bulgarian, Albanian, Polish, Yugoslav.

The attendant returned. He held a neatly wrapped bundle of newspapers.

"Here you are, Mrs. Balodis," the man said. The animosity had left his voice. "We just received it this morning. We hadn't put it in the fish case, yet." He smiled. This transaction was probably one of many similar transactions that he endured over the course of a day. I had a vision of an army of middle-aged Eastern European mothers—all jovial and abusive—demanding products that were not on display in the front of the store.

That night, we ate herring in mustard sauce, a particular favorite of my mom's. My dad used a stale piece of rye bread to soak up the mustard. After he finished this, he licked each of his fingers—carefully, very carefully—and carried his dish to the kitchen. He poured himself three inches of bourbon.

"It keeps the stomach digesting," he said, somewhat grimly, and walked out onto the balcony. My dad held a position as a part-time night janitor at Jack Baldwin Chevrolet—a car dealership on Milwaukee's Auto Row. He was preparing for work with a shot of bourbon; on the nights he worked, he liked to be continually and slightly intoxicated. He'd come home around seven A.M., saturated with alcohol's scent.

Summer evenings could be balmy and pleasant in the parts of Milwaukee where the wind came off the lake and the paper mills didn't pollute the air. We lived just over a mile from County Stadium, the old ballpark where the Brewers used to play. Occasionally you could hear a cheer from the stadium bleachers, as the Brewers scored a run or struck someone out. The noise would float toward you, disembodied, the clamor of a thousand voices, now faint as the voice of a single bird.

I went into my bedroom and retrieved my ragged copy of *Crime and Punishment*. I was reading it for the first time—stunned by the drama of the language. I brought the book into the living room and sat on the carpet in front of the television. I began to read. The TV was on and tuned to *Wheel of Fortune*. I tried to block out the noise, focusing instead on the book and the sounds of my mom doing the dishes. I was reading in front of the television at her request. She was suspicious of my books, and she felt no worries about telling me this. In my mom's eyes, loneliness bred independence, and independence, in Latvia during the Soviet '60s, meant nothing but trouble. The culture she'd been raised in—I was led to believe—had emphasized communal life. Privacy was not something that she'd been raised to treasure.

"Yuri," she'd say, "why are you always reading, reading, reading? So quiet, away in your room. Why not come out here and join us, when we are doing things in the kitchen or watching the television?"

When I was being particularly quiet, my mom would show me a

photograph she'd kept—a black-and-white picture of the sprawling housing developments outside of Riga where she'd grown up. The buildings stretched to the limitless horizon, fifteen stories each, dropped on the treeless earth by some demented construction deity. It was George Orwell meets Walter Gropius meets industrial concrete, and it always terrified me.

"In here lived four thousand people," my mom would say. "The walls were thin as flour." This was a favorite expression of hers, "thin as flour," and I still believe she is solely responsible for its invention. "Everyone was quiet, all of the time," she'd continue, "because if you said anything, made any noise at all, someone would make a note and call the secret police and you would disappear. So be happy for reading in here with me and being together with all of this nice electricity."

I was to live in the open and be free to say everything I wanted—openly—in the living room of our house, as loudly as I wanted, with the windows open even, and with the television on, and with the record player playing, if I so desired. I was to be a typical American teenager and not worry about matters of nationality or language or anything as complicated as this. I was not to worry about speaking Latvian; I was to simply enjoy network television sitcoms and dramas. Sometimes, I confronted my mom about this:

"Mom," I'd ask, "why can't I learn Latvian?"

"Latvian?" my mom would answer. "But you are an American, Yuri, are you not?"

"Well, sure," I'd say. "I'm an American. But—"

"There is your answer. Americans speak American language, which is English. Do you see many Americans running around speaking Latvian? Do not be ridiculous."

I was a lonely kid, I suppose, but in my loneliness I took some solace from the city. We lived in Milwaukee's Third Ward. The Third Ward in 1989 was not what the Third Ward is today—an aggressively reclaimed urban neighborhood, home to a slew of fashionable houseware boutiques and gourmet coffee vendors. In 1989, the Third Ward was just what you'd expect from the tenth-poorest urban area in America: an expanse of boarded-up warehouses, a sprawl of low-rent tenement buildings, a mixed commercial and residential district that over-flowed with trash and potholes.

The Ward itself was a peninsula, bordered on two sides by the Mil-waukee River—that sad, gray, industrial waterway—and on a third side by Lake Michigan. But Interstate 794 cut through the center of the dis-trict, and so our section of the Third Ward had the feel of an island. Water on three sides and the overpass on a fourth. Roughly thirty-five square blocks, all of it paved, all of it lit, at night, with bulbous electric lights, lights that made everything blossom with shadows.

That night—a Wednesday night—I couldn't sleep. The herring and mustard sauce churned unpleasantly in my stomach. I could feel the school year approaching, and a formless sense of anxiety settled over my limbs, sheathing my skin with sweat, sending cramps up the sides of my calves. I squirmed uncomfortably in bed for a few hours. Mid-night turned into one A.M. turned into two A.M. turned into four. Finally, I resolved to go out onto the balcony—to breathe in the warm summer air that would be tinged with the carbon scent of exhaust.

The balcony was strange and expansive without my dad's presence. I stood against the rail and watched the city beneath me. I could see little pieces of the streets that cobbled outward into our section of downtown. I had the sense that the streets might be infinite—that they might stretch into the limitless distance—and that they held a vastness of possibility. They seemed to glitter, almost, to beckon me down and into their body.

Why not go for a walk? I suddenly thought. What could happen? I was an observant, careful kid. I'd watch my back. Maybe a walk would calm my nerves, make it possible for me to get some rest before sun-rise. I turned and crept silently back to my room, where I changed my clothes and slipped on my shoes. I'd never been this excited by the idea of being awake at four A.M. I unlocked the front door, tested the doorknob, and carefully descended the staircase to the parking lot of our building.

The street was beautiful at night. I was a little nervous—downtown Milwaukee wasn't known for its safety—but I figured that most every-one would be asleep, that the bulk of the illegal activity would be over by this part of the night. I walked in the middle of the sidewalk, observing the shadows of objects and buildings, listening for the distant hum of the awakening city. The sidewalks were broad. Awnings hung down from every façade. The city felt like a gelatin silver print, black and white and a little mysterious. I walked along East Chicago Street to North Van Buren Street and headed toward the highway. I could smell the mix of lake air and car exhaust; it was a salty-sweet smell, and it made me a little dizzy.

After a few minutes I reached a broad series of warehouses, old brick holdovers from the nineteenth century, warehouses that were, for the most part, empty. The main exception was the building that housed the Third Ward's biggest landmark—the Tropic Banana Company. The Tropic Banana Company was an old-fashioned produce vendor, and easily the most vigorous business in our neighborhood. Everybody knew about Tropic Banana; it was the anchor of the community, the engine that kept the Third Ward running. And in the early hours of the morning—the hours that I happened to be there—it took deliveries from across the country.

I found an unobstructed viewpoint behind the chain-link perimeter fence and watched the trucks stream in. I counted eighteen trucks— one every three or four minutes. They pulled in to the building's loading bays; they hauled vats of tomatoes or oranges or heads of cabbage or sweet corn. I orbited the margins of the loading area—ignored by the workers—and watched the produce being bought and sold. People were bargaining for goods, right there, yelling back and forth across the rhythm of the deliveries. Buyers prowled from bin to bin, looking skeptically at a handful of kale or a bunch of plantains. Money changed hands next to the crates—with the yard manager accepting bundles of bills and stuffing them into a zippered pouch.

I looked away from the scene at Tropic Banana and focused on the boarded-up windows and broken stoops of the other buildings nearby. Sure, Milwaukee was a sad place. Manufacturing, I knew, had made the city its fortune. I'd certainly heard enough lectures on this topic from my dad. Manufacturing had lured swarms of immigrants from Europe in the second half of the nineteenth century. When manufacturing jobs disappeared, when the factories and breweries and textile mills closed, the working class also disappeared. Now, the Third Ward functioned as a ghostly memorial for the factories. Stenciled across brick walls, and fading year by year to nothing, were the logos of these corporations: Bucyrus Shovel, Briggs & Stratton, EP Allis Company. Goods manufactured in Milwaukee had dug the Panama Canal, had mowed America's lawns, and had helped mine the Canadian interior. Now, the city produced almost nothing other than beer—vats and vats of cheap, watery, macrobrewed lager.

I was trying to absorb all of this when I heard something unusual—a girl's voice moving confidently through the darkness.

"*Socialist Worker!*" she yelled from around the corner of the building. "Fifty cents! Support organized labor. Every quarter counts." I was intrigued, of course, and so I walked toward the shouting.

Several scruffy-looking people stood in a little cluster to the left of the entryway to Tropic Banana. They mostly wore baggy jeans and T-shirts printed with political slogans. A few of them clutched bundles of newspapers, which they appeared to be selling, though no one was buying.

This was certainly unusual. I watched a succession of workers walk through the gauntlet of salespeople. None of the employees of Tropic Banana seemed interested in socialism. Or, if they were, then they were extremely subtle about this interest—they expressed it by refusing the newspaper, by shouldering the vendor out of the way, and surging angrily into the main lobby of the building. Poor socialists, I thought. They were failing so miserably.

I counted nine of them—nine vendors yelling their slogans in the Milwaukee day. They certainly seemed confident; their faces glowed with smudgy energy in the partial, early-morning light. I looked closer. With a shock, I realized that I recognized one of the people in the cluster. She was a girl from my school, Alexander Hamilton High. Alexander Hamilton was a big school—it had more than two thousand students—but still I knew her face.

I hesitated near the corner of the building, frozen, unsure what to do. I decided, after some internal debate, that I'd walk over and say hello. I'd intervene. How often, I rationalized, did I see someone I knew in this part of town?

"*Socialist Worker?*" the girl said, waving a newspaper at me as I approached. "Fifty cents?"

"Absolutely," I said, pulling two quarters from my pocket.

She seemed surprised by the gesture, and brushed an unruly strand of brown hair back from her face. "Here you go," she said. "Are you familiar with our coverage of the war in Nicaragua?"

I had to admit that I wasn't. This didn't seem to surprise her. She nodded in a way that acknowledged that, indeed, very few people were familiar with the *Socialist Worker*'s coverage of anything. "What about our efforts to get a living wage for migrant workers in California?" Her eyes were tailpipe blue—they radiated a blue vapor of intensity.

She opened the newspaper that I was buying. "Susan Emerson has a great article on page four about apple orchards in the Sacramento Valley," she said.

"Don't I know you?" I said. "Don't you go to Hamilton High?"

She paused and lowered the paper slightly. "I do," she said, and nodded. "I'll be a senior in September." She shook her head and looked at me quizzically, trying to place me in her past. "I'm Hannah Graham," she said.

Hannah's hair seemed to teeter on the brink of explosion. She was wildly attractive, I thought—with an angular jawline and high, elegant cheekbones. She reached out to shake my hand and—in the process of this—the stack of newspapers tumbled from her arms. Copies of the *Socialist Worker* caught the wind and swept through the air. They floated along North Van Buren Street like aimless marionettes. The socialists leapt into action. The papers were clearly precious to them— a precious commodity. Eight socialists scurried up and down the alley, chasing the thin newsprint as it rose and fell with the gusts of wind. I didn't know what to do. I stood there, mute and unhelpful, and watched the scene unfold.

Hannah seemed content to stand there beside me. I held my copy of the *Socialist Worker* in my hand. I didn't know what to say next. I leafed through the newspaper, searching for an article to discuss.

"What about this—" I started to say. But a gruff voice cut me off.

"Come on, Hannah. Let's go."

The voice belonged to an older, paunchy man. He wore circular glasses and a beret. His yellow T-shirt said FREE MUMIA in large, red letters. It was tucked into his jeans. He was, I would later learn, Hannah's father. He beckoned her toward him.

"I'm sorry," she called over her shoulder as she left. "We have to hit

the Pabst brewery by five thirty." I watched her walk away. The socialists, it seemed, traveled on foot. They bobbed down the street; Hannah was pulled along with them, drawn like driftwood into a receding
wave.

The summer of 1989 was the end of the road for a certain type of Eastern European communism. Though I was only fifteen, I felt this end
profoundly. My parents scanned headlines for any mention of the
USSR, or the Baltics, or even the various Soviet satellites. Throughout
that summer, I'd feel a shiver of emotion whenever I heard the news
from East Germany. The Soviets, embroiled in their own economic crisis, could no longer funnel aid to the Eastern Bloc. The East German
government couldn't fund even the most basic state services. Tired of
years of oppressive policing and state control of social life, the East
German people were angry. They were beginning to demand political
reform. Or so the story went in the mainstream American media.

My dad's take on communism was simple. "Yuri," he often told me,
"communists are like goats. They come into your house. They eat
everything. They sleep everywhere. They make an awful noise. Then,
just before they leave, they shit on the furniture."

It was difficult for me to argue with this. The Latvian Soviet Socialist Republic had, after all, confiscated his family's property. It had
reeducated his uncle and shipped several of his other relatives to
Siberia. The sting of the Stalinist past was contained in the lines of his
face—deep trenches of worry cut into his forehead, small webs of
worry hung at the corners of his eyes. He felt the legacy of the Stalinist past in his left hand, which had only two fingers, the others cut off,
I imagined, in an underground KGB interrogation room.

But the pages of the *Socialist Worker* didn't seem to focus on communism, or on the promulgation of communist values and ideas. It certainly didn't mention the Soviet Union, or any of the other communist
countries in the world. Instead, the *Socialist Worker* seemed to concentrate on the problems with the American system—on the difficulties
facing America's cities and America's workers. It had editorials on
unionization and corporate tax breaks. There were two impassioned
articles demanding an end to executions. There were a couple of pieces
denouncing the policies of our capitalist society. Its policies, the paper

argued, were going to ruin America's urban centers. I'd been reading as I walked, and now I stopped and looked around me. To my left was an abandoned warehouse. Graffiti covered its brick façade. A line of police tape sealed off the boarded-up doorway. CONDEMNED, said a bright red placard posted on the glass. Judging by the city of Milwaukee, I wondered if it wasn't too late for America's urban centers. Most of the buildings had plywood in their windows. Each piece of plywood looked like a scar.

But by now it was almost six o'clock. I had to sneak back into bed. On this Wednesday night my dad was working at the dealership, so there was a danger that if I lingered too long, he'd catch me. My mom, also, was an early riser. If I didn't hurry, then I'd have to explain where I'd been, a prospect that I didn't particularly enjoy. I closed the *Socialist Worker* and paused at the doorway to my building. In the distance, between the boxy warehouses, I could see a sliver of the lake. It was radiant and gray and seemingly infinite. I liked the way that I could pretend it was an ocean. On the other side, I could imagine, there was another continent, distant and foreign and awaiting discovery.

The next morning I was out on the street again at four A.M. As I left our building I heard a police siren warble in the distance. These were our native birds—the sirens of the Third Ward.

The socialists were clustered at the main gate to Tropic Banana, just as I had hoped they would be. Hannah stood at one edge of the group. I was nervous as I walked toward her. I'd brought my copy of the *Socialist Worker* with me. If all else failed, I figured, I could ask her questions about some of the articles.

"Hi," she said, as I walked up to the group. "Good to see you again." I distinctly felt the focus of eight other sets of eyes. Hannah smiled. "Yesterday morning," she said, "I didn't get your name."

Her teeth were bright and slightly crooked. They made her face seem honest, I decided. They were honest, proletarian teeth.

"I'm Yuri Balodis," I said, pronouncing my last name with a Latvian flourish, imitating the way my parents said it.

The air felt cool and pleasant on the skin of my face. The sky still bore a few stubborn stars, and the moon hung there in the gray—a fat circular moon, a distant milky eye. Once, my dad had spent two or three hours lecturing me drunkenly about the moon. He named all of its seas, in Latin, and explained what each name meant. Standing there in front of Hannah, I wished I'd listened to him. I wished that I could've pointed up at the moon and described its cartography. But, then again, that might have made me seem a little strange.

After it became clear that Hannah was in no danger—that I wasn't some sort of vagrant wandering the streets of the Third Ward before dawn—the socialists thinned out to continue peddling the *Socialist Worker* to the mostly puzzled and annoyed employees of Tropic Banana. Hannah and I talked about the paper and her passionate dedication to the socialist cause. She mentioned, offhand, her knowledge of the works of Trotsky and Lenin and someone named Gramsci. Did I know, she asked, that Milwaukee elected the first socialist mayor in America? I said that I didn't. As early as 1888, she told me, a socialist ran the city. I asked her how she'd become interested in radical politics. The question seemed to offend her.

"I don't know what you're implying," she said. "The ideological commitment is all mine."

I said that I didn't doubt her. She said that after she graduated in May she was going to go travel in the Soviet Union, so that she could see a country where equality was the most important part of daily life. I looked around. Things didn't seem terribly unequal to me. The daylight, for instance, was preparing to break very equally over all of the paved streets of downtown Milwaukee. The streetlights—and I pointed this out to Hannah—were there for everyone to use, for everyone to enjoy. She sighed.

"You have a lot to learn," she said. "What are you doing for the rest of the morning?"

This is how I became—at age fifteen—a vendor of the *Socialist Worker*, America's leading biweekly work of communist propaganda. I was ensnared by Hannah's blue eyes and her slightly off-center teeth and her uncombed hair. In the USSR, I'd come to learn, the name of the government-run paper was *Pravda*, or *Truth*. While I was skeptical about the truth of some of the stories in the paper I sold, at least they had energy, an indefinable vigor that swept me into its enthusiasm.

Hannah introduced me to the group. They were cheerful, mostly, if a little bit wary. I had, after all, approached them on the street. I got the sense that they were institutionally paranoid. One or two of them gave me nervous looks; I was sure that they'd already decided that I was some kind of FBI informer. A small and young—but perhaps young and dangerous—tool of the Milwaukee establishment. The idea of this amused me greatly.

For two weeks I sold the papers without incident. Each day, Monday through Friday, we stomped through the warehouse district, targeting the few businesses that remained in downtown Milwaukee. I traversed the landscape of decaying buildings and cracked pavement, holding a heavy stack of newspapers, offering the *Socialist Worker* to everyone for the meager price of fifty cents.

But no one wanted it. No one cared. In the first nine days I was out there, I didn't sell a single copy. And, from what I could tell, nobody else was selling them, either. A few workers did come up to us and give us small donations—one dollar, two dollars, fifty cents—but none of them wanted the paper in return. I think that this bothered the older activists in the group. They were feeling, I believe, increasingly irrelevant. No one was interested in what they had to say—and this was the worst thing that could happen to a political organization.

Sometimes we'd split into smaller clusters. I'd invariably manage to finesse my way into Hannah's group. We'd walk through Mitchell Park, offering the *Socialist Worker* to a succession of early-morning joggers and bicyclists. We'd walk over the green, grassy hills, lost in a wash of ideas. We'd walk beneath the glassy reflection of the park's three climate-controlled domes—domes that served as hothouses for the Milwaukee Horticultural Society—precarious and glimmering in the first pale sunlight of the day. Sometimes, we'd walk as far as the Wisconsin Gas Company Building, with the three-color flame on its tower, or Kehr's Kandy Kitchen on West Lisbon Avenue, where the air was filled with the delirious thick scent of chocolate. The city was a boundless set of possibilities—a seemingly endless reserve of people who would politely refuse our offer of the newspaper.

I loved the sense of companionship that I had with the other vendors. Though I didn't know much about them beyond their names, we still shared a sense of communal struggle, of communal labor. My home life was solitary. I read and read and read. Occasionally I surfaced to go to the store with my mom or listen to one of my dad's drunken stories. But I didn't have much in the way of community.

Was I doing this solely for the love of socialists and the *Socialist Worker*? Of course not. But through my conversations with Hannah, I did realize that I had no opinions about dozens of issues, issues ranging from free trade to protection of the environment. I considered myself a fairly savvy fifteen-year-old. But I had no idea that public university tuition had increased by 80 percent in the past ten years, or that the war on drugs was putting people in federal prison for possession of tiny amounts of marijuana.

How Hannah had managed to develop these seemingly comprehensive opinions was a mystery to me. Then I got to know her father—Dr. Gerald Graham. Dr. Graham was a media studies professor at Marquette University. Marquette was located in the neighboring zip code—53201—but this one digit formed, in my mind, a vast and practically unbridgeable gulf. The university was framed by a massive tangle of highway overpasses. I knew that the quad was grassy and idyllic, but this beauty seemed foreign to my life, with its warehouses and abandoned, weed-infested lots.

Hannah's father was always there—a constant presence watching over his daughter. He had the charisma and energy of a zealot and he seemed to be—if nothing else—in charge of the group's enthusiasm. He'd traveled throughout the Soviet Union in the 1960s, I learned through conversations with Hannah and the others, and he'd met with Khrushchev and Brezhnev and a young Mikhail Gorbachev. He'd lived in Moscow for a summer, and he'd worked in a tractor factory. This fact, above all others, was the most frequently related part of Dr. Graham's past. What job, after all, was more appropriate for a socialist than working in a Soviet tractor factory?

"It's a pleasure to make your acquaintance," Dr. Graham had said, when Hannah had introduced us to each other on that first day that I sold the paper.

I'd wondered, for a moment, how exactly an acquaintance was made, but I'd smiled and discussed Alexander Hamilton High School with Dr. Graham, who said that while the level of education was prob-ably higher at a private institution, he believed wholeheartedly in the public education system.

"But isn't Marquette a private university?" I'd asked.

Dr. Graham had blushed and laughed in a loud, nervous way.

"Touché," he'd said, and turned quickly away from me.

Dr. Graham clearly enjoyed organizing things. He liked to call the vendors together and deliver a speech. I imagined him at home, gazing into a mirror and rehearsing.

"Foot soldiers," he would call, and everyone would assemble in a circle around him. "Foot soldiers, we are not having much luck here today. But tomorrow, tomorrow will be a better day. We are fighting for justice. We are fighting for dignity. We are fighting against capitalism, and its brutish abuse of the common man. Above all—my compatriots and patriotic American comrades—we are fighting."

Invariably, the group would issue a ragged and discordant cheer. To me, this cheer sounded more pathetic than inspirational, more like an emphasis of weakness than an expression of power. But Hannah's face, on these occasions, filled with a certain joy. Dr. Graham was her father and, I could also tell, he was a heroic presence in her life, a wellspring of emotion and physical awe. It didn't matter that his rhetoric was obviously just that—a linguistic empty set, as meaningless as any bit of political jargon. She listened to him. She loved him and respected what he said.

My relationship with my dad was a little different. I listened to what he said, but often because I had no choice—because he was physically restraining me, holding me by the shirt collar or blocking me out on the balcony with his well-padded, alcohol-soaked bulk. He'd smile and say, "Let me tell you now a story that you have not heard," and I'd have heard it, but I'd be forced to listen anyway. At least sometimes he shared his bourbon.

The last day that I secretly sold the *Socialist Worker* in the streets of Milwaukee was Friday, the first of September. The day itself was muggy; the air felt hot and uncomfortable, even at five in the morning. It was the kind of day that bred flies, spontaneously birthing them out of the fabric of its own heat. By noon, I could tell, the asphalt near the railroad tracks would be melting.

That day was also notable because it was my first sale. We were camped at the entrance to the Pabst brewery. I wasn't really sure why. I figured that Hannah and the other socialists liked the acrid odor of the fermenting yeast—that warm, beery smell that hung over these blocks near the waterfront. But the Pabst employees weren't overly friendly or left leaning. Our luck was no better with them.

Nonetheless, on that Friday morning, a worker stopped as he walked past me. He was wearing black jeans and a hat that said, improbably, Virginia Is for Lovers.

"*Socialist Worker?*" I asked him, not wanting to appear too stunned that he'd stopped. He stared at me, his eyebrows raised. For a moment, I thought he might attack.

"You know," he finally said, "the air-conditioning broke in there yesterday."

"Really?" I said, scrambling for a follow-up. "It must've been hot."

"Damn right," he roared. "With all the machinery—it was over a hundred degrees on the line." He leaned toward me and lowered his voice. "But you know what? The beer is air-conditioned." He shook his head. "They keep the beer nice and cold, but I lost nine pounds in there. That's one pound an hour, just from the heat."

He reached into his pocket and pulled out a crumpled bill. "Here you go," he said. "At least you guys care." He folded the paper and put it in his pocket as he walked away.

I watched him enter the Pabst building. Suddenly, I felt terribly guilty. I wanted to go in there and return his dollar. I wanted to tell him that no, he was wrong, I didn't care, really. Not really, not in the way he thought. I wanted to tell him that I cared much more about this girl, Hannah Graham. I wanted to say that if she hadn't had blue eyes and crooked teeth, then I probably wouldn't have been standing there, selling that paper, with its biased perspective and its consistently contrary ideas.

But Dr. Graham was calling out to the group. "Foot soldiers," he was shouting, and the rest of the vendors were clustering around him. "Foot soldiers," he repeated, "today was a decent day. Yuri, I noticed, made some sales." There was a polite spatter of applause. "Now, let's head for City Hall!"

"City Hall?" I said, but no one appeared to be listening. It must have been close to six thirty by the time we left the brewery, walking toward City Hall on East Erie.

Thinking back on it now, I realize that I should have been more careful. I should have considered how close we were to my neighborhood. I didn't see my dad until it was far too late. I heard the release of the brakes on the bus. I watched distractedly as the white-and-blue behemoth pulled away from the stop. I didn't expect what I saw next: my dad, wearing his light blue work coveralls and safety goggles, tipping back a can of Pabst Blue Ribbon, singing softly to himself in the muggy early morning. I froze. The group of socialists was walking right for him—they'd pass each other in the crosswalk—and I had to figure out what to do. I weighed my options. I could try to slip away. There was a chance that he wouldn't see me. He was, after all, already a little drunk. I could detach myself from the group as casually as possible, and then try to beat my dad to our apartment. Or I could try to saunter by him, hoping that my face would blend into the crowd of other, socialist faces.

My options, however, quickly narrowed. My dad's eyes were sharper than I'd imagined. Within seconds he'd spotted me. He waved to me and called my name as he approached. The group of socialists parted to let him pass. He looked like a drunk Moses, parting the sea of reds, bearing the staff of beer before him. All he was missing was the flowing white robe.

"*Gemütlichkeit*," my dad said. He smiled and handed me a can of Pabst. "It is German word for 'beer, sausage, and fresh air.'" He tipped his can and swallowed its last, foamy bubbles. "What are you doing here?" he asked. He sensed, I think, that something unusual was going on. He was being as neutral and polite as possible. The socialists had formed a little crowd around us.

"What am I doing? You're the one who's drinking on the street," I said.

"Do not worry so much about laws and regulations," my dad said. He gave me a look as if he were imparting some sort of great wisdom. He didn't seem to question my presence there, almost as if it were perfectly natural for him to have found me, standing in the middle of East Erie Street at six thirty A.M.

"Did you know," he said, hiccupping gently, "that before Prohibition the Pabst brewery had so much money, my darling, that they tied a real blue ribbon on every bottle, by hand?"

"I didn't know that," I said. My stomach churned with anxiety.

"What is that newspaper you are holding?" my dad asked.

I thought of a variety of lies. It's just a neighborhood bulletin, I imagined myself saying. Or perhaps a newspaper affiliated with my high school. Or some sort of special foldout from the *Journal-Sentinel*. He would've believed anything probably, in his slightly intoxicated state. But I sensed the pressure of the socialists gathered around us. They were staring at me, wondering why it was taking me so long to answer my dad. I hesitated.

"It's the newspaper of the International Socialist Organization," Dr. Graham volunteered, stepping forward. "We're unifying all forms of struggle against the oppressive tyranny of the corporation."

If it is a beautiful, clear day on Lake Michigan—if there's been a recent rain and the air is relatively free of smog—then the water of the lake can give you the sensation of endless life. It offers you this sensation just for looking, just for considering its body, its aquatic span, which vanishes into the distant horizon. On clear mornings in the spring, I'd often stand on any one of the numerous concrete piers of downtown Milwaukee and just look into the watery distance. It gave me a sensation of smallness, of insignificance, a sensation that would simultaneously scare me and also make me feel fully alive and sad. This is approximately how I felt at that moment on East Erie Street— while I waited for my dad to beat the stuffing out of Hannah's socialist father.

Instead, my dad took me by the arm and pulled me aside. He grabbed the newspapers out of my hands. "What are you doing with these people?" he asked. "Do you know who gives them money?"

"Workers," I said, feeling belligerent. "Socialist workers."

"Wrong," he said. "The communists, Yuri. The Soviets. They are funded through a complex network of banks and embezzlement procedures." He strained to look me in the eyes. "What is wrong with you? Do you want to be on a list that the government keeps?"

My dad had no ability to modulate his voice. Whether he was talking or singing, it almost always came out the same. In this situation, he refused to acknowledge that there were other people standing within feet of us. He hovered above me, and his breath was all alcohol.

"Let us leave, Yuri," my dad said. "Let us go home."

"You should allow your son to think for himself," Dr. Graham said. He reached for my other arm, trying to coax me from my dad's grip. My dad didn't react well to this. With the exaggerated movements of someone who'd been drinking, he slapped away Dr. Graham's hand. He tightened his hold on me and started to steer me down the block. For a moment I thought about resisting. I thought about tearing myself away and making some sort of dramatic declaration in support of socialism or the socialist cause. But then I thought of the Pabst employee, and the way he'd walked into the brewery earlier that day, despite anticipating ten hours of labor in saturating, thick heat. I wasn't any sort of authentic political activist, I realized. I wasn't legitimate. Any statement I'd make would be an inauthentic one. I wasn't fighting this fight—not really, not authentically.

"Foot soldiers," I heard Dr. Graham call in the street behind me, "we must help our comrade-in-arms."

There have been many great occasions in the history of the socialist movement, worldwide. Millions of men and women have given their lives for the socialist cause. They've died on battlefields; they've died in alleyways; they've died the thousand minuscule deaths of the passionate, hopeful, idealistic heart. But the socialist brigade that briefly chased my dad and me through the streets of Milwaukee's Third Ward was easily the sorriest example of this struggle, to date. They caught us at the door to our building. My dad clutched my arm. I wasn't sure if I was being liberated or kidnapped.

"Leave him alone!" someone called from the back of the crowd. "Tyrant!" someone else yelled. And then, perhaps more imaginatively: "Mussolini!"

"Stay away from him," my dad said. He pawed in his pocket for the keys to the front door. I briefly caught sight of Hannah. She'd averted her eyes. She was focusing on anything but the profoundly embarrassing spectacle on the stoop in front of her.

"Wait," Dr. Graham yelled, forcing his way to the front of the socialists. "All we're asking, Mr. Balodis, is that you give your son a chance to speak." Hannah's father badly mispronounced our name, giving it a clumsy, American varnish. But he continued: "Ask him, Mr. Balodis, if he'd like to continue helping us—continue helping the socialist cause, worldwide."

My dad shuffled through his enormous ring of keys. Finally, he found the one to the front door. I can still see the glint of sunlight that reflected off that key. I can still see the dirt on his cracked nails, the broad borders of dirt and grease that he could never quite scrub off his skin. I can smell the stale, dusty scent of his clothes—that scent like the inside of a vacuum—and I remember the way his coveralls felt in the palm of my hand.

"Ah, comrade," he said, the metallic tinge of derision rising into his voice, "you are truly an idiot." Then, with a swift, abrupt gesture, he pursed his lips and spat in Dr. Graham's face.

"Come on," my dad said to me. He put the key in the lock, turned the doorknob, and shoved the heavy door open. As he struggled to pull me inside, one last, unopened can of beer fell from his pocket. It hit the concrete and exploded, spraying the socialists, I imagined, with a downy film of Pabst Blue Ribbon.

2

Friday, september 1, 1989
7:00 A.M.

The first travel writer, quite possibly, was the Greek philosopher Xenophon. In the year 400 BC, Xenophon walked through the Achaemenid Empire, through what is now western Iran and eastern Iraq. He saw the sights, drank the wine, sampled the food, and, not surprisingly, wore through a significant number of sandals. What he also did—much to the chagrin of future generations—was define temperance. "Temperance," Xenophon wrote, "is moderation in all things healthful, and total abstinence from all things harmful."

My dad, of course, would have argued that bourbon *was* healthful—for him—and that he did in fact enjoy it in moderation. If pressed, he might admit that bourbon was not, strictly, a vitamin, but he would argue for its medicinal qualities. "Bourbon is good for the legs," he would tell me with a solemn nod, "and also for the skin and the nails."

But Milwaukee has never been a center of moderation. The hub of twentieth-century America's brewing industry, Milwaukee once supplied 30 percent of the nation's beer. In the early 1900s, the missionaries of sobriety descended on the city, en masse, hoping to reform and revitalize and remake. They came to the eastern coast of Wisconsin by the thousands, campaigning and pamphleteering up and down the Lake Michigan shore. Poor, poor Milwaukee, they said. It was a town run by the lust and greed of alcohol. The streets were violent and soaked in liquor. In 1902, Carrie Amelia Moore Nation—Carrie A. Nation, the founder of the Woman's Christian Temperance Union—said of the city: "If there is any place that is hell on earth, it is Milwaukee."

My dad, obviously, disagreed. He loved Milwaukee. It was his city, his adopted city, and the center of his life in his adopted country. He felt a pang of sadness whenever Milwaukee's sports teams lost. He drank local beer with pride—when he didn't drink Heaven Hill Kentucky Bourbon—and he augmented his diet with a fair amount of Milwaukee-made bratwurst. He reveled in the city's street festivals, which tended to feature sauerkraut, and he owned at least one brown sweatshirt that bore the city's official motto: MILWAUKEE, A GREAT PLACE ON A GREAT LAKE.

But on that morning, my dad dragged me inside and locked the door behind us. My mom was in the kitchen when we arrived. She was scrambling eggs, and she held a little bucket of bacon fat in her hand. This bucket was small, about the size of a milk jug, and she kept it under the sink. Whenever she fried bacon in our cast-iron skillet, my mom would pour the hot fat into this bucket, where it would sit and congeal and become opaque. She'd then use it as cooking oil. When she cooked eggs—or fried potatoes or fish on the stovetop—she'd spoon some of the bacon fat into the pan. It would sizzle with appropriate vigor. If you stood too near the fire, the fat would leap from the pan and scald your skin.

"Yuri," my mom said, "what were you doing outside?"

"That is an excellent question, Mara," my dad said. He motioned for me to sit on one of the chairs at the kitchen table. "It is a question that I, myself, asked him. I am feeling that you will be surprised by the answer, in my opinion."

I sat sullenly at the table. What could I say? I wasn't ashamed of what I'd been doing. It wasn't like I'd planned any of it. It had started with the herring in mustard sauce; indigestion had led me, unintentionally, to the socialist cause.

"Go on," my dad said. I continued staring at the floor. The fibers of the carpet, I noticed, were long and ropelike. I had a brief image of the carpet as a living, growing entity, one that stretched its fibers toward the sunlight, just like a plant. Since I obviously wasn't going to say anything, my dad volunteered the information.

"He was walking around with socialists. He was selling a socialist newspaper on the street."

"*Vai dieninas,*" my mom said, which was what she said whenever she was overwhelmed by particularly dramatic news. The rough translation of this phrase was "Oh daytime," which always seemed like an odd way to express surprise. "Where are there socialists around our neighborhood?" she added, turning off the stove and peering fearfully at the door, as if she imagined that a pack of them, wild and blood-thirsty, were about to break into the apartment.

"They are everywhere, Mara. Do not be so naïve." My dad sighed and waved his hand dismissively. "They are probably down there right now."

My mom went over to the balcony. She slid open the door and stepped outside. She looked down at the city, scanning it, from left to right, for socialists. She turned around. "None that I can see," she said.

When my mom returned to the apartment, my parents began a long discussion. They asked me about my political beliefs, and about the extent to which I was involved with the *Socialist Worker*. I told them, mostly, the truth. Occasionally, I told a lie. I said, for instance, that I'd been reading Lenin and Trotsky for a number of months, and that they seemed like brilliant economists and philosophers. This was not tech-nically true, since I'd never read any communist thinkers. But Hannah and the others were so conversant with them—reciting lines from *Das Kapital* at moments of indecision or crisis—that the work of these writers seemed familiar to me.

"The tradition of dead generations weighs like an Alp upon the brains of the living," I said to my parents, remembering a sentence that Hannah had said, again and again, over the past twelve days. I crossed my arms and scowled, trying my best to look revolutionary.

"Ah!" my dad yelped. He held his face in his hands. "He is quoting Marx," he said. He sat heavily on the floor, a very real sorrow on the features of his face. "We have lost our darling son."

The rest of the morning went much like this: I sat at the kitchen table and listened to my parents harangue me about the socialists. They never expected this from me, they said, especially not here in America. Here in America, there was no need for socialists, my dad said, this was obvious from just looking around. Why would I be inter-ested in such a miserable group of people? Did I understand what socialism meant? What communism meant? How would the workers be better off, my dad asked, in a socialist state? After an hour or so, I couldn't take it anymore. I fled to my bedroom and closed the door. I sat in the middle of the floor in stunned silence. My mind was blank. I focused on my breathing and my heartbeat. I sighed, inexplicable shivers moving up and down my spine. Finally, I took a book down from my shelf—*Crime and Punishment*—and began reading.

The pages moved quickly. I neared the end of the book. Raskolnikov was wandering around St. Petersburg. He was twenty-three years old and a murderer and delirious with poverty and rain and his wild intellectual theories. I watched him seek redemption in the Russian Orthodox Church. I read with shock as he slipped the crucifix around his neck and confessed his crime. I was on the last page of Part Six when I was startled by a knock on the door.

"It is noon and I am going to work," my mom said. She poked her head into my room. She sighed heavily as she looked at me. She seemed to be on the verge of tears. "Do you want me to bring you any books?"

For the past eight years, my mom had worked as a clerk at the Milwaukee Public Library. Her job helped fuel my addiction to literature. She'd frequently bring me stacks of books, as many as she could carry at one time, and drop them on the floor outside of my bedroom. She wanted me to read them in the main room, where I could keep my parents company—sure—but as long as I did this, then my reading was fine with her.

"How about Stalin's memoirs," I suggested. "Or Emma Goldman's autobiography. The socialists suggested that one, especially."

"Do you like to hurt your mother? Do you enjoy to make her feel so sad?"

"What about *The Communist Manifesto?*"

"I will bring you a nice book by a patriotic American," she said, as she shut the door. "Someone like Dwight Eisenhower, or possibly Senator McCarthy. You need a book like this, in my opinion."

It wasn't that I wanted to make my parents unhappy. I'd just been stunned by the violence of my dad's actions. I could see him pursing his lips, could see the saliva shooting out of his mouth and landing squarely between Dr. Graham's eyes. I could hear Hannah's horrified gasp, and I was profoundly embarrassed by what he'd done. I envisioned leaving the United States with Hannah, defecting with her to the Soviet Union, where we would live honest, proletarian lives, and perhaps even work with our hands, on a communal farm or factory. I had friends in high school who were planning to spend a year on an Israeli kibbutz. I imagined that this was the type of life for me: communal living, communal work, communal satisfaction. Sure, my dad had hated it. But he was older, less flexible, less improvisational, more drunk. He deserved a communist son—just for acting the way that he did.

The day passed like this, lost to my compulsive reading. I finished *Crime and Punishment* and moved on to the next book on my list—*Portnoy's Complaint*. I went out into the living room with this one, just so my dad would be a little less disappointed in me. My mom, I knew, would be home around six. Her shifts were short, and the downtown branch was within walking distance of our apartment. My dad, I could see, was drinking from a bottle of bourbon on the balcony and reading the newspaper. As the sun sank lower in the sky, my dad looked almost like a statue, his skin burnished by the yellow light, shadows painted across the planes of his face.

I fell asleep. I had fragmented, confusing dreams, many of which were haunted by disembodied images of Stalin. In one of the dreams, Stalin lectured me on the proper way to sell a newspaper. It was all in the flare of the voice, he said, and the way in which you shouted the paper's name. In my dream, I nodded and listened and worried about the health of my subconscious.

When I awoke it was six P.M. and my mom was opening the front door. She had a little box of books tucked under her arm. "I have many wonderful books for you!" she said, by way of greeting. "I have a Young Adult biography of Ronald Reagan, and it has lots of excellent photographs."

As soon as my mom arrived home, my dad began to stir. He dropped the newspaper onto the wooden planks of the balcony; one section of the *Journal-Sentinel* blew over the rail. I imagined the paper on its wind-aided journey, floating through the city streets in a way I never would. I was intensely jealous of this newspaper; I longed to rise out of the apartment and soar into the evening air.

We ate dinner at eight. Dinner was a thick beet stew—scarlet colored and full of soft, warm beets and pliant boiled potatoes. This was a favorite meal of my mom's. She'd always attributed the recipe to her own mother—invoking this inheritance tearfully as a part of the pre-meal prayer—but on this evening she gave the blessing a new twist.

"Thank you, God, for this delicious beet stew," she said, "which came to us from my mother in the Soviet Union, who cannot be with us, because she died under communism, sad and longing for freedom, unlike her ungrateful grandchildren, who don't even read the books I bring them about Ronald Reagan."

My dad ate quickly and within a half-hour he was out on the balcony again. I helped with the dishes and then took the biography from its stack in my room. I walked back into the kitchen, bearing the book in front of me, a talisman against my mother's anger. "Like Abraham Lincoln or George Washington or Thomas Jefferson," I read aloud as my mom dried the last pieces of cutlery, "Ronald Reagan was born to humble beginnings. Though his family wasn't rich in money, they were rich in love, and—as we all know—love is the most important thing of all." I snapped the book shut and sat at the table. "Mom," I demanded, "do I have to read this?"

"It will be educational for you, Yuri."

"But I don't want to be educated," I said. "I would rather remain uneducated. Hannah says that education is simply a tool of the corporate state—that education is how America enslaves its middle class."

My mom sighed and dried her hands on her apron. She moved steadily from task to task. Now she was reorganizing her spice rack, turning all of the little bottles in the same direction, making sure that her system—organization by the color of the spice—was firmly in place.

"Who is Hannah?" she asked.

"Nobody," I said. "But still—doesn't this seem a little ridiculous? How many American flags can they fit in one book? The cover is an American flag, the title page is red and white and blue."

"The flag is an important symbol of a patriotic state," my mom said. She dusted off her little container of celery salt.

I played with the binding of the book, peeling at the edges of its Dewey decimal sticker. I felt like I was awash in propaganda, bobbing from the left to the right, from the left to the right. Was there any middle ground? I wondered. I looked at my mom—who was now methodically sweeping the kitchen floor—and sighed. But then my dad's voice bellowed through the darkness.

"Mara," he yelled, "let the boy outside."

I'm not sure why I wasn't capable of going out onto the balcony myself. My mom swept into action, though, and left the kitchen and crossed the living room and opened the screen door. "Outside, *bucina*," she said with a flourish. *Bucina* meant "little kiss" in Latvian, and to my teenage mortification it was her favorite name for me.

"Out," she repeated, and waved me through the door. "Go and drink and listen to your father."

I scurried onto the balcony.

"Do you want some bourbon, Yuri?" my dad asked me as soon as I emerged. He'd already prepared my glass, a small, clean one that stood by itself on the wooden railing. I nodded. The liquor splashed from the bottle, a full measure of it, and my dad swept away a cloud of mosquitoes with his other arm. The mosquitoes were everywhere during August and September—surging green clouds of mosquitoes, eager for our blood.

We waited together on the balcony, saying very little. I sipped the bourbon. My dad, however, gulped it with enthusiasm and speed. "You will enjoy the hair growing on your chest from this drinking, in my opinion," he said. "This will help you avoid the communist menace, I am certain."

I'd grown accustomed to the oaky sear of the alcohol from sips my dad had given me over the years, but still I couldn't drink without grimacing, the way actors could drink in the movies. My dad could almost do it, but that was after a lifetime of hard alcohol. Even so, he winced slightly when he drank, his eyes narrowing a little, the edges of his mouth hanging slightly open.

"Drinking is good, here in the Beer City, yes?"

I nodded slightly, but continued to stare at my glass, which I held between my palms. I pressed inward on it, sloshing the golden liquid over the ice cubes. My dad kept pushing me.

"What a wonderful night to see all of these stars—so beautiful in the sky."

"Look, Dad," I said. "I'll stand here, I'll drink the bourbon. But I don't want to pretend that everything's fine."

I shot a glance up at him; his face had softened with the bourbon. I was ashamed of what had happened earlier that day. To be honest, I'd always thought of my dad as a bit of a lush. But he'd never done anything as hurtful or injurious as what he'd done that morning on the street. He ran a hand over his thinning hair; he looked tremendously old and fat, a relic of a time that had disappeared.

"Oh, Yuri," he said, "there is so much to tell you. How can I make you understand?" He put down his glass on the rail of the balcony. He cupped my shoulders in the palms of his hands. "My darling," he said, "have I ever told you the tragic yet captivating story of Yuri Mishkin, after whom we name you?"

My parents' English was a strange beast. They'd learned it together, during a time when the government of the Latvian Soviet Socialist Republic officially discouraged English, and when a single English-language textbook cost more than a month's salary. As a consequence, they'd taught themselves the language mostly from magazines, from a range of prohibited American and English periodicals. Frequently, they used words like *whom*. Frequently, they added grafts from Russian, such as the ubiquitous "in my opinion," which hung at the end of their sentences like a passive-aggressive pit bull.

He'd told me about Yuri Mishkin numerous times, of course, too many to count. But still I shook my head and focused on the floor.

"Ah, Yuri Mishkin," my dad continued, emotion swelling through his voice. "He was a great man, and so kind. The kindest, greatest singer to perform in the bars of Riga. A voice like a siren, and so sad. Just like heartbreak, every time." Slowly, and with many gestures and smashings of mosquitoes, my dad told me for the twentieth time the story of Yuri Mishkin, Latvia's greatest country and western singer, circa 1959. In it, he seemed to imply, there was a great lesson for me, a lesson that would help alleviate my anger, and help explain his behavior on the street this morning.

THE TRAGIC YET CAPTIVATING STORY OF YURI MISHKIN, AFTER WHOM WE NAME YOU

"You see," my dad said, spreading his arms wide, gesturing to the open air, "when Stalin died in 1953 I was twenty years old. I'd just started at the Ministry of Culture, the Kulturas Ministrija. I was at a low level. All I did was sign papers. Piles and piles of papers crossed my desk each day and I signed them, scrawling the same signature each time with the same black pen. It was a great job, you know, one of the best I could hope for. My own father had arranged it for me, bribing many officials in Latvia's Communist Party.

"One day, after I had been working a few months, I noticed that overnight they had changed the decorations. Instead of the two pictures of Stalin behind my desk, as usual, now there were four. I looked around a little and I noticed that this had happened in the whole ministry—and it seemed to have gone by some kind of math formula. Where there had been one photo, now there were two. Where there had been four, now there were sixteen. Some walls were entirely covered in small photographs of Stalin. He smiled at all of us, you know. He watched carefully and with a thousand eyes.

"Of course, one week later we learned he was dead. In Riga there was a big funeral, one that was attended by thousands of mourners. It was early in March, and the air was tremendously cold. Snow fell on Lenin Street—swirling clouds of snow. The whole city was there. But if you find any of the photographs, you'll see that no one was sad. No one was crying. No one dared to laugh—this is true. But no one was sad, either. We were all relieved.

"Then Khrushchev came. When Khrushchev came, we thought, okay, it will be different now. He was small and fat and smiling, whereas Stalin was just like his name: Из Стали, *na stalyeh*, the Man of Steel. Now, with Khrushchev, there would still be the ideals and there would still be the Party but maybe we would be happier. Maybe we would have a chance for free expression. That is all we wanted. A chance for free expression—a chance to say what we believed. We wanted to speak Latvian; we wanted the Latvian language on the billboards and in the official papers of the government and on the menus in the bars and cafés.

"At any rate, I received a promotion. I was suddenly in charge of approving the set lists for all of the musicians in Riga."

My mom chose this moment to interrupt.

"Do not lie to him!" she shouted from inside the apartment. She had a plate in her hand. Perhaps, I thought, she'd been reorganizing the dishes in the cupboard to the left of the sink.

"Mara, leave me alone. I am not lying. It is all true."

She opened the screen door and gestured disdainfully toward the sky. "True? What is true? How could he know what you make up and what you tell exactly?" She threatened to fling the plate at us. "You make the past happy and good and funny, like a fairy tale," she said, wiping her mouth with the back of her free hand.

"Happy? You call this happy? You wait, Mara. You come out here and have a drink and wait. You will see how I make it."

My mom issued an exasperated noise and retreated back into the apartment.

"Do not listen to your mother. She is being too crazy for us, right now. Listen to what I am saying. Relax. Have some drink." He cleared his throat and began again. "You see, my darling, musicians could not play whatever song they wanted, as they can here in Milwaukee. Because songs were powerful. Who had a television? Nobody. Songs were the news. They were patriotic and emotional and they could catch on. A government could rise or fall because of a song. I do not know why. That is just how it was. So the musicians would come to the ministry and they would submit a song list, and I would make sure they were not playing 'God Bless America,' and they would get a certificate and leave. I met many musicians this way. Suddenly, I was spending my time in bars. This is how I met your mother, too. She was a drinker, let me tell you, and a smoker."

This was my cue. "A smoker?"

"Of course. We all smoked Riga cigarettes. They were so cheap, less expensive than a cup of black tea with milk. But they tasted like cardboard. We smoked them anyway. I smoked and drank and went to the bars and listened to the music and the night I met your mother—he was playing."

"Who?" I said, although I knew the answer.

"Yuri Mishkin," my dad said. "Ah, Yuri Mishkin. He first came into my office on a rainy day in the summer of 1956. He looked a lot like me, you know. We both had blue eyes. He had brought his guitar with him. When I looked at him I could have sworn I was looking at my double. He smiled and handed me the list and I puffed out my vest and tried to look official. The truth is I never had to refuse a list—they were all too afraid of deportation to play anything controversial. The police would arrest you and then, within weeks, you'd be on a train heading for a Siberian gulag.

"But as I looked at this paper, I saw that there were religious songs, many of them, and songs that criticized the government. 'How can you play these?' I asked him. 'You could be arrested, in my opinion.' He looked at me, and then—and I will never forget this—and then he played the whole list. Right there, from beginning to end, in my office. A crowd gathered, just to listen to his voice. He was mournful, and sad, and his translations from English to Russian were so beautiful. I approved the list right away."

"But you knew you would get in trouble?" I asked. I always asked this. My dad enjoyed this question because it made him seem more heroic.

"Of course, of course. But what could I do? He was a genius. So I went to all of his performances, just in case there was any trouble. And for two years, everything was perfect. Khrushchev gave us some freedoms. We printed books and newspapers in Latvian. Some people began to suggest, just perhaps, that Latvia could be free again.

"Mishkin was the most famous of all our cultural heroes. We loved him, simply because he had a sorrowful voice and songs that were soothing. Also, he looked quite good in a suit and cowboy hat.

"But then, in 1959, something happened."

"What?" I always asked. I never got a satisfactory answer.

"Well, my darling, it was simply this: Khrushchev went crazy. He banned certain kinds of music, certain kinds of dancing. He closed all the newspapers. He deported the writers and editors. The Thaw was over. Then, he came to the Baltics—Estonia, Latvia, Lithuania—on a tour, to put his popularity, how do you say, in cement.

"Of course, the one song you could never play was the old Latvian national anthem, 'God Bless Latvia.' No one dared to even whisper it. The night before Khrushchev arrived I was in a bar on Lenin Street, drinking with some friends. In walked Yuri Mishkin. He saw me and came over and sat at our table. We were all happy to see him, you know.

"He sat down and right away I could see he was depressed. He drank quickly—bourbon in tall glasses. I knew that in the next morning he was scheduled to play a few songs at the reception for Khrushchev. This was, of course, a great honor. I had arranged it for him. I had recommended him to my director, who had in turn recommended him one level higher, and on this milk road Mishkin had received an invitation."

"Milk road?" I asked. "What's a milk road?"

"It is an expression. Do not worry so much about it. So, anyway, Mishkin the next morning was late, of course, and he had clearly been drinking all night. He stank of it. Anyway, he stood on one side of the stage and Khrushchev stood on the other. This was in front of the Railway Terminal, downtown, where so many people could gather together to see. The Party band played the Soviet anthem, and we all saluted. Then Mishkin got his cue and tuned his guitar. We cheered. We were all so happy."

My dad paused here and looked out over the banister. He tapped his hand against the wood of the railing. He used his good hand—his right hand—to massage the stubs of the fingers on his left.

"It happened so quickly that I didn't even realize at first. Mishkin started to play the other anthem, our anthem, 'God Bless Latvia.' Everyone was shocked, of course. Khrushchev looked like he had a bursting ulcer. Mishkin was singing and it was beautiful, though I have to admit his voice sounded better for Hank Williams's 'Jambalaya.' Suddenly the whole crowd started to hiss, to yell at him to get off the stage. We loved it, yes, but cheering would have been like suicide.

"They took him away in handcuffs. They put him in prison. When I showed up to work the following day, an unmarked van was waiting at the door. They took me, and my director, and my director's director. We spent nearly two years in prison. Your mother—though she had no idea where I was, and though she was only my girlfriend—your mother waited for me all of this time. I was lucky, really. I survived. I only got this," he said, pointing to his wounded hand.

My dad's disability wasn't shocking to me anymore, though depending on my mood it could be gruesome or pathetic or strangely foreign. He was missing two fingers and his thumb on his left hand, and the scars were flat and clean. The fingers had clearly been cut off, and though he could be cloudy on the details, I was sure that he'd been tortured.

"They did the same thing to Mishkin," he concluded. "He came back a broken man, with seven fingers. He never played again."

By the time he'd finished the story, it was after eleven. My mom had gone to sleep, and her absence weighed on us, a disapproving emptiness into which our energy ran. She'd been wrong, of course—the ending was never happy—but I think that she'd objected simply to the telling of it, really. It was a dredging up of unpleasant memories. I was on my second glass of bourbon, and we threatened to finish the bottle. The world was terribly wobbly.

"Yuri?" my dad said, and paused. He seemed to be standing on wheels. "I am sorry to tell you such a story before you sleep. Are you awake?"

I nodded. "I'm inspecting the floor," I said.

"The floor? Ah, the floor. Yes, it is very nice in the dark, this wooden deck, do you not think so?"

I looked up toward him, my voice rising, suddenly out of control and filled with alcohol and anger.

"I don't get it, Dad. Why weren't you angry at Mishkin? I would have been completely furious—"

"Furious?" he said. "Furious at Mishkin? *Ai*, my darling, it was not so simple as this." He shook his head and smiled sardonically. "Furious," he said again, and there was a certain amount of amusement in his voice. He poured himself the last of the bourbon. "Who drank all of this?" he asked no one in particular.

"You did," I volunteered. "Like you always do."

He paused. "What is your meaning?" he said, very carefully.

"I meant exactly what I said. You drank all of the bourbon because you're a drunk."

My dad looked shocked—but shocked in a sleepy, sad way. Then, very slowly, he shrugged. "You are right after all, you know," he said, and then, with one fluid motion, pitched the empty liquor bottle up into the night air.

It landed with a solid crash, the sound of glass exploding, and my dad smiled at this, shook his head a little sadly. He finished his drink. "I am going to sleep," he said, and left me standing on the balcony. Standing there in the darkness, with the little pieces of glass on the asphalt below me, I suddenly felt terribly guilty for what I'd said. I'd called my dad a drunk—and though this was technically true—it didn't change the fact that he was my father. A wave of shame rose and washed over me. What was wrong with me? Why did I always say just the wrong thing? I sighed and turned and walked back to my bedroom. I curled under the covers and went to sleep—still wearing my clothes.

In the two or three hours that I slept, I dreamed many confusing, incoherent things. I had a few nightmares, all of them indistinct and gray, based on a formless sense of fear. The one dream I remember most clearly, though, involved a juggling competition at my high school, and my coach who—in this situation—happened to be Joseph Stalin. All the other kids were juggling bowling pins or beanbags or, at worst, oranges. I was juggling raw steaks. "They will stick to your hands like the glue," Stalin yelled at me in my dad's accent, even as I dropped steak after steak. "You will win this contest for sure, in my opinion."

I awoke to my dad's alcohol-laced breath, hot and overly close to my face.

"I am not always only drinking, you know," my dad said, unprovoked. "I am not only good for nothing. You will see the something I am good for."

I sat up on the bed. I was wearing shoes. I looked stupidly at my feet.

"I just put them on for you, while you were sleeping," he said. "Now, we will go. I will show you a surprise at the car dealer."

I sighed and looked at the clock. I guessed that my dad felt bad about what had happened earlier that day—and that he wanted to make up for it, somehow. But why now? Why now, when the clock read 2:32 A.M.? It was my fault anyway; I'd said something that was completely improper.

"Dad," I began, "I want to apologize."

"Be quiet, Yuri. Do not speak. You will wake your mother."

"But I—"

"Shut up. And don't be loud," my dad whispered as he turned to leave the room. He looked purposeful and resolute. "I said that your mother is sleeping."

What could I do? He was wearing a lavender sweatshirt. He was my dad, Rudolfs Balodis, and we were going on a drunken midnight field trip. He wanted to do this, I could tell. He wanted to seem like a leader, like a good father—or at least his idea of what a good father could be.

We crept through the dark apartment. I tried to make large amounts of noise as I walked. I hoped to awake my mom. I didn't want to go. I wanted to be back in bed, sleeping under the blissful covers, dreaming contentedly of something pleasant. If I woke up my mom, she'd probably be furious. We'd have to stay home.

"Can't we wait until tomorrow?" I asked.

"This is a thing that I can only show to you at night," my dad said.

"Is it a night-blooming flower?"

"Ha ha," he said. "No, it is not a night-blooming flower."

We were out in the hallway, now. My dad had silently closed the door, sealing my warm bed behind a layer of lacquered particleboard. It was hopeless. He ignored me and began walking. We descended the staircase. I worried about what would happen once we reached the dealership. What could he possibly need to show me, what was so important that it couldn't wait for the morning?

We walked through the dark, negotiating a landscape that was part lunar crater and part strip-mall neon. It was a warm summer night and there was some traffic. Cars drifted by with rumbling mufflers, the deep bass of their radios spilling out into the air. I huddled against my dad's side, matching his steps as closely as I could, my head still aching slightly.

I suppose that it was some sort of irony that my dad, who worked at a car dealership, had never been able to afford the monthly payments on a car. He'd dreamed of it, sure, but it had always been unattainable, an unfulfilled desire.

We stood at the bus stop. He peered at the schedule, checked his watch, peered at the schedule again. He turned to me: "Ten minutes we wait," he said. I turned and looked at the strip mall that loomed behind us. The things it promised me, the teenage consumer, were quite remarkable. I could get my ear pierced or rent a tuxedo. I could buy one-dollar Chinese food or receive free Christian Science literature. I could walk away as the proud owner of a new Walkman, or a new vacuum cleaner, or a new pair of shoes from Volume Shoe Source.

Our bus exhaled when it came to the stop—a great hydraulic sigh—and the doors snapped open. The driver was surly. He didn't even look as my dad let a dollar's worth of coins clatter into the fare box. He ripped two transfers from his booklet and handed them to us. "These won't be any good," he said. "I'm the last bus of the night."

There were no other passengers, and the lights in the bullet-shaped compartment were bright white tube fluorescents. They made my dad's face look sallow and tired. His eyes—rimmed with ample pouches of skin—struggled to stay open. For the first time that night I was conscious of his stench. The air around his body was a dense cloud of alcohol. He'd taken a bag with him, a little brown backpack, and now I noticed that it contained another bottle of bourbon. The cap was just barely visible. Six miles of the inky black night later, we were standing in front of Jack Baldwin Chevrolet.

This particular dealership stood at the heart of Milwaukee's Auto Row—a long chain of dealerships, located one after another after another, acres upon acres of gleaming aluminum and steel and glass. We ducked under a waist-high chain and walked quickly through the lot. I let my arms dangle at my sides. My fingers skimmed against the slick new paint of the Luminas and the S-10 Blazers. The dealership at night was beautiful, I decided, a quiet and shadowy paradise of cars that you could someday own. Their colors were suffused with a dark glow. Someday I'd purchase one of these cars for my parents—the nicest Chevrolet that money could buy—and they'd drive it around Milwaukee, proud of this thing their only son had done for them.

"Later you will thank me for this, I am certain," my dad said, as we stood at a side entrance in front of a big metal door. Beside the metal door there was a little white box, the top of which my dad presently lifted. As steadily as he could—concentrating on the work of his good right hand—my dad punched a code into the little white keypad of the alarm system. He swayed and pecked, slowly putting together the chain of numbers: 1 . . . 2 . . . 3 . . . 4. The door buzzed. He grasped its handle and pulled it open. Why even have a security system, I wondered, if the code was this simple?

We were in the body shop. The reek of motor oil and cleaning solvent filled the air, overpowering even the smell of the bourbon. It was cool in there, and the air felt good against my skin. Everywhere there were cars in various states of disassembly. Some of them were covered in blankets or raised on pedestals. "Be careful," my dad whispered to me, and then: "I'll be right back."

I nodded. Although there were no windows, the single bulb my dad had turned on gave off a feeble light.

Being alone in the dealership wasn't that bad. I felt cocooned, safe inside the protection of the building. Or at least safer than I'd felt outside. Outside, walking through the lot, I'd felt extremely nervous, sure that we were about to get caught. I'd been angry at my dad, mad that he'd dragged me out of bed and subjected me to the fluorescent-lit bus ride and his dubious odor. He was insistent, and stubborn, and he wouldn't let me apologize. But now, I felt almost at ease. This was a large space, nearly the size of the bus terminal downtown, and it was impressive to be alone in here.

Hoses trailed everywhere, and massive electronic panels were scattered throughout the room. One wall was entirely motor oil, or at least something that seemed like motor oil, arranged in glass jars on a series of shelves. I took one of the jars down and looked at it more closely. I unscrewed the lid, smelled hesitantly at the liquid, coughed. I dipped my finger in the jar. It felt like lukewarm honey.

When I tried to replace the lid, however, I somehow lost control of it. It spun out of my hands, clattered to the cement floor, and rolled across the room. It rolled and rolled and rolled. It rolled out through the repair bay and into an open pit.

I put down the jar and scurried over to the pit. I looked over its edge. There, on a platform just a few feet below me—the lid glimmered. It taunted me. I reached for it. I stretched as far as I could go. I could feel the ball of my shoulder start to burn. I could feel the cramp spiraling through my rib cage. I lunged. I toppled. I fell.

When I awoke, my dad was looming over me, a strange creature smiling at the top of the pit.

"Would you enjoy a soda?" he asked.

I was dazed. "Yes, I would enjoy a soda," I replied. I realized, with a shock, that I'd been knocked unconscious. I'd been lying there for some significant amount of time—how long, I wasn't sure. It was good that he'd found me. Otherwise, I might have stayed there all night.

He reached down into the repair bay and grabbed me by the front of my shirt. I'd always been a thin kid, but still I was startled by how easily he lifted me. I could feel my forehead throbbing.

My dad handed me a Dr. Pepper. "You're bleeding." he said. "What happened?"

"I don't know," I said. Really, this wasn't a lie. "I think I slipped."

"You could have died," he said. He hiccupped. "Oh, well. You are okay now."

I steadied myself against a nearby car. "Dad," I said as I opened my soda, "I think I want to go home."

My dad looked at me coolly, as if he was coming to some sort of assessment of my worth. "Follow me," he said.

I followed him through a labyrinth of hallways down into the dealership offices and the showroom. The first thing I noticed was that a wall was missing. My dad had opened one side of the showroom—a floor-to-ceiling glass panel that slid on grooves—and a light breeze blew through the aperture. It felt pleasant in my hair, and soothed the cut on my face. The second thing I noticed was the Corvette.

Now, in some ways, 1989 was not a particularly good year for Corvettes. They were—and still are, really—the automotive translation of the teenage male mind. Overly hormonal and angled in an awkward way, this particular Corvette was parked on the edge of the showroom. It was dangerous there, on the cusp of the dealership, two wheels in, two wheels out. It was certainly shiny. It was also a convertible.

"It is so nice, yes? The red is just like a watermelon."

I looked at him. "A watermelon?" I asked.

"Okay, no. Maybe a different red fruit."

I nodded. "Dad," I asked, "did they have cars like this in the Soviet Union?"

He didn't answer at first. Instead, he walked over to the Corvette with its gleaming narrow whitewall tires and sharklike hood. He reached inside and produced a dealer plate and a set of keys. "No," he said. "Get in."

Where were we going? Why were we going there? I didn't really care. Nothing mattered but the scent of leather and new car and Dr. Pepper that enveloped me in a soothing medicinal cloud. My dad jumped in the Corvette without opening the door.

"Just like *Dukes of Hazard*," he called out over his shoulder. He turned the key in the ignition. It roared powerfully to life. "Careful," my dad whispered to himself as we eased through the maze of cars on the lot. "Careful," he muttered as he engaged the blinker and pulled out onto the street. "Careful," he shouted, as he floored the accelerator and shifted from first to third to fifth, and the breath caught in my throat, and I fell back against the seat, flattened by the force of liftoff.

We tore through downtown along Forty-fourth Street and merged on Highway 41. We drove northwest. The tires squealed on almost every curve. From time to time I looked over at the speedometer. The news was never good: seventy, eighty, ninety, a hundred.

"Look in the glove box," my dad shouted over the roar of the road. I struggled forward, popped the latch, and there—of course—was an audio cassette. It was one of my dad's favorites—Moon Mullican, the King of the Hillbilly Piano. I put the tape in the stereo. My dad sang along.

It was a king of a night, a queen of a night. If I ignored the slight deviations to the left and the right of the road—and the fact that we were in violation of probably a dozen laws as we soared along 41—I could feel a certain wild pleasure, a reckless joy in the way we were moving. I also felt a searing sense of guilt and disappointment, but in a way that sharpened everything, made it that much more poignant. Why not steal a car and drive north? What could stop us? The Canadian border? The Arctic Circle? Polar bears? We'd circumnavigate the globe, a drunken Magellan and his teenage son, filling the gas tank with luck or hope or raw life. I felt my anger relent, slightly; the knot in my stomach eased somewhat.

I should never have relaxed. I shouldn't have let go of the tension. I shouldn't have drawn the grass-scented air deep into my lungs. I shouldn't have smiled a little and thrown my head back and looked up at the night sky and listened to my dad singing country and western in his Soviet accent. I shouldn't have struggled to remember that line I'd read just a few nights ago—*the heaventree of stars hung with humid night-blue fruit*—and I certainly shouldn't have closed my eyes to let my other senses absorb this unexpected event. I should have been watching for the police.

When we passed the cop, we must have been traveling at close to seventy miles per hour. This was lucky. My dad had just slowed down to finish his drink, and if we'd been going any faster, the cop would've pulled us over right away. As it was he just swung out behind us. His headlights cut through our rear windshield, making strange shadows on the dashboard. He was within five or six feet of our bumper. My dad immediately slowed down to the speed limit.

"Damn it," he said. "This is quite poor. Look innocent." He took the empty soda can and tossed it on the floor. "Sit up straight," he elaborated.

The cop followed us, followed us, followed us. My dad—inebriated as he must have been—did a remarkable job of driving within the lines. I waited for the howl of the siren, for the swirl of red and blue lights. Would they handcuff my dad? Throw him to the ground? Toss him in the back of the squad car? In a distracted way, I wondered if I, too, would be arrested.

"Okay," my dad said, punctuating every word with a quick glance into the mirror. "If he pulls us over, we will switch seats very craftily."

"Craftily?" I demanded. I must have been yelling. "How can we switch seats craftily?"

"With great craft," he said, and nodded, and swallowed hard.

But there was no siren, no flash of lights. We reached the county line and then—as abruptly as he'd appeared—the cop pulled back off of the road. I resumed breathing. My dad took the first available exit. He pulled onto the shoulder and killed the engine. He sat in the driver's seat, shaking, his head thrown back, his mouth open, his fingers rubbing at the front of his chest. He was clearly in pain. I wondered if he was having a heart attack. After some time he turned to me. "Let us go home," he said. "Never do this yourself."

We returned to the dealership without further incident. As we'd pulled into the lot, as we'd opened the glass wall of the dealership, as we'd washed the car, as we'd dried it with towels from the body shop, as we'd guessed wildly at the Corvette's previous placement in the showroom, as the clock had moved closer and closer to six thirty, I'd been increasingly surprised. No one was going to catch us. We'd logged just under sixty miles on the odometer, a number that the dealership, my dad told me, was unlikely to notice. I was filled with a buoyant effervescence. We'd done something dangerous and we'd made it through.

My dad was crazy, sure, but what a magnificent crazy man he was. It didn't matter, really, what he'd put me through that morning.

We were just about finished—the car was in position but the panel was still wide open—when a man in a navy suit walked around the corner of the building. He was tall and wide, and his forehead had a bright pink splotch. He looked a little like Mikhail Gorbachev.

My dad spun around as soon as he realized we weren't alone. He was holding a towel in his hands, which he quickly used to dust off the front fender of the Corvette.

"Mr. Baldwin," he said. "Good to see you, sir."

So this was Jack Baldwin. His hair was greasy. He had a remarkably phony smile. His teeth were small and his gums were broad oceans of pink.

"Balodis?" he said. "Finishing up so late?"

"Yes, sir." The combination of fear and alcohol, I imagine, had turned my dad perfectly white. I could see the veins in his forehead quite clearly, a maze of narrow blue lines. Sweat dripped from the side of his face.

"You work so hard, Balodis. You should take some time off, you know. And this is your son, I suppose?" Mr. Baldwin pointed to me.

"Yes, sir, that is Yuri, my son. He came to work with me today. You know," he added, gesturing to the showroom and the Corvette we'd so recently stolen, "so he could see what I do each day."

Mr. Baldwin smiled again and nodded and started to walk toward the stairs that would take him to his office. At the bottom stair, he paused and turned, a quizzical expression on his face.

"Is that blood on your son's forehead, Balodis?" he asked.

"Blood?" My father looked surprised. He grabbed me by the shoulder. He licked his finger and rubbed it over the cut. "No, no," he said, scrubbing at the cut with the edge of his sleeve until it burned terribly. "It is only just motor oil. You know kids—always getting into things."

They both chuckled. The pain filled my eyes with tears but I, too, managed a smile. Baldwin receded into the dealership. My dad and I slid the glass panel closed and we began walking back to the bus stop.

"Do you think he suspected us?" I asked. I couldn't stop staring over my shoulder. I was terribly worried that Baldwin had known something was not right. I figured that he'd at least smelled the scent of alcohol that was billowing from my dad, the scent that hung around him like a saint's aura. What kind of saint, though, drank bourbon habitually? There were not, I guessed, a large number of drunken saints in the Catholic Church. I was pretty sure, actually, that temperance was a saintly virtue.

I stood at the bus stop. I felt like an extra for a horror film about the walking dead. My head ached from the combination of the alcohol, the fall, and the lack of sleep. Each of the vertebrae in my back throbbed with a separate pain. Though I didn't close my eyes, I still felt like I was dreaming. Everything had a surreal, almost fuzzy shadow. I was hallucinating, I realized. Nothing substantial, just little exaggerated details, little things that didn't seem quite right. I imagined turning to my dad and resting my hand on his shoulder: "Why are you making my life so difficult?" I'd ask him. He'd be taken aback by this question, of course, and he would catapult into guilt, and apologize profusely for what had happened on the street that day.

This was not, of course, what happened. In reality, we were embarrassed and somewhat chastened by the experience. The sky clouded over. Rain drizzled on us. My dad, it seemed, was determined not to talk. We caught the bus home. There were only a few other passengers. The day was taking hold of the sky, as full of promise as anything I'd ever seen.

3

saturday, september 2, 1989

That afternoon my dad had a fierce hangover. He lay on the couch in front of the television, asleep. His stomach rose and fell with an irregular rhythm. It heaved with each intake of his breath. He had a strange, vinegary odor about him—almost like a jar of olives—and his hair was matted with streaks of dirt and grease. I watched him sleep. I remembered how regal he'd looked, holding the steering wheel of the stolen car. But now he seemed meager and overweight and tired. I felt a piquant sadness.

I didn't return to the street the next morning and sell the *Socialist Worker*. Something stopped me from seeking out the socialists. I missed their companionship, sure, but I also felt like I owed my dad something. He deserved my respect, despite the fact that he'd behaved so barbarously with Hannah's father. So I stayed at home, letting summer's last few days expire. On Wednesday, the sixth of September, I turned sixteen years old. On Thursday, the seventh, I passed—on the first try—the driver's license exam for the State of Wisconsin. I had no car to drive, sure, but at least I had a license.

It was difficult, though, to avoid resenting my dad. We stopped talking. We negotiated the apartment in near silence when my mother was away—the only sounds coming from the distant spiral of a police siren or the occasional jet bound for the Milwaukee Airport. I could feel my dad's shame. "You are both quiet like a sponge," my mom would say, exasperated. She took to watching TV at unusually loud volumes. Then, on the twelfth of September, I began my junior year at Alexander Hamilton High.

Inner-city kids who rode the municipal bus to school were given a bus pass on the first of each month. I used mine as much as I could. I enjoyed abusing the only privilege, as far as I could tell, of living in the stadium district. The bus was never crowded, and I usually had a seat to myself. I pressed my forehead to the window and quietly narrated the passing traffic, imagining destinations and personalities for the drivers. Time passed. I enjoyed the cool feel of the glass against my skin, and the way my breath fogged the little pane. Before I knew it, the bus had come to my stop.

Ah, the rough-hewn glory of Alexander Hamilton High School. The school itself was a crumbling monument. The bricks sagged. The windows leaked cold air even when shut. The floors were thoroughly cracked and worn with grooves. The entire spirit of public education seemed concentrated into this building.

Nobody likes high school, and I went into it aware of this fact. I'd been warned by things I'd read or watched, by Pencey Prep and Ridgemont High and *Less Than Zero*. But I wasn't like any of the characters in the books I read or the movies I watched. Maybe I was an exceptionally geeky kid, the kind some parents might call precocious, but I loved my classes. I enjoyed learning long lists of simple Spanish vocabulary. I liked memorizing the dates of all the major battles in U.S. military history, one after another after another, for no discernible reason except that then, thank God, I'd know the dates of all the major battles in U.S. military history.

For most of the first day, my classes were uneventful. I took a quiz in Spanish on the verb *volar*; I listened to a boring introductory lecture about *The Sun Also Rises*, and then a boring lecture about some aspects of the early days of the Revolutionary War. I ate lunch. In fourth-period geology we discussed the different kinds of rocks and the significance of their appearances. The teacher showed us some images of a soil sample on the overhead projector. She fizzed with enthusiasm for her subject matter. But still the rocks looked like the pizza I'd just purchased in the cafeteria for a dollar twenty-five.

Then, in fifth period—unmitigated disaster. I'd known, for three weeks now, that I had gym scheduled for fifth period. But I'd blocked this fact from my mind. I had tried not to worry about the moment when I'd have to leave the main part of the school and enter the passageway to the gymnasium—where I'd be channeled into a locker room and forced to change my clothes in public. I hated the very idea of gym. Gym was a murderous torment—one that had been taken directly from the circles of Dante's *Inferno*. Or if not the *Inferno*, then some other dark place, where mold grew on walls and the screams of the damned intermingled with the grunts of physical labor.

I changed as quickly as I could. All day, I'd worn my gym uniform under my exterior clothes, so I peeled off my jeans and sweater and stuffed them in an empty locker. I ran up the stairs to the gym floor, where I felt almost naked in my sheer white T-shirt and green athletic shorts. I tried to look confident—as if I had some hope of playing flag football without knocking myself senseless—as I loitered near the doorway. The coach blew a whistle and took attendance. This first day, he said, would be spent taking fitness assessments.

We split up by gender. A team of assistant coaches—God knows where they'd come from—suddenly appeared on the gym floor. They moved among the students, poking and pinching and making notes on clipboards. Every one of them, I saw as I looked around the room, was wearing athletic goggles. They looked like bugs.

I was among the first to be assessed. A coach walked up to me and asked my name. He nodded and made a check mark on his clipboard. Then he scanned me carefully, judging me like a cut of meat in a supermarket display case. He grabbed the meager flesh of my stomach and frowned. He shook his head. "We'll cut down on that body fat, for sure," he said.

"Body fat?" I objected. "But I'm dangerously thin. I'm a wafer."

"Son," the coach said, tapping his clipboard, "I will tell you who is, and who isn't, a wafer."

"Hey," I heard a voice call as the coach walked away. "Yuri!"

There—looking adequately charming in her white T-shirt and red athletic shorts—was Hannah Graham. For a moment, I couldn't breathe.

"I can't believe that you've got this class, too," she said. "They're making me take it to graduate." She shook her head. "It's the tyranny of the majority—making rules for the unwilling minority."

I nodded. This was exactly the kind of thing that Hannah was prone to say. But she seemed genuinely happy to see me, which was a surprise. She glanced nervously around the room. "I have an idea," she said.

She grabbed me by the wrist and pulled me through the double doors at one end of the gym. We bolted down a fluorescent-lit hallway and through a second set of doors. We passed a sign that said Do Not Enter. We walked through a third and final doorway and suddenly we were standing beneath the bleachers. I gazed up at the wood and metal structure—a darkened architecture of boards and brace beams and stanchions. Slivers of light slipped through the bleachers, cutting into the darkness, truncating it. I extended my arm. I looked at it in the pale light. My skin was dark and then light and then dark. I thought of my geology class and sedimentary rocks. We could hear the voices of our classmates. They were almost ghostly—even though they came from only the other side of this structure.

"Let's climb it, Yuri," Hannah said. I must have looked shocked. "Don't worry," she said, "I've done this before."

I never determined under what circumstances Hannah had climbed these bleachers, or how she knew about the little alcove at their top, the alcove where we could sit and wait for the class to end. But I chose to accept this as my good luck, and I quickly adapted to my new environment.

Hannah hated gym, although her reason for hating it wasn't a lack of athletic skill. She simply believed, in the most profound depths of her being, that gym taught violence. That it was all about the survival of the fittest. Why not have a class period devoted to the study of wildflowers, or butterflies? she wondered. Until this happened, until choice existed, she was going to boycott. On that first day of class, Hannah and I covered a range of subjects. She described the celebration her family had had for Labor Day, when all the socialists had gathered together at her house in the suburbs to tell stories about work. They'd talked about what it meant to labor, about how satisfying it was to labor collectively, about how eagerly they looked forward to the day when America's economic infrastructure would be collectivized—and all the bourgeois professionals would be reassigned to the tractor factories. Then, working in a tractor factory would be a great accomplishment; everyone would build tractors with pride. Her father had led them in song.

At the mention of Hannah's father's name, I felt a deep sense of embarrassment. I couldn't help but remember the sweaty sheen of my dad's lips, and the way that his saliva had clung to Dr. Graham's fore-head. Humiliation filled my mouth; I could feel its coloration spilling over the features of my face.

"Yuri," Hannah said, and leaned forward. Her eyes were pale and concerned. "Why'd he do it?"

I looked down. I wanted to tell her that my dad had felt bad after-ward, that he'd been terribly disappointed in himself. I wanted to tell her that the incident on the steps had sent him on a massive drinking binge. That he'd sequestered himself on the balcony and consumed most of a bottle of bourbon. I wanted to describe the awful fear I'd felt when the cop followed us on Highway 41. But my loyalties were divided.

"What do you mean?" I asked. I figured that if I pretended I didn't know what she was talking about, she'd abandon this line of conversa-tion. Instead, she pursued it further. She described her own anger, and the way she felt watching my dad drag me down the street. He'd abused me, she said, and he'd assaulted her father. How could I live with him?

"I don't know," I said. I couldn't find the right words. "He was just drunk."

Hannah shook her head. She started to say something and then fal-tered. She cleared her throat. "How serious is his problem?" she finally asked.

I didn't know how to answer this question, either. I closed my eyes and leaned against the wall. I could feel its press against my shoulder blades. I emptied my mind of everything except the image of my dad, holding the bottle of bourbon in his hand, wobbly and smiling. But I could smell Hannah's scent—the mixture of her perfume and sham-poo and the saline odor of her skin. It was intoxicating. The texture of the memory somehow became charged with a new eroticism, a strange secondary valence above the shame. But still it made me angry.

"You know," I said, "it's really none of your business."

Hannah's eyes widened and she eased back from me slightly.

"Why are you yelling at me?" she said.

"I'm not yelling at you."

"Yes, you are. Do you want them to hear us?" Hannah pointed

toward the gymnasium where—in distant and softened voices—the damned were enduring their daily rites of torture. I looked at her. I felt resentment rise up inside of me, mingling with the attraction, making her, in some ways, even more attractive.

"Look," I said, "I have to live with him. I have no choice." I looked at my feet. They suddenly felt alien and foreign—my arms, too—foreign objects that were attached to my body through some sort of accident, an enigmatic and unknowable accident. I thought about my dad, and how he'd actually lived much of his life under communism; his body was scarred because of the actions of a communist state. But how could I explain this to her without sounding aggressive or pedantic? Hannah shook her head.

"But he drinks," she insisted.

"He drinks too much. But that doesn't change things. He's still my dad."

Hannah nodded. We sat there for a few moments in silence. Desperate for a change of subject, I started talking about my classes. I described the sedimentary rocks in detail, boring Hannah with a roster of words that had stuck in my memory: *shale* and *limestone* and *sandstone* and *gypsum*. She listened politely. She even seemed slightly interested. She stretched her legs out in front of her. I strained not to look at her skin—at the long, delirious, full measure of her skin—focusing instead on the lacquered pine of the bleachers. I carefully regulated my breathing. Each breath tingled slightly as I drew it in. After some time my emotions—the anger and the desire—were in check. The bell rang, sounding its plaintive note from deep within the sarcophagus of Alexander Hamilton High. We hurried back to our separate locker rooms, blending into the crowd of students, changing as quickly as we could.

Despite its rough beginning, this escape became our habit. We'd flee to the top of the bleachers, where we'd talk for fifty minutes. We were only inches from the ceiling, and the volleyballs or basketballs or badminton shuttlecocks would come within a few feet of our hiding place. We'd glimpse only the tops of their highest arcs. The coach didn't seem to notice our absence; he had eighty students in this class, alone. From time to time, we wondered if perhaps this was a mistake, if perhaps we should rejoin the legions of students in the other sections of the gym. But eventually we decided we were fine. This would be our gym experience. We would accept responsibility for our actions. If we were caught—fine—we'd argue against the system. Until that day, though, we would enjoy this version of the class, suspended high above the floor, on the little platform near the ceiling.

4

thursday, november 9, 1989

The rest of September and October pushed past in an array of home-work and Spanish quizzes and unfulfilled, confused desires for Hannah. Each school day seemed to pivot around fifth-period gym. On the days when Hannah was absent, I was lost. I'd escape to the bleachers anyway—and just lie there, staring up at the ceiling's acoustic tiles. On Halloween, my dad wore a fake mustache and rented a Soviet army uniform. He wrote JOSEPH STALIN on a scrap of paper and pinned it to his lapel. "Is scary, no?" he said. And then: "Is the scariest thing I could think of, anyway." He drank his bourbon and waited for any kids who might happen by. None came. "I was going to scare the hell out of them with this costume, in my opinion," he said at the end of the night. He passed out on the couch, the mustache partially in his mouth, a bottle of bourbon cradled to his chest.

Then, on Thursday, November 9, 1989, the Berlin Wall fell. My fam-ily watched it happen live, narrated by Dan Rather. He was fine and moving and eloquent, but what really was remarkable was the noise of the crowd, chanting and singing and cheering as loud as they could. My mom cried and my dad cried and—because they were crying—I cried, too. It is one of the clearest memories I have from the autumn of 1989. I remember this night with a certain, lustrous vividness. By this point, we were nine weeks into the semester. Already the weather was frigid; the holidays loomed in each inch of snowfall, in each morning when the temperature sank below freezing.

When the Wall fell, my parents drank bourbon and kissed each other drunkenly on the lips. It was embarrassing. Who likes to watch their parents kiss, moist lip to moist lip? I squirmed on our overstuffed sofa, trying to focus on the television, with its grainy feed and bubbly news anchors. I cleared my throat. I drummed my fingers on the pleather. I cleared my throat again.

"You guys, please? It hurts to watch."

They kept kissing. My mom's mouth was open and I could see the edge of her tongue, pale pink, almost like an unopened tulip. I imagined tulips. Dewy, budding tulips.

"Hello?" I said. "Could you please stop? Please?"

My dad disengaged and lurched down the hallway, a dazed smile hanging on his lips. "Champagne!" he gasped. "We need champagne." He rummaged through the cabinets while my mom wiped her mouth. "Aha!" I heard him exclaim, and in a few moments he returned with a dusty bottle of Korbel and two coffee mugs full of ice. The cork popped in a lackluster way. My dad poured the champagne.

"To the fall of communism," my mom said, as their porcelain mugs clinked together.

We continued watching, transfixed. We skipped around from network to network. The anchors struggled to match the tumult and energy of the pictures on the screen. My parents sipped their iced champagne and I got a soda from the fridge.

"Here we are . . . in East Berlin . . ." the on-scene reporter for ABC intoned, each of his words rising into a slow and melodramatic chant. The reporters loved to say, "East Berlin," as if, with this single phrase they could lay claim to gritty realism.

At one point, a German standing on top of the Wall quite clearly began to make obscene gestures at the cameras. The news anchor scrambled to interpret the images. "The residents of East Berlin," said the somewhat panicked reporter, "are waving with joy, or at least what appears to be joy, at our cameras. Well, hello to you too, East Berlin!" Shortly thereafter the network broke for a commercial.

The networks struggled with the situation. If they descended into the crowd, they lost perspective. Their expensive equipment would be soaked with beer and jostled by the celebrants. They preferred to observe from the rooftops. The result was a strange, zoom-lens sense of the scene. Zoom and focus. Zoom and focus. I was queasy for hours.

We saw some wonderful things, though. Falling, a cameraman caught someone pounding at a patch of graffiti with a sledgehammer. As he fell there were hands and legs and illuminated faces. Later, another network filmed some teenagers kicking him and stealing his camera. The teenagers then set the damaged camera up on the wall, and began filming the crowd.

"Someday . . ." the news anchor told us, "those children . . . will be the journalists of Germany's tomorrow . . . and they'll remember this day . . . and that camera that they borrowed . . . as the start of a new life." A good portion of which, my dad pointed out, could be spent in prison.

"This is so nice," my mom said. "It is just like Christmas."

"Is there film in our camera?" my dad asked, looking away from the television in a startled way.

"What are you wanting to take pictures of?"

"Of the television, Mara," he said as he stood up. "It is historic event. Where is the camera?" he asked as he headed toward their bedroom. "Is it in the drawer with the bills and—"

The phone rang, cutting him off midsentence. My dad changed his course and sauntered over toward the powder blue receiver. We'd bought the thing—a rotary dial telephone—for two dollars at the Salvation Army.

"Hello?" he said, and waited.

I remember watching his face, which was blank. "Hello?" he repeated, covering the phone with his meaty palm. "Nobody's there," he said. "Hello? I can't hear you. You are very unclear. Hello? Who is this? Are you talking in English?"

His eyes opened with shock and suddenly I heard him speaking Latvian. Within seconds, my mom was at his elbow, listening attentively.

It was frustrating for me because I had no idea what was going on. I strained to recognize any word. After a while I gave up. I sat on the couch and stared into the kitchen.

After a few minutes, the conversation ended. "Hello?" my dad said. "Hello? Hello?" And then he turned to my mom: "Cut off," and he threw his hands in the air with frustration. They stood there for a long time, quietly. My mom looked worried. She cupped one elbow in the palm of her hand and propped her chin on the palm of the other. My dad sighed and replaced the receiver. He swayed a little, standing there, and he stared at his reflection in the glass of the balcony door. They both looked old. I muted the television without their noticing.

For a few moments we occupied that space in silence. When I asked them who was on the phone, neither would answer.

The next day was a Friday, the tenth of November.

I woke up early. My mom was making breakfast as usual, but she had a distant, exhausted look about her. I watched her brew the coffee, and then watched as she cracked two eggs directly into the toaster.

"Mom, no!" I unplugged the toaster and turned it upside down, letting the egg run out into the sink. She smiled gently and ruffled my hair.

"I am sorry, *bucina*," she said, in a submerged way, "but you will have to make your breakfast for today. I am too tired." She walked back to the bedroom.

I decided to skip it. I was eager to leave the house, anyway. No one had said a word to me, really, since last night. I'd turned off the TV myself. My parents had vanished into the back of the apartment. Unsupervised, I'd taken the bottle of champagne to my room and finished it. I'd listened to the murmur of their voices filter through the wall. Now I had something of a headache and my stomach felt unsteady.

At school, I stumbled through my classes. The students seemed mostly indifferent to what had happened. Nobody talked about the news in the hallways. A few teachers tried to initiate class discussion about the situation in East Germany, but no one seemed informed or willing to inform others. Hannah, of course, was the exception.

"Did you watch it?" she asked as soon as we were alone in the bleachers. She could barely stop herself from shouting. "It was the victory of mass-market special interests. The media was awful."

"Awful" I said, and shook my head. "But the people of Berlin did seem happy."

"I don't know," Hannah said, squinting. "Was that a representative sample? What about everyone who wasn't there? What about everyone who isn't celebrating the end of communism?" She paused. "I thought of you. I tried to look you up in the phone book, but I didn't know how to spell your last name."

I spelled it for her. She laughed. "I wasn't even close," she said. "What did your parents do? What did your mom say?"

"She was crazy. They both were tremendously excited. They couldn't stop laughing at first."

I told her about the kissing and the champagne. Halfway through my description of the kiss, I noticed that Hannah was staring intently at me, watching my jaw as it formed the vowels and consonants of the English language. I briefly considered the press of her lips, and how it would feel to touch them against mine. I sighed and described the mysterious Latvian phone call. She couldn't think of an explanation.

"Who do you think it was?" she asked.

I paused. "I don't know. See, the frustrating thing is they won't tell me anything at all. Well, my dad will, now and then. But my mom, it's like she was reborn when she came to America. She hates Latvia. She never wants to go back. That's why it was so weird to hear her speaking Latvian to someone on the phone."

Hannah sighed. We sat there in silence for a minute. She inched forward, peering over the edge of the bench. "God. They're all exactly the same, aren't they? The girls, the guys—they're exactly identical."

I didn't like going near the edge. Not only was I afraid that the coach might spot us, but I was slightly afraid of heights. "The same," I murmured. "But don't you wish, sometimes, that you were one of them?"

She laughed at this, assuming that it was a joke. I looked at my watch. It was getting close to the ten-minute whistle. We'd have to rejoin the class soon, and try to look like we'd just spent forty minutes sweating.

"Are you going to the demonstration next Friday?" Hannah asked, even as I was preparing to inch back along the top of the bleachers.

"The demonstration?" I said. Her demeanor seemed to imply that it was a well-known public event, and that of course I would have heard of it by now. She intended for us to go together—to accompany each other to the demonstration. And this was one topic I was not comfortable discussing with her. Any sort of conversation that might possibly involve dating—I was deeply allergic to this sort of talk. I'd begun to wonder if I was slated for a life as a monk. Why not? Good food, nice robes, beautiful stained-glass windows, peace and quiet. There was a lot to recommend the cloistered life. Although a demonstration wasn't exactly a date.

"You know," she said. "A protest. Communal action, uniting all forms of potential struggle. We're picketing Pick N' Save."

"Picketing Pick N' Save?" I asked. "The grocery store? Isn't that a little ridiculous?"

"They have unfair labor practices," she said. "They don't allow their employees enough sick leave. We'll gather together, picket, and get the attention of the police. Maybe they'll brutally break up our demonstration and we'll spend the night in jail."

"You make it sound so appealing."

"We could make the news," she said. "Are you going?"

"I do love to picket," I said. "I am a picketing fool, after all."

Hannah laughed again and I felt compelled to stand up, to mimic a labor protest for her. Stooped over so that I wouldn't bump against the ceiling, I chanted mute slogans and pumped my fist. I held an imaginary placard on my shoulder, hoisting it from time to time in solidarity with my picketing brethren. I got carried away. Too close to the edge, I slipped on a seam in the wood. I began to lose my balance and topple downward. Why did I always seem to be falling? Was I doomed to stumble and tumble through life, uncoordinated and wobbly?

But Hannah was there. She snagged my arm and braced herself, in turn, against a beam. I didn't fall.

"You're so stupid and clumsy," she said, still holding me by the arm. And then she kissed me.

I was stunned. But within seconds, it seemed, we had to scurry down the bleachers and into the locker room. I wandered through the halls of Alexander Hamilton in a daze, trying to remember what class I had next. U.S. history? No. Math? That was it. I stumbled to the class-room door, barely making it inside before the bell.

To me—a frightened teenager with an overprotective Eastern Bloc mother and a drunken father—sex was an inconceivably distant event. It wasn't even something I considered, really. I knew that someday I would have sex, if I didn't become a monk, and that was that. My luck was quirky. This would never change, and a lot of teenage sex seemed to be about just that—luck. Who would be in the right place at the right time? It was entirely unpredictable, for both sexes. I'd kissed only a couple of girls. One of them had gone so far as to let me take off her shirt, and that was in the darkness of a friend's bedroom during a party, and we'd been interrupted by the unexpected return of this friend's parents. Perhaps predictably, the trauma of the interruption had ended our budding relationship. We never talked again.

I didn't allow myself to imagine having sex with Hannah Graham. Kissing her, however, was an entirely different matter. I couldn't stop thinking about it, actually. I had to fight—desperately fight—to avoid an erection as I solved an equation on the chalkboard.

$$X^2 - 4X = 21$$

the equation said. And then:

Solve for Sex

I blinked. What did that say? I looked again.

$$SEX^2 - 4PLAY = 21$$

Solve for X

This very thing had happened to a kid in another class—he'd given an oral presentation in biology with an erection clearly visible to the students in the front row—and within days everyone was calling him Woody. I couldn't even remember his real name. I took a deep breath. I put chalk to blackboard, trying to remember something (anything) about quadratic equations.

But I survived—unstimulated—and made it to the bus. The secret was mine. I was safe there—hunched in my seat. Memory enveloped me. Despite the other odors that wafted through the air, I managed to remember the scent of Hannah, slightly flowery and almost salty, and the way her smell had clouded around me when we'd kissed. I anguished over the brief touch of her lips. I struggled with the brush of her hair, one errant strand of it, against my cheek. I forgot entirely about the collapse of the Berlin Wall.

I was reminded, however, as soon as I came in the door.

My parents were sitting on the couch, staring at the grainy TV. It was Tom Brokaw this time, and he was still struggling to describe the images. The borders had opened, apparently, and refugees were swarming out of the East. I caught a brief glimpse of thousands of people walking to some Western goal, carrying bundles and boxes and suitcases of belongings. But I didn't have much opportunity to watch.

"Yuri!" my mother said as soon as I appeared. "We have been awaiting your arrival."

"Yuri!" my father said, standing up and walking over to me. "It is good to see you, son."

I put down my backpack. I unzipped my jacket, draped it over the back of the chair. "What's going on?" I asked.

"Oh, nothing," my dad said. "We are just happy to be together, the three of us, all together here. We will make some pasta for dinner, you and I and your mother."

I nodded. I walked carefully over to the dinner table. The mail was piled in one corner, a little collection of flyers and bills. I looked closer. Nothing interesting. I sat down. Both of my parents joined me.

"So," my mom asked, "how was your school today?"

"Fine," I said. "Normal." I paused. "What's going on, guys? Why are you acting so weird?"

"Weird?" my dad said. "We are not acting weird. Your mother and I were just talking a little bit about how proud we are of you. You are working so hard at school and getting such good grades."

"That's all?"

"That is all."

"Okay." I stood up. "Then I'm going to my room." I would lie on my bed, I had determined, and close my eyes. I would close my eyes, forget my family, and think of Hannah.

"Wait," my mom said. "Your father has something to discuss with you."

Immediately my dad was upset. "Mara!" he said, and issued a quick burst of Latvian words, words that sounded accusatory and guttural. My mom looked down at the table, where she'd placed her hands. She was spinning her wedding band around and around her ring finger, twirling it with the nervous tips of her fingers. My dad turned to me: "It is nothing to discuss, simply something to chat about. Let us go out on the balcony and chat a little bit."

I was used to my dad's talks. He was prone to lecturing, and had a variety of opinions about almost anything. But usually the lectures were accompanied by alcohol, at least on his part. Now, as far as I could tell, he was totally sober. He even smelled good, a pleasant mix of soap and aftershave.

We walked out onto the balcony. It was a good evening, for November. Clear sky, temperature hovering around freezing. He cracked his knuckles and then his neck, his bones popping in their sockets with arthritic joy. I leaned against the railing.

"What's up?" I asked. Usually, this question bothered him. "What is up are the clouds," he would reply. "Or possibly the ceiling is up? I do not know. Sometimes I look but recently I have not been interested. Maybe you could tell me what is up, yourself?"

Today, however, he was more subdued. He demurred. "Nothing is up, really," he said, and then he commented on the cold November day. He cleared his throat. Then he said, "Did I ever tell you the somewhat tragic yet amusing story of how we came to America, including the time we spent in a shipping container full of pigs, and also the funny thing about my cousin, Ivan?"

"No," I said. "You haven't mentioned it."

"Ah," he said. "Good, good. You know, a drought in summer could lead to a shortage of corn."

"Dad?" I said, indicating my impatience by crossing my arms.

"Okay, okay," he said. "I will tell you now."

THE SOMEWHAT TRAGIC YET AMUSING STORY OF HOW WE CAME TO AMERICA, INCLUDING THE TIME WE SPENT IN A SHIPPING CONTAINER FULL OF PIGS, AND ALSO THE FUNNY THING ABOUT MY COUSIN, IVAN

"So, my darling, what I never tell you is how we come to America, which is in a strange way the most beautiful story of my life—"

"And my life," my mom said as she slid open the screen door. She stood on the balcony somewhat hesitantly. She looked, I reflected, like a bull elk. Large and regal, yes, but also ready to flee, if necessary, at a moment's notice. "I brought three sodas," she said, and sure enough, she'd brought three sodas. She handed us each one. They were cool and damp and pleasant to hold even in the November cold. I shivered a little, wishing briefly that there was some bourbon on hand.

"Our life and your life also, Yuri. But this is not the story. You see, after I came back from prison I did not want to do anything at all. I was so sad about my hand. I had lost my job, and I lived again with my own father and mother. I only wanted to sleep during the day, and during the night I would walk. I walked a great deal in those days, through the city of Riga, mostly through the old section, where the streets were narrow and there were many alleys. Your mother was worried about me—"

"Not so much worried, really," my mom said.

"Not so much worried?" my dad asked.

"I liked you very much, yes, so I was worried. You almost never came to visit me at my apartment. But I knew it would all be okay, at the end. *Es tureju ikski.*"

My dad looked moved by this. For a moment, I thought he was going to cry. What the hell was going on? I wondered.

"Your mother believed everything would be okay. But I did not. I walked and walked and one night I went down to the Daugava. I stood on the stone bridge that crossed the river and I looked down into the water. I was thinking very darkly. The water was so pretty, but it was also reflecting the city, and the city was all concrete then. New Soviet buildings. There was only one tree. I looked at the tree and it looked so hopeless and lonely. I thought about how the government was putting up so many new concrete towers, so quickly, and not planting any trees. This made me so sad, you know, and then I realized something important. It was something I could not tell you exactly, even now, because I am not sure what are the right words. I tell you I was thinking very darkly, though. Then I thought, Maybe I will jump. So then I heard behind me a voice saying, 'Why do you not simply jump and end it all, you stupid idiot.'"

"Approximately," my mom interjected. "This is approximately only what I said."

"You see, Yuri," my dad continued, "only thirty minutes before, Mara was sitting at her window and looking at the street. She saw me walk slowly by, and stop."

"He stood under the streetlight," my mom said. "I thought he was going to come in, but then he was only looking at the ground. He looked crazy, like he was talking to himself. Then he left, and he did not even say hello."

"So she followed me," my dad said quickly. I could tell he didn't know quite what to do with my mom's interruptions. "She caught me at the river. If she had not caught me, who knows what could have happened?" He stopped.

"Then what?" I asked. "That's not a story about you coming to America."

"Please, have some patience. You have no patience, in my opinion. That is the problem with you, in general, Yuri. No patience. What happened was that she came up to me, and then I kissed her, and I was suddenly sure of what I had to do. I told her that we were leaving the Soviet Union, and that we were going to America. She laughed."

"I laughed," my mom said, and tipped back her soda.

"So I began to look around. But I had to be very careful. I could only tell, one, two, three people. If they found out you wanted to leave, your life was over. They would put you in jail and you might never get out. So, two more years went by like this. By now it was 1964, in October. Rumors started flying around again, this time about a coup, and about Brezhnev replacing Khrushchev. People wondered what it meant, and sure enough, on October fourteenth, it happened. This was what I had been waiting for.

"You see, my darling, when the first secretary of the Central Committee of the Soviet Union changed over—and it only happened twice while I was living in Latvia—there was a big chaos in all the parts of the country. Big celebrations had to be planned. It was like a carnival.

"Now, I had a friend who was a pig farmer. He shipped pigs from the countryside, near Riga, to the port, where they load them onto boats for Finland. We have prize pigs in Latvia you know, they are the best and most delicious pigs in the world. Finland would buy pigs from us, and sometimes we would send them still alive, for breeding. Sexy pigs, only. We would send sexy Latvian pigs to Finland to mate with the Finnish girl pigs.

"My friend, for some money, agreed to let your mother and me sit in the container and we could be also shipped to Finland. It was easy, except for the smell. Also, the pigs were getting very sexy with each other. I am not certain if there were female Latvian pigs in there, too, but if there were not, then I can tell you that the Finnish pig farmers had something of a problem coming to them on this particular boat.

"Finally—on the day before the celebrations for Brezhnev—I passed word to the pig farmer. This was it. We would slip away in the confusion. I told my mother and father. They were old and we knew that we would probably not see each other again. Mara told only her mother, since her father had been deported to Vorkuta, to the gulag there, in 1945 and probably was dead. Then I made a mistake. I told my cousin, Ivan.

"Ivan was my good best cousin, the closest to me and my thinking. We were big friends for drinking, also, and he liked tremendously the country and western music. The night before Mara and I left—the night before the big celebration for Brezhnev in downtown Riga—he and I went out drinking. We went to all of the old bars, all of our favorite places. At the end of the night I told him that your mother and I were leaving in the morning. At first he didn't understand, but then quite suddenly he became furious.

"We were in the hallway outside the apartment of my parents. He started yelling. 'They will hunt us all down,' he said, 'they will hunt down the whole family.' Which was actually a good possibility.

"Ivan would not stop screaming. I tried to calm him down but he was slightly intoxicated, perhaps. The neighbors were all coming out to watch. He would not shut up. I tried, Yuri, to get him to shut up. There was nothing I could do." He paused. He looked over at my mom, who nodded. "So I stabbed him."

I gaped at my dad. My jaw felt like it was on a hinge. "You stabbed him?" I cried. "You stabbed your own cousin? Wait, wait—never mind that. You stabbed anyone at all? With a knife?"

"No, my darling, no. It was not so bad. You see, I only had a little knife, a pocket knife for opening envelopes or whittling at the wood. I stabbed him gently, in his thigh, and I apologized as I was doing it. It was very kind."

"Did he think so?" I said. "Is that what he said as the knife went in? 'You are so kind, Rudolfs. Thank you so much for this gentle stab wound.'"

"No, no. He vowed to kill me. So I ran. I ran to the apartment of Mara. We left early, on foot. We had planned to take the local train—the pig farm was not many miles away—but I was too afraid of being caught. Someone had surely called the police.

"Once we made it to the pig farm, everything went exactly in the way which we had prepared. No problems, except of course that the container was poorly ventilated and we only had one suitcase—and in that suitcase, very few clothes. So for two weeks we smelled like the secretions of the pigs."

"I can't believe you stabbed him," I said, still in shock. "Why didn't you just run?"

I looked out over the balcony rail. The sky was turning a pale gray color, and the scent of evening was settling over everything. My dad hitched his pants over his gut. He massaged the back of his neck with his hand.

"It is complicated . . ."

My mom answered for him. "No, *bucina*, because Ivan would have turned him in to the police—"

"No, Mara," my dad said, "that is not certain."

"I am certain of it," she said, and spat. The saliva landed next to my shoe. "He would have turned us both in and then we would have both gone to Vorkuta."

"Well, I am not certain of that," my dad said finally. "But I was scared of the consequences. At this point, you do not ask yourself, Why? You simply run."

I shook my head. "Okay. But why are you telling me this now, Dad?" I asked.

My dad looked at my mom. They both seemed embarrassed.

"It is important for you to know," he said, "because your cousin Ivan is coming to visit."

"Visit?" I demanded. "When? What do you mean he's coming to visit? It's not like he can just come over whenever he wants. He can't just pop in for dinner. He's in Latvia. It's behind the Iron Curtain, remember? Iron. Not paper. Not glass. Iron."

"Yuri," my mom said, "what is all this talking about iron curtains? It is not polite to yell at your father."

"Why not?" I demanded. "He yells at me." I started to go back into the apartment. I wasn't sure why I was leaving the balcony, or where I was going, or what I would do when I got there.

"Wait, Yuri, wait," my dad said, and I paused at the doorway. "Do not go."

"When is he coming?" I asked.

"Soon, soon," my dad said, looking away from my questioning face.

"Soon?"

"I am not certain exactly when," he said.

"The phone calls are censored," my mom added helpfully.

"What do you mean the phone calls are censored?"

"It is simply that when he calls," my dad explained impatiently, "he is cut off after a small amount of time."

I slumped against the doorway.

"I guess it's not so bad," I said, "if you're not worried about revenge for the stabbing."

"Revenge?" My dad smiled. "No, no, no. Look," he continued, "allow me to tell you another story, so that you will know that my cousin does not only hate me."

He was in his element—he had a rapt audience—and my dad continued talking, telling a long, rambling tale about his drinking days with Ivan in the bars of Riga. Halfway through, I drifted out of focus. I kept replaying the stabbing in my head, imagining the dim light of the apartment-building hallway, and the mixture of regret and nervousness that must have hung on my dad's face.

Eventually, my dad's voice gave out, and we went inside to dinner and a little network TV. My parents shuffled off to bed. Alone in the living room, I decided to go out onto the balcony. I stood there enjoying the way the lights of downtown were reflected up into the sky, suffusing the edges of the clouds with an orange-yellow glow. The cold air spun along my skin, reaching under the collar of my shirt and pooling between my shoulder blades. Was my cousin coming to exact revenge on my poor dad? What would I do about Hannah? Was I falling in love? Was it supposed to snow? I could smell the dry scent of it in the air, almost like the scent of fresh cream.

5

Friday, november 17, 1989

But the problem. for me. was less than obvious. I was sixteen. and girls were mystifying—a baffling enigma with no seemingly correct explanation. I had gym class every day with Hannah, and we still escaped to the bleachers, where we'd sit and talk and tear verbal holes in the fabric of Alexander Hamilton High. We were friends, good friends—but after the kiss, it just didn't seem like enough. The physical part of our relationship remained undefined. She wouldn't make another move, and I was paralyzed by a sudden and formless anxiety.

I tried several times to kiss her. Or, more accurately, I tried to gather the courage to kiss her, but failed. The thought never went further than an impulse, really, and the days blended into each other. I worried that our one kiss would stand as just that: a distant impulse, a pleasant anomaly, something that I'd remember years from now in an offhand way, or possibly forget.

Furthermore, the matter with Ivan remained unresolved. The mysterious call on the night of the ninth had been Ivan. He called a few more times in the following days. Each time, he and my dad talked for exactly two minutes. Then, the censors cut the line. Ivan was coming to visit, sure, but when was he coming?

The next Friday, the day of the demonstration, Hannah and I skipped sixth period—for me it was math; for her, Russian—and rode the bus to the Pick N' Save. Hannah had memorized the route that we needed to take to get to the store; we transferred buses at the downtown station, sprinting to make the connection in the dirty, aging terminal.

It was a gray, cold day, the kind of day that seemed to characterize Milwaukee in November. The bus let us off on the southern outskirts of the city, near Goldmann's Department Store. Hannah was tired. She hadn't eaten all day; she'd spent the whole morning in the library, fashioning the placards that she now carried, disassembled, in her backpack. I suggested that we stop at Goldmann's lunch counter and get something to eat. She agreed.

The days of the downtown department store are, in all likelihood, over. Unless American cities reinvent themselves, unless the car loses its primacy in American life and suddenly Americans flock to buses or trains, unless the suburbs stop barreling outward, the last of the urban department stores will close it doors, and that will be that. It will be a quiet day in some quiet month of some quiet year in the near future, and the final Goldmann's employee will sigh and lock the vaulted aluminum doors, and a part of America's past will be irretrievably lost.

In 1989, Goldmann's had a certain dusty charm. Founded in 1896, it had more than sixty thousand square feet of floor space on two sprawling floors. It had served millions of the citizens of Milwaukee— providing their wedding gifts and birthday presents and the appliances for their first homes. It also sold large-size clothing and suits in unusual colors and school uniforms and bulk candy. The upper-floor balcony still had its original brass and wrought-iron railings.

The lunch counter also felt authentic. It glittered with Formica and polished aluminum. Grease rose in great clouds from the iron-topped grill. The soda fountain still bore the prices from 1936, the year of its installation: two cents for a Coca-Cola, three cents for a Coca-Cola with cherry flavored syrup. The waitresses wore hairnets to keep their unruly perms in place. We ordered two grilled cheese sandwiches and two Cokes. The food appeared within minutes; I worried, for a moment, that it had been premade. But then I decided that it probably didn't matter. Premade would almost accentuate the experience.

Hannah ate her food quickly, without any enthusiasm. She rushed through the sandwich and gulped her drink and paid for half of the bill. We walked quickly through Goldmann's and emerged onto Mitchell Street. The Pick N' Save was several blocks away.

"Isn't Goldmann's great?" I said. "My mom and I come here sometimes on the weekends. It's such a monument to the past."

"No," Hannah said, "it's a monument to the exploitation of workers."

I looked at her quizzically. "What do you mean?" I said.

Hannah talked, in the remaining three blocks, about the way that stores marked up prices and made an unfair profit from the labor of the working classes. One day, she told me, the people would own all the stores in America, the way they did in the Soviet Union—except without the massive produce shortages. We approached the demonstration. She took the signs from her backpack, assembling them and handing one to me. GOOD WAGE FOR GOOD WORK, it said.

I could see the socialists, gathered in a group around one entrance to the Pick N' Save. Some of the store's employees had apparently joined them. All told, a hundred or so people roiled around the automatic doors. A few protestors chanted into bullhorns. It was a disorderly mess.

When we spotted Hannah's father, a spasm of nervousness shot through my stomach. The crowd buffeted him to the left and the right; I wondered how he'd receive me. I imagined his anger over what had happened in September, and I imagined what my dad would have done, if he'd happened upon this demonstration in front of Pick N' Save. Probably, I reflected, he would have wrestled the bullhorn from Dr. Graham's hands and slugged him with it—doling out fair punishment for tampering with the mind of his son. I shuddered as I imagined Dr. Graham's glasses clattering to the cement. I had heard that sometimes a boxer's fillings would fly from his mouth after a particularly vicious uppercut. Did Hannah's father have any fillings?

But Dr. Graham just smiled at his daughter, and nodded at me. He motioned for us to join him. "Isn't this exciting?" he said to us as we approached. "Maybe we'll have a riot."

The prospect of a riot did not excite me. I envisioned a night in jail and a phone call home to my parents. I looked around me. The demonstrators did seem agitated. Maybe, I thought, I should leave as quickly as possible. But then I looked more closely. These people didn't seem like the rioting type. The socialists were invariably pudgy. They wore glasses and clever T-shirts and red Converse All-Stars. A few of them did seem slightly unshaven—but would this be enough to inspire violent rebellion? The clerks seemed very young and possibly unsure of what, exactly, was happening.

We marched back and forth, shouting slogans.

"What do we want?" someone yelled.

"Raises," someone else answered.

"When do we want them?"

"Now!"

It went on like this for some time, point-counterpoint, ragged and dissonant. Then I heard a voice, calling over the commotion.

"Foot soldiers! Foot soldiers!"

Dr. Graham beckoned the crowd to cluster around him. I had to admit that he looked impressive. The cold, late-autumn wind buffeted his graying hair, and he raised his arms above his head as he spoke, almost as if he were invoking the heavens. His speech touched on a few simple themes. A worker should make a livable wage, no matter what his or her profession. A worker should have health care, and dental care, and child care, no matter what his or her profession. I lost myself in the rhythms of his speech, in the way he strung together quotes from communist writers and American politicians, in the sweeping ideas of his rhetoric. Finally, he was done. The audience cheered. He left the microphone, but then came surging back to it—waving his fists to the applause.

"And don't forget," he cried, "to buy copies of the *Socialist Worker* for all your friends and family!"

The demonstration continued until after sunset, but Dr. Graham's speech was clearly the keynote. At some advantageous point, he and Hannah and I slipped away, retiring to the relative comfort of the Goldmann's lunch counter. We drank hot coffee and talked about the process of contract negotiation.

I felt an expansive sense of admiration for Dr. Graham. He seemed passionate—much like my own dad—but passionate in a controlled, measured way. He didn't need alcohol to inspire him. The intensity of his ideas was motivation enough. Of course, I should have remembered who he was, and what the parameters of his life had been. He hadn't lived under communism, except with the option to head home to America if it didn't work out. He was a tourist, in many respects, a tourist of ideas and ideologies. But, in some ways, this was appealing.

As we sat there at the lunch counter, I wanted to ask Hannah's father about that day in early September. I wanted to ask him if he was angered by what my dad had done. But I couldn't form the words.

Instead, I reached under the table and squeezed Hannah's knee, a gesture that almost caused her to spill her coffee. She seemed annoyed, at first, but then her expression softened slightly. She stretched her legs out in front of her, entwining them with mine.

"It means a lot to me," she said, "that you came out here today, with us."

"Absolutely," Dr. Graham added, though he seemed to be suppressing a smile. "Every worker counts. Every person in that crowd was a strike against the heart of capitalism." This was a little ridiculous—but Hannah was nodding as if it was a profound and informative statement. So I nodded, too.

"You see, Yuri, the heart of capitalism is enormous and must be attacked carefully. If you come to my house on Thursday evenings, you'll see." Dr. Graham described his Thursday night reading group—a Stalinist version, it seemed, of Oprah's book club. He whipped out a xeroxed piece of paper folded into a tiny square that had a map of directions to their house—a map I knew I was going to memorize.

I was imagining the skin beneath the fabric of Hannah's jeans. I could feel the strength of her calves, could feel the bulk of her muscle, pressing against the lower part of my legs. We talked for another thirty minutes—thirty minutes of listening to Hannah's father go on and on about his political theories. I nodded and smiled and, from time to time, laughed obsequiously. Occasionally, I repeated the last word of a phrase he'd said, simply to make him think that I was listening. But I wasn't. All I could think about was Hannah, and the steady pressure of her legs beneath the table. My breath came in little gasps; I wonder now if perhaps Dr. Graham thought I was asthmatic.

On the day before Thanksgiving—Wednesday, the twenty-second of November—I was alone in the apartment, reading. I'd moved from *Portnoy's Complaint* to *Humboldt's Gift*, and now I could trace the elements of my dad in the crazy poet, Humboldt. My parents kept popping up in the books I read. Didn't my mother, in some ways, bear a certain resemblance to Mrs. Portnoy? This worried me tremendously.

Thanksgiving at our house was a small celebration. Just the usual thing—my parents and I, sitting around the dinner table, eating our evening meal. Of course, there were also the three days before Thanksgiving, when my mom stayed permanently in the kitchen, broiling and boiling and frying and baking. We had a simple Thanksgiving meal. First there were the traditional staples: the mashed potatoes, the marshmallow-topped yams, the dripping brown turkey, the cranberry jelly, the pumpkin pie. Then the Latvian dishes: marinated mushrooms, fried cheese, baked eel, salmon roe caviar. Of course, these last two were slightly more challenging to find in Milwaukee. There was always Zigorski's—though this obviously wasn't the same thing (God help me if I suggested that it was the same thing).

Also, she baked loaves of fresh bread—one white, one wheat, and one rye. Also, she boiled cabbage and stuffed it with ground beef. Also, she filled savory potato pancakes with sour cream. Also, she produced an apple-honey cake. Also, she offered us several different salads and pickled vegetables—beets and carrots and asparagus and cucumbers. Also, she made a chicken pudding. Also, she made *méle majonézé*, cow tongue in mayonnaise sauce. Also, boiled peas with pork fat and onions. Finally, she finished the meal with *piragi*, a sweet pastry crammed with bits of ham and bacon.

"Please, Mom," I said, for the sixteenth consecutive Thanksgiving. "I can't eat any more."

"Okay then, only one more serving, *bucina*. And don't forget to drink your buttermilk."

Throughout November, whenever my dad was home, he was jumpy. He followed the network news with religious devotion. He bought a map of Eastern Europe at K-Mart and pinned it to the wall behind the television. One by one, he crossed out the Communist states, putting an inky X through Poland and East Germany and Czechoslovakia and Hungary. He circled Romania. "Ceausescu is about to fall like a pin for bowling," he assured me. It would take two more months, but he was right. However, he also said, "Yugoslavia—now there, my darling, is a country which will stay forever together in the Communist hands." And that was that.

On the Friday after Thanksgiving, I awoke early and ate some breakfast. I liked the early mornings on days that I didn't have to trudge to Alexander Hamilton High. I'd sit at the kitchen table or on the balcony and eat breakfast and scan the sports pages. I would enjoy my breakfast at my leisure. If my parents interrupted me in any way, I'd ignore them.

On this particular morning, I figured I'd go for a walk. The demonstration had been exhilarating, and I wanted to be moving, to clear my head so that I could formulate a plan for dealing with Hannah. I left the apartment and headed out to the garden behind the building. This was a space I liked. It was a place where I could think about things—where I could cherish my loneliness and solitude and try to make sense of the world.

Actually, this space wasn't really a garden. It was just an abandoned lot with a small patch of mowed grass on one side, and a number of trees growing deep in its center—a few jack pines and a couple of maples. The lot had been vacant for years, judging by the size of the trees. I always wondered if any buildings had ever stood there, and who owned the lot today, and why they chose to keep it undeveloped.

I'd also been curious about the trees—so I'd taken a cluster of leaves and a section of bark to the library, where I'd discovered that they were hedge maples—*Acer campestre*. I loved the sound of these two Latin words. The sinewy *Acer*, with its noise that moved like a dart through the air. And the foreign-sounding *campestre*, with its implication of another distant world, with its curl of elegant vowels and its clipped energy at the end.

I didn't climb the pines, though. They were too narrow, and their sap was sticky. It would get on my clothes and in my hair, a giveaway. "You stink like a squirrel," my mom would say. "You have been climbing in the trees again like a crazy person." Invariably she would slap me on the back of the head.

Back then I was ravenously addicted to reading. I read constantly, and the books . . . the books accumulated in my head, filling it with a spinning and ever-expanding world of ideas. I read novels and poems and books of philosophy that I only partially understood—books like *The Way of a Pilgrim* or the writings of the Baal Shem Tov. All I wanted to do was read. I'd sit in the hedge maple and read and listen to the sound of the wind through the cones of leaves. Then I'd close my eyes sometimes and imagine that the sound of the wind was the sound of the earth's lost languages. Aramaic, Etruscan, Powhatan—they all floated just beyond the realm of understanding. It was spooky. Maybe I needed medication. But I could hear uncountable billions of words, just barely unclear, twisting together in the air, humming.

Admittedly, this was a little unusual. But it was harmless—*right?*—and I needed something to get my head back to normal. I took *Humboldt* and headed out for the trees. I settled in a particularly large branch, a branch that during the spring hid me very efficiently, giving me an outer shell of maple leaves. But now it offered no protection. Today was a fiercely cold, fiercely sunny day, and my shadow was quite lengthy, broken only by the branches of the hedge maple.

But I couldn't concentrate. I kept thinking about my dad's story, and imagining the knife as it tore into poor cousin Ivan's leg, and imagining Ivan's shock and dismay and pain. The image played again and again in my head. Was my dad truly dangerous? Then I imagined the soft pressure of Hannah's lips, and I lay there propped in the tree, holding the graphically sexual novel to my chest, breathing the air that was so cold that it felt *precise* in my lungs.

I figured that, in order to take my mind off of the pain of unrequited love—not to mention the nearly irresistible pull of physical lust—I should do something athletic. Maybe I'd go to the basketball courts and shoot around for a few hours? Maybe I'd go jogging. I was halfway down the trunk when a voice called out from nearby:

"Balodis? Is that you scrambling down out of that tree?"

I turned around. It was Hammond King.

Hammond was an old black man who'd been born in Indianola, Mississippi, roughly twenty years before the Second World War. He was thin and graying and he often wore a leather jacket with his Air Force service patches ironed on the chest and sleeves. My favorite patch was the one for the 332nd Fighter Group—a medieval crest emblazoned with a fire-breathing beast of some sort. He claimed it was a fire-breathing panther. Underneath, in simple script, were two words: *Spit Fire*. "That was our motto," Hammond would tell me, but he wouldn't elaborate. Unlike my dad, Hammond never told stories. He listened, he commented, he gave advice. But he didn't talk about his own life.

Today, he was wearing the jacket. He came stiffly toward me. "Going to the 7-Eleven?" I asked.

"Of course," he said, and then gestured with his arm to the horizon. "Where else?"

He had a good point. The 7-Eleven was our area's cottage industry. It was the only business that seemed to survive here in downtown Milwaukee. There were two of them within walking distance, but Hammond preferred one over the other, because it had fresher coffee. He gave me a detailed explanation of the need for continuous rebrewing throughout the day. "Even if it causes a great deal of waste, you see, the coffee needs to be changed on the hour. Otherwise it tastes like dirt." Having never tasted dirt, I had no way of telling if his assessment was accurate.

Hammond was in retirement. From what, exactly, he had retired, I was unsure. He was possibly unsure, himself, as it seemed that he'd worked nearly every job in the American economy. He'd been a cab driver and a shoe salesman, a shop teacher and a bailiff, a construction worker and a waiter in a pizza parlor. He'd worked as a draftsman for Lockheed Martin, an office temp in downtown Chicago, a bouncer at several different nightclubs, a short-order cook, and a gardener at a suburban Milwaukee nursery. Also, he'd flown fighter planes during the war. Also, he had a pension plan from his years as a shop teacher. Also, he was the best blues organist I'd ever heard, though I have to admit I hadn't heard many. This was the one job he swore that he'd never quit. Every other Tuesday, he would wheel his Hammond Tonewheel organ out of his first-floor apartment. He'd cart it over to his van—which he'd modified with a ramp—and slowly, laboriously, he'd push the organ up into the vehicle. Then he'd drive to Touch of Blues, a coffee shop in a swankier section of downtown, and set up for the night. Three and a half hours of organ music, melodious and soft-pedaled, and then he'd collect a hundred dollars and his portion of the two-dollar cover. He claimed to be the cousin of Albert King—though not B.B. King—both of whom were born and raised in Indianola, as well.

"You want to keep an old man company for a while?" he asked.

We walked to the 7-Eleven, bought coffee and doughnuts, and walked back to the apartment complex. "Come on in," he said, and motioned me inside. He always came and went through his sliding-glass door.

Hammond and my dad had known each other for as long as we'd

lived in the complex—probably close to fifteen years. They'd met because of my dad's music, and his love of the balcony, where he'd sing the summer away, drinking bourbon and listening to records. Hammond had heard my dad play Lightnin' Hopkins, and he'd come up the stairs and simply knocked on the door. All night they'd talked about the intersection between country and western and blues, and the way the early country stars had stolen their music from the bluesmen of the Mississippi Delta. Or something like that. I think at some point they'd become too drunk to hold a conversation, and there was the distinct possibility that one, or both of them, had passed out in the living room. Hammond King was the closest thing my dad had to a friend, and he came by from time to time, though he was getting older and more frail.

We sat in his large empty apartment. The apartment had three bedrooms, only one of which he used. The primary furniture was a little round breakfast table and the organ—which rose from the wall nearest the doorway. It sat on a wheeled platform, a little portable altar. We drank our coffee and ate our strawberry-filled doughnuts.

"I think I'm in love," I told him.

"What are you telling me for, Yuri? I'm not a confessional. Unless you're in love with me—then I guess I'm the right person to tell."

"No, it's just that I don't know what to do. I'm unsure of myself now."

Hammond looked at me. "Love is rotten, son. You read books—you know that. Now, it's also wonderful, don't get me wrong." He shook his head. "Does the girl in question love you, too?"

I let the steam from the coffee rise into my eyes. The heat hurt a little, but I could take it.

"I don't know," I said. "I think she likes me. She kissed me."

"I see. Remember, now, the kiss means nothing. Have you ever been in love before?"

"Not really."

"I see." Hammond paused, chewed on a doughnut. "You're doomed, Yuri. What can I tell you?"

It seemed like an unfair prognosis. "Doomed?" I said. "Why?"

"It never works out at sixteen."

Hammond stood and walked over to the organ. He turned it on, and I could hear the tubes hum to life, could hear the soft hiss of the speakers. He turned the volume down a little, tapped at the keys. Once the sound was there, he played a long succession of notes. It was a scale, and all of the notes seemed to bridge into each other, to flow through each other with a seamless melody. They teemed with life and lushness and electricity. Then he stopped. He sighed and switched off the organ. He turned around on the bench.

"The middle C is starting to stick," he said. "Could you bring me my coffee?"

I carried it over to him. "Were you ever married, Hammond?" I asked.

He smiled a little. "Never ask a lady her age," he said, and sipped at the liquid that was cooling in the Styrofoam cup.

"What do you mean?" I asked.

"I mean leave me alone."

"Why?" I said, still persistent.

"It's just not a good story, Yuri. If it was a good story, I'd probably tell you."

I stood there awkwardly, my cheeks burning with embarrassment. Hammond cleared his throat. He turned and reached into a nearby drawer, withdrawing a deck of cards. "Come on," he said, "let's play blackjack. Aces high. You deal."

I left Hammond in the late afternoon and walked to the nearest pay phone. I was determined to figure out, once and for all, what was happening with Hannah. I put a quarter in the slot and dialed her number. She answered almost immediately, as if she'd been summoned to the phone for the purpose of talking with me.

"Yuri, you are so sweet," Hannah said when I told her that I couldn't stop thinking about her. I'd laid it out in simple terms. As my heart thudded in my rib cage and my palms sweated, I confessed that I was miserable not knowing if she was constantly thinking about me, too.

"So?" I said. The silence broadened, expanded, grew enormous.

"What am I supposed to say?"

"What you feel, of course," I said, my voice tipping slightly too far—I could tell—into outrage.

"Yuri," Hannah said. "Oh, Yuri. I have absolutely no idea what I feel."

I stared at the face of the pay phone. Maybe if I thumped my head against the keys, the music of the pay phone would lull her into loving me?

"Look," Hannah said, after I didn't appear to be volunteering a topic for further conversation. "I'll totally see you on Monday. Don't worry so much about it. We'll figure it all out."

6

monday, november 27, 1989

But Monday didn't present a solution, either. Whenever I saw Hannah she seemed radiant—she oozed heat and energy and utter desirability. In gym class, she captivated me with an extensive monologue on the myth of courtly love, and the dangers of ownership and desire.

I left school even more confused. My life seemed disorganized. I needed space, personal space in which to understand the inexpressible lusts that seemed to be filling every cell of my body. I didn't get home until six—I went on a long walk, instead, and by then it was already dark.

My mom greeted me at the door.

"Food," she said. "On table." She frowned at me. "I eat already." She turned around and walked toward her bedroom. "Your father is drunk as a bear," she said, and shut the door behind her. "He has bad news for you," she yelled back to me through the thin partition.

My dad was out on the balcony and drinking. He was unusually quiet, though, almost ruminative. He seemed ill.

"Aren't you hungry?" I asked.

"Yes, yes," he said. "I will go inside and eat in just a little time. But first I am sitting here and listening to Hammond. I am not crying. It is the wind in my eyes."

I joined him on the balcony. Sure enough, I could hear Hammond playing the organ much louder than usual, the sound of it rising out of his door and up, past us, toward the hazy winter clouds. I felt a pang of guilt; perhaps I'd caused this mood, in some way, with my questions about his past. "It's so loud," I said.

"I know," my dad said. "That is why I am drinking. I could not leave the balcony when he was playing like this." He paused. "Ivan is coming tomorrow," he said.

I must have looked stunned, because he tried to placate me.

"Relax, relax. Do not look so much like there is surprise on your face. He will be happy to see us. He is lucky, so lucky, to come."

I was panicking. An addition to the household? Why now? Why one more person in my life—just at the precise moment when I craved individual space so powerfully.

"But how? And why? Dad, listen to me. There are so many questions—"

"Questions? Do not worry so much about questions. I will tell you tomorrow morning. Now just listen to Hammond and his piano."

Hammond was playing a blues progression, and its syrupy chords stacked upward toward me. I felt slightly warmer. It was gentle, in a way, but it wasn't sugarcoated. It sucked your sorrow into it—and this is why it seemed so rough. You were aware that it was making some sort of a sacrifice for you. Or was that Hammond, himself? Maybe I was confusing the music with the musician. Or maybe they weren't all that different.

"Did I ever tell you, Yuri," my dad asked, "the story of how we were colonized in our hearts, like pudding?"

"Oh, no," I said. "Can I have a drink?"

"Sure, sure," my dad said. "The glasses are inside."

When I returned with a glass he had the bottle ready. He poured me a conservative amount, something appropriate for someone of my age and tolerance. I didn't move my glass. "More?" he asked. I nodded. He poured again, doubling my shot. Then he settled in the corner of the balcony. He rested his elbows on the railing.

THE STORY OF HOW WE WERE COLONIZED IN OUR HEARTS, LIKE PUDDING

"I am listening to this music and I am thinking about how my cousin is coming tomorrow and I am thinking about my family. So many of us were deported, you know, in cattle cars, in 1945 and 1949. More were also deported. But I was thinking of these, the first ones—Uncle Edvards and Aunt Daina and my brother, Eizens. We all lost so many."

"How many?"

"Too many to count, my darling."

"But what happened?" I said.

"It is the same old story you have heard before. Two in the morning, and the farmer or teacher or writer would have a small knock on the door. He would answer it, or she would answer it, and it would be a few men. Maybe a policeman, maybe two. Definitely an agent from the government. They would say, 'Good evening, I hope you are well. We would like to take you to the police station only simply for some questions. It should take just a few minutes.' And that was that."

"But what if you resisted?" I asked.

"They simply shot you there and took your body to the police headquarters."

"And if you went with them?" I was tired—exhausted, weary, achy, worried about Hannah—but still I couldn't resist. I fed my dad questions, almost helplessly. Now, looking back on it, I figure that I liked sitting out there, listening to him talk. But I just couldn't admit it to myself.

"Then they took you to a detention center. They asked you some questions—unimportant questions—and then they put you in a cattle car with two hundred other deportees. Then you went to Siberia. It was so sad, my darling. In Siberia, you worked. You built things for the Union. Some—very few—came back after ten years. You see, my darling, the Soviets had started a policy they called Russification. Everything was Russification."

"Russification?"

"Russification. More so in Latvia and Estonia than Lithuania—but especially in Latvia. The Russian language, the Soviet flag, the Russian radio—all of it was enforced by law and by the Secret Police. The land, too. The farms were turned into *kolhozes*, run by the Russians. Riga, too, they wanted for themselves. So, once they took over the country in 1945, they immediately arrested Latvians—many Latvian politicians and teachers and scientists and newspaper reporters. This was under Stalin. It was a system. They sent them away for ten or twenty years and replaced them with citizens from the Kirghiz Republic or Armenia.

"We were all scared, sure. But also we were fighting. See, this kind of fighting is something that keeps you alive and with energy. Every day in these years I was fighting. Every day from the first occupation until the day I left for Finland."

"Fighting?" I said.

"Sure, sure. Fighting. It is the most important thing. Once you cannot fight anymore, there is no reason to keep going forward. It is useless to live without fighting, my darling. I would meet my surviving friends and we would talk in Latvian. That was one thing. I would call all the streets by their old names, not by their new Soviet names. That was the other thing. I would say prayers, every morning, and I would even pray for Stalin. That was another thing, also. I prayed for him because I thought it was funny, you know, to offer something up in his name.

"But then I decided that we would leave, if we could. Your mother agreed and so we left. I have told you all of this before.

"So when I arrived here I realized, yes, now I can stop fighting. I can relax and say whatever I want to say. I cannot worry about much of anything, except of course for armed robbery—which happens all of the time, as anyone knows who knows about America.

"But it is very strange. When I stopped fighting in my head—I let go of everything. For some time this was so nice. Every day felt like luxury.

"But everything now is easy. I work an easy job. I have an easy electricity. I have all of the things so easy at the shopping mall, yes? And why use the old words for something, when the new English words are so easy? Why teach you Latvian, when English is surrounding us, and it is so easy?"

Hammond's music was a peculiar background to my dad's voice.

"I did not realize until just not long ago that this is exactly the same thing as the Russification. But it is worse. It is not necessary to move me to Vorkuta or Kazakhstan, because it happens in here, inside, in my heart. I am soft, like a pudding. You can put your finger in me. See? Feel."

My dad extended his belly and encouraged me to poke at the side of it. I did just that, and he was right—it was soft and pliant.

"Just like pudding. My stomach and my heart have been colonized. Jack Baldwin, especially, with his Chevrolet dealership and his easy job. He is a big, fat colonizer in a bad suit."

"What's wrong with his suit?" I asked. This upset my father.

"That is not the point. Do you not see? Listen to what I am telling you. You have to make sure that you are not a pudding. You have to fight against it. All of America wants to make you into a pudding. You understand this—I see—inside of you. So then you follow the social-ists. But this is not right. You have to avoid the pudding in a different way, my darling."

I drank the last of my bourbon. "Thanks for the advice, Dad," I said. "But I'm really tired. I have to go to sleep."

He looked shocked. His mouth hung open for a moment.

"See?" he cried as I walked back into the house. "See? I am right. It is too late. Can you not hear this music he is playing?" Hammond's blues was moving slower now, slinking out into the tired night. "Can you not hear it? You're a pudding, already, in my opinion. My son, the pudding." His voice fell away as I moved farther into the house.

"Hey! Do you hear me! Do not forget! Tomorrow morning we are driving to the airport early!"

In early November—three weeks before this day—I'd found myself alone in the apartment on a Sunday morning. My parents had taken the bus to the grocery store and left me a note along with a plate of cold scrambled eggs: "Eggs to eat. Please wash all dishes first." But washing the dishes before eating breakfast—didn't this seem counter-intuitive?

So of course I ate breakfast first, and then took the opportunity to wander into my parents' bedroom. I rifled through their drawers, looked under their bed, peered into the farthest reaches of their night-stands. Going through their closet, I stumbled upon a box labeled in large red-and-black letters:

PORNOGRAPHY! KEEP OUT! DISGUSTING!

It struck me as odd, labeling a box like this. So of course I opened it. No pornography. Instead, there were books and papers and a few photographs. Photos of my parents when they were younger. My dad's abundant mustache shocked me. There were mostly Latvian books, though—all text and no photos. A few of the covers were etched with Cyrillic characters. I took one back to my room. After unsuccessfully trying to puzzle through it, I placed it under my pillow, where it remained until that Monday, November 27.

In the evening, after having listened to my dad on the balcony, I lay on my bed and tried not to think about Hannah. Her name meant "full of grace, mercy, and prayer," but none of these characteristics were making themselves obvious. I thought she was fickle and danger-ous. I tried to convince myself that I had only one more semester of knowing her, and then she'd be gone for the world beyond high school. It was no good. I couldn't help remembering the gentle pressure of her lips, the hesitant wetness of her tongue. It was a body memory, and it coursed stupidly through my skin. I reached under my pillow, balled it against my face in frustration, and brushed the Latvian book.

I looked at it. *Mazas Piezimes*, it said. *Karlis Skalbe*. But which was the author and which was the title? The language remained strange. Its letters floated at a ghostly level. They were an impossible, black text. How could these sounds form a vocabulary? But also, the book was an unusual size, almost square. For some reason, I found this size tremen-dously appealing, much more appealing than the conventional, rectan-gular paperback. I ruffled the pages with my thumb. A two-dollar bill tumbled out of the binding.

I'd actually never seen a two-dollar bill. I knew they existed, sure. But it seemed fake, this etching of Thomas Jefferson, with the number 2 above it. I shook the book to see if there was any more money inside. No luck.

This was a message from God, I decided. He was telling me, "Forget about Hannah, my son. Go buy yourself a Slurpie." He was telling me not to worry about the impending arrival of my dad's cousin. I should relax. I should treat myself to an overly sweet frozen-fruit beverage. I thanked Him and stuffed the bill—and the book—in my jacket pocket.

When I entered the living room I noticed that my dad had fallen asleep on the couch while holding a bottle of bourbon. The bottle was nearly full. It had toppled out of his hand, and was now lying on the thick shag rug, inches from his twitching wrist.

I stole the bourbon. This was a mistake, of course. But at the time it filled me with a sense of accomplishment and thievery. I waltzed out of the house, my feet tapping a ragged rhythm. I had two dollars. I had a bottle of bourbon. I had the limitless night.

Hammond had stopped playing the organ. Peering through the curtained glass of his patio door, I could see his thin figure moving around his apartment. Though I couldn't be sure, he appeared to be in the kitchen. I decided not to disturb him. I walked through the parking lot and out onto the street.

Once I made it to the 7-Eleven, I loitered outside for a moment, trying to figure out exactly how to proceed. I left the bottle of bourbon next to the mammoth trash bin and entered the store.

The lights flickered in a nauseating way, giving everything inside the sense of stop-action photography. I squinted my way to the Slurpie machine. I chose a flavor—nuclear cherry—and squinted my way back to the cashier.

The cashier was a pockmarked young kid, possibly eighteen or nineteen years old. His face had high, acne-scarred cheekbones, and his nose looked a little like an arrowhead. His eyes were a pale brown color, almost gray. He punched some numbers into the cash register in a desultory manner. It beeped.

"Your total is a dollar seven," he said.

I pushed the two dollars across the counter.

"Very funny," the cashier said. "That'll be one oh seven, please."

"Okay," I said. I couldn't understand why he hadn't taken the money. "There you go," I said, smiling. I figured that somehow he hadn't seen the bill—possibly because of the epileptic overhead lamps.

"I'm sorry, kid, but we don't take Monopoly money at 7-Eleven, last time I checked."

I stared at the clerk. "Monopoly money?" I said. "But that's a two-dollar bill."

"There's no reason to shout at me."

"I'm not shouting."

"Just pay me and get out of here," he said. "Just give me a dollar seven."

I couldn't believe it. "That's real money," I said. Now I *was* shouting. I looked around. There appeared to be no one else in the store.

"For your information," I said, "the two-dollar bill is actual American currency."

"Do you want me to call the cops?"

"Fine," I said. "Fine, call them. They'll come, and you'll show them this, and they'll say you owe me ninety-three cents." I balled up the bill and threw it at him.

I ran out of the store holding the Slurpie. I don't know if he chased me, or even if he ultimately chose to call the police. I grabbed the bottle of bourbon and sprinted through the night. Snow was falling, and it made the apartments almost beautiful. I imagined that they were actually Soviet apartments, and that I was a young boy who had escaped from a difficult life on a collective farm in the Latvian countryside. I was coming to live with my distant cousin in the city. I would build myself a new life in the busy streets of Riga. And sure, my life would be full of unexpected suffering—and unexpected sex—but in the end I'd be able to say: "Yes! Yes, I have lived! Yes!" Or something like that.

The more I thought about it—sitting in my hedge maple now and drinking the bourbon-laced nuclear cherry Slurpie—the madder I became. It was a metaphor, really, a clear metaphor. I'd gone and tried to pay for my drink with real money. But I'd been rejected. Spurned. Forced into the street. Wasn't this exactly what was happening to me, otherwise? Hannah was the 7-Eleven of my love life, and my earnest emotional currency was being rejected like a two-dollar bill.

I don't know if it was the combination of the sugary ice water and the liquor, or if it was the cold, sugary scent of the air, but I quickly became light-headed. I scurried out of the tree, worried about falling. I sat on the cold ground, my back propped against the maple. I deserved better than this, didn't I? I needed to take control of my circumstances. I needed to dictate my personal life. I poured some more bourbon into the cup.

If there was one thing I'd learned from reading, it was that in books possibility crowded into every moment. It could unfold like a billowing flag—sudden and suffused with wind and color. In the detective stories I devoured compulsively—the short, tense thrillers by Raymond Chandler and Dashiell Hammett—every hour of the day could bring adventure and danger. Most any plot was a roller coaster ride, up and down and swirling through the S curves. But my own life had failed to live up to these standards. It was pretty boring. Mostly I spent my time in the living room. I relaxed on the carpet. I lounged. I was too damn boring, I decided.

I'd walked all the way out of the parking lot, I realized, and now I was approaching the bus stop. These were the outer limits of my world. Except for a few deviations I lived within these parameters. Nothing changed for me. Every day I steamed and rattled to school in the immense city bus. Every day I wandered through the halls of Alexander Hamilton High. Every day I steamed and rattled home to my parents. On the weekends I played a little basketball, either indoors or outdoors, depending on the season.

But this was all going to change. And I was going to be the one to change it. Right now. I was going to get on this bus and take it into the future. Wait. Did I have bus fare? I checked my pockets. No, I did not have bus fare.

But that didn't matter! I would explain to the driver that today was the first day of my new life, and that in the epiphany business, having a few pennies for the Municipal Transit Authority didn't make or break you. That I was a soldier on the road to a karmic battle—that he should take arms and join me and together we could triumph over the wage-labor system that indebted us so heinously to the moneyed classes.

This was actually quite close to what I told the driver. I also may or may not have said something about the Navajo vision quest, and the rites of passage that befell sixteen-year-old boys in turbulent, modern America.

"Shut up and sit down where I can see you," he said.

I sat down where he could see me. Almost immediately, I felt sleepy. The bottle of bourbon sagged into my lap. The label was visible beneath the bottom seam of my coat but I didn't care. There were no other passengers—only the driver. We rumbled along. A bus that does not have to stop to pick up people is a terribly exciting thing; we roared bigly through the strip malls; we cruised through yellow lights, a transit leviathan.

The potholes kept me awake. After some time—and a hazy waking-dream about artillery fire—we were at my intended destination.

"I need to get off here," I said, and the driver grimaced and pulled wordlessly to the next stop.

As the bus sped away, I realized that I was alone in the thin, chilly air. I shivered. I felt the solid pressure of the Heaven Hill bottle against my ribs. This soothed me slightly. It was a comforting presence. I tried to remember exactly why I'd come to this lamp-lit place: the sprawling parking lot of Milwaukee's finest purveyor of quality GMC vehicles, Jack Baldwin Chevrolet.

7

tuesday, november 28, 1989
1:00 A.M.

ANATOMY OF A CAR WRECK

fiesta!

For some reason, this was the first word that popped into my head as I pulled open the door to the body shop. I'd easily remembered the security code. They hadn't changed it in three months. This—I realized—was an example of poor dealership security. If I'd been auditing the safety of Jack Baldwin Chevrolet, I'd have made a note of it.

As it was, I barely realized that my dad wasn't working, and that another janitor might be roaming the halls—sweeping or dusting or scrubbing the windows. I took a swig of the liquor and hid behind a partially dismembered car. I couldn't feel the bourbon anymore. It tasted just like water. Sweet, delicious water, and it satisfied a deep and persistent thirst.

I listened for any sounds in the dealership. I could hear the wind buffeting the corrugated steel and concrete of the building's walls. Other than that—nothing. I felt safe. I emerged and made my way through the maze of the hallways.

Finding the keys proved to be tremendously difficult. For what seemed like thirty minutes I peered through window after window. Finally, I found them—they had a room all to themselves. It was an alcove really, off to one side of the break room. I checked the door. It was a flimsy aluminum partition, and it had a thin window in its center. It was also locked. No problem, I thought, and lurched back to the body shop.

The impact of the tire iron shattered the glass into a galaxy of fine, white slivers. I'd taken the iron from a shelf in the body shop, and now

I'd used it to commit my most serious crime of the evening thus far. I punched a hole through the glass and, reaching carefully through, I unlocked the door. It swung open.

The keys hung from a thousand hooks arranged on the wall. All of the hooks were numbered. It was a little bit like choosing a snack out of a vending machine. I chose B-4, a Chevrolet Monte Carlo. I didn't know what this car looked like, but I liked the sound of its name. It seemed sophisticated and continental. Who drove a Monte Carlo? Why, only the most extravagant of the truly wealthy, of course. Who else? Also, I didn't want to take a car from the showroom, since I figured stealing something from the lot might be less noticeable. Also, I didn't know how to open that glass wall.

As I went to leave, I remembered: dealer plates. This was one of the reasons my dad hadn't been pulled over in September. I rummaged through a desk in the key alcove and sure enough: a laminated cardboard placard that was labeled WISCONSIN DEALER'S PERMIT #04215, along with a small blue aluminum box labeled PETTY CASH. Inside were three crisp twenty-dollar bills. Perfect. Everything was ready.

Standing there, on the cusp of my first felony, I was seized with the urge to write something, to scribble a journal entry or a quick, impromptu poem. I rummaged through the nearest desk and found a piece of paper and a pen. I'd never written anything before, really, nothing creative, even though I'd spent most of my time submerged in books. I felt a little ridiculous—but hadn't Kerouac written in all sorts of unlikely places? Street corners and alleyways and coffeehouses. A car dealership was just like a coffeehouse, wasn't it? But what should I write? I wondered.

A poem. This was easiest, right? I could write a poem in a few seconds. It wouldn't take very long to write a few lines, would it? I thought of an opening image:

The night is like a giant dusty tomb,

Who could argue with that? I put a comma at the end of the line. It seemed like the right thing to do. Was my grammar any good? I liked the image of the tomb. But what about *me*? I needed to make an appearance.

And I am just a person walking in it.

Hey! Not bad at all. Now I needed to rhyme, right? But wait. How could I be in a tomb *and* narrating the poem? I'd have to be undead. An undead narrator! What a great idea! But it would take a little more explanation. I crossed out the period and changed it to a comma. This would, I felt, give me a certain flexibility.

I want to sweep it all out with a broom,

Was this iambic pentameter? I tried to remember what iambic pentameter was.

What I needed now was a big finish. Every poem needed a big finish, right? Mine was no exception. I stood there for a moment, looming over the desk. Someday, perhaps, my biographers would look back to this moment and nod knowingly.

But I can't. My hands are wrapped in linen.

Admittedly, that wasn't the greatest rhyme: *in it/linen*. But it was serviceable. And it had a great metaphysical twist. I imagined the dead, pulling themselves out of their coffins and sweeping their own tombs. And then narrating poems. How gothic! Sure, it didn't relate exactly to my life. But still, it was a certain kind of accomplishment. I looked at what I'd done. *But a poem needs a name!* I thought for a moment, then scrawled at the top of the page:

Untitled

I cleared my throat and read the poem aloud. It gave me a slight, drunken thrill. I folded the paper and put it in my shirt pocket.

I retraced my steps back through the body shop and into the frigid night. I ditched the bottle of bourbon in a convenient trash can.

I had thought about it frequently—the feeling that I'd had as my dad and I drove through the open air last September. Though he was outgoing, though he told stories and talked a lot and was generally pretty social, my dad was difficult to really know. He was more of a presence than a person. On that night I'd felt close to him, really close, bonded by some sort of outlaw recklessness.

But in the months since then, things had gone back to normal. Occasionally he embarrassed me with the extent of his drinking. I'd begun to remember that night as an unfortunate misadventure, one that had almost ended in my dad's arrest.

But now, standing in front of the shimmering red Monte Carlo, standing in front of space B-4, I realized that he'd been trying to tell me something. Forget about the rules, he'd been saying. The rules are for suckers. Get away with as much as you can. Get it quick and enjoy it.

Thanks, Dad, I thought as I unlocked the door.

The ignition swayed to the left and the right as I tried to insert the key. The steering wheel swayed a little, too, but eventually I had them under control and steady. The motor roared to life. It was a V-8. This was the first car I'd driven since the day of my driver's exam, and the feeling was exhilarating—a feeling of pure power.

Traffic was a blur of lights. My destination was simple: Hannah's house in the suburbs. I would throw rocks at her window and woo her out into the November night. I was a little disoriented, though, and I strained to remember the roads I needed to take from the map Dr. Graham had pressed on me after the demonstration.

On the way, I stopped at a gas station and bought a cup of coffee and a strip of beef jerky and a pack of gum. I figured that the mint from the gum by itself might not cover up the taste and smell of the alcohol. Beef jerky, I knew, was the most odorous substance a human could eat. I would smell bovine, not drunk.

The rock-throwing plan was hampered by the fact that I couldn't positively identify her window. Her house—large and imposing and ringed with evergreens—sat on a little hill within the neighborhood. I walked around its perimeter, wading through the soft drifts of snow.

One window was lit from within. This has got to be Hannah's room, I thought. There was a patio in the backyard—right below the lit window—and the builders had filled the patio's foundation pit with rocks. I selected a small one, one that could cause a minimum of damage. I aimed. I fired. I remembered the sound of shattering glass from earlier in the night. Thud. The rock hit the aluminum siding, three feet to the right of the target.

Another rock, another miss. Another rock, another miss. I tried again. Another miss. But apparently the sound of the rocks hitting the siding had captured someone's attention. I saw the curtains move. A face peered out into the darkness. I smiled and waved, trying to seem as friendly as possible in the dimly lit suburban night.

"Yuri? Is that you?"

It was Sara, Hannah's sister. Sara was one year younger than Hannah, a junior like me. We'd taken driver's ed together.

"Hey, Sara. Is Hannah around?"

"I think she's asleep. Do you know what time it is?"

"After midnight," I guessed.

"Are you drunk?"

I laughed. "No, no, of course not. Can you get her?"

Sara seemed to consider this for a while. I continued smiling. "Hold on," she said, and disappeared.

As I stood in the cold I noticed that the top of the snow was shining, an iridescent, frosted shine. Was Sara going to call 911? Wake up her parents? Get a rifle from the gun rack in her dad's study? Instead, Hannah appeared. She looked sleepy. She wore an oversized blue sweatshirt.

"Yuri?" she said. "What the hell are you doing here?"

"Come downstairs," I said, my voice a theatrical whisper. "I have something to show you." I wondered if I seemed creepy.

"Downstairs? You mean, outside?"

"Yeah. And don't wake up your parents." I could hear her sigh as she closed the window.

Within minutes she'd appeared. She was still wearing the same blue sweatshirt, but now with jeans and heavy winter boots. The effect was devastatingly attractive. She smiled when she saw me, something that caught me off guard. I guess I'd been thinking of myself in grim terms—a criminal, a thief, a drunken renegade. I gave her a hug and inhaled her perfume—clearly she'd just sprayed it on her neck. Oranges, I thought, and I stood there breathing the scent, letting it saturate the night air.

"What's going on?" Hannah asked. "Why so mysterious? How'd you get here? Why do you smell like beef jerky?"

"All of your questions will be answered"—and here I bowed deeply and gave a flourish of my hand, pointing at the Monte Carlo that I'd parked to one side of her driveway—"when you see this gleaming piece of machinery."

At first Hannah didn't seem surprised. She walked over to it, using the path that someone had so carefully shoveled through the snow. She circled the Monte Carlo, almost as if she was appraising its value. She stretched out her hand and ran a finger along the clean paint. She opened the passenger door, put her head halfway inside. Then she leaned back and looked at me.

"You stole this car?" she said.

"Absolutely not," I countered. I realized then that I needed some sort of explanation. "My dad bought it, at Jack Baldwin. He's been saving his money, you know, to buy it. He's been saving for years, actually."

"You stole this car," she said again. "It has no tags. It has no registration. It does have a dealer plate, though, and its sales sticker—right there in the window. Either you, or your father, stole this car right from the dealership." She looked at her watch. "I'm guessing within the hour."

I suddenly felt sober. What had I been thinking? Had I been thinking at all? Why had I thought she'd like it? She was a normal person. Normal people didn't like stolen cars.

"Okay. You're right," I admitted. "I stole it. But my dad doesn't know. He had nothing to do with it."

Hannah looked at me. She'd been very serious, almost accusatory. She'd seemed displeased with the situation. I couldn't blame her. How would I have reacted—I wondered briefly—if she'd been the one who had appeared outside of my window? I might have been happy, sure, but possibly not.

As I watched her reaction, though, I saw her face soften. Now she glanced quickly at her house, presumably scanning the windows to see if we'd awakened anyone else.

"This is so bad ass," she said. "What an awesome subversion of the capitalist social order. I've been waiting for you to do something like this. Let's go."

Relief flooded through my body. I jumped into the driver's seat and we careened out into the night. The Monte Carlo was an automatic.

Still, it accelerated quickly around the corners, and the tires made pleasant squealing noises as we spun from tract development to tract development. I could feel my heart beat in each of my fingertips.

"So is this a date?" Hannah said, and laughed. She put her hand on my leg, simply resting it there, as if that were the most natural place for her hand to be. "Where are we going, anyway?" she asked.

"I don't know," I said. Then, a thought came into my head. "Gambling? We could go gambling. Isn't there an Indian casino over by Menomonee Falls?"

"No," Hannah said. "It's not open yet. They don't know when it's going to open."

"Damn," I said. "We can't go drinking. We can't go gambling. What else is there to do?" Hannah shifted in her seat.

"Let's just drive," she said.

And so we did. We drove out through the edge of Milwaukee's suburbs, out into the broad valleys to the west of the city. I had no music, but we were talking, so the radio wasn't necessary. Our conversation was a string of jokes—some funny, some not—and its rapid movement exhilarated me. I watched carefully for the police, though, and kept my speed within legal limits.

The feeling of driving a car that you own cannot compare with the feeling of driving a stolen car. In a stolen car, everything seems dipped in mercury. The air you breathe, the touch of every surface, the sounds of driving—all of these are so spark-filled that they threaten to erupt, to blast up and over you and consume you in some kind of invisible fire. I don't mean to sound phony. But really—it's a breathtaking feeling.

After we'd been driving for some time, I said, "I wrote a poem tonight."

Hannah turned to me. "I didn't know you wrote poetry," she said.

I cleared my throat and nodded. "Oh, sure. Absolutely. Hundreds of poems."

She nodded. "Can I read it?" she asked.

"Sure," I said. I took the poem from my shirt pocket. She unfolded it. "It's short," she said.

"But long on feeling," I said.

She read it out loud. At the end, she giggled, which I didn't take as a good sign. It was supposed to be a haunting conclusion. It was supposed to illustrate the great metaphysical dilemma of modern life. It was not a giggling matter.

"Oh, Yuri," she said, "it's such an awful poem."

I was crushed. I'd made a terrible mistake, I realized, in showing it to her. It was a simple fact. Girls never liked the guys who wrote them poetry. But then Hannah said, "It's an awful poem, written by an interesting man." She looked over at me and smiled.

You consider me a man? I thought, greatly pleased with the idea. If Hannah Graham thought of me as a man, I reasoned, my life had reached a pinnacle of success.

"Interesting?" I said.

"Sure," she said, "complicated." She moved nearer to me on the bench seat of the Monte Carlo. "Attractive."

She lingered on the word. I could feel the heat of her breath on the skin of my neck. My throat constricted. She leaned over and—straining to the limit of her seat belt—she kissed the edge of my jaw. Her tongue lingered there, and for a second I thought it might sear its way through the boundaries of my skin.

I couldn't help myself. She was sitting so close to me, pleasant smelling and soft and utterly tactile. I turned my head and kissed her. Our mouths opened; our tongues staggered against each other; they collided and twined together. I struggled to breathe through my nose. But breathing doesn't matter, I thought. If I suffocate this way it'll be worth it.

I suppose it was stupid to make out with Hannah Graham while I was driving. But what else could I do? I wasn't the most experienced of sinners, after all. I had no history of temptation; I hadn't been confronted by vice in any form. Much less a soft, voluptuous, somewhat punkish, pleasant-smelling form of it. All I could think about was the sensation of the kiss, and the way it seemed to fill my entire head with gauze. I relaxed my grip on the steering wheel.

In the fifteen years since the accident, I haven't ever been able to determine the exact order of events. Mostly it's blotted from memory. Remembering critical moments such as this one, I've found, is often more painful than informative. But one thing is certain. The car veered off the road while Hannah and I were kissing. Of this there can be no doubt. One moment we were eagerly exchanging our saliva, and the next moment we were plummeting onto a dairy farm.

The smaller highways outside of the cities of Wisconsin are bordered mostly by dairy farms. The grass of their rolling pastures often extends to the very edge of the road surface, deep green against the shocking black of the asphalt. In this case, our stolen Monte Carlo left the roadway, hurtled through a little wooden fence, rumbled through a pasture, flipped, rolled, and finally crashed through the exterior wall of a barn. We came to rest on our side, propped in the middle of the walls. It was a miracle that no cows were injured. It was a miracle that at least part of the barn didn't collapse. It was equally a miracle that both Hannah and I were alive.

Hannah was the first one out of the car. I was still dazed and sitting in the driver's seat, hanging in the harness of my seat belt. The engine was on, and smoking, and I tried—I still remember this clearly—to drive my way out of the situation. I pressed down on the accelerator. The transmission struggled to mesh its gears; the engine cavity roared. Hannah was at the window, then, and she was screaming at me to turn the engine off. I didn't understand. Why turn the engine off? We couldn't just stay here, could we, upside down in the wall of a barn? We had to head for safety.

It was then that my driver's ed class came filtering back to me. I remembered the videos they'd shown us, videos with titles like *Anatomy of a Fatal Car Wreck*, videos that were invariably prefaced by disclaimers stating that a portion of the footage we were about to see was real, and that some of it was graphic, and that many of the people involved had died, most of them in severely painful ways.

Ghostly apparition of CHARLIE. Low-budget video effects make him translucent, like an angel. He is wearing oversized, cardboard-and-feather wings.

CHARLIE
If I'd only turned off the engine, then the car wouldn't have exploded. I'd still be a person, and not an angel, like I am today.

CHARLIE'S FAMILY standing on the front steps of their ranch-style rambler. CHARLIE'S WIFE is noticeably pregnant. Include SEVERAL YOUNG CHILDREN and a GOLDEN RETRIEVER.

ALL

We miss you, Daddy. We wish you weren't an angel.

GOLDEN RETRIEVER barks. Fade to black.

I turned off the engine, but it was too late. The car had already started to smoke.

"It's on fire, Yuri," Hannah yelled. "Get out now!"

My driver's side window had shattered. Its particles seemed to be mostly on the roof of the car, though I could feel the tiny dots of safety glass on the skin of my face. I took a quick inventory of my limbs. Both legs: check. Both arms: check. I seemed to have no broken bones. I braced myself against the partially flattened roof, the glass pinching at my palms. I unbuckled my seat belt and slumped heavily downward.

Crawling out proved surprisingly easy. Hannah stayed next to the smoking, burning car, which amazed me. Would I have done the same for her? Probably. I hoped so. She stood there—despite the heat of the growing fire—and tugged at my arm as soon as it poked through the broken window. Within twenty seconds I was free. The cows were in an uproar. They'd clumped in the far corner of the barn. Hannah and I left them behind, staggering clear of the situation.

We ran about five hundred yards. Only then did we turn to look at what we'd left behind. The fire was not a large one—the car hadn't exploded—and the flames seemed to have mostly dissipated into thick white smoke. Above the smoking car, the maroon-colored barn was stenciled in barely visible, tall white letters:

Lincoln Quesnell, Dairy Cows

And there was Lincoln, now, or some descendant of Lincoln perhaps, emerging from his house in pajamas, heading directly toward the scene of the accident. He hadn't seen us yet.

"I think we'd better run," I said.

"To where?" Hannah asked.

"I really don't think it matters," I said, already heading for the woods.

We must have run for an hour. I was in decent shape, and so was Hannah—but even so, it tested the limits of our endurance. We'd headed out and over the dairy pasture. Within seconds we'd crossed over the top of a little hill and slipped out of sight of the accident scene. We'd followed the pasture over a series of minor hills and valleys, and ended up on the banks of a creek that was half-frozen.

"Let's follow the creek," I said, "in case they send out the dogs."

"The dogs?" Hannah said. "Are you crazy? This isn't a movie. We're not escaped convicts. They don't just have the dogs ready at two A.M."

I wasn't so sure. This seemed like just the sort of thing for a K-9 unit. Besides, I'd seen it so many times that it just seemed like protocol. Of course the dogs would chase us. How could they not? Hannah gave in. We walked down the creek's shallows. Whether this would be effective in throwing the dogs off the trail, I didn't know. Could they smell our footsteps through the ice? I stumbled again and again on the half-broken slick surface, sprawling into the shallow creek. I was soaked. My muscles ached. Eventually we reached a bridge.

"Come on, this is far enough. Let's take the road," Hannah suggested.

It was Highway 83. Immediately after the bridge we encountered a tall green road sign. WELCOME TO MUKWONAGO, WISCONSIN, it said. POPULATION 4,495.

"Mukwonago?" I said. "Where is Mukwonago?"

We were crossing a set of railroad tracks.

"Right next to Phantom Lake, apparently," Hannah said, and pointed to the nearest billboard. While vacationing at Phantom Lake, it told us, we could rent a Jet Ski for just thirty dollars a day.

Not surprisingly, the town of Mukwonago was small. We found the only gas station, which was thankfully closed. A phone booth stood in the corner of its parking lot. The booth was shiny. The phone was a rotary dial. I used a quarter that Hannah gave me and dialed her home number. Hannah and I had agreed that this was our only viable option.

Sara answered the phone groggily. She'd clearly been sleeping. The whole world, it seemed, was asleep. Except for Hannah and me, of course, and probably Lincoln Quesnell.

"Sara? Thank God you answered the phone."

"Hello?" It was Dr. Graham.

"It's okay, Dad," Sara said. "I've got it. It's for me. It's Yuri Balodis."

"Yuri? Do you have any idea what time it is?"

I didn't say anything. Sara, fortunately, came to my defense.

"I've got it, Dad. It's okay."

"I'd expect more from you, Yuri," Dr. Graham said. He slammed down the receiver.

"Jesus," Sara said. "What's wrong with you? It's three thirty in the morning. Where are you? Where's my sister?"

"I know it's late, Sara, and I'm sorry. But we're in a difficult situation. Otherwise we wouldn't have called."

The explanation took a few minutes. I skipped the kissing, just for the sake of politics, but also to make us seem more like innocent victims. Sara said she knew exactly where we were, and that she'd come get us. She'd sneak out of the house and take their parents' car. She'd be here in thirty minutes.

While we waited, Hannah sat on the curb outside of the gas station minimart. Her arms were crossed and she was staring at nothing in particular. I was soaked and freezing, and I was certain that I'd soon be hypothermic. Without warning, Hannah started screaming at me.

"You know, Yuri, you're a complete idiot. Firstly, I can't believe I came with you. Secondly, I can't believe we left the scene of the accident. We're dead if they find us. My parents will kill me. They will slaughter me."

I stood there and stared at her. She looked decent, considering what she'd been through. Just one cut above her eye. The blood had dried, but the scab was a little muddy.

"I'm sorry, Hannah," I began. "I didn't mean to—"

"I don't care what you meant to do. Please, Yuri, please, please do me a favor. Never drop by at midnight with stolen cars. Never even call me again. Never ask me to hang out in the bleachers during gym. I don't want to see you. I don't even want to talk with you. You are a completely crazy, stupid, ridiculous, annoying fool."

She was done. There was nothing I could do. I cleared my throat. I coughed. I wandered away. I stood ten or twenty feet from her. I counted the stars. There was the Big Dipper. There was Orion. I sighed. My breath rose upward in a plume, tumbling and expanding and then dimming to nothing.

Sara did indeed arrive in thirty minutes. Hannah sat in the front seat, silent and foreboding. I sat in the back, trying desperately to warm myself. We drove silently back to Milwaukee.

Mukwonago turned out to be just off of Interstate 43, roughly twenty minutes from downtown. The strip malls started almost immediately, as well as the suburban developments—Glen Oaks Estates, Tess Corners, Hales Corners. I pressed my head against the glass of the car window.

What were the chances, I wondered, that they'd manage to trace the stolen Monte Carlo back to me? The main problem, as far as I could tell, was that I'd used the alarm access code to enter the building. Had this been recorded in some computer? Could the police find out exactly when the alarm had been deactivated, and by whom?

After a while, I figured out what I had to do. I had to make it seem like a break-in, like an extremely savvy—or lucky—thief had smashed his way into the dealership and stolen the keys to the Monte Carlo.

I asked them to take me to Jack Baldwin Chevrolet. My dad was working, I said; my dad would take me home. But they were unsure. Sara didn't want to go anywhere near the scene of the crime.

Unexpectedly, Hannah came to my defense.

"Just do it," she said. "Please? Let's just get rid of him."

"All right," Sara agreed. "I'll take you. But we're dropping you off down the block."

They did just this. I don't think that the vehicle even came to a complete stop. I jumped out as it rolled slowly along the boulevard. By the time I turned to wave, it was speeding madly away. Dawn had come to the edges of the sky. It had to be close to six.

Like most strip malls, this one was built on the edge of woods. The woods were a reminder of what the land used to be like, before they'd come in and paved it and covered it with cars. I scouted around and found a few big rocks. There was also a chunk of crumbly asphalt and half of a brick. I walked back to the front of the dealership. I threw a rock at the rolling display window.

Nothing. Not even a mark. Damn. I threw the ball of asphalt. A crack sprung from the window, shooting up toward the pale gray sky. I threw the brick. It crashed through the span of glass, landing just inside the shattered panel. Then—knowing that every second was bringing me closer to arrest—I kicked at the window. Shards of glass hurtled through the air. After a few more kicks the hole was big enough to seem like the entryway for a very small, or limber, criminal.

I ran. I ran as quickly as I could, brushing the glass from my sleeves, feeling the small sharp moments of pain as it pricked my palms. I made it to the bus stop. I stood there, exhausted, hands on knees, soaked and shivering, gasping for breath, waiting for the bus. I'd be home in twenty minutes, I calculated—plenty of time to shower and get ready to leave for the airport.

People are not going

To dream of baboons and periwinkles.

Only. here and there. an old sailor.

Drunk and asleep in his boots.

Catches tigers

In red weather.

—Wallace Stevens. "Disillusionment of Ten O'Clock"

part 2

tuesday, november 28, 1989
6:30 A.M.

When I knocked on the door to the apartment, I heard my dad say, "Never mind, Mara, do not call the police. Here he is. I am sure of it."

The door swung open.

"What happened to you? Where are you until six thirty in the morning?" he demanded.

I guess I should have been contrite. I should have been upset or sad or full of regret. I should have asked for forgiveness. But I was really, really cold. I couldn't think of anything but the truth. Or at least a part of the truth. "I fell in a stream," I said.

"You have a black eye," he said.

"I hit a log," I said.

"You are wet like a goose," my mom said.

"I know."

"You will be sick for sure," she added.

After thirty minutes I'd been immersed in steaming hot water, toweled dry, and dressed in bulky winter clothes. "I know that the story about where you went is not short," my dad said, "so it will have to wait until after Ivan leaves."

Whoever said that great historic facts and characters recur twice—once as tragedy, and again as farce—never met my dad. More important, he never met my dad's sweatshirts. They displayed the elements of farce as soon as you saw them. And they were definitely a tragedy—a garish, slapstick tragedy. They simultaneously made a tragic first impression *and* left a memory like the memory of a circus. On this particular morning my dad was clad in bright yellow, and consequently he looked a little bit like a vat of mustard. Also, he wore green pants, green pants that glowed with a verdant, silky sheen. He looked like an entire condiment table, actually—mustard and relish and his lips like shiny ketchup. As we'd left our apartment I'd asked him why he'd chosen these particular colors.

"After twenty-five years," he'd said, "would you recognize me as myself? I am old and fat. When I left I was young and supple. Now my clothes need to tell him, 'Look, is that not Balodis?'"

My mom was eating a pack of Milk Duds. Occasionally, she would grab my arm and twist it and force a Milk Dud into my damp palm. "They are good to make your teeth more strong, in my opinion," she would say, and I knew that this meant that I was required to devour the little caramel in seconds. I'd tried to point out that refined sugar caused tooth decay, and that I already had a mouthful of fillings, but she'd silenced me with an angry glare. "Hush," she'd said, "you will enjoy this candy if you chew it in a careful and proper manner."

It was seven fifty in the morning—an idiotic time for a flight to arrive. I was trying to forget the details of the previous night—the residue of which was the awful headache that hung behind my eyes. I was groggy; my parents were groggy; all the employees in the terminal of General William Mitchell International Airport were groggy. Who wanted to be awake and at work this early? The whole situation was a mystery of modern commerce. I told this to my mom while chewing carefully on one of the Milk Duds.

"You know, Mom, this is a mystery of modern commerce. Why do people agree to do these things at times when it's clearly unpleasant for them? If they engaged in some kind of communal movement, a real broad-based kind of action against the airlines or the Milwaukee County Airport Authority, then they'd be able to get decent hours and save everybody a lot of trouble. You know, Mom, Marx said that we have to make our history with our hands, that we have to—"

"Hush," she said, "or the candy will pull out your fillings."

"No, it won't," I said. "And you just said the candy was good for me."

"Simply shut up, Yuri. I am telling you this as your mother."

On the way to the airport, as I shivered in the backseat of the taxi, my dad had explained what he'd been able to piece together through his two-minute phone calls from the Eastern Bloc. Ivan Ozolinsh and his wife, Guna Ozolinsh, were visiting us for six days as part of an exchange program coordinated by the State Department's Bureau of Educational and Cultural Affairs. They were his cousins: Ivan by blood, Guna by marriage. This made them both my second cousins.

Guna was a professor at the University of Latvia; in the course of her visit, she'd be lecturing at Marquette—and also talking to a few classes. It was simple, a short trip. They would arrive today, Tuesday, the twenty-eighth of November, and next Monday, the fourth of December, they would leave. My mom would take a week of vacation from the library to help show them the sights of Milwaukee. My dad would continue working the night shift, but he'd still spend his days with us.

My dad assured me that the visit was open and legitimate and nothing to worry about—since this bureau also coordinated the Fulbright Program for scholarly study abroad. He'd done some research. "It is the International Visitor program," he'd said, and then nodded in a way that was meant to reassure. "It is organized by the United States Information Agency."

"What's the United States Information Agency?" I asked.

"The United States Information Agency?" my dad said. He paused. He was clearly unprepared for this question. "I do not know exactly. It is a division of the Bureau of Educational and Cultural Affairs. I read a brochure, however, which said that they promote international understanding."

I nodded and sank into my seat, putting the pieces together in my (aching) head. For the past few weeks, we'd only been able to talk to Ivan in a series of echoing and scratchy phone calls. This had raised speculation on a range of questions. How had they obtained our phone number? Our address? Now, it was all starting to make sense. Guna had contacts at the BECA in Washington; they'd done the legwork for her, obtained all the information about her only American cousin, her husband's cousin who lived in the northern Midwest. Perhaps they'd structured the visit around this fact—wanting Guna to be near her American family—or perhaps Guna and Ivan had requested this, themselves. The remaining questions, I figured, would sort themselves out.

Somehow, my dad implied, Ivan and Guna's appearance in the

United States was directly tied to the fall of the Berlin Wall, which had wrought a massive change in the minds and hearts of the Soviet people. They'd heard about it on Radio Free Europe, my dad insisted, and they were uplifted. This was why they were coming—my dad informed me—because they'd been uplifted.

"Uplifted? But, Dad, look, it's the twenty-eighth of November. The Wall only fell three weeks ago. Ivan called us the day it fell. How could the two events be tied together, at all?"

"Tied," my dad maintained. "Tied together like bandages."

"But don't you think they planned this in advance?" I asked. "Don't you think they've been planning this for months?"

My dad, however, was nothing if not stubborn. He insisted that Ivan's arrival was part of a new dawn of freedom around the world. These were the words he used. "New dawn of freedom," he said. "Just like in that movie, with the gorillas."

"You mean *2001*? But that's about outer space."

"Exactly. It is new dawn, because it is just like from outer space."

That we'd even been able to hear Ivan's voice was something of a marvel. There had been no phone access to Latvia for decades. Gorbachev's perestroika and glasnost had only recently eased things somewhat. News reports were circulating that Baltic republics could soon be free again, and that the USSR was on its way to unraveling.

Their names rang through my memory: Ivan and Guna Ozolinsh. They were connecting to Milwaukee from Detroit, a short commuter flight after their lengthy overnight flight from Eastern Europe. "In Latvian," my dad had informed me, "Ozolinsh means, 'Little Man of the Oak Trees.'"

For me, this translation had spawned a lot of images of hermits and elves, and I'd figured that Ivan would walk off the plane wearing wooden clogs, or a pointy red hat shaped like a waffle cone. His wife would be sprightly, perhaps, and her eye shadow would glitter. She'd hand me a garland woven from basil and hibiscus, and if I ever wore it to sleep, I would dream of the Old Country. Or something like that.

Standing in the airport, I felt a surge of nervous nausea sweep over me. I was a fugitive from justice, a criminal fleeing from the law. My dreams of a future life—my hopes of one day becoming a writer, or a lawyer, or a religious mystic—vanished into a swirl of imaginary police lights. The lights would flood the terminal; I'd hear the police sirens approach from a distance, just like in a movie. "Are you Yuri Balodis?" the arresting officer would ask. "Yes," I'd say, my head hanging low. "Yes, that's me." I was certain that I was about to be imprisoned.

I waited with my parents. My skin itched and felt as if it were much too small. We waited; I sweated; we waited some more. Where were they? Their Boeing 737–300 had nosed toward the gate more than thirty minutes ago. It had configured its belly with the accordion seal of the passenger walkway. Baggage handlers had started offloading the luggage. Still, no passengers. My parents clustered around the gate. In some ways, they'd been waiting for this moment for twenty-five years. Refugees from the Soviet Union themselves, they'd lost contact with their families the moment they crossed the Latvian border.

"What is happening?" my dad asked the gate agent. Someday, I told myself, I would gently convince him that there was nothing wrong with the apostrophe.

"A routine delay, sir," she replied, focusing on her screen. Her fingers were a blur of efficiency. If she was writing a novel, I calculated, she'd written at least twenty pages while we'd been standing at the gate.

"A routine delay?" my dad said, his voice gradually getting louder. "A routine delay? Let me see now. What kind of delay is routine? This is a difficult question, no? But wait. I have for you an answer. I see now that it is easy, so easy, like a child playing." Now he was shouting. "All you have to do is simply tell me—that is all—simply tell me that the flight is coming later. Then, I am thinking that the flight is coming later. I come to the airport—and here is the key—*after* the routine delay. So now, for me, the flight is on the time, and I am on the time, and now everybody is happy and poof, no more routine delay."

"Rudolfi!" my mom snapped, and launched into an abusive stream of Latvian phrases. I tried to seep into the carpeting. After a few moments my dad started looking sheepish. He waved his hands in a conciliatory way. "Okay, Mara, okay," he said, and he repeated it again. "Okay, Mara, okay. You are right."

"And?"

My dad turned to the gate agent, who hadn't looked up from her laborious secret novel. "I am sorry," he said. "I should not have yelled at you."

The gate agent nodded. Her computer beeped. She picked up a telephone receiver and had a brief, quiet conversation. With one smooth, smiling motion, she swept past my dad and over to the doorway. She slid her security card through the scanner and there—like a miracle from the belly of the whale—came the passengers.

It was strange that—meeting for the first time after not seeing each other for twenty-five years—my dad and Ivan did not speak Latvian. Maybe it was the pressure of America, this new and overwhelming country, or the shock and commotion of the airport, but they greeted each other with resounding *hellos*. My mom started crying as soon as she saw Ivan—or at least the man that I presumed was Ivan—and she rushed forward to greet him, nearly knocking me to the ground.

Ivan was a tall man, and not at all sprightly. His belly—a beachball–sized stomach—protruded firmly from his shirt and he waddled slightly when he walked. He wore shiny slacks, too, although his slacks were brown. He had stiff, well-greased hair that he'd combed directly back from the forehead. He had a nose like the knob of a baguette, bright blue eyes, and a neatly trimmed black mustache that could only have been dyed.

Guna was not sprightly, either. She was a pillar of a woman, a Grecian column that descended from shoulder to toe. She'd clearly once been stunning—and still was, really, with regal gray hair and a quick, full smile. The lines of her face were set into a sort of cheerful optimism, and the bright orange color of her ankle-length dress reflected warmly in her eyes.

My dad spoke first. "It is excellent to see you, Ivan," he said. "How are you feeling?"

"I am feeling well. But my leg is acting up again, you know. But what can you do about that?"

"Nothing," my dad said. "That is life."

"That's life," Ivan concurred, laughing and throwing his hands up as if my dad had revealed a central truth of the world. It was clear that Ivan spoke better English than my dad. Even his accent was less noticeable—a fact for which I had no explanation.

"This is my wife, Guna," Ivan said. "She is the intelligent one. I am the fool."

My dad smiled politely and extended his hand.

"I am pleased to meet both of you," Guna said. Her English was flawless, a remarkable counterpoint to my dad's muddled delivery. She smiled and shook each of our hands. She complimented my mother on her lovely amber brooch. I looked guiltily over toward my mom; I hadn't even noticed the brooch. Neither my father nor I had commented on it.

"Thank you, Guna," my mom said, arching her eyebrows toward us. "It was my mother's. My grandfather found the stone near Jurmala, on the Baltic Sea, after a storm." My mom seemed to imply—without saying anything—that both my father and I were worthless and unobservant and hopelessly male. She took Guna's hand in hers. "Do you have much luggage?" she asked.

"Well, yes and no," Guna said. She paused, looking nervous.

Ivan gave us a drowning look. This was the first indication that anything unusual was happening. It was only after this look that I focused on the broader world of the terminal. I noticed the two people standing just behind them. A thin boy in a leather jacket—perhaps seventeen or eighteen years old—stood there, holding the handles of an airline-issued wheelchair. In this wheelchair sat an older woman with a wrinkled face. She, too, was smiling. I had a strange feeling looking at them—standing there at the gate—a strange, visceral sense of completion, almost as if they were the last two elements of a tungsten circuit, a circuit that was coming finally into place, an illumination.

"We have a little bit of luggage," Guna continued, "but my mother and my son certainly have more." She laughed nervously.

"Your mother and your son?" my mom said. She was a little slow to catch on.

"Yes," Ivan interjected with an apologetic shrug. "They also wanted to see the States."

Eriks, the boy, was nineteen years old. Oma Ilga—Ivan's mother—was seventy-four. Despite the airlines' decision to wheel her around, she could walk on her own, and actually could even lift heavy suitcases and lug them to the taxi stand.

Now, coordinating the taxis became a complicated process. Seven people wouldn't fit so well in one cab, but one of the taxi companies had a minivan idling in the long line of cars and we rushed to it and settled inside. My parents split up, Mom wedged into the middle seat with Ivan and me, and Dad in the back with Eriks and Oma Ilga.

"So," my dad said as we pulled onto I-94, "there are four of you?" He said this in a neutral way, as if he were commenting on an interesting cloud formation or the score of an afternoon baseball game.

"Yes," Guna said. "We regret, of course, if this is an inconvenience for you."

"Inconvenience?" my dad said, and laughed, as if this was the most ridiculous thing he'd ever heard. "We will simply juggle a few things around in the apartment."

I thought about our apartment. It was probably less than a thousand square feet. Even at just over three hundred square feet per person, it felt a little crowded. I did the math in my head. We'd now have under one hundred and fifty square feet per person. Though I couldn't quite conceptualize the idea of this many square feet, it still seemed like an unusually small number.

"We can stay at a hotel," Guna offered. "We would be happy to stay at a Holiday Inn for a few days." She was sitting in the front seat of the taxi, next to the driver, who was singing softly to himself, following along with a country ballad on the radio. She turned and looked at me. "You know, Yuri," she continued, "to tell you the pure truth—I have always dreamed of staying at a Holiday Inn."

But my dad rejected this idea immediately. "No, no. You will stay with us, absolutely. It will be no problem, at all."

With this, we headed home. First, though, we had to stop at Pick N' Save.

Pick N' Save was about a mile from our apartment, but it was the closest grocery store, the only grocery store, really, that remained in this part of town. The cab dropped us off in the parking lot. "Why the Pick N' Save?" I asked my dad as we approached the automatic doors.

"Think about it, Yuri. We need a few things that they would like for a breakfast."

"But what are we going to do with the luggage?" I asked. There were a variety of packs and briefcases—in an array of colors and shapes— and right now each of us was carrying at least two bags. For a moment, my dad seemed puzzled. Then, he clapped his hands, triumphant.

"We will load them in a shopping cart and push them around the store."

This seemed a bit ridiculous but, all in all, I didn't feel like arguing. My dad procured two shopping carts for the luggage. We loaded the bags into the silvery metal trolleys. Ivan and Guna, however, had stopped on the grocery store's threshold. They were arguing in rapid, clipped syllables. Guna pointed at the floor and made folding motions with her hands. She seemed exasperated. She stepped on the rubber mat—and the door opened. She waited for it to swing shut. Then she stepped on the rubber mat again. "Don't be an idiot," she told her husband. "It is easy."

Ivan nodded. He inched forward and placed his foot on the rubber mat. The door swung suddenly open. He smiled and walked hesitantly into the Pick N' Save. "Is good," he said, and beckoned for us to follow. Last was Oma Ilga, who crossed herself before inching through the automated doorway.

This was a theme that would repeat itself—with minor variations—again and again throughout the coming days. The smallest appliances or mechanical gadgets would amaze Ivan. One morning I heated a cup of tea in the microwave. He was stunned. "You have such a small and quick oven," he said. "How can it cook so rapidly?"

"It's a microwave," I said.

"How does it work?"

"Like I said—it's a microwave. It cooks the food with micros."

I couldn't explain it. Who knew how a microwave worked, anyway? This wasn't necessary information for living a contemporary American life. You just punched in the numbers and the food cooked. End of story. Of course, Ivan's amazement extended to the garbage disposal and the toaster oven and the remote control for the television. I couldn't explain any of them. I realized that I lived in a world of things that I didn't understand. I didn't even know how an electrical current worked. It all seemed hidden and inscrutable. If I was marooned on a desert island— even a desert island with lots of natural resources and an abundance of industrial machinery—I wouldn't be able to make a lightbulb. Much less a microwave. Or even a pen. I wouldn't be able to hunt. I'd have to gather. The collective learning of the human species, I realized, had somehow missed me. I only knew how to use. I was very good at using.

I began to understand this, however, only after the Ozolinsh family descended on Milwaukee. I didn't see how hard my dad worked to keep me surrounded by these appliances and technical gadgets that neither of us really understood. He was sacrificing his life, day after day after day, sweeping the floors of that dealership, and I did little—if anything—to understand the world he provided for me. Now, much later, I realize that I shouldn't have taken it for granted. He worked hard to give me the opportunities that he'd never had; he loved me absolutely, and I couldn't see that.

But that morning in the Pick N' Save, everyone eventually made it through the doorway. We clustered together in front of the produce—rows and rows of apples and lemons and eggplant and broccoli.

"It is so beautiful!" Ivan cried. He wandered forward. He was walking through the aisles in a dazed way, shuffling across the broad white tiles of the floor.

"American supermarket!" the son, Eriks, yelled. He seemed more at ease with the experience. "I will sing for you now—American rock and roll," he said, and took a banana from the banana display. Using it as a microphone, he began to croon a vaguely familiar melody. I concentrated on it—and tried to ignore the stares of the other shoppers.

"Eddie Money?" I asked. "Are you singing Eddie Money? 'Take Me Home Tonight'?"

"Exactly," Eriks beamed, though the song had been barely recognizable. "It is anthem in Soviet Union. You know this one also?" Again, he began to sing. His accent closely resembled my dad's.

"'Can't Fight This Feeling'?" I said, well after the chorus kicked in for the second time. "You listen to REO Speedwagon?"

"Oh, man," Eriks confided. "They absolutely are the best."

I sought out my mom and walked with her through the aisles. She was filling a little red shopping basket with items. "After I am finished," she said, "you take the basket and then run outside without paying."

I must have looked stricken. She rushed to comfort me. "I am only joking with you, *bucina*. Why are you so serious this morning?"

I was serious, I wanted to tell her, because I was lucky to be alive. I was serious because I'd just committed several felonies, and crashed a stolen car into a barn, while drunk. Also, the girl whom I had just reclassified as the love of my life was intent on never speaking to me again. On the scale of human tragedies, I estimated, these ranked at least in the middle echelon.

"I don't know, Mom. Just tired, I guess."

"You are tired? Of course you are tired. Up all night with girls, swimming with them in heated pools in the suburbs. I am so worried about you, all last night. And you are out with girls, skinny-dipping."

So this was what she'd decided. I'd been swimming in a suburban pool with some imaginary girlfriend. I cringed at the way she said the word *girls*. She gave it a hostile and foreign emphasis—turning the entire gender into an accusation. But an accusation of what? Clearly she believed that I was deeply and salaciously successful with the opposite sex. Why? What evidence for this could there possibly be? I was pimply. I was overly thin. I was quiet and shy and painfully removed from the most popular circles of Alexander Hamilton High.

"Can we get some cereal, Mom?"

"Cereal? But I am buying many eggs. I am sure that Ivan and Guna will not enjoy cereal."

We hadn't had cereal for months. My mom insisted that eggs were the healthiest and most nutritious breakfast food that a human could eat. Also, it was a superstition. *Feed those who are arriving eggs*, she often said, *and those who are departing cabbage*. One time, I pointed out to her that this meant that really I should be eating cabbage for breakfast, since I departed each morning for school. "Shut up, Yuri. You are not taking the true meaning of the saying."

This morning, though, she wasn't difficult to convince.

"But don't forget about Eriks," I reminded her. "He told me that the one thing he wanted to eat in America was cereal. He told me himself, just a second ago. He said exactly this: 'I have heard all about the remarkable variety of your boxed and sugary breakfast foods.'"

"He said that to you?"

"Absolutely."

"Okay, then. It is fine. Then we buy for him cereal."

"Sugary cereal," I specified. "He said he wanted sugary cereal. The more sugar, the better."

Admittedly, we should never have separated. We should simply have walked through the grocery store together, all seven of us, pushing our two carts of luggage and a single cart of groceries. Instead, we scattered like split atoms. Eriks wandered through the aisles unsupervised. More precisely, he strutted through the aisles—the clasps on his black, faux-leather jacket dangling merrily along. When I found him he was standing in the liquor aisle. Wisconsin was a rarity in America—a state that allowed the sale of hard liquor in grocery stores and gas stations. Eriks had unscrewed the top of a bottle of Absolut, breaking its plastic seal.

"It is Swedish vodka," he said, "but it tastes the same."

"Put that back," I said. I snatched the bottle from him.

"I didn't know that the police were so watchful in America," he said.

We went back to the produce section, searching for the rest of the family. Oma Ilga was easy to spot. She had procured a grocery cart. She was filling it with onions, pounds and pounds of onions, and I sprinted over to her. She'd been crying, I could see, and she was short of breath. She was speaking in Latvian—a steady stream of emotional words—as she placed the onions in the cart in a gradually growing tower. Her eyes were puffy and bloodshot.

"Stop," I said. "Wait. We can't use this many onions." I called Eriks over. "Tell your grandmother that she can't buy this many onions. They're a dollar a pound. That's got to be a hundred pounds."

There was a short, passionate conversation. At one point Oma Ilga whipped off her shawl—the shawl that she'd been wearing wrapped around her head—and threatened to whip Eriks with it. After a while, he turned to me.

"She agrees," he said. "She will put them back."

After some time, my mom reappeared. Apparently, she'd found the breakfast foods aisle. Her basket was overflowing with sugary cereals—Cap'n Crunch, Count Chocula, Lucky Charms.

"Okay, Eriks," my mom said. "I have your sugary boxed breakfast foods."

Eriks looked confused. Before he could say anything, I'd taken my mom's arm and was leading her toward checkout. "Excellent," I said. "We're all very excited. Why don't we just buy our food and go home."

At the checkout counter, however, Ivan insisted on paying.

"I'm here as your guest, my cousin," he said. "I will buy this produce."

My dad laughed. "That is very funny, my cousin, but I will not allow a guest to pay."

"Ah, my cousin, you always were such a gentleman. But I'm afraid you will not win this time."

"No, no, my cousin, you are the gentleman, and a gentleman always accepts defeat with a good smile."

"I always smile, my cousin, but I am never defeated."

The clerk was staring at us, his mouth open. My dad waved his wounded hand in dismissal. This was a gesture that he often used, and one that tended to win him sympathy in an argument. He would give in, seemingly, and at the same time he'd draw attention to his disability. His opponent would be wracked with guilt and, usually, my dad would win the argument.

"Fine, fine," he said, "but how will you pay? How much money do you have?"

Ivan raised his chin with pride. "Seventeen dollars," he said.

"Seventeen dollars?"

"Yes."

"That will not pay for these groceries."

Ivan looked crushed. "It won't?" he asked. Note the contraction, Dad, I thought. *Will not* can so easily become *won't*. But Guna stepped forward.

"I will pay," she said. "I have a little more money. And besides, I can always get more money from the BECA or from Marquette. They are big universities and governments. They can handle the extra expense."

"All of you get out of the way," my mom said, and waded up to the register. She deposited the groceries on the moving conveyor belt. "I will pay for them," she said.

My mom stood at the counter and watched the Pick N' Save employee stuff the groceries into plastic bags. She seemed satisfied with her role here. She'd supplanted the men—made them unnecessary, in a way. I stood beside her, proud of what she'd done, proud of how she'd taken control of the situation. Currency changed hands. As we were about to leave, the cashier looked at me more closely. Recognition skittered across the features of his face.

"Don't I know you?" he said. "Haven't I seen you before?"

He undoubtedly had. I remembered him from the demonstration. Even though two weeks had passed, I had a clear picture of this cashier, looking confused and apprehensive, listening to Dr. Graham's speech with his arms crossed over his chest.

"I don't think so," I said, hanging my head and pushing my mom toward the exit.

"Maybe you look like a movie actor," she said as we walked through the automatic doors, carrying our groceries and our relatives' luggage— looking like a family of refugees. "Or maybe you look like a star from the television."

We returned to the apartment. There were seven of us in the little space, and overcrowding was immediately an issue. I wasn't sure where to go. Ivan and Guna and Oma Ilga sat on the sofa. My mom began cooking breakfast. Eriks immediately started rummaging through the refrigerator.

"Heinz 57 ketchup. So excellent," he said, and he took the bottle around the kitchen counter, to the fruit bowl. He selected one of the bananas we'd bought—at his urging—and unpeeled it eagerly. He tapped the ketchup bottle on its side, and within seconds the bright red liquid had drenched the aromatic flesh of the banana. It was like watching pop art take place in my home.

I stared as Eriks devoured the ketchup-covered banana. He finished it in seconds. Over the next week, I would watch as Eriks and the other members of the Ozolinsh family poured ketchup on everything. For them, it was an all-purpose dressing. It was a tasty, sweet-yet-salty addition to a wide range of foods. Eating eggs? Add some ketchup. Eating boiled spinach? Add some ketchup. Eating a peanut butter sandwich? Ketchup would be a wonderful garnish.

Eriks explained that in Latvia there was a certain mystique that surrounded American ketchup. No facility in the Soviet Union produced such a substance. The idea of blending tomatoes with vinegar and sugar and spices seemed broadly enchanting, Eriks assured me, to the bulk of the Latvian populace. I wasn't sure if he was telling the truth. Very quickly I'd learned not to trust him completely. He was too flamboyant to be totally truthful. He had the storyteller's love of the entertaining lie. But I did have to admit that the evidence seemed to support his position. Of this cross-section of the Latvian population, almost all of them had an unusual love for the sauce of Heinz. I could at least verify this much.

"Did you know, though," I said, "that people thought tomatoes were poisonous when they were first imported to America?"

"Poisonous?" Eriks said. "But of course you are joking."

"I'm serious. It's because they were bright red. People thought it was an evil color."

"But this is truly interesting," Eriks said. He turned to his grandmother. He told her this in Latvian. I was able to catch the word *tomato* and little else. To me, the language sounded impenetrably beautiful— like the ghostly face of a model in a fashion magazine—and I was suddenly deeply jealous of their ability to speak Latvian. I should be a Latvian speaker. It was my birthright, wasn't it? My parents had raised me as an American, sure, but what did this mean? That I was entitled to a shoddy public school education? That I could proudly speak our bulky, predominantly Germanic language? English wasn't mysterious. It wasn't ghostly or romantic.

But I was exhausted. Truly exhausted. The day was becoming a sleepy blur. I struggled to keep up with the meandering conversation. My parents served a breakfast of sorts—a widely ranging culinary experience that was shocking in its bounty. My mom had made a few Latvian dishes—*piragi* again, and chicken pudding. There was also *galerts*, a favorite breakfast food of my dad's. *Galerts* was a jelly made of pickled pig's feet. You were supposed to spread it on little wedges of toast. It was actually quite salty and delicious. Then there were the eggs—fried, boiled, and scrambled—and the copious varieties of boxed cereal.

The conversation, however, carefully avoided one topic: why, exactly, there were four visitors from Latvia in our house instead of one. At one point, I thought I'd shouted at Ivan: "Stop, stop what you're saying and explain to us why you never mentioned, in all of your scratchy phone conversations with my father, that you were bringing your whole family." I shook my head and realized that I'd been half-awake and dreaming, and that in actuality, I'd said nothing.

By noon I was falling asleep in one corner of the room. As I slipped from consciousness, the family was discussing the current state of the government of the Latvian SSR. "It's awful," I heard Guna saying. "They are stealing money from the people at every moment that they can. They are pigs."

"Pigs?" I said, half-asleep. I tried to open my eyes but they wouldn't budge. My head rolled helplessly to one side. There was a chorus of laughter.

"Should we wake him?" Guna asked.

"No, no," my mother said. "Let him rest. He had a long night, with his girlfriend in the suburbs." There was another chorus of laughter. I knew exactly what her face had looked like when she said this—raised eyebrows, the curl of a smile on her lips. The image of it haunted my fitful dreams.

I awoke with a cold. My throat ached a little and my head hurt. I was still slumped in the corner of the living room, though someone had tucked a pillow behind my head and covered me with a blanket. I'd coughed myself awake, really. Now I peered blearily out on my world. My dad was blundering through the kitchen and assembling his lunch.

"Where did everybody go?" I asked him. My voice was undeniably raspy. I stood in the kitchen with the blanket draped over my shoulders. "What time is it?"

"It is eight o'clock," he said, "and I am late for Jack Baldwin."

"Eight?" I demanded, though I could barely whisper. My head was pounding. This meant that I'd slept for eight hours. "What happened?"

My dad looked at me—a long appraisal of a look—and he said: "You slept right there, in the corner. We talked." He tossed a banana in his brown paper sack. He picked up a bottle of ketchup—full this morning, empty now—and shrugged and threw it in the trash. "Such a conversation we had," he said. "We talked about so many interesting things. I learned some things about Guna and Ivan that I did not know. Guna is truly an insightful woman, for example."

I nodded. Of course she was insightful. She was a professor at the University of Latvia. The United States government had approved her visa request. It had given her some amount of funding to come to this country. I fully expected her to be insightful. My head continued pounding; my dad continued talking.

"I am certainly looking forward to her lecture at Marquette," he said.

My stomach seized, clenching into an even smaller, nauseous ball. I thought of Marquette and Dr. Graham. I had an uneasy vision of Guna's lecture, one that featured my dad confronting Dr. Graham in an academic setting, wrestling him to the ground on a stage beside a podium, while an audience of grad students watched.

"And Ivan—he is funny as always. We will have some good times before he goes, I can tell you that, for certain." My dad looked at me. "But why are you so quiet? You slept all the day through. I got you a blanket." He cleared his throat. "They are all so tired with the jet lag. So this is why they are sleeping." He pulled the insulated hood of his winter coat over his head. "Now," he said, "I must go." And he went.

I was sorry that I'd missed the conversation, but sleeping had probably saved my life. As it was, I was a little dubious about my survival. I had a fever, I was sure, and my glands were enlarged. I checked my bedroom. Ivan and Guna were asleep in my bed, intertwined and snoring. Eriks slept on the living room couch, I saw, and my mother was sleeping in her bed, next to Oma Ilga. My dad, I assumed, would have to sleep on the floor.

I had nowhere to go. It was awful, really, to feel so awkward in my own apartment. I had no personal space. I was stripped raw and vulnerable. I decided to flee to the balcony—where I could find a sense of peace and perhaps have the chance to reflect on the events of the day.

At least there were no sirens roaring toward our apartment, no squad of police fanned out in formation around the base of our building. I worried, again, about the accident. Why had I been so stupid? My feelings for Hannah seemed completely out of control. They didn't seem reasonable. They choked me, palpably, a knot of emotion that settled at the base of my throat. I struggled to breathe. Anxiety saturated my body. I heard a noise behind me and turned around. Eriks had emerged from the living room. He stood on the balcony, stretching his back, stretching his arms and his shoulders.

"Perhaps we'll go to an outdoor rock concert?" he said. After a few moments I realized that he was joking. I laughed. He seemed pleased, and stood beside me near the railing. He offered me a cigarette. They were European, a brand that I didn't recognize. I accepted anyway. He cupped his lighter in his palm and offered me the flame. I leaned over and lit the cigarette. I noticed the way that the lighter illuminated the skin of his hand, making it seem plush and rose colored in the darkness.

We smoked for some time in silence. The cigarette choked me, slightly, but it also soothed my anxieties. The smoke rose around my head, surrounding me in a miasma of gray. It felt powerful to be smoking on the balcony, to look down at the street through smoky darkness. The buzz from the nicotine made me slightly dizzy. I laughed a little, spontaneously, and Eriks laughed, too.

"What is it?" he asked. "Why are you laughing?"

"It's nothing," I said, shaking my head. "You just wouldn't believe the night I had."

He nodded. "I've had many wild nights, also," he said. He looked at me. "Mostly with my band."

I took the bait. "You're in a band?" I said.

He paused, took a drag of his cigarette. "Volcano of Love," he said, exhaling through his nose. He nodded, as if he'd just made a profound statement on the nature of existence. "Volcano of Love," he repeated, and looked quizzically into the night sky. He seemed lost in that phrase, in the significations and contours of it, and I had no choice but to wait, to contemplate those three words. They were catchy, I had to admit, especially when delivered with an Eastern European accent.

"When they found out that I am coming to United States," he said, "all of the players in the band were jealous." He smiled. "But perhaps we will tour here sometime soon. Perhaps with Guns N' Roses, or with Megadeth."

We talked a little about the style of music that he played. He saw it as classic metal, with a little bit of melody thrown in for good measure. He was familiar with a range of jazz musicians and, interestingly, he cited these men and women as his primary influences. "The music of John Coltrane," he told me quietly, "is always making in me amazement." I nodded. I'd barely heard of John Coltrane—and only in the context of my dad's record collection. I was intrigued and impressed. He seemed terribly sophisticated. I felt the sting of my own impoverished cultural knowledge. Suddenly, I remembered the story that my dad had told me the previous night about Russification. The events of the past day had made it recede into what was seemingly the distant past. Now it rose into my mind, a full memory, a memory of the night, the balcony, and the grain of my father's voice. I wanted to impress Eriks. I wanted him to know that I understood, at least in part, the suffering through which his family had lived.

"I wanted to ask you," I said, "about the deportations under the Soviets, about Russification."

He shook his head. "Russification?" he said. "How do you mean?"

This surprised me. I figured that the term would spark anger in Eriks. I'd pictured him cursing or spitting on the balcony deck, or angrily stabbing the rail with the end of his cigarette. Instead he looked at me questioningly, wondering what I was talking about. I explained what I knew—what my dad had told me about the policies of deportation, about the way that the Latvian language and the Latvian flag had been banned, about the ways that ordinary citizens had been deported to Siberia.

"Ah," Eriks said, nodding. "I see." He coughed a little and flicked the cigarette into the darkness. I watched its ember trace a long arc toward the ground. A beautiful spark, it lit the air as it traveled, lending the smallest illumination to the black. I felt my eyes following the burning cigarette, drawn helplessly to its path, fixed on the only burning thing I could see. Eriks continued.

"There is no name for this in Latvia," he said. He seemed much sadder than he'd been a minute ago, discussing the ways in which Volcano of Love managed to blend Megadeth and John Coltrane. Now he seemed pensive. He patted the pockets of his coat. He found his cigarettes again. I was still smoking my first. I was a little nervous, actually, that I'd accidentally smoke the filter. I didn't want Eriks to know that I wasn't a veteran smoker; I decided to stub it out on the bottom of my shoe. For a moment I worried that I'd scorch a hole in the rubber, but it worked well. I pitched the butt over the rail. It didn't glow; it didn't trace a bright half-circle through the November night.

Eriks started talking, then, and his voice was drawn and sad. He'd become very serious. "I understand what you want to know," he said. "And, if you want to know this, then I will tell you."

Guna and Ivan—Eriks told me in a sober voice—lived in a top-floor apartment in Riga, in a small building, by Soviet standards, in the old part of the city. In their bedroom there was a closet that, when you moved the coats to one side, revealed a narrow spiral staircase leading up to the attic. It wasn't much of an attic, he said, but it was as pleasant as a windowless space could be, lit by a few battery-powered lanterns. On the walls were photographs. The photos were a pictorial history of the Ozolinsh family. Eight family members had their pictures up there, two on each wall, and the frames were all decorated with something, with fabric or bits of glass or colorful buttons. I thought of my world history class, and the way my teacher had described Chinese ancestral shrines. Each of these eight people, Eriks told me, had been deported by the Soviets, six in 1945, two in 1949.

There was also a final set of photos—photos of Eriks's grandfather—who was deported in 1954, and who survived. He'd been given what everyone called a ten-ruble bill—ten years in a gulag outside of Novgorod. His crime, Eriks told me, was simple. He'd stolen cucumbers from a collective farm in order to feed his hungry family. For this, he'd been charged with the theft, and also with Article 58-10 of the penal code, Anti-Soviet Agitation.

"His sentence was easy, actually," Eriks said, "because of other things he was called. He was called, for example, a Socially Dangerous Element, and under Article 7-35, they could have shot him."

"How do you remember the numbers?" I asked, amazed.

"Ah, my friend," Eriks said, "that is not the right question. The question is, How do we forget these numbers? That is what I would like to know."

Eriks continued with the story of his grandfather. He told me that at the end of his grandfather's term, the prison authorities were surprised to find him still living. They shrugged and handed him a month's rations—two smoked codfish in a paper sack—and a blanket. He was free, they told him, free to make his way back to Latvia. How he should cross the four thousand miles of tundra between the labor camp and his home—they said—well, that was his business.

So, with no other alternative, he started walking. It was late spring, and the mosquitoes had just begun to breed. They were dangerous, the mosquitoes. They attacked a man's face while he was sleeping. They sucked the blood from the eyes and the lips, where the skin was softest. Also, there were carnivorous flies, flies that would dig into the skin and leave an infected bite. Without medicine, or alcohol, or even soap, these infections could kill.

The countryside was an enemy as well. It was all stagnant, boggy tundra—cut through with a few dirt roads. Occasionally, a truck rumbled past. Eriks's grandfather waved his arms desperately, hoping that someone would have the courtesy to stop. No one ever did. Once, the driver of a flatbed truck threw something at him, an object that glittered in the relentless sun. It missed his head by inches and buried itself in the wet ground. Eriks's grandfather walked up to it and looked. It was a vodka bottle, empty, with the Smirnoff family crest on the side.

Eriks told me that his grandfather ate the fish slowly, over the first two weeks, and that he saved the eyeballs, keeping them in the pocket of his jacket. He ate one every five hundred miles—every ten days of travel—as a salty reward for staying alive. He gnawed each eyeball to its cartilage core. Finally, when he ate the last one, he realized that, over the course of forty days, he'd made it halfway home. His body coursed with joy. He'd spent nearly six weeks walking during the day, six weeks sleeping in haystacks or peat bogs simply to save himself from the bugs. Now he could imagine a bed, and a blanket other than this scratchy, fetid wool rag.

A few days later, he saw a set of railroad tracks. He followed these to a station, where he waited for two days, begging food and water from the station manager. Eventually, he hid himself in a boxcar heading to Leningrad and then Riga. Eriks paused here. "That is what you call Russification, maybe," he said. "Because when he came home, his farm had been given to the public good."

"But was it really to the public good?" I asked.

"No, of course not," Eriks said. "In the house now lived ten new Russians, swarming over everything, planting little, wasting so much." He paused. "But of course not all the Russians were like this. Many of the Russians, to be fair, planted many good crops."

Eriks threw the second cigarette out over the balcony railing. He looked at me again. The attic above his parents' apartment, he said, was not all depressing. There was one photograph he liked to look at, to study in the middle of all of that sadness. It was taken on the day that his grandfather returned. It showed both of his grandparents. His grandfather was gaunt; he looked almost comical in a suit that had fit him ten years before, but was now seven or eight sizes too large. Though he'd bathed and shaved, he still seemed dirty, somehow, as if the road had permanently stained him, stained his body, somehow, or his spirit. "And my grandmother," Eriks said, "was wearing a beautiful red dress."

"Red?" I asked. "Was it a color photograph? In 1964?"

"No, it wasn't a color photograph. But the dress was there, in the attic, folded in a box and wrapped in tissue paper. I loved to look at it, to feel the fabric of it with my fingers." Eriks shook his head again. "Until the day she died, my grandmother always said that she knew, that morning, that her husband was coming home. She had counted the years, one by one, and she'd believed that he was still alive, and that he was walking home. She woke up and she made a loaf of fresh rye bread and she put on the red dress and also lipstick, which was impossible to get and which she had saved for years. She waited at the front door and then, in the afternoon, there he was, walking down the road, smiling and laughing, so skinny, but so happy to be home. So it was a good story, too, in a way."

I stared at Eriks. I watched his mouth form the language, watched the gentle curl of his lips and the way he seemed to maneuver the English words into place, carefully, like a mason fitting the stones of an archway. I was drawn to him, inexplicably drawn. I felt a pull in the vertebrae of my chest. I tried to clear my head—to make it feel less gauzy and light. He put his hand on my shoulder and squeezed its tendons gently. "But this is too much of a story for such a late night."

We talked for a few more minutes. But the intensity of his words had somehow battered me. I wanted to cry, actually, but I felt embarrassed crying in front of him. After a while, I excused myself and went back into the apartment. Looking over my shoulder, I saw that Eriks had lit yet another cigarette, and that he stood at the balcony railing, smoking, staring into the darkness.

That night, I decided that I'd take my blanket and my pillow to the kitchen. The hum of the refrigerator was somehow reassuring, and I could hear people moving through the kitchens below me. The murr of a garbage disposal, the buzz of a microwave—I could hear the secret language of appliances through the tiles of the floor. I felt comforted by the noise. I was cocooned by it. I lay on my back and, with a visceral shock, remembered the events of the previous night.

Eriks's story about his grandparents had overwhelmed me and, for a moment, I'd almost forgotten about the accident, about the loss of Hannah Graham. Now, my thoughts turned to her, and how angry she'd been on the ride back from Mukwonago. Of course she was really partly responsible, wasn't she? If she'd refused to come with me, if she hadn't kissed me, if she hadn't put her hand on my leg—then maybe we could have averted the crash. Or was I projecting blame? Maybe I should be mad at myself, I thought, for being a ridiculous miscreant. Was that even a word: *miscreant*? It sounded about right, though, even if I didn't know precisely what it meant.

Remembering Hannah's warm mouth, I fought the surge of my hormones. You're lying in the kitchen, I thought. Keep it clean. This is where we eat. The pillow was soft and yielding. I sank my head into it and fell asleep, imagining Hannah's breasts cradling my head. In my dream Eriks was standing on our balcony, and he was playing, on guitar, "Sweet Child O' Mine," by Guns N' Roses. He had a sad look on his face, almost mournful, and with each impact of his pick against the surface of the guitar, a burst of sparks flared into the darkness. Every chord was lit with a certain fire, and the fire rose and consumed him and roared—white noise—behind the melody of the song.

9

wednesday, november 29, 1989

The next morning was more subdued. My dad came back just before seven, and he padded by my new sleeping area in the kitchen.

"Dad," I said. He didn't hear me. "Dad!" I said again, a little louder this time. He turned to look at me, an expression of gentle, distant surprise on his face. I know now that it must have stunned him—this influx of the past—and that it must have felt a little bit like living in the presence of his memories, memories quite suddenly made fleshy and real.

"Oh, hello, Yuri. I did not see you upon entering the apartment."

"Hi, Dad. Listen. I have to be in school today. It's not optional."

I was concerned, in a way, about missing the academic component of school. But more important, I felt the need to see Hannah. Maybe if I apologized to her, things would get a little better?

"What do you mean—*not optional*?" my dad said. "Of course it is optional. It is your decision and my decision. What if you are sick? Just think all day—I am sick, so sick—and then you will not be feeling guilty."

"I'm sure my teachers—"

"We are going to be tourists today, Yuri. It will be like a refreshing moment of rest for you. Tomorrow you can return to your school. I have many activities partially planned. You will find it very enjoyable, in my opinion." My dad walked into his bedroom, ending our discussion.

My throat still hurt, but I'd been helped by the night's sleep. I went into the bathroom and turned on the shower. I let the hot water run over my aching body. I knew that this meant that the other members of my family would have to endure cold showers—but I really didn't care too much about them at this point.

I emerged happily after half an hour. Ivan was waiting at the door. "I am excited for my first American showering experience," he said. He paused for a moment, and seemed to reflect on what he'd just said. "Well, probably it will be the same as in Latvia, don't you think?"

I nodded. "Probably," I said, "except that the water might be a little more democratic." Ivan looked at me strangely. Within seconds he'd closed the flimsy bathroom door and begun filling our apartment with the tenor of some Latvian melody.

Within two hours everyone was ready for breakfast. This was an interesting pattern for me—breakfast then sleep then breakfast again—but I ate willingly. There were fewer Latvian delicacies; the eggs and cereal played more of a starring role. I chewed at my Count Chocula with precision. Sugary residue accumulated on the roof of my mouth. It was a chocolate-flavored paste—and it made my tongue uncomfortable. Overall, though, I was in decent shape. My body ached a little—particularly at the sides of my neck and behind my eyes—but I was beginning to feel excited by the possibilities of the day's tourism.

At breakfast, my dad was especially quiet. It was only after twenty minutes or so that he spoke at all. "The dealership was closed for all of yesterday," he said, through a particularly large bite of scrambled egg. "When I arrived at work, the entire place was covered in police tape. I stayed all night, only to watch what was going on."

I tried to concentrate on my cereal.

"What is police tape?" Ivan asked.

"It is what they use to seal off an area where there has been a crime, so that they can investigate."

"I see," Guna said. "And was there a crime?"

My dad leaned back and wiped his mouth with the back of his hand. Little flecks of egg clung to the edge of his upper lip. "Yes, there was crime." My mom was watching him intently now, as was everyone else except for Oma Ilga, who continued to stare at her plate and eat. Was she muttering softly to herself? It did seem like her lips were moving slightly.

"What crime, Rudolfi?" my mom demanded. "What happened?"

"Well, it simply looks like somebody stole a car from the lot."

"You are joking," my mom said. "Who could do that?"

So they'd traced the car to the dealership. I'd known this would happen. I'd been expecting it. Even so, the words themselves came as something of a shock. Hearing my dad tell the rest of the family what had happened somehow made the experience more real. My guilt blossomed. It filled me with an aching regret and a sense that I'd betrayed my dad's trust. I was in danger. He was in danger. How would he find another job if he was fired? What would I do if I got sent to jail? We were all in danger, really. I was just the only one who knew it. My dad was jovial about the situation. It clearly amused him greatly. If he had any memory of our drunken ride in September, he didn't betray it to me.

"That is why they are investigating, Mara. Do not be so ridiculous. They do not know who did it. But whoever did it also crashed the car somewhere outside of the city."

"Where?"

"I do not know, Mara. I am not the private investigator or police. I only go to work and clean the dealership. How am I to know the answer to all of your questioning?"

Oma Ilga was struggling to follow the conversation. My dad noticed this and began to speak in Latvian. It was a strange experience, listening to the story told again in another language—probably in more vivid and interesting detail. It felt a little like riding on a linguistic iceberg—skittering across the top of a vast ocean of unknowable words, isolated and shivering on a steep promontory. What were they saying? An entire week of this was going to drive me crazy. My parents had kept me from participating in my cultural identity as much as possible. Now the isolation that they had created was evident in my own isolation.

The conversation branched and expanded and I was left with my soggy cereal. At several points I tried to clear my throat, to get their attention. But nobody noticed. Oma Ilga—who'd suddenly sprung to life when the conversation had changed languages—was going on and on in a high-pitched voice. She used her hands to emphasize her points, wagging her swollen-knuckled fingers at her son or her grandchild. At one point, she held the attention of everyone at the table—and she launched into what sounded like a lengthy campaign speech. She smiled as she talked. As soon as she finished, there was a round of laughter.

"What did she say?" I asked my mom, tugging at the sleeve of her blouse.

"It is old Latvian saying. It does not translate well."

"Tell me," I begged. "I want to know."

"Fine, fine, *bucina*. She said, if you are going to the house of your neighbor, wear shoes or you will be stung by bees."

I paused. The conversation continued to swirl around the table.

"Stung by bees?" I asked.

"She meant that it is important to stay prepared. The car dealership was not prepared."

I thought about this for a while. I didn't agree, really. No amount of shoe-wearing would have protected the car dealership from the Balodis family crime syndicate.

"Okay, okay," my dad said suddenly in English. "Are you ready, Yuri?"

What could I say? "Yes, I am ready, Father," I said, mimicking his precise diction.

"All right," he said. "Then let us go. We are going to go out and see the city."

I decided that I had to do something. I had to talk with my dad somehow and straighten things out. Perhaps more important, I needed to devise a way of getting through the guilt. The guilt was not productive. It took an uncomfortable situation and made it close to unbearable. I turned over a few possibilities in my mind. I wanted to go out onto the balcony and think. I needed to escape the symphony of winter-coat zippers. I slid open the door. But as I prepared to leave the apartment, my dad called out, "What are you doing, Yuri? It is time. We are all ready to go."

It was my dad's idea to tour the brewery. "They will enjoy seeing the process of the creation of a fine American beer," he'd said. I couldn't argue with him. At some level, I did find the idea of a brewery tour appealing. Not that I could explain why. But the image of the brewery percolated with a certain romantic energy. It would be fun, wouldn't it, to see the vats where some fine American beer fermented?

After the brewery tour, my dad philosophized, we should go see the Milwaukee Bucks, who were playing the Detroit Pistons this evening at the Bradley Center. It was a good matchup—Isiah Thomas and the Pistons against Sidney Moncrief and the Bucks. We'd probably be in the playoffs this year, though we were usually in the playoffs. Seats would be hard to come by, but my dad claimed that he could swing the tickets. "I know a salesman at work who is a friend with a big-time ticket scalper," he said. "I will make a call to him in a few moments and then—like magic—we will have the excellent tickets."

It was also his idea to rent a van. "We should get a vehicle for driving all of us, together," he'd said. He'd come out onto the balcony with the powder blue telephone clutched in his hand. He looked vaguely hopeful, and showed no sign that the stolen car at Jack Baldwin Chevrolet had caused him any anxiety.

I pointed out to him that neither he—nor my mother—possessed a driver's license. "But you have one, Yuri," he said.

"So? I can't rent a van."

"But I will rent the van and then I will use your license to drive. If we get pulled over, I will simply say that I looked much younger on the day of that photograph."

"Dad," I said. "First, that's totally illegal. Second, they won't let you rent the van. They'll ask to see your license. It's a basic precaution."

"Oh," he said, clearly disappointed. He stood in the balcony doorway, the phone in his left hand. He looked confused. Earnest and confused. I will always remember him this way, standing there and clutching a light blue phone, an expression of befuddlement blotted on the features of his face. In some ways, I envied my dad's separation from the larger part of American life. He lived within certain limits. He worked; he returned to his home; he drank bourbon and sang. It was a small life. It was simple. What else could he hope for—so far from his homeland, so isolated from his first language?

"Hammond owns a van," I said, and my father leapt to life at the suggestion. He was animated and excited. We could invite Hammond to come with us, he suggested, and also invite ourselves into the use of his van. It was the perfect solution.

So—after my dad made a phone call to his salesman/ticket scalper connection—we trooped down to Hammond's apartment, all seven of us, the sound of our footsteps echoing on the stairs. We went outside and around to the sliding glass patio door. He answered quickly—how could he not have heard us coming—and listened to my dad's explanation. When the part came about the unexpectedly large number of relatives, Ivan elbowed his way through the rest of us. He smiled and reached out his hand.

"My name is Ivan Ozolinsh," he said, "and I am proud to shake the hand of an American black man."

"Ivan!" Guna said. "Don't be foolish."

Hammond looked surprised. "Well, fine," he said, squinting a little, unsure what to make of this situation. "That's what you're doing. But you're also squeezing so tight that you're cutting off my circulation."

Ivan recoiled and made apologetic noises. He slipped back into the sea of Latvians.

"So," Hammond said, "before Yuri told you that you couldn't rent a car, you weren't planning on inviting me. But now that you've got this situation, you want to use me for my van?"

My dad peered at him. "Yes," he said. At least he was honest.

"Okay," Hammond said. "Let me get my coat."

But we just barely fit in his van. The adults occupied whatever little seating there was.

"We are old and we have weary knees," my dad said. "So we will share the bench seat."

Oma Ilga sat in the front, and from what I could hear, she seemed to carry on some sort of a conversation with Hammond. Eriks and I had to sprawl on the floor of the cargo bay. Over the course of the afternoon, I experienced the woeful inadequacy of the municipal Milwaukee road system firsthand. I cringed through every pothole. I winced over every speed bump. My spine jangled with each uneven patch of roadway.

We'd decided that the brewery to tour would be Pabst, since this was the largest one downtown, and the one most tied to the cultural heritage of the city. Or so I argued, and my dad agreed, nodding his head and looking official. So the van sputtered toward the Pabst brewery— Hammond behind the wheel, seven Latvians squeezed into its hull. I was a little apprehensive. The employee at the Pick N' Save had recognized me. What if someone at Pabst did the same? Milwaukee had suddenly become a small town. I wondered if this was what membership in a radical organization tended to do—contract your world, narrow it down to a few ideas and locations.

"Did you call ahead and check to see if there is a tour?" Guna asked as we pulled into the mostly empty parking lot.

"Ah, Guna," my dad said. "You are a wonderful woman. I love you like a sister. But perhaps you do not perfectly understand capitalism. There must be a tour. They would not miss any opportunity to take your money from you, in my opinion."

There was, of course, no tour. "Not much to see here," said the receptionist. She looked like the female version of a young Marlon Brando. Her broad forehead gave way to a massive nose and a catfish-like mouth. With a certain sense of amazement, I watched her lips work through the syllables of the English language. She seemed to move only her lower jaw. Her name tag said:

CANDY

"I could call a manager if you'd like."

"Certainly, Candy," my dad said. "That would be quite excellent."

After about fifteen minutes, a young man arrived from the cata-combs of the building. If he was anything, he was a mailroom clerk. Nineteen years old, maybe twenty. He had a broad swath of pimples on his forehead. His name tag said:

CHET

The likelihood that his name was really Chet seemed to me compa-rable to the likelihood that he was about to hand out eight sets of wings and fly us through a Pabst brewery tour. Clearly this was a made-up name for a made-up manager.

It pained me to watch my dad explain that his family had come all the way from the Soviet Union, and they'd wanted—above all else— to tour the Pabst brewery. That they longed for one taste of the freshly brewed beer. That they would love to see the yeast and the hops and the barley, in which, he was sure, they would find the taste of freedom. No one else seemed to grasp that this was high comedy. Even Candy ignored us. She concentrated on her phones. They rang madly.

"But we can't just give you a tour," Chet explained. "What if every-one who showed up at the brewery got a tour? We'd have an endless stream of people—all of them just pouring through our plant. We'd drown in tourists. This is a workplace, not a water park." At least his metaphors were consistent, I noticed.

"I promise you we are not spies," my dad said. "We will bring no notes back to Soviet Union for better brewing technologies."

"I'm not saying you're spies," Chet said. "But, then again, I'm not saying that you *aren't* spies."

My mother chose this moment to interject. I expected her to apologize. I expected her to marshal us together and take us, one after another, back to Hammond's van. "Do you have perhaps a manager with whom we could speak," she said instead, and at that point I knew that this was going to get ugly.

Much to the exasperation of the rest of us, we saw not one, but three different levels of managers that afternoon. All of them were young, all of them were pimply—*did the beer breed acne?*—and all of them had the same message for us. There was nothing to see. We were wasting our time. Pabst was a workplace, not a water park. Finally, after much persistence, my parents arrived at:

LARRY

Larry, it seemed, was actually a manager. He was at least thirty-five years old. He wore no name tag. "I tell you what I'll do," he said. "I'll see if I can't make you happy."

He disappeared into the catacombs again. We waited for what seemed like thirty minutes. Was he never coming back? Was this how they planned to get rid of us? Just disappear and hope that we'd wander away? I could sense that even Oma Ilga was getting frustrated. She sat in one of the waiting room chairs and flipped through *People* magazine. *People* magazine—I remember thinking at the time—transcends all language barriers.

Finally, Larry returned, carrying a large cardboard box. He placed it on the edge of Candy's desk. "Here you go, folks," he said. "They should enjoy these back in the Soviet Union." He opened the box and withdrew several six-packs of nicely chilled Pabst. "I'm assuming that you're all of age," he said, eyeing me suspiciously.

"Absolutely," my dad said. "He just turned twenty-four," he added, pointing at me.

The manager seemed to accept this. He wanted to get us out of the brewery. "I also brought this," he said, "for you to remember us by."

He pulled out two hard hats from the box. They seemed to be actual hard hats, as opposed to souvenir hard hats, which I imagined would be much flimsier. They were emblazoned with the brewery logo—a bright red swirling *Pabst*—and looked quite official.

"Hard hats?" I said, elbowing my way forward.

"We're making some repairs in the brewery," Larry said and shrugged. "These were just lying around."

Guna stepped forward. "I would like to thank you, sir, for enduring our presence here this afternoon."

Larry looked pleased at this. "Why, thank you, ma'am," he said. He smiled at Guna. "I'll definitely recommend that we add a tour area to the new building." He talked for a little while about the new facilities. Pabst was going places, he said. It was going to be the most popular beer in America, once again. He addressed most of this speech to Guna, who nodded whenever it seemed appropriate, listening with what seemed like avid attention to the most mundane construction details.

My mom took one of the hats and put it on her head. It looked like the cap of a mushroom—bulbous and white—and she smiled in a strange way. "I love it," she said, and that was that. We gave the other hard hat to Hammond. It only seemed fair.

We exited the brewery—without a tour, after all—and headed directly for a late lunch. It was close to three o'clock. We'd been in the Pabst brewery for nearly two hours. We stopped for lunch at McDonald's. This was at the request of Eriks, who insisted that ordering food from the drive-through window at McDonald's would be the culmination of a long-held dream of his. My dad approved. "Also, we must drink this beer before it becomes warm," he said, and so Hammond drove to a secluded parking lot near the Bradley Center. We disembarked, and handed out cheeseburgers and fries and cans of Pabst to everyone. We had four six-packs—which amounted to exactly three cans per person. It was clearly the strangest tailgate party in the history of organized sports. My mom was still wearing her hard hat, but Hammond had put his under the front seat. It was freezing cold; I shivered desperately, slurping my beer in a futile attempt to warm myself with alcohol.

"This is good," Eriks said. "But it is not rock and roll experience."

"Eriks, wait," Ivan said, "have patience. Tonight we will have a great time, I have no doubt."

But I had no idea how my dad had managed to get the money for the tickets. To be quite honest, we were close to broke. There was not a lot of room in the Balodis family budget for eight tickets to see the Bucks. In fact, in the days before Thanksgiving I'd asked my mom for some money to buy books. I'd read about a few new hardbacks in the *New York Times Book Review*. I'd imagined them sitting colorfully on my bookshelves, promising me a glamorous world of ideas. When I'd asked for the money, she'd suddenly started screaming.

"I have no money to buy even a simple bag of marshmallows. I have nothing to give you. Nothing." She'd stood in the kitchen and started sobbing.

"Mom?" I'd said. "Is everything okay? Why do we need marshmallows?"

"Marshmallows?" she'd demanded. "Why do we need marshmallows? Why do *you* need to buy books? Do you want to eat the books for Thanksgiving? That would be a terrifically delicious casserole, in my opinion. Aristotle and onions and cream, just like everybody makes in America." She'd stormed off to her bedroom, leaving me alone with my guilt.

However, on this afternoon, even as we finished the beer and walked toward the arena, even as we met the scalper as my dad had arranged, met him on the corner of Fourth and Highland, I had doubts. Enormous doubts. My thoughts wandered toward Hannah, and the investigation of the theft of the car, and Eriks's strangely alluring magnetism. I felt a certain nervousness move through my body when I thought of him. I imagined him lighting my cigarettes for me; I imagined the reflection of the lighter's flame against the skin of his palm. Guna's voice startled me—quiet and very close to my ear.

"I don't have a good feeling about this," she said.

"About the game?" I asked.

"No," she said, pulling me to the rear of the pack. "About the tickets. That man your father is talking to—he looks like a criminal."

In all honesty, I'd been extremely nervous about the situation. My dad had forced us to hide in an alley behind a pizza parlor while he met his ticket connection.

"Why can't we wait in the parlor, itself," Guna had asked, and he had silenced her with an angry glare.

"We cannot do that because it is too obvious. I am very worried about the police perhaps catching us and throwing us in jail."

But we were even more conspicuous in the alley, I quickly realized— seven of us bunched near the corner. Guna and I crouched closest to the front. We had a view of my dad as he met a bulky, hooded character, a chunky man in a sweat suit who smoked a rather offensive-smelling cigar. "He is not a good man," Guna said, and I whispered my agreement. After exchanging the tickets for the money, my dad's connection jogged off in the opposite direction. My dad checked over his shoulder for police and then sauntered over to us.

"Now we have tickets," he said, opening them into a little fan.

"How do you know this guy?" I demanded.

"Is he honest?" Guna said.

"He seemed like he was a member of a motorcycle gang," Eriks offered.

But my dad demurred. This connection was a friend of a friend—he left it at that.

We arrived at the gate about an hour before tip-off. We stood in a long line, my dad at the front, and began to move through the turnstiles. The attendant took my dad's ticket first. His face clouded over as soon as he saw it. "I'm sorry," he said, "but you'll have to wait here a moment."

My dad turned to us and shrugged. I watched the attendant walk back to a little booth just inside of the gate. He had a long discussion with his supervisor. He handed her my dad's ticket. He pointed to my dad, who was standing, helpless, halfway through the turnstile. They both walked back over to him.

"Where did you purchase this ticket, sir?" the supervisor asked.

My dad sensed something was wrong. "From a good friend of mine," he said, "who lives in Detroit."

The two gate attendants exchanged looks. "Well," the supervisor said, "your friend sold you a fake ticket."

"I am sorry?" my dad said.

"It's counterfeit. Void. Useless. It has no hologram. Wait here." She walked to the next turnstile over, and tapped its attendant on the shoulder. She grabbed a bundle of tickets that the attendant had wrapped with a rubber band. She returned to our turnstile and held the tickets out toward my dad. She riffled through them with her thumb. "See," she said, as if she were offering him a glimpse of a sacred relic. "Holograms, every one."

Even if we'd wanted to buy tickets at the gate, we couldn't. All seats were sold out. The Bradley Center was a new building—it had just opened last year—and the Bucks were the most popular professional sports franchise in town. They'd been sold out for months in advance. No amount of persistence would get us tickets to the game. We'd be smart, the turnstile manager said as she confiscated all eight of our tickets, if we left before she called the police.

My dad sputtered and fumed in the little entryway. I tugged at his sleeve.

"Come on," I said. "Let's go, Dad." His face was bright red, almost the color of a Coca-Cola label. His arteries and veins showed through his skin. He waved his hands with derision.

"We do not even want to go to your awful professional sports demonstration," he said, yelling. "You have expensive tickets for the rich and the famous." He backed slowly away from the gate. I tried to soothe him and put my arm around his shoulder. He brushed me away.

"It is like Soviet Union!" he yelled. "It is like the Politburo and the embezzling of pork!" This was, of course, my dad's favorite insult. In his eyes, comparing anything to the Soviet Union was the most slanderous of invectives.

Ivan tried to comfort him.

"Don't worry, my cousin," he said. "We will find something else equally exciting to do this evening."

I doubted that, of course, but I continued walking away from the Bradley Center with the rest of the group. I figured that the more distance we put between ourselves and that building, the better off we'd be. We came around the corner, a tightly bunched group of Latvians. I watched my dad as he slowly returned to some semblance of calm. He turned and began talking to Ivan. At first he spoke softly, but gradually—as he realized what he was doing—his voice grew and rumbled out through the gathering night. His words gained a certain sense of theatricality. My dad was, quite suddenly and in an improvised manner, giving us a tour of the city. We squinted at the buildings in the vanishing light, struggling to discern the things that he showed us. He was trying bravely—fighting against the diminishing day—and his voice shook with the energy of this effort.

He loved Milwaukee, in some ways. Though he spent little time in its streets, though he moved within a fairly limited world, he read extensively, from books my mom got him at the library, about the city in which he lived. So as we walked—and shivered—I was entertained by a litany of facts, a roster of dates and names that echoed and seemed to form a luminous list in the air. Was I hallucinating, or were those names really floating there, in a billowing smoke font, a rising history of the city? We walked toward the Captain Frederick Pabst Mansion. Though he'd never been there, as far as I knew, my dad pointed at the building and described its architectural tenor.

"It is work of Flemish Renaissance Revival architecture," my dad said. He waved his hands grandly in the air. "I do not know honestly what this is, but I am certain that it is very important."

Ivan and Guna nodded and squinted at the mansion. Eriks did not hide his disappointment. He sulked at the back of the group, just behind me. "Do they play Flemish basketball inside?" he muttered. I heard the soles of his shoes scuff against the pavement. He was, I noticed as I looked quickly over my shoulder, staring darkly off into the Milwaukee cityscape.

But my dad was taking to this new and unexpected role with a certain amount of gusto. He was smiling, now. The confusion at the Bradley Center seemed forgotten. He pointed to the Pabst mansion. It was almost rose colored in the dying light of the winter day. A broad set of steps led up to the gargoyle-framed main doors.

"It was only lived in for some time by the beer family," my dad said. "And then it was bought by the church for the archbishop."

"Did the archbishop also brew beer?" Ivan asked.

"No," my dad said. "He did not brew beer."

"Not even for himself?"

"Not even for himself, Ivan. He only drank the wine, at the communion."

Ivan seemed to ponder this. He nodded in a ruminative way.

"I would like to go to church, perhaps," he said. "Perhaps we could go this Sunday?"

My dad didn't answer him, though. He was pointing vaguely at the back of the building. "I think there used to be a stable for horses behind there," he said. "They had many horses. They were very rich from brewing the beer."

"Is this the same beer family from earlier?" my mom asked. I looked at her. The hard hat made her look kind of sweet—almost like a very curious dumpling—bobbing along the streets of Milwaukee.

"Yes," my dad answered. "It is all the same beer family. The Pabst beer family is very large. And Milwaukee is a very drunk town." He grinned. "That is why I love it."

He coughed and rubbed his hands together for warmth. We were all standing quietly in front of the mansion. It was a grand, imposing structure, and its wealth almost stung the eyes, in a way. I compared this residence to our apartment building, or any of the numerous, shabby tenements that crowded our section of downtown Milwaukee. I remembered the photograph of my mom's building—the Soviet highrise outside of Riga where she'd grown up. What was she thinking? Was she jealous of these people, with their unattainable lives of wealth and Flemish Renaissance Revival architecture? What were Ivan and Guna and their family thinking? I tried to read something in their faces, but no emotions were readily visible.

We continued walking. We were getting farther and father away from the van. I felt like the day was an asymptote—we kept progressing, but we would never reach its conclusion. My dad continued narrating.

The city, I learned, was founded in 1818 by a fur trader named Solomon Juneau. It was a small fur-trading area, my dad said. "There were numerous creatures of many different furs bought and sold in the markets." He described to us, in detail, the differences between the coats of the martin and the minx and the beaver and the stoat. The information, I marveled, seemed to be endless. Where was it coming from? Was it always there—submerged under a sea of bourbon, invisible beneath the layers of his addiction?

Then, my dad said, the Germans came. Then—after the Civil War—the Poles. The Poles brought the labor unions, he said. Then, there were Lithuanians. They brewed beer and worked in the meat-processing plants. I thought of Jurgis Rudkus in Upton Sinclair's *Jungle*. I remembered reading about Jurgis and his terrible life, as he toiled in the slaughterhouses of Packingtown. But the Lithuanians also worked on the docks, my dad said. Often they were crushed by the crates, he told us, crates full of cargo that were moving up the St. Lawrence Seaway.

"Of course a few Latvians came at that time, also," my dad said, and shrugged his shoulders.

"How many?" Guna said.

"I do not know," he said.

"Not many," my mom said. She'd been quiet up until then. "Not many at all. There are not very many Latvians anywhere," she said. This seemed to make her sad, for some reason. She slowed down and looked toward Guna in a wistful way. "If we were in Latvia," she said, "there would be many more Latvians than there are in Wisconsin."

After a few more minutes of walking, Eriks suddenly stopped. "I will not walk anymore," he said. "This is stupid and boring."

My dad seemed shocked.

"What do you mean?" he said. "Why is this stupid and boring? Do you not enjoy this cultural education?"

"Sure," Eriks said. "It is wonderful. Simply wonderful. I am trembling with anticipation and joy for what you will imminently say to me."

My dad seemed stung by the sarcasm. He'd led us, I realized, in something of a circle. We were fairly close to the van. Hammond also realized this, and I could hear him twirling his keys in his pocket. He'd been fairly quiet. Mostly he'd walked next to Oma Ilga, making the occasional remark. She'd smiled at him and nodded appreciatively. How much she understood, I was unsure.

"We must have a conference," my dad said, and beckoned for everyone to huddle around him. I felt like a member of some sort of a fat, Eastern European football team. We were about to storm onto the field, in our brown leather loafers and various winter parkas, and win one for the Soviet squad. Or was that the ex-Soviet squad? I wasn't sure. Neither was my dad. A slew of Latvian suggestions rose through the cold November night. I stood on the peripheries of this, wishing—

almost desperately so—that I could understand what was being said. Finally, there was a consensus.

"We will watch the basketball game," my dad said triumphantly, "on network television."

We drove back to the apartment. Hammond seemed to be driving much faster—the van teetered around corners, its tires squealing and giving off a pungent smoke. Our building was almost anticlimactic.

"So, Dad," I said as we got out of the van, "how much did you pay for the fake tickets?"

"Ten dollars each," he said.

"I see. Ten dollars? Where did you get the cash?"

"Do not worry so much, Yuri. Maybe it was fake cash, too. Fake cash for fake tickets—a big joke. Only know that you would have enjoyed those seats very much. They were excellent seats," he said. "All of them together, right there in the first row." He walked toward the building. "Such a shame," he called over his shoulder.

We thanked Hammond for putting up with us and driving us around the city. Hammond nodded and shook Ivan's hand again and kissed Oma Ilga gently on the cheek. Shaking his head and smiling, he walked slowly back to his apartment.

We trooped up the stairs, the sounds of our footfalls rising and tumbling in a rhythmic chorus. At the door to our apartment my dad turned. His face was illuminated with the joy of an idea. "Here we are!" he said, and swung the door dramatically open. Everyone surged forward, trying to squeeze through at once. My mom bumped her hard hat on the side of the door.

"I forget," my mom said, and smiled. "I forget all day."

The last thing I wanted to do was watch a professional basketball game on our grainy TV. Playing basketball was fine—when the play wasn't enforced by a surly gym teacher with a whistle and a clipboard. Watching basketball in person was fun, too. The sound of the shoes on the court, the scent of the beery crowd, the deafening roar that enveloped you. It was as pleasant a communal experience as you could find. The highly salty foods—the pretzels and hot dogs and peanuts—only made it better.

But televised sports were invariably disappointing. I felt totally detached from the spectacle of it all. The announcers were phony and artificially inflated with hype. The seventeen-inch television screen was a poor substitute for attending the game in person. Not everybody felt this way, though. The game came on, and my mom made some microwave popcorn. As gradually as possible, I drifted back toward my room and slipped inside, grateful that it was unoccupied for what seemed like the first time in days.

I sat on the bed and tried to collect my thoughts. I imagined this process literally, as if the thoughts were brightly colored stones or interesting shells on the beach. I took them and placed them within certain boundaries. I made little colorful stacks of thoughts, smooth and orderly and pleasantly pastel. I breathed slowly. I tried to relax the tension—a fierce tension—that I could feel pulsing beneath the tendons of my neck. I tried to screen out the enormous number of people who'd descended on my life. Didn't I have homework to do? I was still a student at Alexander Hamilton High School, right? I sighed—a long ragged sigh. I was self-indulgent, sure, but I was also sixteen.

But that night, with the Milwaukee Bucks game blaring in the living room, I took *Breakfast at Tiffany's* down from the shelf. Maybe I'd reread it when I finished *Humboldt's Gift*. It was different than the movie, absolutely. It was darker and lacked the Hollywood ending. It was unequivocally about sex. Holly slept with the men she dated. Then she disappeared. She didn't choose sentimentality and courtly love in the end. She evaporated, JETS TO BRAZIL. An airplane transported her into the iridescent blue future. The book was so much better in this way. It was tougher and colder. But still it had somehow absorbed the glamour of the movie. Holding it in my hand was like holding a little glittering corner of Hollywood. Even the pages smelled somehow more appealing.

The more I thought about it, the more Hannah reminded me of Audrey Hepburn. There was something of a physical resemblance. Her hair—if combed—would look just like Audrey's. Her eyes, admittedly, were blue, but still—her nose, the high cheekbones—there was something else there. She oozed that very particular thing—that cinematic magic—that had animated Hepburn's career. She had a certain breathless wonder about her. It was in every look, every pose they threw out at the world. Not that this theory was based on any evidence. I had no proof that Hannah was anything like my imagined Holly Golightly. Did she even drink cocktails?

Looking back on it now, I guess that I was particularly susceptible to thinking this sort of thing. It had all started when I'd stumbled across *Breakfast at Tiffany's* in the supermarket video aisle. I'd stopped cold— something about Audrey Hepburn's eyes had frozen me in place. I'd demanded that my parents rent the film for our dinosaur of a Betamax tape player.

"You have to rent it. Please, Dad. I need to see this movie."

"Okay, okay. But it is black and white, is it not? It is so old. There are many new movies made even this year, and they are all in color. What about *Moonstruck*? It has that singer your mother loves, what is she called? She only has one name."

"Cher."

"Exactly, Cher. We would all like that movie *Moonstruck*, in my opinion. It would be much more colorful than that old black-and-white movie which you are wanting."

"*Breakfast at Tiffany's* is not black and white."

"No? But still, you would like Cher. And your mother, in my opinion, would also. You would be making her very happy."

But he'd given in and we'd rented it. I was enraptured, of course. Soon, we'd checked out all of Hepburn's films. Over the past few months we'd watched *Roman Holiday* and *Funny Face* and *Love in the Afternoon*. I'd found out that there was a book, too, and I'd read Truman Capote's novella, *Breakfast at Tiffany's*, in a day. What could be better? I'd thought. It was the pinnacle of the form, I'd decided.

I had also imagined myself into its story. Someday I'd be a young artist living in a brownstone in the East Seventies—a Manhattan Island regular. Why not? Someday I, too, might stumble across a Holly Golightly.

Why were other people so endlessly mysterious and perplexing? Was it a gender-based code? Why was I thinking of Hannah and Eriks constantly? What was that phrase? Like a shout in the street? Love is like a shout in the street? I couldn't remember. I buried my head in the pillow. Who needed books about war and peace? Why not a book about Poor Yuri Balodis, who suffered the scorn of teenage girls and battled valiantly to entertain his three Latvian cousins and his Latvian great-aunt, and ate all manner of Latvian breakfast foods, without complaint? There was a knock on the door.

"Come in," I said, my face still in the pillow. I looked up to see Eriks, towering in the doorway.

"What is happening, man?" he said.

I sighed.

"Have you ever seen *Breakfast at Tiffany's*?" I asked him.

"I'm sorry?" he said. "What did you say?"

"Never mind," I said. "It's not important."

Eriks raised an eyebrow. "I am supposed to tell you," he said, "that your mother wants you to come and join us and to watch the end of the game."

"I see."

"She seems very eager for this to happen."

I turned away from him. "Tell her I'll be right there," I said.

Even my bedroom—I realized after Eriks left—wasn't a sanctuary. It wouldn't save me from the attentions of my inquisitive family. I needed some space. I took my winter coat from my closet and bundled my head in a hat and a scarf. Even though it was freezing cold, I gathered up some materials. I grabbed a book off my shelf—the *1989 Farmer's Almanac*—and I shoved it into my backpack. I grabbed a pen and a flashlight and a little notebook. I also picked up my algebra textbook. I strode purposefully through the doorway and out into the hall. I made directly for the front door.

"Where are you going?" my dad cried as I opened the door.

"To study," I said, brandishing the math textbook over my shoulder.

Except I didn't know where, exactly, I was going. I walked down the stairs and out into the cold. I stood in the mouth of the stairwell, breathing the cold night air. The hedge maple. That's where I'd go. I walked through the little abandoned lot and scrambled up into its branches. It was glacial. I shivered and coughed. My throat still ached; I still felt sick from the night that I stole the car. But I wanted to push on. Maybe it was good for me? Maybe it would be physically and mentally healthful? Maybe through shivering in the dark cold night, I would move somehow toward patience and understanding? No, probably not. I would probably just worsen my cold.

I turned on the flashlight and directed it at the page. I sank into the text. I felt free and buoyant again; I was alone with a book. The almanac overflowed with specific information, with tide tables and weather forecasts and lists of the best fishing days for bass and grouper and trout. There was a long article, I saw, about gardening. It was wonderful—page after page about seeds and bulbs and soil. The text opened and enveloped me. I thumbed through the charts—finding the moon schedule for December, the twelfth month. "December," I read, "hath 31 days." But what would each of those days bring?

I stared up at the stars, framed in the brace of the essential dark. They glimmered half-heartedly in the sky—muted by Milwaukee's light. They were pale. I counted twenty-two of them. They were like little white letters, the fragments of a forgotten alphabet. I rested my head against the corrugated bark of the tree.

10

thursday, november 30, 1989

There was not, of course, salvation in the almanac. It was a diversion, but it offered no revelations. Or at least nothing that I could put into words. Looking back on it, I'm sure that sitting in that tree was my attempt to get a handle on the situation, to relax and allow myself space to adapt.

The next day, I prepared to go back to school. After the dual disasters of the brewery and the basketball game, my dad felt a little sheepish about showing our guests the sights of Milwaukee. I was allowed to return to my classes, though I would spend much of the day explaining my disappearance to my teachers. My dad, of course, wouldn't give me a note covering my absences. "You are a smart boy," he said. "You will certainly enjoy inventing some stories for your teachers to believe."

Guna had a long list of errands to run. She was going to meet her hosts at Marquette—she was due in the International Studies department at nine o'clock—and she was going to lead two sections of a Soviet History seminar, responding to the students' questions and offering her perspective on recent developments, on Gorbachev's policies, on the détente between the Soviets and the West. Finally, she had a late lunch scheduled with the provost and the vice president of Academic Affairs. They were eager to meet her, and—she told us—had extended an invitation, in writing, to any other members of her family who might want to attend.

Even with all of this, something didn't seem quite right. Though Marquette was a good school—even though it was the academic pride of Milwaukee—I couldn't imagine that they had enough important funding to bring someone from Latvia to the U.S. just to attend a few speaking engagements. Especially not someone who wasn't well known, outside of certain academic circles. Gorbachev, maybe, or even Sol-zhenitsyn, but Guna? I thought, briefly, about calling Dr. Graham and confirming that my suspicions were valid.

But my mom was thrilled by the prospect of lunch. "I would absolutely love to attend this lunch," she said. She bubbled through the apartment, ebullient in a way that I hadn't seen her since the Berlin Wall fell. Her reaction to Guna had been palpable—starting in the airport when Guna had noticed the amber brooch—and now my mom seemed somehow brighter and more eager to move through the day. She concentrated less intently on my behavior. She hummed qui-etly to herself as she prepared breakfast at the stove. She'd gone to the 7-Eleven last night and bought a handful of plastic-wrapped Ecuador-ian roses, which she'd arranged in a little vase on the counter next to the sink. She spent ten minutes discussing, in great detail, what she should wear to lunch.

"I have always wanted to go to college, *bucina*," she said to me as we were eating our breakfast cereal. "It is so exciting to imagine listening to Guna talk."

As I was leaving, my mom met me at the door and gave me a hug.

"Have a wonderful day at school, my darling," she said, and tousled my hair playfully.

I scrambled that day—devising a litany of excuses, all of them involving sick grandparents or destructive pets, or both. I lied to all of my teachers, reminding myself that this was my own father's advice, and I promised that I'd be much more attentive to attendance and homework in the future.

As the last bell rang on Thursday, I was filled with a hopeful but slightly worried sense of anticipation. When I exited the school build-ing I was surprised to see Hannah, loitering in the shadow of a tree. Her presence itself wasn't overly unusual. She'd met me there before. But I hadn't expected her to ever talk to me again, really. It was my first day back since the accident and she'd been secretive and solitary, assiduously avoiding me. She wouldn't even look at me when we passed each other in the hallways. She'd skipped gym.

"Mind if I ride home with you?" she asked, without any explanation, and I quickly said that I didn't. Sure, I was mad at her for being so rude to me on the night of the crash. But I couldn't be angry forever.

Once we were on the bus, I could tell that Hannah wasn't herself. She looked pale and drawn, almost sickly. Once the bus pulled away from the stop, she leaned toward me, whispering in my ear.

"I'm freaking out. I keep seeing stuff in the news about"—she lowered her voice to a conspiratorial whisper—"the accident."

I looked around us. There were six other passengers on this, a full-sized city bus. I didn't think that secrecy was warranted. Besides, she was liable to attract more attention this way. The way not to attract attention on a city bus is simple: Act like you want attention desperately. Everyone will ignore you.

"Stuff?" I said. "What stuff?"

"It's all over the news," she said. "The story is totally out of control. It's like . . ." Here Hannah paused, the gears of her mind struggling to mesh. "It's like a gondola at a mountain resort—you know, like one of the ones for sightseeing—except it's totally going out of control and . . . it's about to crash, and nobody can stop it."

"Are you done?" I asked.

"Yes."

"Okay. Well, then, I can tell you that you have nothing to worry about. I'm sure the fire was big enough to burn away our prints." This was probably a lie. But it sounded feasible and I actually took some comfort from it. "Even if it wasn't, there's no way they can trace the investigation back to you. To me—well, there's a slight possibility. Very slight. But to you—no way."

Hannah shook her head and sighed.

"I'm just telling you what I see. Every time I read about it, the story gets worse. It gets bigger or more frightening or closer to me."

The bus rumbled up to my stop. We climbed off in silence.

"Come upstairs," I said, not wanting this moment of contact to end. Hannah looked undecided.

"I don't really want to." She paused. "Looking at your face, actually, still makes me kind of queasy."

"I'll cover my face, then. With a towel. I can talk through a towel."

Hannah almost smiled. The corners of her lips twitched slightly.

"Fine," she said. "I'll come up for a few minutes."

"Great," I said. "I'll introduce you to the rest of the family."

We labored up the stairs to the apartment. Once inside, I immediately offered her something to drink. To my surprise, she took a few crackers covered in pig's-feet jelly. She chewed them gingerly at first, but then with greater eagerness. "I didn't eat this morning," she said— and by implication I sensed that she hadn't eaten in a couple of days. She did look noticeably thinner. I was pleased that she liked the *galerts*; it wasn't every day that you got to feed the hooves of livestock to your friends.

Hannah and I were, however, disappointed on one count—the apartment was oddly empty. Only Eriks loitered in the front room. "Where's my dad?" I asked him. "Where's your grandmother?"

"He is asleep," Eriks said. "And Oma Ilga left a few minutes ago. She went somewhere with your friend, the black gentleman with the van."

With Hammond King? That was odd. Hammond didn't go places, as far as I knew. He had certain immutable rituals. Picking up my great-aunt who didn't appear to speak English and taking her some- where—this was unusual.

"Did they say where they were going?"

"I don't think so."

Hannah appeared behind me, still chewing on a cracker. The pig's- feet jelly gave her mouth a filmy sheen.

"Hello," she said, "I'm Hannah."

"Nice to meet you, Hannah." Eriks stood up. It seemed, to me, that he raised his eyebrows a little—that his body gave off a little crackle of energy. He also looked a little desperate, almost like a caged animal. This was understandable, really. Here he was, surrounded by America but unable to experience it. Or at least unable to experience it the way he'd imagined—on the back of a Harley, the wind flattening his hair into a bug-filled crust.

"You like the *galerts*?" Eriks asked. "It is a fine delicacy in Latvia."

"I love it," Hannah said. "I mean, I think it's a little gross that it's made from the hooves of pigs, but it has a really nice salty flavor."

"So salty, yes." Eriks walked toward us. "It is ancient Latvian tradi- tion, you know, from when we were all pagans."

"Pagans?"

"Yes, absolutely. We were pagans and we worshipped the gods of nature."

Hannah seemed awed. Her jaw hung slightly open. "Totally," she said, nodding to confirm that she was in that camp, that she too would gladly worship the gods of nature.

"We slaughtered the pigs at night," Eriks said, "and then we pickled them. We would bury the pig legs in big wooden buckets, and then cover them in layer after layer of salt. Then we would rotate the legs every few days, taking the leg that is on top and putting it on the bottom. Then, when they were ready, we would rub them with oil and vinegar and cut them up and put them in a jar."

"Intense."

"Then, after a few months in the cellar, the jelly would be ready." Eriks smiled, satisfied with himself. "This is how we did it when we were pagans."

Hannah and Eriks started to talk about the ways in which the ancient Latvians were pagans. It was disconcerting in a way, but then again, I had no control over Hannah Graham. She could talk to anyone and everyone. She could debate the merits of Latvian pagan foods for hours. I had no say in the matter. While I certainly would have preferred it if she'd decided that she desperately craved my scrawny body, and that she simply *had* to force me into my room and strip off my clothes and take advantage of me, I couldn't do anything about it.

Hannah was excited, and when she was excited, she was a roller coaster of language. I watched her hold forth on pagan rituals and the essays that Marx wrote about ancient tribal life. Eriks seemed captivated. I knew what it felt like to be ensnared in Hannah's ideas. I drifted away from the conversation. I poured myself a glass of water. I ate a little of the *galerts*. Eriks and Hannah drifted out into the living room. I heard the balcony door open. I looked up to see them walking outside. They both lit cigarettes. I felt excluded. I strained to hear the conversation through the thin glass door. I wasn't certain, but I thought I caught the words *neoclassical* and *deconstruction*. At one point Eriks exclaimed, "Rock and roll." The echo of the phrase spiraled off into the gathering urban night.

I went to my room and took *Humboldt's Gift* from the shelf. I debated barging out onto the deck, trying to interpose myself between the two of them. I would captivate them with a story, or with my juggling abilities. I shook my head. That would do no good. Instead, I sat at the kitchen table and pretended to read. I thought about Hannah and Eriks—both of whom I hadn't even known in July. Now, they felt like two of the most important people in my life. I felt conscious of my self—of my body, my ideas—and felt like that self was floating out there on the deck. I was intensely jealous that they were talking to each other, that they were exchanging odd bits of cultural knowledge or outright Soviet propaganda. What would Eriks make of Hannah's ideas? He'd lived under communism for his entire life. He knew its effects firsthand. He'd tried to be objective, tried to say that some of the country's collective farms generated high-quality produce. But I could tell that he had nothing but derision for the Soviet system. That he regretted the suffering the Latvian SSR had caused for its civilians.

As if on cue, I heard an exclamation from beyond the sliding glass door. "No, no, no," Eriks was saying, and I inched forward. I ached to go out on the balcony, to join them and listen to their conversation. I was too scared, though, to actually open the door and go out there. I don't know why. I hesitated near the sofa. Within seconds, Eriks was pointing at me, calling me out there in a brash, confident voice. I tossed my book onto the sofa, eased the door open, and stood on the cold wood of the balcony.

"Yuri, tell her, tell her that you don't believe these things that she is saying." Eriks was smiling, playful but serious, his eyebrows cast into a broad arc.

"What things are those?" I stood next to Hannah. I could smell the thick scent of her perfume—delirious perfume—clouding around me, saturating my space and taking it over, turning my air into her air, a pure ownership. I wondered about women's perfume. How was it so intoxicating? Why was the sense of smell so powerful, so principal among the senses? I felt eviscerated by the smell, totally helpless before it. I contemplated throwing my arm around Hannah's shoulders. I settled for leaning against the balcony rail.

"That the Soviet system," Eriks said, "is a worker's paradise." He was clearly amused. Hannah wasn't taking it well, at all. She was seeing her opinions ridiculed in this—somewhat public—forum. She fought back.

"What about America? It's not any better. Look at the workers' plight, look at the waitresses, look at the food-service workers, at clerks in stores and shopping malls. They have no hope. They will never see the best that society can produce."

"In Soviet Union," Eriks said, "it is exactly the same thing."

I looked at them. Hannah and Eriks were both so passionate; they were young and vibrant, and they both had a riot of opinions on the world and the nature of living. I wasn't like them. I was a quiet, guarded individual. To me, the world seemed like a terribly painful place. Why get involved with it? I figured. Why make myself vulnerable to the intricacies of entanglement with other people? I was much happier in my books. I could read, feasting on written words. I didn't need to complicate my life. But then I thought, for a moment, about Eriks's charisma. He was compulsively interesting; he occupied a space in the world that was so different from mine. Eriks had seen things, been places—he'd lived in the presence of great historical forces. His daily life had been touched with deprivation and suffering. What had I done? I'd burrowed into my little Milwaukee apartment and attended an American public high school. So had Hannah, admittedly, but at least she'd had the courage to have new ideas, to think in ways that didn't seem to fit within the mainstream of society. Also, she was beautiful and, for some reason, this mattered. I was gangly, awkward, and sprinkled with acne. Eriks was beautiful, too, in a less contained sort of way. They would probably fall in love, passionately in love, and I'd be left behind, a footnote to their lives together.

"I don't know the answer," I said. "You guys fight it out." I went back inside. I crashed onto the pleather sofa. I looked up at the walls, scanning this odd environment in which I'd been raised, glancing at all the framed advertisements for consumer goods. I just sat there, drifting in and out of *Humboldt*. I could see, with my peripheral vision, the flick of Eriks's lighter, the flame that marked cigarette after cigarette— too many to count. Finally, after what must have been an hour, the sliding glass door opened. Hannah stood there, blinking at the dim interior of the apartment. She moved purposefully across the room. She was leaving. With only a nod in my direction, she was going to slip off into the November evening.

"Wait," I called to her. "Where are you going?"

"I'm leaving," she said. "I have to get home."

"Home? That's ridiculous. You come over here for an hour—barely talk to me—and then you leave? Tell me how that's okay."

Hannah hesitated near the doorway. She struggled with the buttons of her coat.

"Look," she said, "I don't know what I'll say. I feel a little unbalanced, right now. I'm usually balanced, right?"

I didn't say anything.

"Fine," she said, "fuck you, too. But at least I normally feel like I'm in control of things. There's a great line in Trotsky: The overwhelming control of the smallest situation leads to greater control of the larger situation."

"I'm a situation?" I asked.

"No, you're not a situation," she said. "But you are completely out of my control."

I was angry again. "You know," I offered, "you can quote Trotsky all you want, but how about this. My dad always says: When lightning strikes, the rich think that God is taking their picture."

She tapped her foot on the carpeting. "And what does that mean?" she asked.

"Nothing," I said. "I don't know. Look. How about I walk with you?"

"I'm not sure that's such a good idea," she said.

But by then we were in the stairwell. Our voices spun and echoed through the enclosed space. The acoustics of it were marvelous. My voice suddenly seemed unusually powerful. I resolved to be somewhat cheerful. Even if it wasn't an accurate reflection of how I was feeling, I figured that Hannah wouldn't want tears—or even small-voiced whining.

"Why not? See—it's already happening. You're walking with me right now," I said. "See. It's not that painful, is it?"

We emerged from the building. My life felt episodic. I was living from swatch of time to swatch of time, from moment of shock to moment of shock. I felt disconnected and unsure of why I was even walking with Hannah. After all, I'd nearly killed her. Under my supervision we'd rolled a stolen car into a barn. I needed to say something suave, something that would show her that I was stable, something that would reassure her that I could easily salvage our relationship, that it was no problem at all.

"You see," I said, "the problem is this. I'm in love with you."

Looking back on it now, I cringe. This moment—among all the moments of November 1989—is perhaps the most painful to recall. There's no real excuse for having said something like this. I guess that I was displacing what I wanted to say, saying the right thing to the wrong person. When I should have been telling my dad that I loved him—or at least surrendering myself to his care—I was doing something else entirely. Why? Now I realize that I didn't understand my dad and his sacrifices, didn't understand how weary he must have been, dragging his aching body to the dealership night after night. I was foolish and short-sighted. Fortunately, Hannah was not in a loving mood.

"You love me?" she said, and laughed. "I worry about your future, Yuri, if this is what you do to the women you love."

I fell slightly behind her, trying to process this insult. It was, I thought, a terrible thing to say.

"That's a terrible thing to say," I suggested.

"It's true," Hannah said.

"What do you mean, it's true?"

"If you'd really loved me, you wouldn't have put my life in danger."

I thought about this. It seemed true, on some level. But then again, wasn't danger exciting? Hannah clearly didn't seem to think so. Or at least not the kind of danger that we'd experienced. She walked away from me, heading toward the bus stop.

"Wait," I said. "Come with me to 7-Eleven."

"7-Eleven?"

"You know," I said, "a minimart. It sells a variety of prepackaged foods. You can get a corn dog."

I looked at Hannah. She seemed to smile slightly, the faintest sliver of a smile, and she walked back toward me. I was happy that she was here, sure, but I was still confused. She seemed to be unsure of what she wanted; one moment, I was someone to be spurned and ignored, the next moment I was somebody who deserved affection (or at least attention). Odd. As we walked to the 7-Eleven, I made a short internal catalog of my merits. I was almost attractive, right? Or at least I would be, in a few years, once my gangly body grew into itself, once I became a near approximation of an adult. Also, I could occasionally be a funny guy, though the humor felt like a wildfire in a windstorm—never pre-dictable, wholly beyond my control. More often than not I just said stupid things, or did stupid things, or dreamed stupid dreams about seducing women who were beyond my reach.

"So," Hannah said, as we came within sight of the neon-lit convenience store, "what's Eriks like?"

"Eriks?" I asked, even as I held the door open for her. "What do you mean?"

"You know what I mean," Hannah said. "Does he seem like a nice guy?" She paused. "He was so combative. I've never had anyone talk to me like that."

"He says what he means."

"He's sort of boorish," she said.

What could I do but agree? "Absolutely," I said.

"And a little magnetic."

I looked at her. I wondered how to respond. "Sure," I said. "I can see that magnetism, too."

"What does he want to do?" Hannah asked as we neared the store entrance. "I mean, does he have plans for the future—that you know of? Does he want to stay in America?"

"Wait," I said, as we walked through the door. "I think we're in trouble."

I'd carefully chosen which 7-Eleven to patronize. I wanted to avoid the one I'd gone to on the night of the theft, simply because I was worried about the cashier. He'd remember me as the kid who'd slipped him the two-dollar bill, and who knew how he'd react. So I'd chosen carefully, trying to remember where I'd been, trying to avoid the repetition. But as Hannah and I entered, I saw that it was the same cashier. He had the same arrowhead-shaped nose, the same pale brown eyes. *Damn.* How was this possible? Could he move between locations, shuttling from one 7-Eleven to the next? I walked over to the magazine shelf. I turned my back on the counter. I nervously paged my way through a copy of *Muscle & Fitness*.

But Hannah ignored me. "Why'd you need to come here, anyway?" she asked. It was, I figured, a fair question.

"Soap," I said. "We're out of soap. I have to pick up a bar." I continued flipping through the magazine.

"Okay. I don't have all day. Let's go. Get your soap and let's get out of here."

I weighed my options. I could just walk up to the counter with the bar of Ivory and hope that the cashier didn't recognize me. Perhaps he would even apologize. Perhaps he'd been disciplined by his manager for harassing an honest teenager. Perhaps this was his punishment— working at this particular 7-Eleven, which was somehow inferior to the other, superior convenience store. I decided against it.

"Never mind," I said to Hannah, even as I turned and began to hurry out of the store. "I like being dirty."

We wandered back toward the bus stop. I figured that I should talk about how I felt, but something stopped me from saying anything. I waited with Hannah until the bus arrived. She gave me a hesitant hug as she left.

"Don't worry," she said, "this will all work out somehow."

That night, my dad focused his energies on something that he knew would turn out exactly as he planned: a Thursday-night dinner at Kentucky Fried Chicken.

"Is it not so nice that this chicken is served in a bucket?" he said. We'd ordered two fifteen-piece family meals, and they'd come with a mountain of biscuits and a bounty of small, individually wrapped segments of corn. The chicken had been lovingly fried and salted by the fine folks at KFC. Each thigh and wing dripped with nutty-tasting oil. Each bite of corn oozed sweet butter. The salt lingered on your fingertips. For just under twenty dollars, this seemed to be the quintessential American eating experience.

Guna and Mara returned home at nine o'clock. Guna sat in the kitchen and told stories to my mother—who watched her intently. From time to time, my mom would break into laughter, long rolling loops of laughter, and she would get up and walk to the refrigerator and pour herself and Guna glasses of soda and ice. I lingered on the margins of the kitchen, ensnared by my mother's transformation, captivated by the way she seemed somehow lighter, almost buoyant.

My mom couldn't stop talking about her day at Marquette. They'd started with the lecture, which, my mom said, was the most enlightening experience you could imagine. Guna blushed when my mother said this. She took a sip from her glass of soda and turned bright red. My mom continued talking, describing the lunch, which was privately catered, in a room beside the vice president's office in the administration building. The building, she said, had a view of downtown and the lake, and the bank of windows beside the dining room table was twice as tall as she was. The provost, it turned out, was an expert in the field of Soviet affairs. He'd worked, at some point, for the Peace Corps. He'd traveled throughout the southeastern part of the USSR. "He was such a handsome man," my mom said, and then glanced guiltily toward the living room, where my dad was watching a sitcom with Eriks and Ivan and Oma Ilga.

They'd eaten venison—a delicious venison with a cherry sauce, cherries from Door County in the northeastern corner of the state. "The pride of Wisconsin," my mom said. "But how did they have cherries so late in the year? I don't know. It was wonderful, however, *bucina*. You would have truly enjoyed both the lunch and Guna's speaking."

"Hush, Mara," Guna said. "You are too kind to me." She turned toward me. "Don't listen to her, Yuri. She is exaggerating. I simply tell the truth, that's all. I tell them what it is like in the Soviet Union."

"I'm sure it was great," I said. I leaned my back against the kitchen counter. I was full of greasy chicken and corn and butter-soaked biscuits. I felt tired, but also, I felt the desire to stay awake, to soak in this rare glut of people who'd descended on our lives. Suddenly, though, my mom was standing and waving her arms in the air.

"I have a wonderful idea," she said. I braced myself. This couldn't be anything but disastrous. "Why doesn't Guna go with you to your school tomorrow? Do you have anything planned, Guna?"

Guna seemed shocked. She clearly didn't know how to respond. "Not until the evening," she said. "I have a lecture in the evening."

"We're all going to that lecture," I said, scrambling. "There's no reason to force her to do more than she—"

"No, no, no," my mom said. "I'm sure she would love to come with you. Is that not right, Guna?"

"Actually," Guna said, her face lighting up, "I would love to see the American school system as it truly functions—from the point of view of the student."

I stared, openmouthed, at my mother. This was, quite clearly, a terrible idea.

"And I'm the student?" I said. But my mom barreled over me.

"Then it is settled," she exclaimed. "She can take the city bus to school with you in the morning. She can meet your girlfriend, then," my mom said, and winked at Guna. "The one who is living in the suburbs."

Just before bed, I went out onto the balcony with my father and Ivan and Eriks. My mother and Oma Ilga and Guna stayed inside. I sat on the balcony deck, sipping a bourbon, and watching while Eriks smoked numerous cigarettes. He had a seemingly endless supply—and no desire whatsoever for moderation. I demurred when he offered me a cigarette, casting a quick glance over at my father, who was embroiled in a passionate conversation, in Latvian, with Ivan. "It is a suit for yourself," Eriks said, and lit the cigarette with his pale gray lighter.

We talked about Guna's upcoming lecture. In my nearly boundless anxiety about the car accident and about Hannah, I'd almost forgotten that tomorrow would likely bring a second meeting between Dr. Graham and my father. I braced myself for a confrontation. If the fistfight was quick, I reasoned, then there wouldn't be any need for the police to become involved. With the moon hanging fat and pale yellow in the sky, I imagined a long chain of events, wherein my dad's temper led the police to our door, and I was imprisoned for the theft and destruction of the property of Jack Baldwin Chevrolet.

"For the lecture tomorrow," Eriks said, breaking through the surface of my anxious thoughts. "Marquette is nearby?"

"Yes," I said. "It's not far. It's a beautiful campus." I paused. "What's your mother's lecture topic?"

Eriks nodded. "The Soviet press," he said, "and what it can teach the world."

I sighed and sank against the balcony rail. Tomorrow would be a long day, I imagined. Why had I so completely lost control of my daily itinerary? At least, I rationalized, every day that passed bore me further and further from being caught for the theft of the Monte Carlo. It seemed as if I had—just like my father—committed a crime that would go unpunished. Of course, what I'd done had been slightly more extreme. But at least now I could imagine the possibility that I'd get away with it. I watched the moon slowly rise and fade to white; its glow gave Milwaukee an anemic, ethereal tinge.

11

Friday, december 1, 1989

It would strain the limits of credulity if any of the scenarios that I imagined that night actually occurred. I concocted a variety of situations as I tried to sleep on my pile of blankets in the kitchen, all of them involving Guna at my high school—humiliating me, or herself, or a variety of other individuals. I couldn't sleep, so instead I decided to count the stains on the kitchen ceiling. I moved my eyes back and forth, hoping that this counting would lull my mind and somehow trick me into rest. Eventually, after many hours of worrying, I fell into an approximation of sleep.

We awoke, all of us, to the sound of my mom singing in the bathroom, singing some sort of Latvian drinking song, something with the pitch and rhythm of the sea. She seemed to be slapping the sink along with the meter of the tune, and she sang the male and female parts of it, dropping or raising her voice through the registers. She stormed into the kitchen, still singing, and kicked at me—gently—until I turned over.

"Get going, Yuri," she said. "You have much to prepare."

And so I did. I felt like an engine was driving me toward some sort of final conclusion, an engine with my mother's features, with her increasingly boisterous singing, with her big, floral-print dress—a dress she'd dug out of the depths of her closet, one that I'd never seen before. We would go to the main office, my mom decreed, and we would ask for a visitors' pass.

I hoped that it wouldn't be this easy, and though I agreed with my mom's plan—though I cheerfully ushered Guna onto the bus and to the school and through its labyrinthine hallways—I suspected that the plan would unravel once we reached the main office. But instead I met with the cheerful building secretary, Mrs. Glover, who smiled and assured me that this kind of observation occurred all the time, and that Guna didn't need any sort of special permit or approval from the principal. As long as the goals of the observation were constructive—and as long as each individual teacher approved—I was set.

"Honey," Mrs. Glover said, tapping five French-manicured fingers on the wooden surface of her desk, "we do this all the time. Especially for at-risk students."

"But I'm not at risk," I said. Panic surged—a sea wave—through my gut. "I'm not at risk, at all."

"That's okay, sugar. I'm sure that we can make an exception for you. Especially since your visitor has traveled such a long way to be here." At this, Guna smiled obligingly. My fate was ordained.

"I will meet all of your friends," Guna said. "This will be very exciting. I will get a true interior view of the American school system."

The day—however—didn't go as badly as I'd feared. Guna surprised me by speaking fluent Spanish to my Spanish instructor, explaining who she was and what she was doing in the United States. My teacher—Ms. Engert—was charmed to use her language skills in a setting other than the one devoted solely to instructing teenagers. She loved Guna; she delayed the beginning of class by fifteen minutes, just so that she could have a conversation with her about her impressions of America. Though I could only partially follow along, the conversation did delay our daily quiz, and so—at least in the eyes of the other students—I became something of a hero.

My American literature class was reading *The Great Gatsby*. Guna raised her hand at the beginning of the discussion section. My head sank onto the table. Though she'd done so well in Spanish class, I was still wary, and I resented standing out from the group, resented losing the safety of my anonymous life. Guna commented that in the Soviet Union, *Gatsby* was a morality tale, that it was used to instruct children and young teenagers about the evils of capitalism. My teacher—Ms. Fortenbras—was enchanted by this idea. What, she wondered, did the Soviets make of Fitzgerald's life and the way he lived—drinking excessively, dying young and unhappy?

"That is also instructional for them," Guna said. She continued talking about American authors, who were often held up as examples of the sorrows of capitalism. They were artists, she indicated, but they had to write for the demands of the open market. These demands, the teachers in her high school had always maintained, ruined the lives of writers. F. Scott Fitzgerald, she said, was only one example of an American writer who'd turned to drinking for solace from the marketplace.

"But in the USSR," Ms. Fortenbras said, "authors are censored, aren't they? They can't write what they want to write, either. There are Soviet writers who are alcoholics, too, correct?"

"This is true," Guna said. "But the study of these writers is, how do you say, discouraged." She continued talking, citing a few examples, giving short life studies. If she'd been closer to my age, if Eriks had accompanied me to school, for instance, the teacher would have shut her up long ago. But since she was an adult—a member of the privileged class that walked among the chaos of teenagers—she was allowed to speak. What she said was interesting; I glanced around the room and saw that almost everyone was listening to Guna. Again, she took up a large section of class time, something for which my fellow students were grateful, I am certain.

In U.S. history, we'd progressed from the Revolutionary War to the Civil War. All of our history was cast in this light—a great bloody illumination—as war after war unfolded, slaughtering generations in the carefully illustrated pages of our textbooks. Guna listened quietly. She didn't say anything. Afterward, she confessed that she was intimidated both by the subject matter and the man teaching it—a beefy, former professional linebacker, a barrel of a man who strode around the classroom and made proclamations in a booming baritone. "In the Soviet Union," she told me, "more History teachers were shot than any other kind of teacher." I thought about this for a moment.

"Even science teachers?" I asked.

"Certainly. There was something about history, I think, that made Stalin nervous."

Of the four classes that we attended that day, geology was the most uneventful. "Rocks are rocks," Guna said to me afterward and, sadly, I had to concur.

During lunch, I had tried to unearth the particulars of Guna's stay with us. I wanted to know, for certain, on which flight she was leaving, or which city she was scheduled to visit next. She'd been evasive, and her answers had been circular, couched in metaphors and lengthy discussions of the history of Latvia. I became ensnared in these discussions. I let them distract me. I sat on the little immobile cafeteria chair and listened, transfixed, as she described the dying days of Karlis Ulmanis, the final president of Latvia—who was captured by the Soviets on a boat in the Gulf of Latvia as he tried to escape to Finland. I forgot to chew my lunch as Guna described the way he was arrested and shipped to Siberia to die, anonymous, with thousands of others in the Gulags.

We waited for Hannah at the door to gym class. She showed up—much to my surprise—and we were able to draw her away, to take her on a walk along the perimeter of the school's athletic fields. The security guards—what few there were—kept at a distance because of the presence of an adult. With Guna accompanying me, I realized, I could do almost anything. I wished, briefly, that she could attend my classes each day. This was where I wanted so badly to be—within the world of adults. My time in high school seemed, to me, like an expulsion from my rightful place, like a banishment.

I introduced Guna as Eriks's mother. This had an effect on Hannah, who seemed slightly nervous—seemed a little bit uneasy when she launched into her rants about the lack of collective action within the student body, about the ways that the curriculum was designed to reinforce the political and social and economic structures of the capitalist state. Hannah listened as Guna talked about her son's high school experience. Guna said she'd enrolled Eriks in a musically oriented high school and that much of his training had been practical, vocational music training. He'd learned the specifics of composing for film, or television, or the necessities of playing in an orchestra. Now, though, she worried, he didn't have a comprehensive sense of the world.

"Don't worry," I said. "Neither do we."

The bell rang after what seemed like only a few minutes. We started walking back toward the high school building. I'd given Guna directions to the apartment complex. She needed to prepare for the evening's lecture, so she'd take the bus home. She was comfortable with buses, she told me. All of Riga ran on buses, big diesel buses that turned the air in the city gray. She said good-bye and walked back across the field toward the bus stop. Hannah left me and headed to her last class. All that was left for me was math. I hadn't done the homework, but that didn't matter. In my mind, I was already home, surrounded by my new and burgeoning family, listening to the babble of their multilingual voices.

The hall that Marquette had chosen for Guna's presentation was quite large. We arrived several hours too early, just after four o'clock, and we were easily the first people in the auditorium. Guna left us and walked to the department offices to meet her hosts. She carried a small, laminated map of the university. She'd marked off her route with a bright pink pen. I stood with Ivan and watched her leave. She shuffled out of the hall, bent assiduously over her map.

We sat in the front row. This was Ivan's suggestion. "Let us sit near her, so that we will provide a row of family support, in case she needs it." I sat next to Eriks, on the very end of the row. I could hear my dad and Ivan talking about basketball and brewery tours.

"It would be so much better," my dad's voice asserted, "if they combined professional sports with professional places of drinking. They could play basketball in the brewery, or baseball on the vineyard. It would be so nice, then, for the fans."

I sighed and stared up at the ceiling. It was beautiful. From what I'd read about architecture in my world history class, I decided that the ceiling had been painted to mimic a European cathedral. There were raised moldings, slathered in gold paint, as well as a fresco—a biblical fresco, complete with cherubim and seraphim—fluttering there in tasteful reds and blues. Eriks slumped in his seat while I contemplated the painting. The seats were narrow, though, and as his head turned it brushed against mine—the slightest brush of hair. I could sense the warmth of his body, so close to mine. I felt a brief spasm of desire, and then a deep flush of embarrassment. I shifted my position in the seat and tried to concentrate on the winged Pegasus that appeared, in this fresco, to be carrying the baby Jesus on its back.

People began arriving about twenty minutes before the presentation. They filled the auditorium. I was impressed by the size of the crowd that had come to hear Guna Ozolinsh speak. Just before Guna arrived, I spotted Hannah and Dr. Graham. They'd slipped quietly into the back of the room. I tried, with too much subtlety, to get Hannah's attention. I demurely waved my arms, hoping that my dad wouldn't notice, wouldn't follow my gaze and storm to the back of the room for a confrontation.

Guna looked professional, entering from the side of the stage, standing with a cluster of professors and discussing something in an official manner. She'd worn a bright red suit, and the sizzle of the color animated her face, gave her skin a subtle, roseate glow. She seemed entirely at ease, comfortable in front of the lecture hall, comfortable and eager to give public voice to her ideas.

The introductions were extensive. As an instructor of Soviet literature and culture at the University of Latvia, Dr. Guna Ozolinsh was respected as one of the foremost scholars in the field of Soviet letters. I learned that she'd had numerous articles published in the leading journals of the Soviet state. With the mention of each scholarly magazine, a wave of head-nodding swept the audience. Everyone seemed eager to affirm the importance of the *Soviet Studies Quarterly*, and *Moscow Today*, and *Proletarian Lives*, *Proletarian Writers*. Guna thanked her hosts and thanked the generosity of Marquette University, which—she said— was a wonderful venue for the exchange of ideas.

When she stood behind the podium, Guna took on a quiet intensity. She held the lectern in both hands, and she shaped her English with a precise, consistent energy.

"I have no notes," she began, "because I could bring no notes with me from the Soviet Union." Emotion moved through her voice. "They searched all of my bags, they searched my coat, they searched my briefcase.

"Of course, when I came to Milwaukee on Tuesday, I could have made notes for you." Guna shook her head. "But this would be wrong. In Latvia, if I want to make a presentation on something important, I have to do it all from my head, and leave no evidence afterward."

Guna talked about her experiences with *samizdat*—the underground publishing industry in the Soviet Union—and the way in which books had taken on, for her, an almost holy air. I found myself nodding, mesmerized by her talk. Something about this, about her love for the book as an artifact, was so appealing to me. There was nothing like *samizdat* in America, Guna said, and this was certainly, in some ways, a good thing. But then she described a year in which the thing she'd been most proud of was her production—on her tiny underground printing press—of four copies of Solzhenitsyn's *Gulag Archipelago*, translated into Latvian. She'd given the copies to four friends, who had, in turn, passed the copies to four other friends. These books, she said, circulated at great risk. They were the Soviet Union's drugs; for even the smallest amount of possession, you could go to jail for many years.

Guna left the podium and walked over to a little table on the corner of the stage. She poured herself a glass of water.

"A friend of mine," she said, "during the Second World War, gave shelter to five refugees. The Germans came into Latvia from 1941 to 1944. My friend hid three men and two women in his attic, behind an artificial wall." She drank from the water glass. "Today those people, those five, they have seventeen children and nine grandchildren. That is thirty-one people he saved—just like that. And how many more in the next generation? This is the way in which we saved books and ideas."

Eriks turned to me at this point and whispered in my ear, "There is probably a KGB informer in this room." He pointed to an older man, who was frowning and listening attentively to Guna's talk. "Him, maybe." Then he pointed to a woman, wearing a polka-dot dress and sitting to one side of the auditorium. She had an angry air about her, as if she was offended, somehow, by the content of the presentation. "Or maybe her." I doubted this, but I didn't say anything. Instead, I listened to Guna as she described the pseudonyms she used to publish articles that were critical of the government—at the same time as she published celebratory articles in *Pravda* under her real name.

She talked for forty minutes. In this time, I gradually came to realize that there, on that stage, was a woman of roughly my mother's age, a woman who was sleeping in our apartment, now, and eating most of her meals at our kitchen table—my relative—who was a crusader for freedom of speech. I imagined myself scurrying through alleys, passing around copies of Roth or Bellow or Salinger wrapped in butcher paper. I imagined what my life would've been like—if I hadn't been able to buy whatever I wanted at the bookstore, or check out whatever I wanted at the library. It crushed me. I felt the surprise and shame of learning a fact this important for the first time. Why hadn't I known about *samizdat*? I wondered. Why hadn't I learned about it in school?

When Guna finished, applause poured over her. She smiled and seemed genuinely shocked by the warmth of the reception. She fielded a few questions. The professor who'd started it all thanked everyone for coming. There was a wine and cheese reception in the adjacent room, he said, to which we were all invited. At the mention of the word wine, my dad cheerfully jabbed Ivan in the ribs. He stood and picked up his coat and brushed some dust off of the lapel. I walked over toward him and we assembled into a little knot of people—Oma Ilga, Ivan, my father, my mother, Hammond, Eriks, and myself. Guna had joined us and we were about to leave when I heard a familiar voice.

"Yuri," Hannah said. "Wait."

I turned to see Hannah. She was making her way through the crowd, shoving her way past the people who lingered in the aisles, talking. She held her dad's hand, pulling him toward us. He didn't seem eager to follow.

"It was a pleasure making your acquaintance earlier today," Hannah announced as soon as she arrived. "Yet I have some practical questions about the presentation."

Guna smiled and nodded. "Absolutely, Hannah," she said. "I would love to hear further about your reactions to the words I have said."

But then—before Hannah could begin to object at the unfair treatment that Guna had given to communism, or stress the importance, in her opinion, of a free press when America, too, was ruled by the Communist Party—my dad lumbered over and made his presence known.

"Well, Yuri," he said, "aren't you going to introduce us to your friends?" He paused, an ebullient smile on his face. He nodded with encouragement. Not exactly sure what else to do, I made the introductions. Dr. Graham visibly blanched when I said his name; he clearly anticipated that my dad would attack him at any moment.

And, in some respects, he was right. The conversation moved quickly from pleasantries to particulars—diving into the specifics of Guna's talk. Dr. Graham wouldn't back down. He said, "But don't you think you overemphasize the lack of individual freedoms in the

USSR? I mean, we all know that the people are better off than you contend."

"Well," Guna said, "maybe I do. But then again, perhaps you haven't really lived in the Soviet Union. Perhaps you don't know how life there truly goes."

"Or maybe," Dr. Graham countered, "you are motivated by your own self-interests. Maybe you're trying to use this speaking tour for your own economic gain."

My dad flinched, and leaned perceptibly toward Hannah's father. I imagined my father's hands reaching out and encircling Gerald Graham's neck. His arms twitched. I braced myself. "Trust me, Dr. Graham," my dad said, rocking on the balls of his feet, suddenly reaching out and poking Hannah's father squarely in the chest. "Conditions in the Soviet Union are fairly poor today." Guna nodded, as if to confirm the veracity of what my dad had said. She turned around and shook the hand of an elderly man who'd been waiting patiently nearby. She was clearly a celebrity—at least in this room.

"But at least the Soviet people are happy," Dr. Graham said.

"They are not happy, Dr. Graham. Quite the contrary."

"What do you mean?"

"I simply mean that it is idiotic to suggest that they are happy, Dr. Graham."

Hannah's father turned bright red. I assumed that, in his professional life, he was not accustomed to people calling him an idiot. The conversation went back and forth like this for quite some time. They traded barbs and half-concealed insults. Finally, someone announced that the lecture hall was closing and asked everyone to please adjourn to the wine and cheese reception. Without saying a word, my dad turned away from Hannah's father. He eased out through the doors and down the hallway. He disappeared into the postlecture crowd. All in all, I reflected, the scene hadn't been that drastic. No punches were thrown. No one had wrestled anyone else across the stage, knocking over the lectern and overturning Guna's pitcher of water. It had all been quite civilized.

Later, I found my dad in the corner of the room, sitting on a folding chair, drinking from a plastic cup of red wine and staring into the distance. His lips were stained bright purple, and he'd managed to smear his cheek with a streak of onion dip. He ruffled my hair when I walked up to him.

"So," I asked, "what did you think of Dr. Graham?"

"Dr. Graham?" my dad said, frowning. "He is an idiot. He is the bastard who sells that communist newspaper. You must love him, my darling son. You must love his ideas like you do not love the ideas of your father."

This hurt me. I was still angry that he'd been so rude to Dr. Graham. Why couldn't he be a gentleman to people with whom he disagreed? Had his life been so tough that he couldn't just talk politely with Dr. Graham and respectfully disagree? Looking back, I realize that I was wrong to judge him this way. I should have given him more leeway. But instead I corrected him: "Socialist," I said. "It's a socialist newspaper."

"Socialist, communist—same thing. No difference. But I am not going to make a problem for you, Yuri. I lived through communism, you know. I chose to raise you as an American." He coughed. "You are free to make stupid choices, my darling."

My dad stood and sighed and swished his wine from left to right. It looked remarkably like a cup of blood.

12

saturday, december 2, 1989

By the next morning it was clear to me that the Ozolinsh family was not leaving. No clothes had been packed. No arrangements had been made for a trip to the airport. My dad, however, seemed confident that our relatives were about to depart. He arranged to go in to work late on Saturday night, and he planned an elaborate farewell barbecue, complete with Pabst and steaks and pork ribs, which he promised to grill himself, in the cold. He wouldn't tell them, of course, that this was their farewell barbecue, but he hoped that the implication would be clear. I doubted this. But I kept quiet.

"How will you grill these in the cold air at night?" my mom asked him when he described the plan to her. "We will not be standing out there on the balcony with you, I can tell you that, in my opinion."

But Saturday night came and the meats had to be barbecued. My dad braved the frigid temperatures and produced a plate of steaks and two enormous racks of pork.

We assembled in the living room and started drinking and eating. Suddenly, I was overwhelmed by a sense of family. I was in my home, surrounded by a large group of noisy blood relatives. It was a buoyant feeling—a slightly aggravated but buoyant feeling—one that I'd never felt before. So much of my life with my parents had been solitary. We were a small kernel of Latvians, buried deep within the folds and seams of the broader American culture. We hadn't had an opportunity for this sort of joyous living. We hadn't had a chance to be festive; we'd been too busy just getting along. But now, as I sucked the meat off the charcoal-flavored pork rib, as Eriks picked at a sliver of meat that was stuck between his front teeth, as the heat from our food and our bodies accumulated on the windows in clouds of opaque condensation, now I felt at home. I felt at ease.

"Your father was the best country and western singer in all of Eastern Europe," Ivan said, brandishing a forkful of steak for emphasis. "His voice was the best—by far the best—in all of the Soviet Union, did you know that?"

"Ivani, stop," my dad said, looking embarrassed.

"No, my cousin. They should know. You are a singing genius."

"Stop, my friend, stop." Now my dad seemed to be actually getting angry. The secondary conversations in the room seemed to fade away. I could feel a slight current of tension—slight but palpable—radiating with the waves and the particles of light.

"No, no," Ivan continued, "there is no reason that they shouldn't know the whole story."

"Look—" my dad began, only to be interrupted by a loud knock at the door. Oma Ilga's face wrinkled into a smile. She exclaimed something in Latvian and struggled to stand up.

"What did she say?" I asked Eriks.

"She said that she invited him."

"Invited who?"

I turned to see Hammond walk into the room, holding an enormous bouquet of white carnations. "I brought these for you, Mara," he said, kissing my mother on the cheek. "And for Ilga"—Hammond brought his other hand out from behind his back, revealing a second, enormous bouquet of red carnations—"I brought these."

"*Vai*," Oma Ilga said. "*Vai, vai, vai.*" She took the carnations and admired them. She brought them to her face and inhaled deeply. She walked immediately to the kitchen and cut the stems with a knife. My mom handed her a vase. "*Vai*," she said again. "*Vai, vai.*" She took Hammond by the hand and led him to one side of the room. They sat off to one side and began talking.

Talking? I inched closer, confirming what I'd suspected. She'd say something in Latvian, and he'd reply with a sentence in English. It was truly remarkable. They didn't seem to speak each other's language but they were still able to communicate.

After dinner there was bourbon and more beer and the volume of my dad's voice increased steadily. His face brightened. He seemed younger. His heart distributed the bourbon throughout his body, giving him new energy. He and Ivan discussed the future of Eastern Europe in loud, broken English. I couldn't shake the idea that maybe—though it was doubtful—maybe this performance was for me. Why wouldn't they just speak in Latvian? It was a mystery. Whatever the case, Ivan was getting more and more restless. At one point, I thought I saw him rubbing his thigh and grimacing—though I couldn't be sure. The story of his stabbing flooded back to me. I noticed the way he was fingering his steak knife. He was slowly stroking the blade, almost petting it in a way.

My dad laughed sadly when Ivan said that he thought the day would come—within ten, maybe twenty years—when Latvia was free again. Ivan claimed that there was a real energy in the young people in Riga. They wanted to speak Latvian, to relearn Latvian customs, to fly the Latvian flag rather than the flag of the Soviet Union. All of these things were forbidden, of course, but still Ivan thought that soon they'd be allowed. My dad disagreed.

"You cannot say that, my friend. Just look at the facts. Forty-four years of occupation. Even a young boy who remembers the free country is now an old man."

"So what?"

"So they do not remember freedom. In thirty years, everyone will be proud to be Soviet citizen. I guarantee it. Latvian citizens will be like an inconvenient memory."

I thought about this. I didn't necessarily agree, but I didn't feel like contradicting my dad. He could be so loud when he was drunk.

"No," my dad continued. "The Soviet Union will never die. I am telling you this now. You remember it. The Soviet Union is too powerful. It will never end."

"The Soviet Union is a dead idea," Ivan said, and he rose to his feet dramatically. Didn't I see him reaching for his knife? This is it, I thought. This is the payback. My father is about to be stabbed in the leg.

But my dad stood up also, and extended his hands.

"Ivani, my darling, calm down. Have another Pabst."

Ivan seemed stunned by his own outburst. "I am sorry," he said. "I am forgetting myself. I've had too many Pabst, perhaps, already."

He sat back down. There would be no second stabbing, it appeared.

My dad cleared his throat. For the first time in recent memory, he seemed to be at a loss for words. He poured an inch of bourbon into his glass. He sighed. He stretched his legs out in front of him. No one was talking. Even Hammond and Oma Ilga were staring at him, waiting for some idea as to what would happen next.

"Everybody, come on," he said. "We should have good time. We are all here together. It is such a happy occasion. Why so much unhappiness?" An idea came to him. "Have I ever told you," he suggested, "the story of McKinley Morganfield and the Longing for Home?"

"I've never heard the story," Hammond said, "but I know who McKinley Morganfield was."

My dad nodded toward Hammond and smiled and leaned back in his chair.

McKINLEY MORGANFIELD AND THE LONGING FOR HOME

"You see, my darlings," he said, "when I think about everyone who has traveled so far to be here today, and when I think about the way that we are all sitting in this room and it is not Latvia . . ." He paused, and seemed to be on the edge of crying. I wasn't sure what he meant, exactly, but this didn't bother me. He was my dad and I gave him a certain amount of latitude with incomprehensibility. He sighed and shook his head.

"McKinley Morganfield was born in the Mississippi Delta, in 1915. He started playing harmonica when he was twelve and guitar when he was seventeen. He played with the neck of a bottle—he called it the bottleneck style—truly, and he moved the bottleneck up and down the strings, to make a sound that was a little like crying.

"He loved Mississippi, but he wanted to be a recording artist. Believe me, I know what this is like. It is sharp desire, right here." He pointed to the bottom of his throat. "It is not like anything you could feel on a normal day. Not like love for a woman or a man. It is not like love for a country. It is different, in my opinion.

"So he left and went to Chicago in 1943. He was twenty-eight years old. He changed his name to Muddy Waters. He invented a new personality for himself. I have his first record. *Aristocrat 1305*. 'I Cannot

Be Satisfied' and 'I Feel Like Going Home.' I will play them for you later. But he became so famous. He made more money than I will ever make, even though he was not completely a moneybags."

"Moneybags?" Ivan asked.

"It is expression in the United States. It means very wealthy."

Ivan nodded.

"But always he wanted to go back to Mississippi. Sure, he went back a couple of times to play concerts. But still, he never had the same feeling as when he was young, and playing in the local bars, all for his friends. He was never as happy again."

"How do you know?" I asked. It was as if I was hardwired to ask the obnoxious questions.

"Exactly, Yuri. A good question. I am sure because I went to the library the other day, and I do not remember why but I was reading all of the newspapers from Chicago. You know how they have them on file in the library. At any rate, I like to go there and read all of the reviews, from the 1930s and 1940s, when blues was starting in that city, and all of the records and clubs were always in the paper. So I read an interview with him, just a few months before his record was released. It was a short column, only few inches long. He was still using his old name, McKinley Morganfield. But he talked about the song 'I Feel Like Going Home,' and he said how much he missed Mississippi. That was the whole interview.

"And then, of course, in his last concert—just before he died in 1983—what do you think was the last song he ever played in public, when he came back onstage for an encore?"

I guessed. "'I Feel Like Going Home'?"

"No, it was 'Stormy Monday.' But his regular set list . . ." Here my dad paused, for emphasis. "It ended with 'I Feel Like Going Home.' He didn't know for sure if he would get to play an encore, you see."

"That is so sad," Eriks said. "I am very interested by this sad highlight from the life of one of the fathers of American blues music."

"So you see," my dad continued, straining to come to a conclusion, "what do you gain—you know—if you leave behind everything, no matter how successful you are?"

Everyone was listening. Reflecting back on this night, I see it now as a point of departure. I was learning things that would be critical to me in the future, but—as usual with my dad—I had no idea that I was learning them. He was elusive and charismatic and drunk and captivating.

"So you are telling me that I should have been happy in Latvia," Ivan said, "for the past twenty-five years?"

"No, no, no," my dad replied, but it was clear that he didn't have much more to elaborate on this point.

"So then you are telling me," Ivan said, puzzling this one out, "that I should be happy here?"

My dad smiled. He looked directly into Ivan's eyes. "Exactly, Ivan. That is exactly what I am trying to tell you."

How, exactly, he was saying this—again, I was unclear. But Ivan and my dad seemed to be communicating on a level that was beyond my understanding.

"I agree with you, Rudolfi. It is all a mystery. Here, let us smoke a cigarette on the balcony."

They went outside and smoked and talked for a long time. We were all full and sleepy. A few of us actually fell asleep. I slipped in and out of a dream in which Hannah and I were at a picnic, drinking wine and eating sandwiches on delicious French bread. The bread was unbelievably fresh and the sandwiches were made from the finest-quality meats and cheeses. But the more we ate, the larger the sandwiches became. I couldn't stop eating, I knew, because then I'd lose Hannah. So I ate and sweated and ate and sweated and ate. My stomach hurt. I awoke suddenly, gasping for breath.

I looked around. Everybody had left. Oma Ilga was nowhere to be seen. My mom had returned to her room. It was almost midnight. Ivan and Eriks were standing on the porch, smoking and talking. My dad, I assumed, had left for work. I grabbed a pillow off the couch and retired to the kitchen. I was beginning to like sleeping on the tile floor. I closed my eyes again. What would I dream of this time? From beneath the kitchen floor, I heard the slow, almost medicinal sound of Hammond's playing. It was a river of music, a river of blues, and it enveloped me in the soft murmur of its chords, in the steady accumulation of its sounds. I imagined the Milwaukee River, sloshing its way through the Third Ward, rolling from bank to bank, bearing its boats and barges to Lake Michigan. I floated along with the music. I let it filter upward and wrap itself—a full measure of blue—around my body.

13

sunday, december 3, 1989

Sunday was beautiful—a glorious, sunny day. All in all, I felt like the sky was mocking me. Why was it so beautiful when things seemed to be going so wrong? I ate my breakfast sullenly. I watched a little network television. Then, just before noon, I stood up and started to walk toward the bathroom. The shower was free, and I was going to prepare myself to face the rest of the day.

All morning, I'd been sitting on the couch worrying about the future. I was concerned about a number of things—not the least of which was the progress of the investigation into the stolen car. Should I just confess to my dad, I'd wondered. Maybe this would ease the pressure of the guilt. I thought briefly about calling Hannah and asking her advice on the subject. But I knew this would just upset her further. She was already fairly upset.

I knew that something was wrong as soon as I stood up. My legs felt rubbery, and dizziness seemed to generate at the base of my neck and flood outward through my body. I wobbled. Everything felt like a Polaroid snapshot—precise and shiny in its center, faded and indistinct at the edges. I staggered toward the kitchen.

"I think I'm fainting," I said, to no one in particular.

I caught a glimpse of Ivan's concerned face, and I heard Eriks say, "He is falling!" Then, darkness.

I awoke to Ivan slapping my face. "Wake up," he'd say, and then slap me gently with the back of his hand. "Wake up." Slap. "Wake up." Slap. "Wake up."

"Okay, okay," I said, catching his hand before he slapped me again. "I'm awake." I struggled to sit up.

My dad had appeared from his bedroom. He'd been sleeping off his night shift. "What is going on?" he said. "Are you all right?"

"I'm fine," I said. I had no explanation for why I'd passed out, other than the sense of overwhelming powerlessness, the sense that everything was unraveling around me. I felt unstable and queasy. Anxiety bloomed in my gut, an algae of anxiety, squishy and expanding and almost certainly green.

"Get him water!" my mom said, and sure enough, within seconds three glasses of water were arranged beside my reclining body.

"I'm okay," I said. "Don't worry. It's nothing." But they didn't believe me.

"We should call a doctor, perhaps?" my dad ruminated, and looked toward my mom. She shook her head and shrugged her shoulders.

"How will the doctor help?" she said. "We can handle this ourselves."

I was carried to my bedroom, where I was placed in my bed and told to rest. But I couldn't. I was oppressed by the apartment. Even the walls were driving me crazy—pressing against me with what seemed like claustrophobic intensity. So, I got out of bed and threw on some clothes. I heard them all talking in the living room about a TV show that was about to come on. I snuck out of my room and crept into my parents' bedroom. I stole four dollars from my mom's purse. I crept back down the hall and, when everyone was paying attention to the television, I snuck through the door.

I headed for the bus stop. I would spend Sunday, I'd decided, at the Milwaukee County Public Library. Normally, when my mom was working, I spent at least one afternoon a week at the library, wandering through the stacks, idly sifting through the volumes. Now I missed it. I took great solace from the library. It was immutable and constant. Barring some sort of large-scale catastrophe it would be here forever, quietly accumulating books, slowly expanding. The library could be scathingly cynical or beautifully naïve. I sat in a comfortable chair and started reading newspapers from around the country.

On some level, I worried that I'd become one of the homeless people I saw in the public library. (They were almost always men, rarely women.) They took elaborate notes in little stained notebooks and muttered to themselves about the hidden truths of life. They wore dirty clothes. They were all—and I was certain of this—concocting expansive theories of the universe and the meaning of existence. They were crazy, sure. But how had they reached this point? How had they come to this stage of total degradation? They'd been kids, too, right? What had happened to them that couldn't possibly happen to me?

One particular man was seated near me at a long, rectangular table. He had the odor of dirty clothes and cigarettes and alcohol. For five or ten minutes he'd scribble wildly on a yellow legal pad. Then he'd stop and sigh. He'd look critically at what he'd written. He'd clear his throat. He'd drum his fingers on the tabletop. Then—with great precision— he'd tear off the sheets and crumple them and throw them in a nearby trash bin. After he'd done this four or five times, he caught me staring at him. My mouth must have been hanging open.

"I'm a poet," he said, in a voice that was deeply offended. He gathered his notebooks and stormed off, heading for the deeper recesses of the building.

After I bought a hot dog for lunch (ketchup and relish and onions— no mustard, no sauerkraut) from a street vendor, I ambled back inside and found the library's copy of *Humboldt's Gift*. It had been checked out twice, most recently in 1982. I finished the last hundred pages. I cried at the end. What could I do? I was a teenager.

I wandered into the section of the library where they kept the reference books and encyclopedias. For some reason, this section was the most appealing to me. It was pleasant to read the short paragraphs on anything—little snapshots of information and color. I wished, briefly, that there could be an almanac for everything: an almanac of the senses, a map of the emotions, an almanac of love. Then I'd more fully understand my feelings for Hannah. I'd look them up, right between the horoscopes and the weather predictions. The day wandered quickly by. *So*, I thought, as I took the bus home in the evening, I've committed a serious crime—quite possibly a felony. My apartment is overrun with relatives.

I needed to take action of some kind, I realized. I needed to do something definitive or dramatic. But what? I slipped unobtrusively back into the apartment. My mom was in the kitchen, boiling something in a kettle at the stove. She nodded to me as I came in. "Yuri, you look much better," she said, touching my cheek with one hand, stirring the liquid in the kettle with the other.

I cornered my dad before he left for work. He, too, told me I looked better and seemed cheered by my presence. It was seven at night. I suggested to him that we go out into the hallway, just to chat for a moment. I meant to confess, I really did. But it was too difficult. Once in the hallway, I suggested that we walk down the stairs. Once down the stairs, I suggested we walk to the bus stop. He agreed, though he must have been curious as to why.

"Dad, I'm worried," I finally said, as we walked through the softly falling snow. "I don't think that they're leaving."

He sighed. "It is a beautiful night, do you not think so, Yuri?"

"Dad, I'm serious. I don't trust Ivan at all. Did you see how angry he was last night? He was furious. I thought he was going to kill you."

My dad stopped walking. "This is important point, Yuri, so I will emphasize for you. Ivan would never kill me. He would perhaps stab me in the leg, yes. But he would never kill me."

"Stab you in the leg?" I protested. "Are you kidding me? How can you live in the same apartment with somebody who might stab you in the leg?"

"It is to be expected," he said.

"Are you kidding me?" I repeated. "Besides, didn't you say they were supposed to leave tomorrow? Have any bags been packed? No bags have been packed. They may never leave. Do you envision the seven of us living in this apartment forever?"

"You are being ridiculous, Yuri."

"Ridiculous? How am I being ridiculous?"

We'd reached the bus stop. I felt guilty for yelling at him, but what choice had he given me? I waited for him to explode. His blistering anger—in situations like this—was almost a matter of contractual obligation. This time, however, my dad was surprisingly calm.

"My darling, Yuri," he said, "it is cold tonight outside. You should go home, where it is warm. But you think about this: When a guest comes to your house, is it your duty to tell him when he should leave?"

"It is if he's planning to move in with you."

The bus pulled up to the stop. My dad shrugged his shoulders. "I guarantee they are not moving in with us," he said as he entered the hydraulic doors. He looked tired and old, backlit by the dim light of the doorway. I could see the neck of a bottle of bourbon sticking out of the pocket of his winter coat. "You should be grateful to have your large family visiting you from so far away."

That evening, Ivan and Guna went walking. I didn't feel like pointing out to them that it was close to nine thirty, or that the weather forecast was now calling for six to nine inches of snow. They were on their own. If they got trapped in a snow drift and preserved until spring, that would be their fault, not mine. Eriks was watching network television in the living room, together with Oma Ilga. My mom came into the living room. I was sitting propped against the wall, staring into space.

"I am going to the 7-Eleven," my mom said. "Does anyone need something from the store?" She'd made a borscht for dinner and she was planning to serve it tomorrow at breakfast. All she needed, she told me, was a tub of sour cream. "It is a short walk, anyway," she said. "You watch over everything while I am away." The door swung shut behind her.

This was my opportunity. Perhaps it would be my only opportunity. I bolted into my parents' bedroom, where Ivan and Guna had stashed their luggage. I tore frantically through their shirts and socks and pants and underwear. Trying to be as quiet as possible, I rummaged among their Soviet deodorants and toothpastes—marveling only briefly at the Cyrillic characters on the outsides of the bottles. Finally, near the bottom of one black bag—the bag that Ivan himself had carried off the plane—I found what I was looking for.

Four passports, all bound together with a rubber band. The stubs of plane tickets. Luggage receipts. Boarding passes. Papers—a thick stack of papers—many of them on official U.S. Government stationery. There were letters from the State Department, letters from officers in the Bureau of Educational and Cultural Affairs, all of them addressed to Dr. Guna Ozolinsh.

I was lifting the last letter from the pile when I heard the front door to the apartment swing open. "Hello," an accented male voice called out through the apartment. It was Ivan. Damn. I stuffed the passports back into the bag, covering them with a layer of socks. I slipped the letters under my shirt.

I hurried into the hall, hunched over so that no one could see my bulky figure. I got lucky; Ivan and Guna had stepped into the kitchen.

I managed to make it to my room unseen. I threw the papers down on the carpeted floor of my closet. I walked back to the door, opening it slightly.

"Sorry, everybody, but I'm asleep in here." I slammed the door shut.

With what I imagined to be the attention of an archaeologist, I unraveled the mystery of Ivan and Guna and Eriks and Oma Ilga Ozolinsh. It took me a while to piece it all together, but by eleven o'clock I'd established a map of the important dates. I'd also developed a name for the whole situation—trying to stay within the boundaries of the spy-novel genre. Carefully, with red ink and block-capital letters, I'd written:

THE OZOLINSH FAMILY INFILTRATION PROJECT, DIRECTIVE FOUR

I discovered that Guna had been in this country for weeks. I discovered that my impulse—that the BECA wouldn't pay for her flight if she was only speaking at one university—was right. This much was certain. Milwaukee was the fourth stop on a speaking tour that had taken her to three different states and five different universities.

I found the remnants of their airline tickets. She'd landed at Detroit Metropolitan International Airport on the twenty-eighth of October, a Saturday. She'd stayed with Janis and Marija Kiegelis—faculty within the University of Detroit's Eastern European Languages Department. Besides the ticket stubs and letters from the American Latvian Association and the Bureau of Educational and Cultural Affairs, I'd also found letters from Western Michigan University, Beloit College, Marquette, and the University of Chicago. So she'd been partially honest with us, only partially, and she'd left out some critical details.

Ivan and Eriks and Ilga had arrived much later, only one day before they'd come to Milwaukee. They'd flown from Moscow to Detroit, just like Guna. Then the Ozolinsh family had stayed for one night at the Airport Holiday Inn. I found the receipt: two rooms, ninety-one dollars, paid in cash. Though I searched and searched, I couldn't find any return tickets back to Latvia. All of their tickets were one way. They were staying forever. I wanted to call Hannah and let her know what I'd discovered, but how could I use the phone in my house to make this call?

I didn't know what to do—didn't know how to use this new knowledge to my advantage. Although it was late, I had an idea. I went into the living room and approached Eriks. I suggested that we walk to Zigorski's, the Polish deli that my mom and I sometimes frequented. It would be open for another hour or so. If we hurried, we could buy some pickled eggs and cups of chicory coffee. Eriks nodded and slipped into the kitchen, where he rummaged in one of the cupboards. He returned with a little thermos full of what I could only imagine was bourbon. "For the coffee," he said.

We passed my mom in the kitchen as we left. "Where are you going?" she demanded. On the counter was a little white plastic bag emblazoned with the 7-Eleven logo.

"Out," I said. We didn't break our stride.

"Out where?"

"Las Vegas," I called back over my shoulder. "We're going to hit the casinos and play roulette all night."

As we walked, Eriks and I talked about his mother. He'd heard her give that same speech many times, he said. I pressed him for dates. He was vague. Many times, he said. Too many to count. That was why she seemed so comfortable, he said. Language became easier through repetition. This was how he was going to learn to sing in flawless English, how he'd master the art of English rock 'n' roll songwriting.

We crossed the Milwaukee River as the snow began to fall, walking through the little patch of land that was dominated by the Port Authority's shipping bays. It was a landscape composed of concrete and steel. Because of the containers, though, it could be quite colorful. A bright red container would rest next to a bright blue one—and they would both have a pale glow in the darkness, lit primarily by electric lamps. It was almost lunar, this landscape. We crossed the Milwaukee River again; we stitched our way deeper into the industrial center of the city.

My goal for the night had been to get the truth out of Eriks. I'd imagined apologizing to him for rummaging through his family's belongings but then justifying myself by pointing out that they hadn't been entirely truthful with us. But as we walked, I focused on the rhythms of our walking, and the sound of his voice, which seemed almost hypnotic in the thin darkness. We walked all the way to Zigorski's. The proprietor was sweeping snow from the sidewalk in front of the deli. He looked surly and unwelcoming. We slipped into the store. I checked my watch. Ten minutes before midnight.

We poured ourselves two small cups of the powerful, chicory-flavored coffee from the pot at the back of the store. We walked slowly up toward the register. We waited in front of the display case. The pig's brain bobbed there—antiseptic and white—and I saw Eriks staring at it quizzically. I looked at the case while we waited for the proprietor to finish sweeping. There was an empty plate on the top shelf. It was labeled with a small cardboard sign. POTATO KNISH, the sign promised, 80 CENTS.

Finally, close to twelve o'clock, the proprietor reappeared. He shook his head and squeezed his bulk behind the register. He punched desultorily at its keys, ringing up our coffee. "One dollar," he demanded, extending his palm.

"I'd also like a knish," I said. "A potato knish."

The proprietor scowled at me. He gestured with the broom. "We have no knishes. You can see for yourself."

I could feel Eriks shifting uncomfortably on his feet. I turned and winked at him. "Don't lie to me," I said to the cashier. "I know you have them," I added.

The proprietor looked confused. "No," he said, "actually we don't."

"You're lying."

"No, I'm not. Why would I lie to you?"

I winked at Eriks again. "Because you're a lying bastard," I said. "Because you're a lying, stupid bastard of a shopkeeper."

I'm not certain exactly how the coffee ended up on the front of my shirt, soaking me to the skin and threatening to inflict third-degree burns. I'm also not certain precisely how the proprietor of Zigorski's managed to lift us both off the ground—one in each arm—and heave us through his doors and onto the newly blanketed street. I'm also not certain precisely what language he used when he cursed at us, for almost an entire minute, shaking his fist and yelling until his voice degenerated into a series of incoherent coughs.

I sat on the sidewalk where I'd landed and checked myself for cuts or, perhaps, broken limbs. Finding neither, I turned to Eriks and began apologizing. He looked upset, and I tried to explain the story behind what had happened, tried to explain that my mom had done the same thing, but with drastically different results. At some point in my explanation, his body collapsed into a fit of laughter. He whooped and cackled, sitting there on the curb in the pale almost-darkness of neon lighting, his voice rising into the Milwaukee night.

"Jesus," he said, "I was afraid for a moment that he would kill us with the broom."

Eriks continued shaking his head. He patted the pockets of his leather jacket until he found his cigarettes. He lit two of them at once and handed one to me. I felt the slight dampness of his saliva on the filter. He withdrew the thermos from his pocket. He took a sip and handed it to me, too. It was indeed bourbon, as I'd guessed, but with a twist.

"Lime?" I asked. He nodded.

"It's a delicious citrus fruit."

We sat there and smoked and drank in silence. Unlike my father, Eriks seemed like my friend, my ally, my coconspirator. After a while, the silence gave way to easy conversation. We talked about the deli. Eriks was amazed at the variety of products he'd seen, many of which had been covered in Cyrillic script. The Cyrillic had been a shock to him; he thought that he'd left it behind him, in Latvia. After some time the proprietor of Zigorski's scurried onto the street. We watched as he turned the hand crank and lowered the grating over the doorway to his shop. He didn't seem to notice us, or, if he noticed us, he didn't care. He locked the grate in place and walked off in the opposite direction.

Eriks and I passed the flask back and forth, sitting there in Downtown Milwaukee, on the border of the Third Ward. The night seemed munificent and full and insulating; it rose around us like a cocoon. Eriks asked questions about Milwaukee. He wondered how much a person paid for rent in a section of the city like this one. I didn't know. He wondered what the average wage was here, for a laborer. I didn't know. I felt a little useless. I tried to steer the conversation back to literature. No luck. Eriks didn't feel like discussing books. He was interested in visceral life, in the teeming possibilities of walking through the city, in the lifestyle of the *flaneur*, the tramp, the rock-star hobo.

Then I asked him about the story he'd told me—the one about his grandfather and deportation to the gulag. What had it been like, I wondered, to return to Latvia after ten years in Siberia? What had it been like to try to live in the civilized world again?

"No, no," Eriks said, suddenly less excited. He stubbed out his cigarette on the snowy street. "There was no coming back. He could not come back, not truly. He could not truly be happy anymore. He would always remember the terrible things he had seen. He could not truly laugh anymore."

Silence fell over us again. The snow had stopped long ago. After some time, I stood up and stretched the aching muscles of my back. Eriks stood and stretched as well. We started walking quietly back to the apartment. I hadn't managed to force a confession from him; I wasn't any closer to knowing when the Ozolinsh family was planning to leave our apartment.

As we crossed the Milwaukee River for the final time that evening, Eriks stopped, and turned toward the railing. I stood beside him. The river unfolded beneath us in a sheet of luminous light, twisting and rising with each small wave. Eriks seemed like he had something to say. He hesitated. He shrugged his shoulders. "What is funny is this," Eriks said as he looked at me, a crescent of a smile moving across his face. "My grandfather never laughed. But he was always telling jokes about the government."

We walked home. I felt a closeness to Eriks—a sense of shared experience that I hadn't felt before. When we returned, the door to the apartment was partially ajar, and everyone inside was asleep. We sat at the kitchen table and talked, sipping the bourbon and lime, slowly getting drunk.

14

monday, december 4, 1989
7:30 A.M.

Though I didn't remember collapsing on my makeshift blanket-bed in the kitchen, I awoke the next morning wrapped in the covers, miraculously lacking a hangover. My dad—I realized as soon as I awoke—would be home any minute. He was already late. When he returned, I'd show him all of the letters and ticket stubs. He'd know what to do. He'd know just how to confront Ivan and Guna with the truth. Then we'd get a better sense of what we could expect from December and January and the rest of the cold, long winter.

I was still tired but I couldn't sleep. I stood in the kitchen and wobbled sleepily from side to side. I decided—after much reflection and consideration—to brush my teeth. The mint would soothe me. I walked to the bathroom. I stood at the sink and cupped the water in my palms, splashed it over my skin. I wanted to submerge myself in that water completely. I briefly fantasized about slipping quietly under the surface, simply dissolving away to nothing in the cool, clear liquid. I turned off the faucet, sighed, and ambled out into the hall. I was stopped by a bellowing voice just outside the front door.

"Yuri," my dad yelled as he surged into the room, leaving the key in the lock. "Where the hell are you?"

"What is it, Dad? What's wrong? I'm right here."

I hadn't seen my dad this drunk in a while. His drinking intensified and slackened, depending on various unknowable factors. This, however, was an all-time low. He swayed as he stood in the doorway. His eyes looked like pure jelly. There was no way he could focus on me, I was certain. He slammed an empty bottle of bourbon on the kitchen counter. Ivan and Guna were in the far corner of the room, staring at him with shock. They'd clearly just awakened. Behind me, I heard the latch on the bedroom door click shut. Thanks, Mom, I thought, for all your support.

My dad turned and pointed in the direction of the members of our extended family. Oma Ilga—who had been sitting quietly—made a soft exclamation of surprise. "I am taking my son out onto the balcony to kill him," he said. There was something malicious in his tone, something dangerous. None of us laughed. For a moment as he steered me outside—gripping my shoulder with his clawlike injured hand—I thought that he might actually kill me. He could easily have shoved me over the edge of the balcony.

It was freezing. Absolutely freezing. I wasn't wearing very many clothes, admittedly, but still, the sweat froze to my skin. I could have scraped it off. My dad, for his part, slouched into the corner of the balcony, his elbow draped over the rail. He looked like an aging prizefighter.

"So, my wonderful son," my dad said, and stopped, almost as if he was thinking about this word, this *wonderful*, as if he was turning it over in his mind. "So, my wonderful son," he repeated. I was suddenly full of shame, a deep churning shame.

"What's wrong, Dad?" I asked. Then: "Do you need a drink?"

His knees seemed to buckle at the mention of alcohol. "A drink?" he said. "Well, now, wait one moment. This is a good idea. Get me a bourbon, would you. There is a bottle behind the television."

Sure enough, there was a bottle behind the television. It was half hidden, tucked into the back of the entertainment center. Ivan and Guna had disappeared—they'd probably gone into my room. Eriks slipped into the kitchen. "Why is your father so angry?" he asked. He'd brought me a sweater for the cold December day.

"I don't know." I put on the sweater. Ice cubes, glassware, bourbon. I poured a full glass of Heaven Hill. I headed back onto the balcony.

"Yuri, my darling," my dad said as he drank the bourbon, "I am curious to know what you think of this?"

He slipped his hand into his back pocket. He pulled out an indistinct object—something small and square—and dropped it on the deck. He kicked it toward me. "What do you know," he asked, "about the Latvian writer Karlis Skalbe?"

I stared at the book. Though it had been slightly charred—the bottom edge of the cover had burned away—it was still recognizable. I realized that it must have fallen out of my pocket at some point during the confusion of the accident.

"What do you think of that?" my dad said. His speech was loose and disjointed. He seemed to be speaking from the base of his throat.

I didn't know what to think. Until that moment, I'd forgotten about the book. As soon as I saw it, though, I remembered everything. The details tumbled back into my memory. They were all there at once, crowding into my mind simultaneously, a tumbling array of pictures that I'd tried to forget. It had been completely unintentional. I'd just slipped the book into my pocket on a whim. I couldn't believe that everything was unraveling because of this single detail.

"At first," my dad said, "they thought the author was Swedish. I do not know why they thought he was Swedish. Swedish names look nothing like Latvian names. Very strange."

I agreed. The less I said, I'd decided quickly, the better off I was.

He'd gone in to work last night like always, he told me. Jack Baldwin had met him at the door to the dealership. This was my dad's first sign that something was wrong. Mr. Baldwin had taken him to his office. No one else was there. He'd started with a long speech about trust. About how trust was the most important thing in business. That without trust all of the economy would be in shambles. Without trust, Jack had said, a business deal could never be accomplished.

"Sure it could," I said. "You can't just base a business deal on trust. That's why you sign a contract, that's why lawyers—"

"Shut up," my dad interrupted. His voice was throaty and mucus filled. He spat an ice cube over the edge of the deck. "Listen to what I am telling you."

He continued the slow narration of his conversation with Jack Baldwin. Mr. Baldwin had been evasive at first. He'd seemed almost playful. Then he'd pulled the book from a drawer and dropped it on the table. He'd asked my dad if he could read it. "Is that writer from *your* country, Balodis?" he'd said. Of course my dad had said yes. Why wouldn't he say yes? Mr. Baldwin had said that he was glad that my dad was an honest man. Honesty could save you in a difficult situation. Mr. Baldwin had leaned forward. I could visualize him clearly—the pink splotch on his forehead radiating red energy.

"Why'd you do it, Balodis?" he'd said. "I thought you had pride in the company."

"I do have pride in the company," my dad had said. "What are you talking about, sir?"

My poor dad. He stood there in the corner of the balcony, drink in hand, drunk and off-balance. His eyes swelled and moistened and a few tears spilled out. He explained to me how Jack had accused him of stealing the Monte Carlo, how he'd put my dad on immediate unpaid leave, how my dad had protested, sworn his innocence, demanded a lie detector test. All of the things you saw in the movies. My dad explained it all to me. *Explained* is the only word for it. He wasn't telling a story. When he told a story there was a certain exuberant joy at the edges of his eyes. When he told a story his movements were animated by the energy of the telling. Now, he was just talking. He was downcast, dejected, sullen. Loud but sullen.

Because of a variety of factors, because he was a marginal employee who worked at night, because of the book they'd found in the car, written in the relatively obscure and rare Eastern European language that he spoke, the police had demanded that my dad be brought in for questioning. They'd wanted to arrest him immediately. Lincoln Quesnell was particularly angry. None of his cows were giving milk; they'd been frightened dry.

But Jack Baldwin was a magnanimous, kindhearted man. He'd told the Mukwonago police that my dad would agree to go of his own volition.

"What happened?"

"What do you think? We went down there together," my dad said. "We drove out there in his car. Totally silent. He did not say one word to me. The detectives were waiting." He coughed. "They said, 'Are you ready to confess?' I said, 'No, I am not ready to confess because I am innocent.' So they just sat me in a room and asked me questions. It was just like the Soviet Union. Except, after some time, one of them brought me coffee. In the Soviet Union, they never brought you coffee.

"I started to wonder if maybe—because of the drinking, you know—I had done this but I did not remember." For a few moments, my dad was unable to talk. He kept swirling the liquor in his glass. It made sloshing sounds.

At the unusual sound of my dad's voice, my mom had come out from behind her locked bedroom door. She leaned on the wall, hovering on the margins of the balcony.

"What is wrong?" she asked my dad.

"Nothing," he said. "Nothing is wrong."

He was near the end of his story. He needed to sleep, he said. He needed to think things over. They'd interrogated him for hours, he said. Only at the end of it all had they asked about me. They'd wanted to know my whereabouts on the night of the crime. He'd laughed, actually, and said that I was asleep, in my bed, as usual. Then he'd remembered the night it had all happened, and the way I'd shown up at six thirty A.M., and a sickening feeling had spread through his stomach.

"A sickening feeling, Yuri. It spread directly through my stomach."

He stood up straight, then, and handed me his empty glass.

"So I am waiting for them to call. They will let me know in forty-eight hours if I need to come back. They will probably be filing charges against me, they said."

I stuttered, trying desperately to form some sort of a response. Many, many times in the years since then I've wished that I'd managed to confess. I've wished that, standing there on the little wooden balcony, I'd managed to summon the courage—not much courage, really, all things considered—to tell my dad what I'd done. It might have changed things, somehow. Maybe things would have worked out differently. Instead, I tried to change the subject.

"I've got news," I said, my voice a little ragged. "I've discovered secrets about Ivan and Guna and the rest of their family."

"I know, I know," my dad said. He shook his head. "Never mind about that. Leave me alone right now. I need to be alone."

He walked into the apartment and disappeared into the bedroom. My mom followed him, looking quickly over her shoulder to see what I was doing. For my part, I was standing silently on the balcony. I looked at my dad's glass. The ice cubes were slick and shiny and still laced with bourbon. I emptied the glass over the railing. Ice falling on snow—one altered element was added to another.

I waited on the balcony. I looked at the sky. In some ways, I wanted to stay out there. I didn't want to leave that space. But I wasn't going to solve my problems by sitting on the balcony all morning—that was certain. And I definitely wasn't going to school today. This wasn't an ordinary Monday morning. I needed advice. But where could I turn? I needed Hammond.

I walked downstairs to his apartment. I knocked on the glass of his patio door. Within seconds, I could see his tall, thin frame moving hesitantly toward me. "Yuri," he said, peering out into the morning light. "Is that you?"

"It's me," I said.

"Wait one second. Hold on while I get my glasses."

Hammond returned and led me inside and sat me down and boiled some water for tea. It was peppermint tea, and the smell of our steeping tea bags filled the apartment. "Good for the vocal chords," he said, as I took my first sip.

"My vocal chords are fine," I said. "It's the rest of me that needs help."

"You'd be surprised," Hammond said, "by how influential the vocal chords are." We'd actually talked about this many times. His theory was that the vocal chords were the center of one's being. They vibrated with the energy of life—language—and they could control the energies of the rest of the body. Balance started with the vocal chords, he claimed. Why else did monks take vows of silence? Hammond maintained it wasn't just so that they could reflect on the divinity of silence and the uncluttered world. It was because they recognized the power of the vocal chords.

"I've got a problem, Hammond," I said. He nodded. He could tell by my face, he said, that it was serious. I cleared my throat. I sipped my tea. I sighed. There was no way to do this, I realized, except by telling the whole truth. So, over the next twenty or thirty minutes that's exactly what I did. I recounted the accident in great detail. I included what it felt like—for those several moments—to be suspended upside down in a motor vehicle. I felt like Hammond was becoming my therapist. I briefly wondered if I should offer to pay him an hourly fee.

After I finished, Hammond sat very still on the sofa. If his eyes hadn't been open, I would have wondered if he was asleep. His breathing seemed perfectly measured and controlled. Then, finally, after what seemed like hours, he took a sip of his tea.

"Well, then, I don't know what to say. What can I say? You're doomed."

"Damnit," I said. "Not again. Why, for once, couldn't you just say that everything looks okay? Why am I always doomed?"

"Do you want the truth?"

"I want advice."

"Well, advice often contains the truth. That's actually the ideal kind of advice. I could give you advice based on lies, but I don't think you'd be satisfied." He was angry. He took a gulp of his tea.

"But all you say is that I'm doomed," I said. "You don't elaborate."

"The details are too sad to elaborate. Wouldn't you rather just sit here and sip some peppermint tea?"

I agreed with him. I needed to consider Hammond's apartment a sanctuary. It was spacious and fairly empty. It had a certain soothing energy which I found pleasing. Also, it had the Hammond Tonewheel, which sat to one side of the room. It looked a little bit like an immobile statue of Buddha.

Hammond put his bony hand on my shoulder. "You came here for advice," he said. "But now I'd like to ask you for some." He leaned closer to me. "Tell me, Yuri, is Ilga married?"

It took me a moment to figure out who he was talking about. "Oma Ilga?" I asked. "My great-aunt?"

"Exactly," he said, and smiled.

"No," I said. "I'm pretty sure she's not. She was at some point, I think. Why?"

"It doesn't matter," Hammond said. He leaned back, straightened his shirt, adjusted his belt. "Look," he continued, "like I said—you need to tell your father. This is a serious matter. You need to be careful how you handle it. I think you could be in a lot of trouble. Your father will help you, Yuri. He'll figure some way out of this mess."

I nodded and thanked Hammond and left his apartment. I decided that I'd go out to the hedge maple, though, and see what its opinion was. I stood at the base of the tree and leaned against it. I felt a little ridiculous, sure—but paying homage to something always felt a little ridiculous. The bark was ridged and rough under my hand. The tree seemed sleepy. It didn't offer any communication. This one was up to me. The maple was cased in winter. It was waiting for spring.

I ran into Ivan and Guna on the first-floor landing. They were on their way out. They seemed surprised to see me. I barely even noticed them. "We are going walking for a short time," Ivan said, and smiled nervously at me.

"Only a short time," Guna repeated, and the two of them walked away.

I climbed the stairs to our apartment. I opened the front door. Oma Ilga was standing right there—waiting with a tray of some sort of pastry. My mom appeared behind her.

"You are just in time," she said, clearly happy that I'd returned. "Your father is asleep. But Oma Ilga," and here my mom looked slightly desperate, "Oma Ilga suggested that we make cookies."

"Cookies?" I said, staring dubiously at the little triangles of pastry that were cooling on the tray. "Those don't look like cookies."

"They are an old Latvian recipe," my mom said, staring me directly in the eyes. "Horseradish cookies. Go ahead. Try one. I am certain that you will find them delicious, in my opinion."

I hated horseradish. But I had no choice. I took one of the crisp little triangles and popped it in my mouth. It was sweet—very sweet—and quite rich. It had a strong, almost buttery flavor. But this flavor, I noticed, seemed to stick to the roof of my mouth. Then I was suddenly overwhelmed by the aftertaste: a direct blow to the sinuses, a liberal dose of horseradish.

"Ah," I said, my eyes watering and my smile wavering. "They are delicious. What's that flavor?"

"Which flavor?"

"The unique, buttery one."

"Lard," my mom said. I wretched slightly, but managed to disguise it as a cough.

"Tell Oma Ilga that I love them," I said. I took another one and walked away. As I knocked on the door to my parents' room, I slipped it into my pocket.

So my great-aunt had decided to make cookies while I was gone. It was probably a gesture meant to soothe the angry, tumultuous household—though I didn't really know how much of the situation she understood. Probably all of it, I realized with a shock.

"Come in," my dad said. He was clearly not asleep. I entered the room to find him sitting at his desk—a little writing desk that they kept in their room in front of the window. He had managed to procure another bottle of bourbon. Probably it had been buried in the clothes hamper. He was drinking straight from the bottle. He'd taken off his sweatshirt; it was crumpled in a ball in the corner of the room.

"Are you okay, Dad?" I asked. I knew the answer to this, but I felt that I had to ask anyway. He didn't turn around in his chair.

"I was thinking about a squirrel," he said. After some time it became clear that he wasn't going to elaborate.

"A squirrel?" I said, trying to encourage him.

"Do you not ever think about a squirrel?" he asked. I started to reply but he cut me off. "You know, there is one squirrel that I can see from time to time out of this window. We are very high off of the ground here, so I do not know if it is the same squirrel, but I think it is. He runs in a very distinctive way." My dad took another swig of bourbon. Even after all these years of drinking, I was still surprised by his capacity for it. "I think to myself, What a pleasant squirrel. It is working hard, in my opinion. It has such a bushy and pleasant tail."

I shifted my weight from foot to foot. I didn't know what to say. I doubted that there was a grand metaphor at work here. My dad wasn't making any comparison between himself and a squirrel, or between me and a squirrel, or between our cousin Ivan and a squirrel. Though, come to think of it, Ivan did have puffy cheeks. I wasn't certain, but it seemed like I remembered him admitting a certain affinity for nuts.

"Dad," I said, "I have something I need to tell you."

His head snapped toward me. "Okay. Wait only one moment. Please help me to stand and then to sit on the bed."

I propped my hands under his armpits. They were entirely soaked with sweat—sweat that was cold to the touch. I steered him to the bed. He collapsed onto it and situated himself in a way that could not have been comfortable. He was still wearing his shoes, and his legs were strangely crossed and tangled with each other. His head hung at a precipitous angle.

"Okay," he said. "Now I am fine. Fire away."

I worried briefly that he wouldn't remember anything that I told him. That even if I confessed my part in the theft of the Monte Carlo, even if I described in detail my emotions for Hannah and the red energy of her lips, even if I profusely apologized and claimed that I never thought anything like this could happen, he'd forget it all by the evening. But then I remembered that my dad was a deceptive drinker. He loved alcohol's release, and he often exaggerated—even to himself— the effect that the bourbon was having on his body. Though he seemed in a disastrous state, he could very easily rally. By tonight, I knew from experience, he could inexplicably be standing in the kitchen, only slightly intoxicated, cooking us dinner and popping Tylenol like candy.

"I did it, Dad," I said. "I'm sure you know already. You probably already figured it out. But I did it. I stole the car and I'm sorry."

He nodded, made a disappointed noise with his mouth, and looked away. Then he sighed deeply. He ran his hand over his face.

"I need to smoke a cigarette," he said.

I was not a seasoned criminal. I was not rebellious enough to withstand the standard impulses of guilt that affect most people—and so my words took a great toll on me. Within seconds of confessing to my dad, I was lying on the bed and sobbing. I had no idea how much emotion had built up within me. There were not adequate words to describe how the anxiety left my body. It was a torrent, a flood, a deluge. There was no cliché strong enough for the way it exited my chest.

"Yuri, my darling," my dad said. Then, in a voice that sounded just like my mom's, *"Ai, bucina."*

He stroked my head with his hand. It felt heavy and thick, like a meaty club moving through my hair. Still, it was comforting. He continued stroking my head and reassuring me, telling me that it would be fine, that I had nothing to worry about.

It was strange, actually, that my dad reacted this way. When I'd imagined telling him that I was responsible for the theft of the car, I had only imagined his anger—profound and expansive—and I'd worried about shielding myself from it. But now, he was almost gentle. It was as if he knew, intuitively, that this was an important moment. Anger, for him, arose from frustration. This moved beyond frustration, somehow. On the roster of his life, it would be a moment that counted, that stood apart from the others.

"Don't you have any questions?" I asked, raising up and blowing my nose with the handkerchief he offered me. "Don't you want to know anything else? I'll tell you anything."

My dad struggled to sit on the edge of the bed. I helped him stand and walk in the direction he seemed to want to go. He stumbled over to the window, where he slumped his head against the glass. I couldn't see his face. I had no idea if his eyes were open.

"Are you okay?" I asked.

"Yes, I am okay," he said. "You go outside with your mother. You keep her company. I need to think of what to do now."

Room to room. I opened the door to my parents' bedroom and walked into the hall. I didn't feel like confronting anyone, so I slipped into my own room. Remarkably, it was unoccupied.

I was overwhelmed. I'd become a juvenile delinquent. I'd destroyed property and terrified innocent milk cows. My situation seemed hopeless. I looked up at my books—the short stories, the detective fiction, the Gothic novels, the comics, the poetry collections, the works in French and Spanish and German which I hoped to someday read. There were Harlequin romances and Hardy Boys mysteries, children's picture books and collections of fairy tales, *The Joy of Cooking* and *The Joy of Sex*. They were a substance of wonder, a carefully arranged and colorful set of ideas. I'd taken solace in the printed page for as long as I could remember.

My breath seized in my throat just looking at them. I loved my books. They'd always be there for me. Books were a constant. I stood up. The bones in my back made a rustling series of pops. I needed to get ready—I needed to prepare a face to meet the faces that I'd meet. I sighed. I opened the bedroom door. I entered the living room.

My mom sat by herself on the sofa. Oma Ilga sat with Eriks at the dining room table, sipping at a cup of tea and eating a horseradish cookie. She was reading a Latvian book of some sort. With a spasm of queasiness I realized that it was the book I'd left in the car—*Mazas Piezimes*, by Karlis Skalbe.

"What's wrong, Mom?" I asked. She'd been crying. I knew perfectly well what was wrong. No amount of baking could erase the fact that she'd heard my confession. She'd probably been listening at the door. Even if she hadn't been listening, the walls of our apartment were incredibly thin. She could have heard me from there—sitting on that sofa, staring at the wall above the television.

"What is wrong?" she said. She chuckled in a bitter way. "What is wrong? You are asking me what is wrong?" She refused to even look at me. This couldn't be a good sign, I figured. I was trying to imagine what to say next when the door to my parents' bedroom flew open.

My dad was singing, though I couldn't make out the words. It sounded vaguely like "I've Got Tears in My Ears," a favorite of his—a song that was written in 1949 by Harold Barlow:

> *I've got tears in my ears from lyin' on my back*
> *in my bed while I cry over you*

My dad had the bottle of Heaven Hill in his hand—though I noticed that it was now almost empty—and he had a huge grin on his face. The grin was infectious. Though my mom and I were both depressed, though we were dealing with a problem that seemed bigger than us, one that seemed like it could stretch infinitely tall and consume us and our little family completely—we couldn't help but smile, too. My dad staggered past Oma Ilga and Eriks, who could only stare.

He'd taken off his shoes. He was a barefoot moon of drunkenness, distended and luminous glowing white. He stood in the middle of the living room. He paused in front of the map of Eastern Europe. Over his shoulder, half-turning his drunken head, he said, "It's pretty damn far away, isn't it?"

I was stunned. Two contractions in one sentence. I started to say something but then he turned toward us, raising his arms gradually, mimicking the movements of a pirouette. When he was facing us completely, he said, "Would you like for me to do a dance for you, now?"

And before we could respond, he was dancing. It was, under any circumstances, a terrible dance. My mom and I found it amusing, though, and soon we were giddy with laughter. It was a release. My dad was happy with this reaction. He continued humming to himself and drunkenly staggering through the room. He came up to each of us and kissed us on the lips. He touched my mom's face when he kissed her, and smiled and ruffled her peppery hair. He opened the sliding glass door and walked onto the balcony.

"What a beautiful day," he yelled loudly, gesturing with a sweep of his hand to the sky. He took the last mouthful of liquor. "Empty," he said and shrugged. He set the bottle down gently on the deck.

"Be careful, Rudolfi," my mom said. He was wobbling noticeably, struggling to even stand on his feet. He smiled again at us, though this time his smile seemed a little different.

"I am normally careful, do you not think?" he said, and then, with one sudden motion, he kicked at the balcony rail, splintering the wood of several slats into a thousand tiny fragments.

My dad was never a violent drunk. This is why I didn't do anything, why I didn't rush out onto the porch to calm him down, why I didn't go out there and help bring him back into the house. I was too shocked to move, really, and even if I had moved, I wouldn't have known what to do.

Though we've never talked about it, I'm sure that my mom had some intuition of what he was going to do. I turned my head for a moment toward her, just for a moment, and I saw her stand from the couch and make a small strangling noise and reach out her right arm, reach for my dad—though he was at least ten or twelve feet away.

No, I thought.

Even as I turned back toward the balcony I could see his smile fade. A new, empty expression settled in its place. His voice was otherworldly.

"I am sorry," he said. "I love you both." He plunged backward through the air.

I cannot bring a world quite round,
Although I patch it as I can.

I sing a hero's head, large eye
And bearded bronze, but not a man.

Although I patch him as I can
And reach through him almost to man.

If to serenade almost to man
Is to miss, by that, things as they are,

Say that it is the serenade
Of a man that plays a blue guitar.

—Wallace Stevens, "The Man with the Blue Guitar"

part 3

15

monday, december 4, 1989
10:00 A.M.

I am not sure, even now, what happened next. I know that some part of me experienced the powerful, visceral urge to jump, too. To follow my dad over the edge of the balcony. To leap off and catch him, perhaps. I was sure he was gone. He'd reduced himself to an absence, a pure absence hanging over everything.

I know that I lurched toward the balcony, because next thing I remember I was standing at the open door, pressing my hand gently against its glass, as Eriks rushed past me to look over the edge. I also remember a tissue of female voices—all of them screaming.

It must have been only seconds after my dad fell, but of course it seemed like much longer. Time broke apart. Moments like this have always convinced me that thoughts move through an entirely separate and invisible world—one that is related to time, but not necessarily a part of it. This world might be a reflection of time—bound up with time, in the same way that a reflection is bound to the object it reflects.

As soon as Eriks and I came out of the stairwell I saw that my dad was alive. He was partially potted, in fact, in a swath of bushes near the base of the building. These bushes were blackberries, and they'd grown in an unkempt tangle beneath the balcony. I'd never really noticed them before. Now, I thanked God for them. I would bake the church a blackberry pie, I thought as I scrambled toward my dad. I would bake a whole vat of cobbler.

My dad was conscious and he seemed to be in a great deal of pain. I could see his right arm waving for help.

"Thorns!" he called out, and I was near him a moment later, gazing through the bushes at his sprawled body. I could see a sliver of his face.

His eyes looked desperate. He must have been in shock—his skin was pale and translucent as wax paper. "I cannot feel my legs," he said. "Oh, no, wait. Okay, I cannot feel one of my legs."

"Rudolfi!" my mom yelled as she, too, came out of the stairwell. She ran over toward the blackberries. She was frantic. She tried to wade through the bushes, but they were too thick and forced her to her knees. She knelt there on the grass, unsure what to do, a panicked look on her face. "You are alive, then, Rudolfi?" she said, asking her question without looking, asking it to the ground.

"Ai!" my dad yelled, by way of reply. He began cursing in Latvian again. "My back!" he yelled. "I am in the sticker bush!"

A crowd of people had gathered. Hammond was among them.

"Jesus," Hammond said. Then: "What happened?"

"He jumped," Eriks said.

"Jumped?" Hammond asked. "What? Why'd he jump? You mean *fell*. He *fell* off the balcony?"

"No," Eriks said, "he jumped. He jumped right into the air, like this." He mimicked my dad kicking the boards and then tumbling backward. He flung his arms in the air as he mocked him falling, and he wailed a little, too.

"My leg!" my dad called out. "Hello? Everybody? It is necessary to call the ambulance, in my opinion."

"I'll call 911." Hammond turned and disappeared around the building.

Sirens and flashing lights are never emotionally powerful unless they are coming for you. Then, they are terribly invasive, proof that you're suffering something unusual. The ambulance lights seemed to work their way into the substance of my eyes—into the irises. The same was true of the sirens. They felt like they were roaring inside of me, roaring outward from my chest and into the frigid December day.

The paramedics arrived and quickly cleared away the bushes, ripping them out of the ground by the handful, using their thick leather gloves to grasp the thorny plants. I tried to help where I could—hovering nearby and reassuring my dad that everything would be okay.

"Okay? I am broken, you idiot, like a Soviet clock!"

Only my mom and I accompanied him in the ambulance. Oma Ilga and Hammond and Eriks agreed to take the van and meet us at Milwaukee General. Ivan and Guna hadn't returned from their walk. In the confusion of the fall and the swarm of the EMTs, my mom and I forgot all about them.

The paramedics, for their part, were terribly earnest. They screamed at us; they screamed at each other; they were overflowing with urgency and a desire to make sure that my dad was okay. I was fairly confident he'd survive, though. His body, scarred and resilient and pickled by fifty years of drinking, was going to make it. In what (slightly damaged) condition he'd reappear—this, I didn't know. They asked my mom a battery of questions. Was he suicidal? Was he a threat to himself or others? Was he violent toward herself or her children? I couldn't bear to listen to her responses, which were wild and full of fear.

The EMTs had subdued my dad with some sort of an IV. He was asleep and breathing pure oxygen through a mask. His body was strapped firmly in place, with buckles securing his ankles and knees and hips and chest and shoulders. The collar they'd put around his neck made him look a little like a pet after an operation. Even if he'd wanted to (and he probably would have wanted to), he would not have been able to move.

"How does he look?" I asked one of the paramedics as we sped toward the hospital.

Just then my mom started sobbing and strained forward to touch my dad's face. She slipped her fingers under the oxygen mask and stroked his lips, which were tinged with pale blue at their edges.

"You rest, Rudolfi. You need to rest. You rest so you can get better."

"To be completely honest," the paramedic said to me, "I don't know." The paramedic was a young man—he couldn't have been much older than twenty-five. "He may have had blunt trauma to the skull or to his spinal column. They'll do CAT scans. It's troublesome that he can't feel his legs."

"Leg," I corrected.

He nodded and turned back to a screen that monitored my dad's heart rate and blood pressure. I was stunned by the level of automation inside of the ambulance. A bank of computer screens hung over us, crowding us into the narrow aisle. Everywhere I turned there was a keyboard of some sort, and I couldn't even begin to guess what many of them controlled. These were still the early days of the PC boom; to me, a computer-illiterate urban teenager, the ambulance felt a little like an extra from *The Empire Strikes Back*.

I looked at my dad, barely recognizable beneath the braces and buckles and tubes and the clear plastic oxygen mask.

He went, of course, directly into the ER. The nurses allowed my mom to accompany him everywhere—as they unloaded him from the ambulance, as they slotted him into his cubicle, as they hooked him up to a new series of machines. I was told to go sit in the waiting room.

The waiting room was a utilitarian area, furnished with a few round white tables and rows of bright orange chairs. These were easily the ugliest chairs I'd ever seen. Was there some law mandating that hospitals buy their furniture in ugly colors? Or was this simply the shade of the cheapest surplus fabric at the chair factory? A variety of sick people were slumped and seated and propped and squeezed into the chairs. Some were pale and silent and some coughed with tubercular fury. Others looked pained, or haggard, or generally down on their luck. One was visibly bleeding—his wine-colored blood leaked through an Ace bandage that was wrapped around his leg.

It was disgusting, really. I felt the overpowering desire to wash my hands. I looked at the walls, hoping for some reprieve. The walls were decorated with pamphlets. This actually reminded me a little bit of home. If I wanted to, I could learn about a variety of diseases and disorders. Why not? It would pass the time. I started reading *The Facts About Smoking*—a lively brochure complete with full-color illustrations. After a few moments, I was sick to my stomach.

I decided to switch to the magazines. Their covers were invariably wrinkled, the pages torn and folded from the attentions of numerous sick hands. What was going on, I wondered, behind the doors of the ER? Was he okay? I squirmed with anxiety and guilt.

Newsweek, I saw, had a story about Germany's pending reunification. I stared at the photographs, barely seeing them. There was a cast-iron Lenin, toppling to the ground, surrounded by a mob of cheering Germans. Someone had fastened a red blindfold over his head. People in the crowd held signs and banners and hung effigies of Honecker. One man, oddly, held a placard that said:

I Love American Ketchup!

He was off to the side, and somewhat turned away from the camera, so I couldn't make up my mind if he was really holding that sign, or if a photo editor at the magazine had just been bored and ahead of deadline. Or maybe I was hallucinating? I held the thin, slightly transparent page up to the light.

"Yuri Balodis?" someone said.

I turned around. A nurse hovered in the doorway with a clipboard. "Your mother asks that you be allowed to come visit your father," she said.

What a strange way to put it, I thought. As I was following the nurse to the hydraulic doors leading into the treatment rooms, Hammond and Eriks and Oma Ilga burst through the doors to the ER entrance and rushed over to me. I didn't have much to tell them, but I promised I would be back soon with news.

After the disorder of the waiting room, the ER itself seemed like an orderly paradise. The nurse led me down a well-lit, antiseptic hallway. "He's in here," she said, and pulled the curtain aside for me.

My dad still wore the oxygen mask. His eyes were closed. My mom stood at the side of his bed. She tried to smile and swept some of his gray-black hair from his forehead. She told me to sit down. A chorus of machines beeped and purred in the background.

"He is asleep," she said. She was whispering. I sat beside her. My dad was terribly depressing in his white gown. He looked sad and pale and utterly fragile. "He is going to be okay," my mom continued, still whispering.

"Why are you talking so softly?" I said.

"I do not want your father to wake up," she said.

I glanced at the IV that dangled from a hook beside his left arm. By the looks of it, my dad was heavily sedated. A marching band could have paraded through the ER and he wouldn't have twitched.

"What will happen if he wakes up?" I asked my mom, forcing my voice into a whisper.

She looked at me gravely. "He will be screaming about the bushes again."

I felt awful. I was ashamed—deeply ashamed—of the whole situation. I'd brought this on, hadn't I? It was my fault, really. I was the guilty one, not my dad. He was a victim.

Suddenly, I receded from it all, slipping slowly away from the scene. My eyes closed. The heat of the room surrounded me and I fell asleep—a thick, dreamless sleep. Immediately I felt my mom's hand on my shoulder.

"Please, Yuri, wake up. I need help with this paperwork."

I shook myself awake. There were, indeed, mountains of forms, all of them affixed to a ridiculously small clipboard. With her shaking hands and wild eyes, my mom was in no condition to concentrate on paperwork. I didn't actually feel much better. Still, I managed to sign waiver after waiver. I provided our names and our address and my parents' insurance information. The numbers aligned in little columns and stretched for pages. All of this precision—I thought—after such an imprecise act.

That night, my mom refused to leave the hospital. This was understandable. In some ways, I didn't want to leave, either. But my mom assured me that my dad would be okay—and the somewhat evasive nurses seemed to confirm this fact. So I walked out to where Hammond and my relatives waited. I told them my father would be okay and we drove home in near silence. What was there to say? Hammond asked for more information about my father's condition. I told him the little that I knew. Hammond nodded thoughtfully. He turned the volume knob on the tape deck. The van filled with the soft sound of Muddy Waters. I turned around to see Oma Ilga asleep against Eriks's arm.

We got home at eleven P.M. Hammond suggested that we all come to his place and have a nightcap. Eriks, and even Oma Ilga, immediately accepted. Even though the thought of sitting in that apartment was abhorrent to me, I said good-bye and retreated up the stairs. Once inside, I poured myself a glass of water and stood at the kitchen counter. Did I want a glass of bourbon? I knew that there were numerous bottles hidden all around the house. I could have found at least one of them. But I decided against it. Somehow I didn't feel up to drinking.

The apartment was empty for the first time in a week. It was also freezing. No one had bothered to close the door to the balcony. The wind moved in and out of the room, covering everything, rustling the curtains, disturbing the papers on the table. I walked directly to the phone. I dialed Hannah's number. Mercifully, she answered and not her father.

"Hannah," I said, my voice cracking, "there was another accident."

"What happened?" she asked. "Did you wreck another car?"

I sighed heavily into the receiver. "That's not funny," I said, and then the story came out—including that image, that terrible image, of my dad falling backward over the balcony rail. I talked with Hannah for hours, well into the early morning. It was soothing to talk with her; no matter what happened between us, I suddenly realized, she would remain my friend, someone with whom I could talk, somebody who would listen to me and offer her opinion. I turned the lights off and sat there in darkness. The only energy was the sound of her voice through the receiver—somehow more elegant in the glassy dark. She didn't judge me; she didn't offer advice; she didn't blame me for the fall. It was therapy, really. I felt tremendously grateful. I was full of longing for her presence, for even one brief lecture on the path of socialism in the world since 1917, or the joys of collectivization.

"I'm so sorry, Yuri," Hannah said. "Do you want me to come over?"

I looked around the room. Everything was a mess. The coffee table had been overturned; food was congealing on plates at the kitchen table. The balcony railing was in splinters. I felt the ache of exhaustion at the sides of my neck, in the weary muscles of my shoulders and my neck.

"No," I said. "You'd better not. I have to get some rest."

We said good-bye and Hannah hung up. I sat there, motionless, listening to the plaintive sound of the dead line.

A few minutes later—after I'd straightened up a little in the apartment—I walked into my parents' bedroom. I wanted to be in there. I wanted to be surrounded by the things that had, for so long, been comfortable and reliable and stable. I lay on their bed. I could smell each of them and it comforted me.

But I didn't want to fall asleep. I didn't want to dream. I had no idea what my unconscious mind might produce, and the thought of it terrified me. I stood and walked over to my parents' closet. My dad's sweatshirts were there, a whole row of them suspended from hangers. I selected one—a bright orange sweatshirt with a duck on the front—and walked over to the window.

I felt my dad's presence in this room. It was palpable. I felt like an intruder. He hung over everything, a mist of him, dispersed and omnipresent. Every surface I touched stung my hand with memory—burning memory, a sear of memory, memory in images and words. I was guilty. I'd caused him to fall. I'd caused his tumble over the balcony. He'd sacrificed himself to save me—it was the only way he could imagine getting out of our dilemma. My dad could have died—and it would've been my fault. The idea bit into my flesh. It ripped open my skin with its invasive teeth. It made my entire body itch. A flame of guilt seared along my backbone.

My parents had set up a little shelf of photographs—mostly photographs of me—but interspersed were photos of them, either by themselves or with each other: a photo of my mom in the park; a picture of my dad in front of a different apartment building, holding a key in the air, brandishing a glittering key and smiling—this was clearly their first American apartment.

Most of these were easy to decode. There were pictures of them at Niagara Falls, pictures of them at a Brewers game, photos in front of the Milwaukee Art Museum. There was a picture of my dad and me—one that was particularly difficult for me to look at. I must have been five or six years old, and I was trying to climb some sort of a playground structure. My dad stood there with his arms extended, an expression of concentration on his face. He was ready to catch me if I fell. I was ignoring him, of course.

I walked back to the desk where there was another photograph, one he'd taken from the box in the closet. It was a faded color picture—vintage 1964—and all of the colors had browned or dimmed away. It was also a little bit blurry, but in the center I could see my young parents, their faces quick and hopeful and shiny.

All at once, I felt ridiculous in the sweatshirt. It was way too big, first of all, but second, it felt almost like a desecration—I shouldn't have been rummaging through his things. But I needed it—I didn't think I could cope without it. Eventually, I did fall asleep.

I dreamed that I was on a tropical island. It was a beautiful tropical island, as far as tropical islands go, and the water was a dark, cobbler blue. I was by myself, of course, and I had a little hut just off the beach where I apparently lived. I could move between this hut and the beach simply by thinking about either destination. It was teleportation at its finest. My body was an almost invisible thing, a nuisance, really—well tanned but inconsequential. I was mostly just thought and ether.

Suddenly my dad was there. He had two coconuts in his hands.

"You can drink from these and it is delicious, in my opinion," he said.

Sure enough, he poked holes in the coconuts with a straw. Then he handed me one. "Try it," he said.

I sipped the coconut water. It was wonderful—sweet and salty at the same time. It was entirely refreshing.

"This is entirely refreshing," I said.

"You know what else," my dad said, "when we are done, we can use them for beach bowling."

"Beach bowling?" I said, and he showed me a long strip of oceanside sand, a strip that he'd groomed like a bowling alley, with ten sugarcane pins at one end.

As soon as I'd finished drinking the coconut milk, we went bowling.

He was great—an expert at the sport he'd invented—and he threw strike after strike. I was no slouch either, and I almost matched him shot for shot. Finally, we came to the tenth frame. Suddenly our scores were tied.

I was nervous, and it was my turn first. My initial shot only clipped five pins. My second shot was off-center, and took out an additional two. I stood aside, knowing my dad needed seven to tie, eight to win.

His first shot was uncharacteristically poor. He hit the pins straight-on, leaving the bowler's worst nightmare—a 7–10 split. Six pins were down and four were standing—two of them in each corner of the lane. Even so, all he needed was two pins. This was actually an easy shot; he just needed to aim at one side or the other.

"Now your father will show you the proper way to lose," my dad said, and smiled. He began moving forward, ready to hurl his coconut down the lane's sandy surface. I was standing to the side of his path, and as he passed me—his eyes focused on the distant sugarcane pins—I stuck out my foot. He tripped. He sprawled forward. The coconut flew into the air. He landed facedown on the beach.

I stood over him. He wasn't moving. I felt terribly powerful at that moment, but also terribly afraid. I couldn't tell if he was breathing, but I was afraid to touch him, afraid to roll him over. I hovered above him, paralyzed, transfixed.

I awoke with a shock. Eyes open. Heart thudding. The sun spiraled through the window. It was the first light of morning.

I stumbled into the empty hallway. I stood at the kitchen counter. The apartment was only marginally warmer. I didn't need breakfast. What I needed was something else, entirely. I needed to go back to Jack Baldwin Chevrolet. I needed to talk with Jack Baldwin.

But first I had to call the hospital. I punched the numbers into the phone, numbers my mom had written down and stuffed into the front pocket of my shirt. I felt a jab of panic as I waited for the operator to transfer me to his room. What if something awful had happened? What if, somehow, he'd died during the night? Things seemed okay— but then again, you never knew. He'd had a terrible fall. He might be fine one second and dead the next, the victim of some unseen internal injury.

"Hello?" It was a man's voice, and heavily accented.

"Ivan?" I said. "Is my mom there?"

I heard the shuffling of feet and the transfer of the receiver from one hand to the other.

"Hello," my mom said, "how are you doing this morning, *bucina*?"

"I'm okay. How is Dad feeling?"

"Well," my mom said, "he fell off of the balcony and nearly broke his neck. How do you believe he is feeling? I think he is feeling fairly lousy, in my opinion."

"But he's fine other than that? I mean, he's not any worse?"

I could hear her turn to look at him. I imagined him as I'd seen him the previous day—the oxygen mask, the gown, the IV. I shuddered. "No," she said. "He looks the same."

I nodded and told her that I'd be ready to come to the hospital in a few hours. I lied and said that I had to talk to a couple of teachers at school. I hung up and bundled myself into my dirty clothes. When was the last time I'd done a load of laundry? I made my way out of the apartment and back down the stairs.

The bus ride out to the dealership was longer than I remembered.

This was the third time in four months that I was making this trip, and the second time in the past week. It was Tuesday, the fifth of December, 1989. It was also nine A.M. The bus filled with commuters; it bore legions of workers to the fast-food restaurants in the suburbs.

This time, I entered Jack Baldwin Chevrolet through the front door. They hadn't repaired the display window, I could see—they'd merely boarded it up with sheets of plywood. This gave the dealership the feel of a construction site. I briefly wished that I'd brought my mom's hard hat.

The receptionist smiled broadly when she saw me. She was obviously unaware who I was. I decided to act confident—maybe this way I'd be able to conceal the nausea swelling up in my gut.

"I'm here to see Jack Baldwin," I said.

"And your name?"

"Yuri Balodis."

At the mention of my last name, the secretary's smile disappeared. She squinted at me, paused for a moment, and then looked down at her desk. She picked up her telephone receiver. She dialed a few numbers.

"Yuri Balodis is here to see you," she said quietly. She paused, listened. "I'll send him back, then, sir." She turned toward me, but failed to make eye contact. Instead, she seemed to concentrate on a point several inches above my right shoulder.

"Mr. Baldwin will see you immediately," she said. "Up the stairs and to the left." She turned partly away from me and pretended to begin some kind of work.

I walked up the stairs and along a carpeted hallway. Somehow, it seemed too silent. I decided that the dealership had double-padded the floor—so the salesmen could sneak up on customers and surprise them like hyenas.

Jack Baldwin's office was unmistakable. It had an enormous golden door. "The road to wealth," said a plaque next to his nameplate, "is paved with honesty." What exactly did that mean? I wondered, as I knocked on the metallic surface. Within moments I heard Baldwin's reverberant voice calling me into his office.

He was seated—as a head of industry should be—behind an enormous, glass-topped desk. He leaned back in his leather recliner, and a faint, sad smile haunted the margins of his face. His hair was carefully arranged on his forehead—it looked like a sculpture of hair, or possibly a wig, perfect and seamless. The smell of cigar smoke hung in the air. Sun came solidly through the broad windows.

"Yuri," he said, "good to see you again. I wish the circumstances were more pleasant."

"Me too," I said, sitting down in a chair near the wall.

"The police called us this morning," Baldwin continued. "I have to say, I'm deeply sorry about this turn of events. I'm very sorry, son, for what happened to your father." Suddenly Baldwin was standing. What was he going to do? Come around the desk and throttle me? Hurl me out of the window? Hold me upside down until I confessed on my father's behalf?

Instead, he merely walked to the corner of his office, where he kept a golf club on a stand. Baldwin grasped the club and walked to the middle of the room, where he assumed his golf stance—feet shoulder-width apart, knees slightly bent, head down. He swung. The imaginary ball arced high into the air, landing neatly on the imaginary green.

"Mr. Baldwin," I began. I'd decided—as soon as I'd awakened—what I needed to tell him. This time, I'd resolved, I was going to do the right thing. I launched into my explanation.

"Mr. Baldwin, my dad's innocent. He's a good man, sir. He'd never do anything stupid like this. He'd never steal and wreck a car. He loves me—and my mom—so much. He's got problems, sir, but—"

"Yuri—"

"No, don't cut me off. He's got problems, sir, but his whole life is dedicated to us. It's my fault. I'm the one who . . ." My voice failed.

Baldwin stared at me. His eyebrows had arched upward, and he seemed to suddenly be interested in what I had to say. I tried to rally the words, to get my tongue to engage and shape the language that would amount to a confession. But no words came out. I was so used to being cut off—so used to being preempted and forced into silence—that now I couldn't bring myself to speak. I felt like I was floating in front of Jack Baldwin's desk—a ridiculous, perspiring balloon—my face hot and sweaty and grotesque.

Baldwin switched the golf club from his right hand to his left. He shifted his weight slightly. He nodded encouragingly. His face seemed to indicate that he would accept my explanation, no matter what it might be. Suddenly, I realized that he possibly felt guilty, too. That he wished he hadn't handled the matter in such a personal way—driving my dad to the police station himself, getting so involved in the entire process.

The truth, I felt, was a necessity. I owed it to my dad. Within hours, I figured, he'd probably be awake again. Once the pain subsided, he would probably start worrying.

"I'm guilty," I said. "I stole the car."

Baldwin walked back across the office. He put the club back on its stand. He turned around. He seemed extremely interested in a speck of lint that clung to the lapel of his suit.

"That's surprising," he finally said. "How?"

So, for the third time in the past few days, I detailed the events of that night. I described, in detail, the way that I stole the keys, the way that I flung the rocks at the display window, hoping to confuse any potential investigators.

"But the alarm?" Baldwin said, at one point, cutting me off midsentence. "What about the code?"

"Ah," I said, scrambling to find a believable answer. "It was just a lucky guess."

He seemed to accept this, and he sighed again—a deep, rumbling sigh—and he came and sat down behind his desk. The silence was enormous. He swiveled his chair toward the window. For a while he just looked out of its glass at the parking lot. A boy was washing the row of cars closest to the building. He looked like an insect of some sort—a symbiotic organism—one that helped keep the cars clean. He darted from vehicle to vehicle with the soapy sponge and the hose. He was all efficiency, all eagerness for work. After some time, Jack Baldwin turned around.

"Come with me," he said, and led me out of the office.

What could I do? I followed. We walked down the corridor and turned left, moving away from the stairwell and the rest of the dealership. We walked to a second set of doors, doors marked:

EMERGENCY EXIT ONLY
DO NOT OPEN
ALARM WILL SOUND

We surged through these, as well. The doors, it turned out, led to the roof. My shoes made crackling noises as they moved along the phosphorescent roofing material.

Jack Baldwin towered over me. He had a strange expression on his face—a combination of sadness and anger, it seemed. My fears returned. I imagined him tossing me off of the roof. I'd fly in a tumultuous half-circle, my body spiraling and spinning through the air. I'd pop open on the pavement, my intestines leaping out of my stomach, spring-loaded and twirling like holiday ribbon. Jack Baldwin would, after all, be responsible for my death. And wasn't this fair, actually? I'd destroyed his property. I could never repay him. I had no money. I'd simply have to pay with my life.

Instead, Baldwin put his hand on my shoulder. "Yuri," he said, "do you see all of these cars?"

Of course I saw the cars. This was—I recognized—a rhetorical device. No answer was required. Listening to my dad's stories had taught me this much.

"There are five hundred and sixty-two cars on this lot," Baldwin continued, "as of this morning."

It seemed like an unusually large number. But how did he want me to react? Was I supposed to be impressed? In some way, I suppose, I *was* impressed. But I was also far too nervous to dwell on this emotion. Jack Baldwin, however, would not be deterred.

"Can you think of how much money that represents? It's quite a lot. Don't do the math."

I wasn't planning on it.

"The Monte Carlo itself," Baldwin said, spreading his hands open, and waving them in what seemed to be a conjurer's gesture, "is a fairly unimportant loss." He paused. His hands fell back to his sides. "At the end of today," he said, "we'll have sold ten or twelve cars. Tomorrow, we'll get ten or twelve cars delivered. We'll always have about five hundred and fifty cars on the lot." He looked at me hopefully.

"Do you see what I'm saying?"

I nodded hesitantly.

"I think so," I said. It was cold on the roof. I could feel the air saturating my clothes, freezing the moisture in my skin.

Jack Baldwin nodded. He was still looking contemplatively into the distance. A pigeon landed beside us. I looked down at its shape—a little gray smear of feathers in the bright morning. It was fluffy and fat. It pecked at the concrete, impaling, perhaps, some microscopic insects. Jack Baldwin shook his head. I'd have to go with him to the Mukwonago Police Department, he told me. We'd have to drive there right now.

The next few minutes were a blur. He led me back through the dealership; he told his secretary that he'd be in a meeting all morning; he ushered me out to his personal car, parked in the back of the building. I imagined my dad in this same situation. I imagined a taciturn Jack Baldwin, leading a member of the Balodis family toward the inexorable bar of justice.

We pulled into the police headquarters—a little, wooden building with ample parking and a brace of cop cars in front. The secretary knew Jack Baldwin by name. She whisked us into a windowless room. Within minutes, we were talking with two detectives. They fit my preconceived notion of what a detective should look like. Thin men— they both had mustaches and suspenders. They oozed procedural exactitude. One of them took notes with a red ballpoint pen. The other operated a handheld tape recorder. Jack Baldwin indicated that I wanted to make a statement. I nodded in compliance.

"I need to notify you, sir," one of the detectives said, "that you are not in custody at this time." He put down his pen. "So, you shouldn't feel that this is an interrogation."

I agreed. I didn't feel pressured to confess. The only compulsion I felt was personal. I needed to erase—if anything *could* erase it—the image of my dad, plunging backward over the balcony rail.

"But, as it is, sir," the detective continued, "we're happy to take your statement." They unfailingly referred to me as *sir*, something that I found both intimidating and annoying. It was a powerful word, a word that I didn't use in everyday life. It floated in the air between us, never fully absorbed like the rest of our language was absorbed, never dissipating completely.

I gave them the full account—the one I'd given Jack Baldwin, the one that entirely omitted my father's role in the affair. It had been my idea, I specified. I was the guilty party.

"And you were alone, sir?" the first detective asked at one point, leaning toward me in a disconcerting manner. I looked to the ground.

"Absolutely," I said. "It was just a midnight joyride."

When I said this, the detectives exchanged glances. They continued asking me questions, though, trying to get as much information as they could. My story weakened when I told them about the hours after the crash. In the effort to get no one else involved, I omitted all mention of Sara. They asked me, of course, how I got home.

"I called a taxi," I said.

"A taxi? That must have been expensive."

"Thirty-two dollars," I said. "Plus tip."

"And what company?"

"I don't remember," I said. "Honestly, sir, I was in shock."

Jack Baldwin sat beside me throughout the whole procedure. At one point, he held my shoulder, squeezing it to bolster my courage. He seemed apologetic and fully human. He clearly regretted these circumstances. He clearly wished that this had all turned out differently. When I finished talking I sighed deeply, a shabby sigh that seemed to carry with it all of my anxiety. I felt utterly debased and depleted.

"What happens now?" I asked.

"Now, sir, we have to read you your Miranda rights." He turned off the tape recorder. "We have to place you under arrest so that you can be charged with a crime."

I felt emotion rise through me. I was so terribly embarrassed. It was humiliating, really, to be sitting here and taking responsibility for such a stupid—if slightly beautiful—series of actions.

"What crime, specifically?"

The detective answered, without a pause: "Wisconsin State Statute 943.23. Operating a vehicle without owner's consent." He pulled on the elastic of his suspenders, imperceptibly raising the waistline of his pants. "This, of course, doesn't take into account the destruction of personal property."

They called my parents at the hospital. They had no choice. Though I begged and pleaded, though I promised to sit in jail indefinitely, willing to endure anything except this phone call, they didn't listen. My mom took it well—all things considered—and she showed up at the station in a few hours. Together with my mom and Hammond and Jack Baldwin, I set up a status conference with the district attorney. No one was overly emotional. They were all exhausted. Jack Baldwin eventually excused himself, leaving with a nod and a terse wave from the doorway. The assistant district attorney set my conference date for February—toward the end of my junior year at Alexander Hamilton. Finally, at four in the afternoon, after an exhausting battery of paperwork and a small fee for the paperwork, the Mukwonago Police Department released me into my mother's custody.

Hammond and my mom dropped me off at the apartment. I told her that I needed some time to myself, that I needed to think things over before I saw Dad again. In reality, I just wanted to be alone. I wanted to surround myself with anything familiar—with my room and my clothes and, most of all, my books. When I got inside, I went straight to my room. Without thinking about it, I ripped dozens of books from my shelves. I piled them around my body—stacks and stacks of books—arranging them in a full circle. I opened the novels and let the deluge of sentences spill over me. Perfect, precise sentences, sentences that sang and resonated and rang with the solace that only well-structured language could provide.

> If you use enough elbow grease even the coarsest wood gets to look like ivory. Warm it and polish it with your hand till it glows like a jewel.
>
> —*Years of Hope*, Konstantin Paustovsky

I lowered my face to the books, inhaled their musk, lost in the sad energy of my day, swept into remembrance of my dad and the feel of the wind over my face in the stolen convertible.

> He drove his Cadillac under the glittering sun. Shadows that might have been cast by all the peoples of the earth flickered over it. He was an American builder and millionaire. The souls of millions fluttered like spooks over the polish of the great black hood.
>
> —*Humboldt's Gift*, Saul Bellow

I wanted nothing more than to sit with my dad on the balcony, listening to his stories and sipping a fiery glass of bourbon.

> *When I thought of death, and I thought of it as soon as darkness enveloped the room, the thought unwound itself, like a roll of black silk thrown from a fourth-floor window.*
>
> —*Garden, Ashes*, Danilo Kis

I wanted there to be redemptive power in these words, in these small black rows of words, arranged in such a carefully and perfectly geometrical pattern on the page. What else was this orderly?

> *And the sky. It will be a solemn sky, she had thought, it will be a dusky sky, turning away its cheek in beauty. But there it was—ashen pale, raced over quickly by tapering vast clouds. It was new to her. The wind must have risen.*
>
> —*Mrs. Dalloway*, Virginia Woolf

I heard a knock at the door. I stood up, still holding a book in my hand. The knock came again and I dropped the book on the kitchen counter. I hoped it was Hannah—the previous morning she'd offered to drop by. I opened the door. It was Eriks.

"Hey, man," he beamed. "Would you like to have a nice, refreshing Pabst Blue Ribbon?" Eriks proceeded to tell me the story of how he'd bought a six-pack of Pabst at the Pick N' Save. He'd bluffed his way past the clerk by refusing to speak English. At one point, he told me, the manager had been involved. Eriks had yelled at them in Latvian and Russian—calling them vile names and invoking the curse of Stalin upon them. They'd sold him the beer, he claimed, just to get him out of the store. I wondered, for a moment, how much of the story was true.

"Your mother told me that you would be feeling lonely," he said, and walked over to the window and pulled aside the curtains. Light tumbled into the room, a broad panel of light, one that lit his edges, gave him a holy appearance, a halo. I remembered photographs I'd seen of medieval illuminated manuscripts. Was this a vision of a saint, sent from my books or from the branches of my hedge maple—plummeting to earth in a time of crisis to offer a token of the divine? "I want to be here for you," Eriks concluded.

We went to the kitchen and sat down at the table and began drinking the beer. We talked about some stupid small things. I told him about the police department. He'd already been briefed, it seemed, by my mom. He nodded and smiled and was quite empathetic. I felt the alcohol in my body. It was a relief to let go of my worries. It was a lightness, almost like a surge of helium.

Eriks looked vaguely hopeful, the way someone might look, I thought, if they were expecting to hear a secret, or listen to a favorite song on the radio. Suddenly I was aware of his breathing, of the simple mechanics of his lungs and his throat and his mouth. I could feel the entirety of my own skin. It seemed to vibrate slightly, to pulse with new animation, new possibility. I watched him talk. He was almost mesmerizing—sitting there and talking and gesturing with the can of Pabst.

I leaned toward him. We kissed.

The kiss was tentative at first, gentle, much slower and more constrained than kissing Hannah. His lips had a rough texture, not abrasive but not totally smooth, a little—I thought—like the skin of a Bosc pear. His breath was slightly sweet and beery. I reached out and took his hand. I held it in mine, tracing the lines of his palm with the tip of my finger. I rubbed his palm, pressing its bones and its tendons and its smooth skin. Then, I kissed his hand. My lips brushed against the can of Pabst.

"But I love Hannah," I said.

"Me too," Eriks said. He kissed me again.

We sat at the table together for some time. We kept kissing, delirious in the sensation of it. He was—I remembered—my second cousin. This was exactly the kind of relationship, I realized, that typified my unfortunate physical career. An affair with a bisexual relative? Why not add it to the list? I was, after all, an omnivorous reader. Why not be omnivorous in other respects?

We kissed for ten minutes. I felt an overpowering urge to pull off Eriks's clothes, to take him into the bedroom and fling his body onto my book-covered floor. But then the phone rang. It was my mom. How much time did I need for myself? she asked. My dad wanted to see me.

She wanted to see me. Hammond and Guna and Ivan and Oma Ilga wanted to see me. "Is Eriks there?" she asked.

"Yes," I said. I hung up and walked over and sat on the couch next to him. The sun was setting in a smudge of bright yellow light. If I closed my eyes, I could imagine that sunset consuming me, could imagine my body burning away, turning into a tiny handful of carbon. Each particle, I realized, could float away with even the smallest amount of wind.

16

tuesday, december 5, 1989

Eriks and I went to the hospital that evening. Neither of us wanted to talk about what had happened, and so the crush of relatives and medical procedures was a strangely comforting development. I tried to understand why I'd been so powerfully attracted to him—sitting there at the kitchen table—and what it was that I was feeling, a mixture of elation and confusion and relief. As often as I could, I looked furtively over at the side of his face, trying to distinguish his emotions from his appearance. He seemed just like he always seemed—smirking slightly at the unseen ironies of America—bemused, in an imperial sort of way.

When we got to the hospital we found that my dad had been transferred out of intensive care. He was now resting in a recovery ward, and we were free to visit him at once. We clustered around his bed. He was groggy and not terribly communicative. His speech was slightly slurred. My mom pulled me aside.

"He looks okay, right?" she asked. She looked nervous.

"Sure," I lied. "He looks fine."

She nodded. She seemed poised on the edge of something. Then, without warning, she started sobbing. She hugged me close to her body. I shook with the force of her sadness. She bit into the flesh of my shoulder, then backed off slightly.

"I am sorry to bite you, *bucina*," she said, and sighed and turned back to my dad.

Thankfully, my dad had his own room. As it was, we all barely fit inside. Everyone was talking, and the tumult spilled out into the rest of the hospital. I looked around. Ivan and Guna had been at the hospital with my parents since hearing the news from neighbors when they returned home from their walk that awful night. They looked the same as always—large and imposing and fairly noisy.

After some time, Guna walked over to me and wrapped me in her arms. Her body was voluminous, and I clung to it, letting my hands sink into the soft flesh of her forearms. She didn't bite me. Her hair smelled like apples.

I stood back and tried to gather my composure. I was aware that all of them were staring at me. "Come with us out into the lounge," she said, and suddenly Ivan and Guna and Eriks and I were leaving my dad's room and making our way to the lounge.

"Would you like a drink?" Ivan asked as soon as we sat down. He pulled a bottle of gin from beneath the flap of his coat.

Though it was the last thing I wanted, though my heart sank at the very thought of it, I remembered my dad's bravado, and the pleasant way he would say, "I could use a drink," even when it was clear that a drink was the last thing he could use.

"Sure," I said. "I could use a drink."

"Of course you could," Ivan said. "I'll be back in only a few moments."

Ivan had apparently learned the layout well enough to know where all of the vending machines were located. He soon returned with four cans of Canada Dry club soda and four paper cups. He mixed drinks for everyone. We sat there in the lounge, exchanging stories.

I drank one gin and soda. Then I drank a second gin and soda. Then I drank a third gin and soda. Everything became much less painful. I actually enjoyed the slightly bubbly taste of the Canada Dry, which Ivan told me could only be found in one vending machine. It seemed the head of the hospital drank cans of club soda and this machine was outside of his office.

We talked for a while about the circumstances of the fall. We agreed that my dad would probably recover—after the bones in his leg had healed. At this point, Guna took my hand in hers. She had something important to tell me, she said, about her family's visit to America.

"Mamu!" Eriks said, his voice scolding. "Wait."

"No," I said. "Don't worry. I know all about it." I told them that I knew that the cultural exchange was over. I told them that I knew all about the speaking tour, about the parameters of her family's visit to the United States. I told them that I understood why they wanted to stay. I told them that I expected that they wouldn't leave. I didn't know what would happen in the next few weeks, but whatever happened, they were always welcome. "My dad will say the same thing." I struggled to keep my voice level. "Really, it's no big deal." They rushed at me, hugging and kissing me and each other. I knew the relief they were feeling. A guilty secret is a burden.

My priorities had shifted dramatically. A short time ago I'd been longing for them to leave. Now I was grateful for their presence. They felt like family. They *were* family. A significant portion of them—two out of four—had slept in my bed.

For the rest of that week, we took shifts at the hospital. My dad was conscious, and alert—but he seemed a little confused, and his speech was slurred at times. The doctors told us that he'd had a small stroke, in all likelihood, when he hit the ground. He'd also badly bruised his spinal column and slipped a disc in his back. He had numbness in his left leg, and the neurologist said that this was undoubtedly a result of the fall. Something—they named several Latinate possibilities— was pressing against a nerve. They would like to operate to relieve the pressure.

But my dad was stubborn.

"How can they know what is inside of me?" he demanded, some of his old strength coming back. "I am the person who knows best what is inside of me." Though he must have known that this was a ridiculous thing to say, he refused to compromise. He hobbled gruffly around his hospital room, intent on somehow fixing himself without surgery.

On his fourth night in the hospital, my dad left his bed in the middle of the night; my mom awoke to find his bed unoccupied. She panicked. At first she thought he'd died and been carted out while she was asleep. Then she called the nurses. The nurses panicked. They searched everywhere. Finally, my mom discovered him in the cafeteria— talking with the workers as they prepared the day's meals.

"What are you doing?" my mom demanded when she found him. "I have been so worried—running up and down the hospital looking for you."

"What is wrong, Mara? Do not be so angry, my plump darling wife. I was merely offering advice to the cook on how to make the borscht."

How could she argue? There, on the day's dry-erase menu, along with the turkey sandwich and the peach cobbler and the lemon sole, was borscht. He'd seen the sign and waited for the cooks to arrive. He was an expert, after all, in the field.

That night, however, ended his rogue hobbling. The doctors were adamant: stay in bed or ride in a wheelchair. Period.

After six days of this he was discharged. If the hospital had operated on a demerit system, I am certain that his discharge would have been dishonorable. Hammond set my dad up in the main room of his down-stairs apartment. Medicare provided an adjustable hospital bed. It went right next to the patio door—so that my dad could have a view of the parking lot and the street.

In order to go anywhere my dad had to use his wheelchair. It was all glittering chrome finish and discomfort, and my dad hated it and cursed at it and begged God for deliverance from the foul contraption. But the break in his leg was a drastic one. He'd shattered his tibia and snapped his fibula in two places. The impact had crushed the medial malleolus and the lateral malleolus. The bones had to regenerate. Any weight on the leg—even accidental—could break it again.

Despite this, my dad still wanted to live an active life, and—within certain parameters—I didn't blame him. He was a little disillusioned that the American medical system could not work miracles and he took refuge from this disillusionment in the city of Milwaukee. We took him to the bratwurst festival, to the jazz and blues festival held on the shore of Lake Michigan. Eriks and I loaded him onto bus after bus, struggling with the chair. Though the Milwaukee County Transit Authority claimed to be handicapped accessible, actually negotiating the bus system was a difficult, time-intensive process. Dad had to be raised onto—and lowered from—the bus on a hydraulic platform, so invariably, he would become impatient and embarrassed, which would cause him to issue a loud string of Russian slurs, cursing his luck, and the bus, and the driver, and all of the passengers. No one, of course, paid any attention. For all they knew, he was aggressively thanking them for their patience. The whole thing was made palpably disgusting by the scent of my father's cast, which had a sweet smell about it, almost like rotting fruit. He seemed to enjoy my expression whenever I had to—gingerly, so gingerly—move the bulk of his leg.

One afternoon, in the days following his discharge, the phone rang. My dad happened to be sitting next to the receiver—almost as if he'd been waiting for the call—and he answered. What followed was a brief conversation, one which he struggled to keep as cryptic as possible. I was reading on the floor in front of the television, as usual. I tried to understand the conversation without lifting my head; I tried to appear as uncaring as possible, so as not to draw my dad's attention. After a few moments, he said:

"It's all settled, then," and he hung up the phone.

He seemed pleased with the conversation, and he spent some time making small noises of satisfaction—a litany of noises that I'd come to know over the years. He sucked the air from his cheeks; he clucked like a hungry hen; he cracked his knuckles with imperious pleasure. Then he rolled the wheelchair over toward me, threatening, for a brief moment, to break my own leg.

"I have, for you, Yuri, something important to say."

I was nervous and apprehensive. My court date was scheduled for the new year—toward the end of February. This impending collision with justice made me jumpy and perpetually nervous.

"I believe," my dad said, "that it is important for you to have a little punishment, my darling." He squinted and nodded in a slow, sagacious way. "I have just spoken with Jack Baldwin. We have come to a further arrangement that will, I believe, be constructive for everyone involved."

While I lay there on the carpet, my dad outlined the plan for what he termed "your little punishment." His absence from Jack Baldwin Chevrolet had created a paucity of cleaning employees; it also meant that our family's income was severely limited. So, in order to solve both of these problems, I was to go—two nights a week, both Friday and Saturday—to the dealership, where I would work as a janitor. This punishment, he maintained, would only last as long as it took for his leg to heal.

"But, Dad," I asked. "How will I know what to do?"

"My darling Yuri," he said. "This is simplicity, itself. I will simply tell you instructions. You can take notes, perhaps. It will be such a wonderful opportunity."

So, over the next few days, I was treated to a series of—sober—lectures. My dad instructed me on how to clean the service bays and replenish the bottled water and vacuum the sales cubicles. He specified which cleaning solutions to use for the windows, and how to get oil stains out of concrete. And I took notes. Copious notes. Notes that—it turned out—were mostly useless, since Jack Baldwin always assigned a second janitor to accompany me when I worked.

This is how I became—at age sixteen—a night janitor at Jack Baldwin Chevrolet on weekends. Unlike my time selling the *Socialist Worker*, however, this job was real. It was mostly numbing and tedious and hard on the back. My ligaments and vertebrae ached—punished by the slab concrete floors. Clouds of cleaning solution seared my nasal passages; the tips of my fingers chafed pink from the Borax; I learned to discern good steel wool from cheap steel wool simply by holding it in my hand; my world, all in all, became a much cleaner place. And of course it's disingenuous to suggest that I changed, somehow, at one specific time, on a certain day in December. But I did realize—in part by going to that dealership and mopping the floors—the full measure of my father's sacrifices for me. And I still feel, today, that he was meant to live a life different from the one that he lived. I certainly could imagine another, more sober, life for him. But then he wouldn't have had that thing he savored—the visceral burn of the bourbon—in his mouth.

One morning just after Christmas, I returned from Jack Baldwin and stumbled into the apartment. I sat at the kitchen table, dazed. It was a beautiful, sunny December day, cold but clear. The sun cast a pale light over everything, giving the buildings of our neighborhood a new, almost refreshing illumination. Suddenly, I was struck with an idea: Why should I go directly to bed? Instead, I decided that I'd go for a walk down to the edge of the lake, where the piers punctured the water with their great metal stanchions covered in a skin of ice. I put on my coat and my gloves. As I stood at the door, Eriks called out to me from the living room, where he slept.

"Wait, I'll go with you," he said.

"You're awake?" I asked, surprised.

"How could anyone sleep?" Eriks said. "You walk like a bear through the kitchen."

I agreed, happy for the company. We walked down North Jefferson to East Park, and then cut over toward North Harbor Drive. The edges of the lake were frozen, and these edges groaned and sighed with a low, muffled intensity. Waves pounded up through the ice, percussive and consistent, a solemn symphony.

"It sounds remarkable," Eriks said, clearly delighted.

As we walked, I told Eriks that I wanted to thank him. He and Ivan were making everything much easier. Eriks looked surprised. He took out his pack of cigarettes. He'd long ago run out of the Soviet brand he preferred. Now, he'd switched to Lucky Strikes—short, stubby cigarettes that were perfectly symmetrical and filterless. I found the Lucky Strikes unusually powerful, but I suffered them with dignity, enduring the burn in my lungs with bravado.

He lit his cigarette as we walked, saying that it was nothing, that it was the least they could do. Living with us was a temporary situation, he said, a necessity for the immediate future. He just wanted to help in any way that he could. Soon, Guna would start at Marquette as a lecturer, and this would help the financial situation. Eriks was looking for a job. He'd applied on Friday to the Tropic Banana Company.

We walked along the lakeshore and talked about his plans for the future. After he got a job, he told me, he'd save the money to bring the other members of his band to the United States. Volcano of Love would surely become massively popular. He couldn't think of any obstacles in their path. He'd bring his brand of Eastern European rock 'n' roll to the American masses. They'd thank him and realize what they'd been missing in their cultural isolation.

I doubted, of course, that this would happen. But what I didn't doubt was his passion. We stopped walking, stopped and looked out over the ice. He lit a second cigarette. He offered me one. I took it and leaned toward the flame of the lighter. As I inhaled the first sweet smoke I looked up and saw that he was staring at me—his palm still cupped around the flame of the lighter. His eyes were unusually bright in the morning light, unusually bright and almost ethereal.

I retreated into the cloud of smoke from my cigarette and thought about Eriks. I wondered about my feelings for him. On the one hand, I was carnally, powerfully attracted to women, to Hannah, to the idea of the other gender, the opposite gender, distant and unknowable, a fascination. But maybe mine was some other, vague, as-of-yet unnamed sexuality. A confusion of desires—a gray zone—a sexuality that was drawn to Eriks's magnetic exuberance. I remembered the passion I'd felt for him; it hovered in my memory, palpable but blocked.

We repaired Lincoln Quesnell's barn. Ivan and Eriks were skilled builders and, with my earnest help, they fixed it immediately, fitting new boards for the wall and bracing the ceiling with a series of extra supports. We waited to paint the barn, though, until a weekend in late January, a weekend when my whole family—even my father—could gather and watch the paint go up. The bright red color spread gradually along the grain of the wood. It was soothing to participate in this progress, a steady progress of color, and our families stood there for hours in the cold January day, sipping coffee and watching us. I had a sense of closure, a sense that wasn't dependent on my upcoming status conference with the Mukwonago district attorney. Whatever punishment I would receive—anywhere, my dad told me, between one and two years of probation—I felt that this experience of watching the barn become whole again was the closure I needed. As I worked, I could smell the scent of oil and gasoline, faint but still present, mixed in with a milky bovine odor and the rich smell of the hay.

Many people have pleasant memories from their childhood. Bathed in the gentle light of nostalgia, they remember family cookouts or nights at the movies. In these memories, they go places or do things with their parents—and the world has soft edges, and the light is lemon colored and speckled with dust. Since these memories are not mine, I can only speculate on the many ways in which they must be pleasant, and buoyant, and sustaining. My memories, of course, are slightly different.

Sometimes, when I was younger, I used to close my eyes and wander around our apartment. I took a certain joy in reaching out and touching familiar things: there was the carefully framed Toyota Camry advertisement, there was the familiar static of the television screen, there was the smell of garlic and butter and bourbon. Things were entirely predictable. I could imagine that if somehow all of us were to disappear, if one day the world awoke to our absence, these things would somehow remain. Perhaps dust would accrue, perhaps yellow mildew would accumulate in the corners of the advertisements, but still, our solid possessions would endure. The carpet would last forever. The drywall was eternal. The balcony if left entirely to itself would stand and stand and stand, a monument to the lives we'd lived on its span.

17

Friday, may 4, 1990

The events of that fall were tremendously emotional—they were, quite simply, some of the most remarkable days I'd had, then or since. But as my dad recovered, slowly letting the bones in his leg heal, I still felt like I was absorbed in the plot, like I was *in medias res*, in the middle of the thing, itself. My emotional loyalties veered from Eriks to Hannah and back again. I had no framework for what happened to me that fall. I needed something to delineate the past from the present, to mark off one segment of my days, and begin another.

Then—on a Saturday afternoon in late spring—Hammond assembled the whole family in his apartment. He told us that he had an announcement to make. He was animated and excited. There was a narrow line of sweat on the side of his face, and he kept tapping his foot on his hardwood floors. He cleared his throat and straightened his sport coat and reached out his hand to Oma Ilga.

"Ilga and I," Hammond said, his voice cracking, "have decided to get married."

I was stunned. Then I thought back to the first days that the Ozolinsh family had spent with us. I'd sensed an attraction between Ilga and Hammond from the beginning. Despite the language barrier between them, they'd managed to communicate and seemed to understand each other. This was more than I could say for myself and Hannah, or myself and Eriks, or even my parents. Hammond looked almost noble in his brown sport coat and green-and-yellow checkered shirt. He stood in his living room and took great pleasure in telling us that they were in love, and that he believed that he and Ilga had waited their entire lives to meet. He said that it was amazing, when you thought about it. I nodded. It was amazing.

"It's almost like a vegetable soup," Eriks said. I was unsure exactly how it was like a vegetable soup, but I just nodded happily.

Hammond and Ilga, it turned out, had both been married before. Hammond's wife had divorced him after the Second World War. "I came back from the war and I was jumpy," he eventually told me. "She didn't like jumpy."

"That's it?" I'd demanded. "That's all? I thought it'd be worse than that."

"It was five years of pure agony," Hammond had said. "By my count that's fairly awful."

Ilga's husband had died in Stalin's 1949 purges of Latvian farmers and intellectuals. These losses had bonded them, as had the ensuing forty years of loneliness they'd both experienced. "Besides that," Hammond confided in me, "she's great looking for an old lady."

Hammond and Ilga decided—with the help of Guna and my mom—to have a traditional Latvian wedding. Because of a lack of money, they also decided to go to the Justice of the Peace, and then hold the reception in a public park on the waterfront.

The ceremony was short but well attended. Somehow word had spread that a seventy-five-year-old couple were to be married on the afternoon of May 4. The judge's chambers couldn't accommodate the crowd of well-wishers. Eriks and I barely had room to stand. The *Milwaukee Journal-Sentinel* had a reporter on the scene and, of course, *he* got a seat.

When the judge pronounced Hammond and Ilga man and wife, an enormous cheer rose from the audience. Flashbulbs cascaded around the room. The bride and groom kissed each other gently on the lips.

The friends and family adjourned to the park. Hannah looked particularly good in a bright red cotton dress—a dress that was far too thin, I thought, for the weather. There were a number of rituals to attend to, and Guna outlined—for me—a specific set of responsibilities, none of which included drinking champagne. I was deeply disappointed. Wasn't this the best part of a wedding? Free champagne?

My dad sat there in his wheelchair, quite content to watch the ceremony and sip at a bourbon and soda. From time to time he would tell a story, or talk with someone who happened to come by. But for the most part he sat there and smiled, looking generally pleased with the spectacle that surrounded him.

First, there was the *mitcosana*, something that I could barely pronounce. This was an interesting process, and one that, I had to admit, captured the spirit of the joy of a wedding. Certain factors, however, complicated this particular *mitcosana*.

Typically, in this ceremony, the bride and groom sat in chairs made from birch saplings. Since we didn't have an abundance of birch saplings at our disposal, we settled for the folding chairs from Hammond's apartment. The wedding guests, according to tradition, then lifted the chairs and heaved the newly married couple up into the air. Everyone cheered as they ascended; everyone held their breath as they came down.

But the objective was not to unseat the young lovers. Instead, the heave was supposed to be gentle, and it was supposed to be repeated a number of times.

"How many times?" I asked Ivan.

"Normally, it is done as many times as the groom is old."

"Wait," I said. "Do you mean years? As many *years* as he's old?"

Ivan looked at me. For a moment, his face was grim. Then we both started laughing.

So we compromised. Though Hammond and Ilga were not heavy, the most we could manage was twenty heaves. Eriks and Hannah helped us, as well. "People got married younger in the past," Ivan said, panting for breath. My shoulders burned for hours. To this day, I don't think that my rotator cuff has fully healed.

Next, there was the breaking of the plates. The bride and groom each took a plate. Then they threw their plates down on a rock. The number of pieces into which the plates broke represented the number of children that a couple would have. Again, in our situation, there were certain difficulties.

"We can always adopt," Hammond said.

"No, wait," my mom said. She had a solution. "I brought plastic plates!" she exclaimed. The problem was solved.

Then there was the matter of the mitten-toss. The bride, Guna informed us, had to stand in her kitchen, close her eyes, and throw a pair of woolen mittens over her shoulder. If the mittens landed on the stove, then she would be a good cook. If they landed on the floor, then she would never learn even the simplest culinary technique.

Guna had brought the mittens. They were quite nice actually, and had a bright red and blue pattern. Of course, we were also in a public park. "I know what to do," my mom said.

She walked over to a nearby hot dog vendor. He was a middle-aged man, balding and slightly portly. I watched her talk with him, watched her smile and laugh and point to us all. In five minutes she was back. She was carrying a hot dog, which she handed to me. "Is okay," she said. "He will let Oma use his stovetop."

So, off we went to the hot dog stand where Ilga flipped a pair of mittens over her shoulder. They landed in the middle of the grill. Everybody cheered, even the hot dog vendor. Nobody thought to take the mittens off the heat. By the time someone did, they'd been badly charred.

"They look slightly overcooked," Ivan said.

Finally, there was the matter of the garland of flowers. This was presented to the bride by the mother-in-law. The bride was supposed to refuse it three times, and then, on the fourth offer, accept it. The reasons for this were murky, but Guna insisted it had to do with luck. Hammond objected, though. "My mother," he said, "God bless her, passed away sixty years ago."

"I can do it, Hammond," Guna offered.

After some convincing, Hammond relented.

"This is all provisional," he said. "But I like it, anyway."

By this time I was sitting on the grass. I'd participated in the lifting of the chairs and I was now free to sip champagne. I watched as Guna offered the garland to Oma Ilga—once, twice, three times.

The wreath itself was beautiful. It was the wreath from our wall, but Guna had added to it over the past few days, laboriously winding forget-me-nots among the stalks of wheat. The sunlight seemed to collect in its curves and on the edges of the light blue flowers.

Guna offered it to Ilga for the fourth and final time. Ilga, of course, accepted. But as Guna went to place it on her head, a gust of wind blew the flowers into the air. They twirled, caught for a moment in a suspension of sunlight, and settled directly on my dad's legs. He shook his head and struggled to stand. Putting one leg in front of the other—laboriously—he walked over to Ilga and placed the flowers on her gray head. For the second time that day, we burst into spontaneous applause.

That night, we played Scrabble in Hammond's apartment. Eriks had decided that this was the best way for him to obtain fluency in the English language. This, combined with old black-and-white movies. We'd rent movies in bulk from the Pick N' Save, and we'd set up our television and Betamax player downstairs. We'd watch Audrey Hepburn and Rock Hudson and play Scrabble. I'd revel in the slumber party atmosphere.

On this night, however, we stuck to Scrabble. Hannah was there, too. We hadn't solved our relationship in any satisfying way. We oscillated between friendship and passion. I knew, absolutely and conclusively, that I would love her forever. But what she thought about me—that was an entirely different matter. Just before midnight, we found ourselves alone together, briefly, in the kitchen.

"I know it's ridiculous," I said, "but I really do love you."

"It's amazing, Yuri," she said, and laughed. "You're so perfectly typical."

Though I wondered what she meant by this, I suppressed my anger.

"Typical?" I said. "How am I typical?"

She smiled. "How am I supposed to know if I love you?" she said. "We're so incredibly young."

We changed the subject. We decided it had been a beautiful wedding. Hammond and Ilga had already left—of course—in Hammond's van. They'd headed for their honeymoon in the Florida Keys. We rejoined the rest of the family in the living room. I sat in front of my Scrabble tiles. My dad thought that the ceremony had been full of integrity and good feeling and tradition.

"What I loved," my dad said, "was how everyone who was crying was also happy. This was perfect, in my opinion."

I nodded. I stretched out my legs, looked at my tiles. I had seven vowels and no consonants. Damn.

"We did not have a lot of money," my mom said, "but still it was pleasant."

"I agree," Guna said.

"I agree, as well," Ivan said.

"I also agree," Eriks said. "We were broke, but—rock and roll—we had a good time."

Sitting there in the living room, looking at the innovative and burgeoning game board, I remembered something that my dad would say from time to time. I looked over at him. He was concentrating on his Scrabble tiles. His lips moved slightly, struggling to imagine English words.

"There is an old Latvian proverb," I could hear him saying, "that every good story has at least one bad joke."

Soviet Humor, Simply Only for You

A Soviet citizen walks into his local post office. He is clearly angry. "These new stamps of Stalin are completely defective," he says. "They do not stick to the envelopes."

The clerk looks at him and replies: "Comrade, the problem is obvious. You are spitting on the wrong side."

EPILOGUE

If the great mythic journey is the journey home, then my dad was a mythic traveler, completing his journey every night, buoyed on his way by a sea of bourbon. Our balcony was his true home. It was where he felt most comfortable. It was where he told his stories. It was where he felt most at ease in a foreign—irredeemably foreign—country that had stupidly decided that his destiny was janitorial.

On our balcony, he was a well-known country and western star. He was one of many stars, actually, the others being simply more distant and suspended by some accident in the sky. Every clear Milwaukee night was his biggest night in Nashville. He closed every show to a galaxy of applause.

"I have many rare recordings," my dad would often tell me. "Many old bootlegs from here and from Soviet Union. I have Howlin' Wolf, I have Lightnin' Hopkins, I have Blind Lemon Jefferson. I have Latvian singers too, like Maris Tuksnesis and Pauls Mezacuka."

But I never really looked through his records, never really examined what he owned. Last year, when I finished this book, I sent a copy to my mom, hoping only that she wouldn't be devastated, or that she wouldn't mail the last of my childhood belongings to me in a series of small cardboard boxes. Instead, I received a two A.M. phone call.

"Yuri," my mom said. She'd been crying. "You have to come home to Milwaukee," she said. "I have to play for you a record."

"What record?" I asked, but my mom had already hung up the phone.

Within a few days, I'd boarded the flight from La Guardia to Milwaukee County, and taken the familiar cab ride from the terminal to the apartment. My dad had died in 1998, at the age of sixty-five; his heart had eventually failed him, swollen and distended by the years of heavy drinking. So much had changed in the world—he'd spent his last years in a state of perpetual amazement.

"Your father and I," my mom said, almost as soon as I walked through the front door, "agreed that we would do this someday if—" she stopped. "I will only play the record," she concluded.

"Whatever happened," I protested, "to a meal for the weary traveler? The least you could offer me is a soda."

"Only shut up right now, Yuri," she said. "Shut up and listen."

"What record is it?" I asked.

"This is Yuri Mishkin," she said, "after whom we name you."

The twang of guitar came first, followed by a little snare drum and the resounding thump of an upright bass. The recording was decent—if a little scratchy. The song was "Your Cheatin' Heart" by Hank Williams. I recognized the tune. Then, Yuri Mishkin started singing. His voice was mournful, sorrowful, full of lost love. I pictured him wearing rhinestone-crusted spurs and a black Stetson.

I looked at my mom.

"That's Dad's voice," I said. "I'd know it anywhere. That's Dad's voice." I listened to the record with unmitigated wonder. How could I have been so oblivious? I couldn't believe I'd never figured it out. My dad, I realized with a soft breath of shock, was Yuri Mishkin.

"But, Mom," I said. "Why? How? I don't understand."

My mom sighed. She explained it all to me, unfolding a series of facts from the distant past. *Yuri Mishkin*, she said, was my dad's stage name, the name he used when he sang in Riga's bars and clubs. But when they came to America everything was different. Who wanted a singer with such a strong accent? He had no chance to succeed in mainstream American pop music. They put it all behind them; all they had to remind them was me—the two syllables of my name. This was why, my mom told me, they were so nervous when Ivan arrived. He worried that Ivan would say something, accidentally—before they had a chance to explain the situation to him.

"But it's not a bad thing, Mom. I mean, Dad was a fairly famous guy. Why'd he hide that?"

"I know, *bucina*," she said. "I know. But he did stupid things also,

you are aware? No? And anyway, how do we know what makes somebody happy or sad to remember?"

I sat in the living room and listened to the end of "Your Cheatin'
Heart." My mom stood up and walked to the kitchen. She rummaged
in the refrigerator for something, then gave up and poured herself a
glass of water. She walked back toward me, stopping to turn out the
lights. Now, the room was illuminated by only the levels of the
stereo—faint green and red flickering lights—and what meager illumination came through the balcony door.

My mom sat on the couch across from me. My dad continued
singing—he finished "Your Cheatin' Heart" and began "Jambalaya."
This was a whole record, I realized, cut from a live performance by my
dad and two (or possibly three) accompanying musicians. I listened as
he reeled through a set of Hank Williams, and then a set of Muddy
Waters. I stood up and flipped the record over. He sang some songs on
the B side that I didn't recognize. They were perhaps originals.

My dad sang these songs in English, except the last song on the
record, which was a Latvian ballad. After it ended, my mom and I continued sitting there for some time—engulfed by the silence. The
needle ran off the vinyl, the sound of the spinning turntable stuttered
through the room. I didn't know what to do. I touched the skin of
my face. I'd obviously been crying—I could feel the moisture on my
cheeks—but I hadn't noticed it as the music was playing. Finally, my
mom looked at me.

"Do you want a cigarette?" she said. "Remember that they are not
very healthy."

I was a little startled. But, then again, it wasn't completely surprising. She'd once been, after all, a smoker. I accepted the offer. I remembered a night in a previous life, years before, when I'd smoked a
cigarette with Eriks, standing on the balcony of this same apartment. I
remembered how that had felt, and what I'd felt—listening to Eriks
tell the mournful story of Soviet Latvia. She took a pack of Camel
Lights from her pocket.

I inhaled when my mom placed the lighter in front of the cigarette.
The smoke immediately billowed from my mouth. I coughed. She
walked over to the record player and lit her own cigarette. She flipped

the record. Again, the same strains of acoustic guitar, the same percussive snare drum and cymbals. She sat down. It was somehow perfect that we'd be smoking cigarettes and listening to my dad's voice. The songs burned away. My mom stood and played the B side once more. We lit a second cigarette.

This time, my mom hummed along to the Latvian ballad. "It is a song about a pony," she said. "It is about a girl who has lost her pony in the fog." She hummed a harmony, carefully mirroring my dad's deep, resonant voice. "In the end," my mom said, "she finds her pony in a field."

The needle thumped against the center of the record. Its noise was disconcertingly loud. It sounded like the flick of a lighter, amplified numerous times. My mom stood up. It was dark, and I couldn't see the details of her face.

"I am going to sleep, *bucina*," she said. She tossed the cigarettes onto the couch beside me. "You can smoke these if you would like." She paused. "But leave one or two for me in the morning."

She stood and walked to her bedroom. She closed the door without another word.

I wanted to play the record again. But our walls were terribly thin. I knew that my mom would hear, no matter how softly I played it. Instead, I took the disc off the turntable. I sat on the carpet just inside of the balcony doorway. I put the record next to me. I smoked a few cigarettes, lighting them one off the other. They burned my throat but, somehow, the pain was satisfying.

That night, I went to sleep in my old bed, but I couldn't get any rest. I was endlessly speculating on the past, on the things that my dad had done and said, on the ways in which he'd told me stories without mentioning that they were stories about himself. I thought about the first days with the Ozolinsh family, and how close Ivan must have come—at various points—to telling me the truth. Finally, I couldn't sleep anymore. I left the bedroom and walked out onto the balcony.

The city was striking from this height. The municipal government had torn down some of the Section 8 housing nearby. This had opened up, unintentionally, view corridors for our little apartment. I could see the dramatic lights of the city—skyscrapers so close that it felt like I could swipe at them with my hand, and even some of the lake in the distance. I sighed. My dad would have liked it out here, even more, with this new vista. After a few moments I heard the sliding glass door open up. I felt my mom's presence beside me. My hands were on the rail of the balcony; she placed her left hand over my right, rested there next to me, admiring our city, our Beer City. Is it not so beautiful, here, my darling? I thought, hearing his voice rise through the darkness. And, all in all, I had to agree.

I'm telling a story now, sure. It's the story my dad might tell, if he were here to tell it. In a way, I had to tell it. I couldn't help myself. But it's a fairly decent story; it's even got a car crash. Unfortunately—and fortunately—it does bear resemblance to actual persons, living and dead. This resemblance is not coincidental.

The salient question, then, is this: Have you ever heard the story of Yuri Mishkin? Not the second Yuri Mishkin. Not the one who was convinced, as a teenager, that there was a chance he'd discover enlightenment sitting in the limbs of a hedge maple. Not the one who recklessly stole a car for a girl and didn't truly love his father—not truly—until it was pretty much too late.

I mean the first Yuri Mishkin. The one who was imprisoned by the Soviets and fled to America and changed his name and drank bourbon on his balcony and sang the forgotten classics of American country and western music. The one who worked as a janitor to support his family and nearly died for his son on a frigid December day.

No? Well, do you have a minute? I could pour you a drink. We could begin again.

ACKNOWLEDGMENTS

First and foremost, I'd like to thank my agent, Renée Zuckerbrot. Without her tireless dedication, the manuscript of *Red Weather* would have never been more than just that: a manuscript. I am deeply indebted to Shaye Areheart—a wonderful editor—and everyone at Random House (especially Julie Will, Sally Kim, Joshua Poole, and Kira Stevens), who've made this process so enjoyable. I'd also like to thank the designers, who've created two beautiful covers, hardcover and paperback.

A massive thanks to my crackerjack publicist, Campbell Wharton.

Finally, I'd like to thank my friends and family—and Claire—for their patience.

And yet my greatest debt is to my teachers: Harris Levinson, Jay Parini, Ron Powers, Daniel Schwarz, Bob Morgan, and Roger Gilbert. Thank you.

AUTHOR'S NOTE

The basement of the Elliot Bay Book Company in Seattle, Washington, has a quality of light that—in my mind—does not exist anywhere else. It is a rare light, a light that has always lingered in my memory: equal parts electric lightbulb, brick wall, chapped wooden floor, and hardcover book. This last thing is especially important, I think: every available flat surface has a book on it; these books execute a particular alchemy, transforming the environment in some crucial way.

It's the afternoon of Saturday, May 27, 2006. I've just read sections of *Red Weather* to an audience of about fifty people (mostly friends and family), and I'm now signing books in a corner of the store's basement. It's something I've imagined doing since I was an awkward, book-loving teenager at Seattle's James A. Garfield High School. I never imagined, of course, that realizing this goal would involve reading sections of my novel in a suspiciously poor Eastern European accent that sounds a bit like Count Chocula's.

My father—my real father, not the father who appears in the pages of this novel—sits in the corner with a group of people, waiting for me to finish signing books so that the family can go to dinner. I can hear him in the middle distance having an earnest conversation.

"Well, you know," he says, his voice rising in intensity and emphasis: "I'm not a drunk."

Ah, yes. The intersection of fiction and real life. *Oh, Dad,* I think at that moment, *I am so sorry.*

At every reading—and in nearly every interview that I've done for *Red Weather*—someone has raised this question: How much of the novel is autobiographical? Unfortunately, in many ways, it's nearly impossible to fashion a satisfactory answer to this question. Because I'm really not sure what to say. Are the events of the book real? In some ways, yes, and in others, no.

Four facts about the novel.

1. The characters are very poor.
2. They live in an urban area—in the crumbling warehouse district of downtown Milwaukee, Wisconsin.
3. Yuri Balodis, the teenage protagonist of the novel, has two Latvian parents.
4. Yuri's father is what could be charitably called a self-destructive alcoholic.

Four facts about me.

1. I was solidly middle-class. My parents were both teachers in the Seattle Public School system; their income was such that I never really had to think about money, to worry about poverty. It's a somewhat forgotten fact that millions of American families struggle even to put food on the table; thankfully, ours wasn't one of those.
2. For nearly all of my childhood and teenage years, I lived in a house that my uncle's construction company built in one of the neighborhoods of North Seattle. Yes, my uncle's name was Juris (the true Latvian version of the novel's Yuri), but other than that there were few similarities to the environment in which my protagonist grew up. The environment I negotiated on a daily basis was made up of manicured lawns and ranch homes; there were no Polish delicatessens or decaying turn-of-the-century warehouses. There were (unfortunately, perhaps) no Pabst breweries.
3. And, yes, I was born to immigrant parents. As a child, I was surrounded by people with funny accents. And many of these accents were Latvian. I did attend Latvian Saturday school every year from the time I was four to the time I was sixteen, sacrificing a childhood of Sat-

urday-morning cartoons to learn the Latvian language and culture and history. But I also had a sprawling Egyptian side to my family. Though my mother is Latvian, my father was born in Cairo, Egypt, in 1932. Hence my hybrid name: Pauls, which is the Latvian version of Paul, and Toutonghi, which is Middle Eastern in origin and means "tobacco grower." So my home life didn't really resemble the home life in this book.

4. My dad is not a drinker.

I think that people believe (at some level) that if they read that "I" in a book, then the events depicted in that book must be true. Or at least close to true. One person, an old friend of mine from Seattle, sent me an earnest email a few weeks after the book came out this summer. "I'm so sorry you were going through all that," he wrote. "I had no idea that your family was so crazy."

While this is interesting, I believe that the novel actually depends— critically depends—on *straying* from the truth for its emotional power. None of the facts of my life that I illustrated were really that interesting; there was no conflict in being comfortably middle class. So I looked for conflict wherever I could find it, wherever I could put my characters in opposition to any element of society. I didn't try to stay close to the truth of my family—because I had hoped that fictionalizing would make for a better book. In *The Art of the Novel,* Milan Kundera writes that "the novel is a meditation on existence as seen through the imagination of imaginary characters."

I started the novel when I was living outside of Milwaukee in Wisconsin in 2002. I fell in love with Milwaukee's history and beery degradation—from an outsider's perspective. I began the process of reconstructing a fictional version of it in the pages of *Red Weather*. In some places, I succeeded. In others, I failed. For those small missed details, I apologize.

But then again, some of the things in the book are true. The car accident, for example, is based on a less dramatic (but still significant) accident I had while driving my parents' Ford Probe to Vancouver, British Columbia, at the age of seventeen.

Nonetheless, the true Latvian immigrant experience to America in the twentieth century was quite different from the somewhat comic version I depict here. But hopefully these characters are vivid and entertaining, and linger after the book is closed.

At least that's what my imaginary father, Rudolfs Balodis, would want: "I am making for you story," he might say. "It should leave delicious flavor, like a refreshing sip of beer."

Pauls Toutonghi
Brooklyn
October 2006

READING GROUP GUIDE

1. What was your opinion of Yuri's father, Rudolfi? Did your feeling about him change as you read the book?

2. Why do you think Yuri started selling the *Socialist Worker*?

3. "I slipped in and out of a dream in which Hannah and I were at a picnic, drinking wine and eating sandwiches on delicious French bread. The bread was unbelievably fresh and the sandwiches were made from the finest-quality meats and cheeses. But the more we ate, the larger the sandwiches became. I couldn't stop eating, I knew, because then I'd lose Hannah. So I ate and sweated and ate and sweated and ate" (page 178). What does Yuri's dream reveal about his feelings for Hannah?

4. Of the many colorful characters in the book, which one or ones stood out for you? Why?

5. Discuss the relationship between Yuri and his father. Would you describe it as typical? If so, in what respects? If not, why?

6. The city of Milwaukee holds a special place in Rudolfi's heart: "He loved Milwaukee. It was his city, his adopted city, and the center of his life in his adopted country" (page 26). But in 1989, Milwaukee was in a depressed economic and social state. What are some parallels between the city and Rudolfi's state of mind?

7. "I was drawn to him, inexplicably drawn" (page 128). What do you think is behind Yuri's attraction to Eriks?

8. Part 2 of the novel begins with an excerpt of a poem by Wallace Stevens, "Disillusionment of Ten O'Clock" (page 105). What does this poem mean in terms of the events of *Red Weather*?

9. How are Eriks's and Yuri's fathers alike and different? How might these similarities and disparities explain why Yuri is fascinated by Eriks but rejects his own father?

10. The fall of communism in Eastern Europe in 1989 is one of the story's central backdrops. How does the author use this event metaphorically?

11. What role does alcohol—and its abuses—play in the story?

12. At several points in the novel, Yuri goes along as another person engages in reckless behavior, against his own better judgment and with disastrous results. Why is Yuri so willing to do dangerous things?

13. The balcony in the Balodises' apartment figures prominently in the story. What does the balcony best symbolize: a precipice, a gateway, a refuge, or something else?

14. What did you think upon learning of Rudolfi's true identity in the epilogue? Did it come as a surprise? If so, why? If not, at what other points in the novel did you find hints about Rudolfi's former life?

15. What does the book's title mean?

ANOTHER AUTHOR ASKS

Darin Strauss on *Red Weather*

1. No denying it: *Red Weather* is funny. But how does Pauls Toutonghi get you to laugh here? Any novelist worth her salt knows how to make a reader cry; it's much harder to be funny. Is it the language in Red Weather? The characters? The situations? Which of these is the most effective way that Toutonghi gets you laughing here? And how does humor on the page differ from comedy in a film?

2. Pauls Toutonghi is an original—even down to his name. (Who has a *plural* first name? Just how many Pauls worked on this book, anyway?) But who do you think Toutonghi's influences as a writer are? No one comes out of nowhere: From what tradition does this book come, and what other stories did it remind you of?

3. It's not a young-adult novel, but *Red Weather* captures—squirm-inducingly—the high-school milieu, the zits-and–driver's permit years of our youth. But would you allow a high-schooler to read it? What lifts it out of the YA genre and into the realm of adult literary fiction?

4. Yuri's parents are well-described in their "otherness," their difference from some of the all-American parents of Milwaukee. But how

so? Is it simply that the author gives them bad grammar—or does he use other techniques to show the Balodis family as uniquely Latvian?

5. In Philip Roth's *The Ghost Writer*, a rabbi gets mad at the Jewish protagonist for writing unflatteringly about some Jewish characters. The rabbi asks: "Can you honestly say that there is anything in your short story that would not warm the heart of a Julius Streicher or a Joseph Goebbels?" Roth then spent the rest of the book—and maybe the rest of his career—arguing against that point. But . . . is this story too hard on the Latvians? Does art have a responsibility to be PC?

DARIN STRAUSS is the author of *The Real McCoy* and *Chang and Eng*.

ABOUT THE AUTHOR

Pauls Toutonghi is a first-generation American. He has been awarded a Pushcart Prize and a Fulbright grant, and he is the winner of the first annual *Zoetrope: All-Story* Short Fiction Contest. His writing has appeared in *Sports Illustrated, Zoetrope, One Story,* and the *Boston Review,* among other publications. He lives in Brooklyn.